Rank Insubordination!

Roland Jaquarello

ISBN: 978-1-917293-06-8

About the author

Roland Jaquarello was born in London in 1945. He was educated in the UK and Ireland. He is a theatre and radio director/producer. His work includes residencies at the Royal Court Theatre, the Abbey Theatre Dublin, the Lyric Theatre Belfast, the Redgrave Theatre Farnham and BBC Northern Ireland, producing for Radio 4, 3 and 2.

He has written two previous books: Memories of Development: My Times in Irish Theatre and Broadcasting and Being Fulham, a supporter's story about Fulham FC's 2016-17 season in the Championship. He has also contributed to the book, Being Irish 101 Views on Irish Identity Today. Rank Insubordination! is his first novel.

Acknowledgements

The author would like to thank the following for their help with this novel:
Tony Coombs and Graham Fawcett for their advice. regarding the public school background of the period.
The late Tim Woodward for putting him in touch with Mark Reeve, who designed the cover.
The World Rugby Museum at Twickenham Stadium, London for giving him access to information about the game.
Mira Faber for her patience.

Quotation:
The author is grateful to Sony pictures for permission to quote from:
THE BRIDGE ON THE RIVER KWAI

To Mandy

Contents

Note

Some of the attitudes and language in this novel are of their time. Over the last sixty plus years, many things have changed but our cultural past still informs the present.

R. J. 2024

An English Public School

Mid-1950s

Michaelmas Term

'Squit!' shouted One Ball, lounging in his bath like a Roman emperor.

As there was no reply, One Ball got irritated and started irrationally splashing water in all directions.

'Squit!' he yelled again as if on some parade ground. In fact, Potts, known as One Ball, after some boys had learned about his unfortunate accident, had a military mind. He hated lack of punctuality, laziness and ineptitude but he revered discipline.

'Were you calling for me?' enquired Hayes aka squit, as he opened the lav end door.

'Yes, I was,' replied One Ball peremptorily. 'Go to the tuck shop and get me a Tiffin and Tizer.'

'I haven't got any money,' stated Hayes facetiously.

'Get it from my breeches pocket, over there on one of the pegs,' ordered One Ball.

Hayes was a fair-haired junior but coming from Battersea he had a certain street sense borne out of dealing with teddy boys on the Latchmere Road. As he rummaged around in One Ball's pockets, he felt a small packet.

'Potts.'

'What is it?' said One Ball, arrogantly displaying his muscular torso.

'I've found some rubbers.'

'Christ. Give them to me.'

Hayes slowly but obediently placed the durex into One Ball's wet, clammy hands.

'I've taken a pound, so that should be enough,' mentioned Hayes, hastily looking to depart.

'Hayes!' yelled One Ball, desperately searching for a place to hide the forbidden object.

‘Yes, Potts,’ replied Hayes with feigned innocence.

‘You didn’t see it. Understand.’

‘Of course not.’

‘And if I find out that you have been telling others about this discovery, I’ll do my best to make your life here a bloody misery. Understand.’

‘Yes Potts,’ acknowledged Hayes with a smirk on his face.

‘Don’t dawdle as I’ve got to get ready for parade.’

‘Ok. I won’t be long’ said Hayes reassuringly as he left the lav end and walked through the senior dormitory to go downstairs.

‘Bloody squits!’ cried One Ball in frustration after Hayes’s departure.

One Ball only got the durex as a precaution. He wanted to engage with one of the younger maids, a French woman, who was working in the school kitchens. He was hopeful that he would get an opportunity to develop this relationship and therefore thought he should take some precautions. When he went to the chemist for the first time during the holidays to get some durex, he got nervous. A shop assistant, a young girl from a local estate, chewing gum in an abrasively sexy manner, asked him what he wanted. Immediately, he panicked and bought a bottle of Lucozade instead of his proposed purchase. Later, One Ball regained his composure and made a second trip to the chemist. Thankfully, it was the acerbic girl’s day off and he bought a packet of Johnnies from a severe, grey-haired woman in brown spectacles, who gave him a look of intense disapproval. One Ball regarded this transaction as a personal triumph.

After his accident, he had an acute desire to make sure his equipment was in full working order. Consequently, he kept his eye on Françoise, a slim French maid with an alluring short-haired, brunette fringe. The only problem was that he’d only spoken to her briefly when she was serving fish and chips and that she was already very friendly with Arthur Rutter. Rutter was a senior monitor at Ironside A, who embodied the lofty values of public school life by being in both the 1st X1 and the 1st XV. However, despite his sporting status, One Ball consoled himself that Françoise would never find him attractive. After all, Rutter wasn't just small, he was a bloody midget. Nonetheless, One Ball hadn't yet devised a strategy to meet her. Such rendezvous were risky and he didn't want to be expelled when he had a good chance of getting to Cambridge. First, he had to hide the rubbers. But where? Then suddenly as he was drying himself with his accustomed thoroughness, One Ball discovered a solution. In his settle, there was a Bible. He wasn't particularly religious nor was his family. They attended their Surrey church more out of habit than conviction but he kept a Bible in case he had to read a lesson or somebody challenged him on an abstruse theological point. One Ball never wanted to appear ignorant as it would be a form of weakness. In any case, what would be a better camouflage for his rubbers than Holy Scripture? Accordingly, One Ball placed the contraceptive packet at the beginning of Exodus and neatly placed the Bible back in his settle. He then patted his face with English Leather cologne and got dressed, neatly putting on his carefully ironed dark blue shirt, white underpants, grey socks, dark breeches and black shoes, which much to his annoyance, hadn't been polished to expectations by his squit. One Ball liked to see his own reflection in his shoes, not polish covering caked mud. He noted this serious aberration and decided to chastise Hayes on an occasion of his own choosing. In the meantime, he had a parade to take. Self-consciously, he bent down and looked carefully at himself in the mirror, which ran across a trough for communal washing. Relieved that he didn't discover any extreme forms of acne, he fastidiously fastened his grey bands around his neck. One Ball then ceremoniously put on his black coat, while proudly gazing at the school's distinctive uniform. After he fastened the coats' silver buttons and his leather belt, One Ball peremptorily left the dormitory like a general about to inspect his troops.

One Ball's study was at the top of the dayroom. He was after all a senior monitor and this meant that he was entitled to such accommodation. The only other study, opposite One Ball's, belonged to Beckett, the most senior monitor and the school swat, who had an amazing photographic memory but little imagination. The dayroom consisted of a series of long rectangular brown tables, where the rest of the boys had to study. While doing so, the incessant daytime din of caterwauling pupils and the sound of rock 'n' roll emerging from the dayroom radio, constantly tested their concentration. One of the tables stretched across the window, next to the two studies, others lay lengthwise towards the end of the dayroom. Benches accommodated all the boys of James B, a house named after a scientist who had emigrated to South Africa. Later, it transpired that this former pupil had disturbingly extreme views. However, the school's establishment rejected efforts to rename James as Gandhi B. They insisted on a British alternative, despite protests from senior boys and more progressive masters, who were seen by the higher echelons as Marxist agitators.

As One Ball lounged in his study, Hayes, holding both a bottle of Tizer and a Tiffin, came strolling through the house porch into a noisy, unruly corridor, to be greeted by the towering ginger-haired figure of Sully, a fellow junior.

'Who's that for?' asked Sully, hoping to be offered some nourishment.

'One Ball,' replied Hayes dismissively.

'I hope it poisons him.'

'Why?'

'He's given me a punishment for nothing.'

'He must have had a reason.'

'Rank insubordination.'

'I don't know what that means.'

'Apparently, it means being cheeky and not knowing your place.'

'Well, One Ball isn't God.'

'He certainly isn't. More like the Devil.'

'I'd better give him his tuck.'

'All I did was disagree with him about whether my coat was dirty.'

Hayes left the aggrieved Sully and departed. He moved through the swing door of the dayroom, past the sporting cups ostentatiously displayed in their shiny glass cabinets and the monitors' desks, which lay to the side of the tables like Stasi observation outposts to observe the house's junior ranks. Arriving at Potts's study, Sully knocked on the door.

'Who is it?' a stentorian voice proclaimed.

'Me,' replied Hayes cheerily.

'Who in the hell is me?' demanded One Ball.

'Hayes,' revealed the junior confidently.

'Come in,' said a vexed One Ball

Hayes opened the door with difficulty, as he precariously balanced the Tizer and Tiffin.

'Put them there,' ordered One Ball, lounging in his armchair while pointing to his desk. Hayes obeyed him and then stood warily by the door.

One Ball, who was irritated that his reading of Colonial Memories by General Lancelot England, had been interrupted, suddenly launched his considerable frame to its full height. He placed his military tome on a bookshelf and then deigned to review the refreshment.

'You've got the wrong bloody Tiffin!' roared One Ball.

'I thought you liked the smaller one better,' reasoned Hayes.

'No I don't like the smaller one better, I like the bigger ones. They've got more raisins.'

'Sorry, Potts.'

'Sorry isn't bloody good enough.'

'Still, the Tizer is ok?'

One Ball surveyed the red coloured drink as if he was inspecting a rebellious brigade.

After a tense pause, he declared:

'It seems satisfactory.' He then proceeded to explain. 'What you've got to realise Hayes is that after a bloody demanding rugby game, in which you may like to know, we won 20-12 and got through to the next round of the cup..'

'Congratulations,' interjected Hayes diplomatically.

'Thank you' acknowledged One Ball, relishing the compliment before continuing. 'What I'm saying is that after such a game, in which I was kicked all over the bloody place, I need sustenance.'

'Sus what? enquired Hayes.

'Food and drink, Hayes. Food and drink,' emphasised One Ball.

‘Of course, Potts,’ responded Hayes with detached servility.

‘Ok that’s all, Hayes,’ said One Ball, waving his hand airily as he moved towards his record player, which he’d placed on a small round table, in front of an imposing poster of Richard Wagner. ‘Get ready for parade, ’ he ordered.

‘Ok,’ agreed the junior.

The opening overture of Tristan and Isolde then enveloped the study, as Hayes left Potts’ Germanic grotto and made his way through the dayroom. As he was about to go through the swing door, he was hailed by Barrett, who was listening to the dayroom radio, which was strategically placed above the surrounding lockers to accommodate the erratic American Forces Network reception. He was standing on a bench with Sully, jigging around to the strains of Lonnie Donegan.

‘Can you hear it?’ cried Barrett, his curly brown hair dangling down over his forehead.

‘What is it?’ replied an incredulous Hayes.

‘What is it? Hayes really. It’s Lonnie. Lonnie Donegan,’ countered Barrett.

‘Oh yes,’ remarked Hayes uncertainly.

‘It’s Rock Island Line. Lonnie is bringing his own brand of blues to Britain,’ imparted an enthused Barrett, evangelising from the pulpit of the bench like a manic preacher energetically selling his beliefs to a bemused congregation.

‘I prefer Elvis,’ divulged the statuesque Sully, superciliously leaning back on the nearby lockers to give himself greater authority.

‘Listen to this,’ screamed an ecstatic Barrett turning up the volume with alacrity. ‘You just can’t beat it,’ he beamed, exuding all the adulation of a true believer.

As Lonnie pounded away in the background, the boys continued this musical conversation, pitching their favourite songs and singers. Hayes had a particular fondness for The Ballad of Davy Crockett, having sung it one summer, albeit badly, in a talent contest on holiday at Herne Bay. Barrett and Sully had no time for Mr. Crockett. In fact, Sully, notwithstanding his admiration for Elvis, was in the school choir. He had operatic ambitions but avoided venturing into conversations about Verdi when the Lonnie Donegan Fan Club was in overdrive.

Just as the boys were about to discuss the respective merits of the Dandy and Beano comics, Pound, a slim, dark-haired monitor of moderate disposition, rang the bell for tea. All the boys from both the dayroom and the adjoining changing rooms, shuffled outside to the forecourt in front of the porch. Gradually, they assembled themselves into a military formation of lines of ten, all standing behind each other. While they waited for the appointed monitor to take the parade, Barrett took the opportunity to extract a Liquorice Allsort from his pocket and munch it voraciously. Meanwhile Sully started a rendition of Jesu Joy of Man's Desiring and Hayes got stuck into a Mars bar he'd bought at the tuck shop, while carrying out his squit duties.

Suddenly, One Ball entered from the porch. He looked grim and mean.

'Barrett!'

'Yes, Potts.'

'Are you eating?'

'Yes, I am.'

'You know you shouldn't be eating on parade.'

'Yes.'

'Well don't.'

'It's in my mouth, Potts.'

'Well get rid of it.'

'Shall I spit it out?'

'No, Barrett. Put it in the bin.'

Barrett made his way meekly to the dayroom, as Hayes swallowed the remaining part of his Mars bar and Sully stopped his rendition of Bach's celebrated song.

'Hurry up Barrett,' bellowed stern Jim Potts, as Barrett reappeared, having deposited his sinful sweet, and returned to his place in the squad.

'At ease,' commanded One Ball.

One Ball was now in full military mode.

A-T-T-E-N-T-I-O-N!' 'LEFT TURN!' 'QUICK MARCH!'

And James B were on their way to tea.

'LEFT WHEEL!' screeched One Ball as the boys came to the end of the drive.

Schoolboys marching into meals was eccentric and bizarre but it certainly got eight hundred boys into the Dining Hall quickly. One Ball revelled in such a military exercise. It inspired his imagination to think of himself as a great leader like Montgomery, who gave the impression that he'd won the war singlehandedly. In fact, One Ball's father had died in the conflict and his mother Martha Potts was left bereft, both emotionally and financially. As a result, One Ball qualified for help from a charity, which helped children from families affected by the war to get a good education. One Ball's father had been a stickler for discipline, and his son, who had inherited this trait, now revelled in administering it.

'LEFT, RIGHT! LEFT!, RIGHT! KEEP THE DRESSING SULLY!' shrieked One Ball.

The boys marched past Morton A, the house directly opposite James B. Morton's senior housemaster, 'Chaps' Le Mesurier, was a modern languages teacher and an ardent European. 'Chaps' was always making a case for the boys to have greater linguistic skills. 'We're going to join the Common Market chaps and we've got to be ready. We can't expect everybody to speak English!'

'LEFT, RIGHT! LEFT, RIGHT! DON'T SLOUCH, HAYES!' shouted One Ball, revelling in being a manic sergeant major.

The boys then passed Jasper House, named after a drug addicted minor romantic poet, who had briefly attended the school. Jasper A's Senior Housemaster was 'Long John' Carson. Long John only had one leg, the other was wooden and hence he was named after Long John Silver. Long John was an English teacher, who had a particular penchant for the plays of J. M. Synge and insisted that his pupils read them aloud, although none of them were Irish and their attempts at the appropriate accent proved to be disastrous. How he got only one leg was a matter of considerable schoolboy conjecture. Some thought that he'd stood on a mine, others that he was the victim of a savage German assault. The less charitable believed that he got inebriated and had a car accident. No one was quite sure and the mystery of Long John's wooden leg was a comic incitement to the adolescent imagination. It gave rein to unalloyed fantasy.

As the boys passed the School Chapel, with its ancient sculptures of various formidable dignitaries peering down on them from on high, they went through a grandiose arch and into the Quadrangle, a big square space, surrounded on four sides by elegant Tudor buildings. It was dark and dank as James B approached the Dining Hall.

'LEFT WHEEL!' yelled One Ball as the boys turned towards the entrance.

'FALL TWO DEEP!' One Ball shrieked to order the boys to move into double formation, so they could enter through the Dining Hall door.

The Dining Hall, with its large arresting paintings dramatically reflecting the school's history, provided for all the many pupils. While the James B squad looked to enter its stirring portals, boys from houses on the opposite side of the Avenue went through a door further away, but closer to their entrance into the Quadrangle. As the hungry boys dispersed to their place on the assembled benches, the noise became thunderous. There were twenty long series of tables, which extended for sixty yards, all placed in a line across the expansive space. At the bottom of the tables, kitchen staff served food. In the centre of the hall, built into the wall, was a huge ornate ascending pulpit with a lit lectern, surrounded by two ferocious wooden lions. This was where senior monitors read grace. Opposite the pulpit was a small dais with an accompanying seat and table. On the table, there was a gavel and wooden block, which was used to get everybody's attention. At the far end of the hall, there was a raised dais with a very large oval dining room table, where at lunch the headmaster would dine with the most senior boys.

In James's case, it was Boring Beckett who could eat with the courteous but aloof headmaster not One Ball, much to the latter's regret. However, during lunchtimes all eyes turned towards the dais when Françoise and her colleagues served the food. Even the righteously disciplined Jim Potts allowed his eyes to wander in that direction, only to discover the dreaded Rutter smiling and chatting to the attractive kitchen maid.

‘What does she see in that bloody idiot?’ One Ball murmured to himself, grinding his teeth in frustration. Such was his anger that Mr Roy, James B’s Junior Housemaster, nicknamed ‘Killer’ because of his propensity for extreme punishment beatings, enquired about his welfare. Killer was sitting at the top of the house table, eating next to the monitors, when One Ball nervously reassured him that he was fine.

Fortunately, this wasn’t lunch and the entrancing Françoise wasn’t present to distract One Ball. Instead, having marched his troops into the Dining Hall, the senior monitor was going to read grace. This was a rare occurrence as seniors from every house took it in turns to carry out this duty. One Ball sat at the top table, waiting to be summoned. Although he’d done it before, suddenly he felt nervous at the prospect of addressing so many boys, even for such a short period. To while away the time, he talked to Pound about the afternoon’s game.

‘We won a lot of scrums today Greg.’

‘Yes, quite a few against the head.’

‘Barrel’s a bloody good hooker even if he was always last to the lineouts.’

‘More interested in girls than fitness.’

‘Really.’

‘Yes, apparently, he’s very friendly with Yvette.’

‘Who’s Yvette?’ asked One Ball.

‘She’s over there,’ said Pound, pointing to a buxom young woman, twiddling a ladle in a huge urn at the end of the table.

‘They share a passion for theatre apparently,’ continued Pound. ‘She’s a friend of Françoise. They’re both taking a year out before university.’

One Ball got excited. Although Barrel or Madoc as he was more formally known, was a fellow senior, he wasn’t a close friend, he was far too arty for that, but maybe he could still get him an introduction to Françoise? His pulses raced as he craved such an opportunity. Then, his initial enthusiasm abruptly dissipated. He remembered that theatre wasn’t his subject, even though he knew a bit about the recent spate of angry young men. He tried to console himself that Yvette might be interested in other things like Sputniks and space exploration. After restraining his impetuosity, One Ball concluded that it was inadvisable to involve the house's rugby hooker or another kitchen maid in his emotional yearnings. He didn't want to risk perpetuating gossip. He decided to deal with his desires more privately. Just as One Ball's thoughts came to a strategic conclusion, the reverberating sound of Mr Smallman, the Dining Hall Warden, banging the gavel on his wooden block, awoke him from his reverie. It was now time for grace and One Ball walked towards the towering pulpit and regally ascended its stairs.

On his arrival, One Ball looked down on eight hundred boys. He relished the awe of such power as he awaited Smallman's cue. Smallman, Senior Housemaster of Ironside A and the school's Cricket Team Manager, taught modern languages. He always wore grey, neatly pressed, turned-up trousers. On this occasion, a white shirt, a dark blue tie and a royal blue blazer with a golden cockerel crest woven into the top pocket, supplemented his regular attire. From the dais, Smallman stared at One Ball through his brown-framed oval spectacles like a peering owl. There was a brief pause and then Smallman banged the gavel abruptly, twice. One Ball then placed both of his hands on the lectern and solemnly intoned:

'For what we are about to receive may the Lord make us truly thankful.'

'A-m-e-n' replied the school in a mock-solemn, elongated reply.

Smallman looked around the school with a menacing stare to show his displeasure at the boys' facetious attitude. He then banged the gavel angrily so that the evening meal could start. As One Ball descended the pulpit, he also felt annoyed by the derisory response. Consequently, he swept all aside as he made his way to the top of James B's table.

'Did you hear that, Greg?' said One Ball, depositing his body imperiously back at his place on a bench.

'I know. Childish,' sympathised Pound as he patted his bread or crig as the school traditionally called it, with some butter or flib, which was another of the school's eccentric synonyms.

'Don't take it too seriously, Jim,' advised Beckett, who as the most senior monitor was sitting in a chair at the head of a very long series of tables.

'I just get a feeling that somebody is spreading rumours about me,' confided One Ball as he leaned forward conspiratorially.

'What kind of rumours?' responded Boring Beckett, who had a reputation for being decent but dull.

'About my family,' alleged an obsessive One Ball.

'Your family?' queried Beckett.

'And its military background,' persisted an offended One Ball.

'I doubt it. Look do eat your fish and chips, I got them especially for you,' implored Pound.

'I know. Thanks, Greg. Still that exaggerated amen was bloody annoying,' maintained One Ball.

'They were just taking the piss, Jim. It wasn't personal,' reassured Pound.

'I'm not so sure,' replied a deeply suspicious One Ball.

Later, further down the table, the juniors were enjoying a special treat. Various leftover desserts needed to be eaten immediately, so they were offered to the boys at tea. As they tucked into their sweets, Sully, was extolling the virtues of his father's war service.

'My father shot down lots of Japs in Singapore,' extolled the overweight junior, while eagerly eating his dessert.

'How many?' probed Barrett quizzically.

'Lots.'

'They were giving the army cover. My Dad was a squadron leader. '

'How many is lots?' pursued Barrett, inquisitively prodding his banana split with his spoon.

'At least three.'

'Three? Are you sure?

'That's what my Dad told me.'

'You know we lost that battle Sully.'

'My Dad got medals. He wears them on Remembrance Sunday.'

'He may have got medals but the Japs battered the RAF.'

'My Dad was a brave man. He was in many serious dogfights fighting for his country.'

'The RAF lost many planes during the defence of Singapore.'

'Not my Dad's.'

'I've read about this, Sully. We lost badly and your Dad and his mates had to retreat, so don't tell me he's Biggles.'

Sully's face was turning red, his ginger hair only contributing to a visage of intemperate anger. Just as he was about to explode into a Churchillian aria about his father's war service, he was interrupted by boys either side of the table, ritualistically passing a message down to the bottom of the table, like a repetitive liturgy:

'Hayes. Hayes. Hayes. Hayes..'

As a junior, Hayes was near the bottom of the table when he got the message. He was looking forward to his semolina. Semolina was one of the desserts provided and his own particular favourite, especially when it was crowned by a bit of appetising red jam. Consequently, he didn't appreciate the interruption.

'I bet it's Potts,' he told Binns, who came from Eastbourne and had a peculiar way of squeezing his hands and shutting his eyes when he got excited.

'Ah, grim Jim.' said Binns.

'I'd better go up and see what the bastard wants.'

Hayes reluctantly left his semolina and sauntered up to the top table.

'Somebody wants me?' quizzed Hayes, casually addressing a group of monitors.

'Yes. I wanted you,' confirmed One Ball, purposefully looking away from his squit.

'What is it Potts?' asked Hayes.

'Come over here,' ordered One Ball.

Hayes moved around the head chair where Boring Beckett was showing a face of diplomatic neutrality, to face the exasperated monitor.

'Yes, Potts?' queried Hayes to a detached One Ball, who still didn't look him in the eye.

'See me back at house.' commanded One Ball.

'About what?' questioned a curious Hayes.

'See me back at house!' repeated a furious Potts, turning to Hayes and staring menacingly into his blue eyes.

Hayes thought that One Ball looked stupid when he feigned anger. His crinkly black hair gave him a clownish look and when he tried to be emotional, he became absurdly splenetic, like a bad character actor in a horror film.

Hayes returned to his semolina, which was now a bit cold, thanks to bloody One Ball.

This didn't stop him from eating it rapidly. He didn't think it was as good as apple pie and ice cream but it was still bloody good.

'What did grim Jim want?' enquired Binns, tucking into his sticky pudding.

'He wants to see me back at house,' replied Hayes, rigorously stirring the jam in his semolina.

'What for?' pursued an inquisitive Sully, munching the remains of his banana split.

'I've no idea,' said a bemused Hayes.

Binns watched the others eating, before mischievously revealing some gossip.

'Do you know that Potts's father got killed during the Italian campaign?' asked a beguiling Binns.

'I didn't know it was there,' revealed Hayes, halting his attack on his dessert.

'Yes, with the 8th Army,' continued Binns, enjoying the attention of the others. 'He was leading a battalion. His father was highly respected as a thinking soldier. Popular with the men. My mother was talking to Mrs Potts during her last visit. A nice woman. Lives in Farnham. She showed us a picture of her garden. She certainly knows how to grow roses.'

Binns punctuated his thoughts on Potts and his family, while devouring the remaining remnants of his pudding. Binns particularly enjoyed studying languages. This particular junior had strong European sympathies and was a supporter of the Common Market. In the future, he wanted to work in foreign climes 'to broaden the mind'. Nonetheless, one had the feeling that even if he went around the whole world, it wouldn't really change him. Despite his commendable continental curiosity, he'd still be seeing everything from the perspective of

Eastbourne. Binns, pudgy with a mop of unruly blonde hair, relished the last slice of his delicious sticky pudding. He was now ready for his prep and launching into the declension of French verbs.

While Binns was destroying the remains of his dessert, One Ball suddenly leapt off his bench, carefully making sure he didn't injure his remaining equipment, and strode to the bottom of the tables with his plate. He then approached Françoise who was cleaning up the serving table.

'Thanks very much. Lovely semolina,' said One Ball.

'Merci.' replied Françoise, as she disinterestedly took his dirty plate.

There was a pause. One Ball became increasingly nervous and abruptly tried to start a conversation.

'Where did you come from in France?

'Pardon?' queried a bemused Françoise.

'Where do you live in France?' continued One Ball, talking slowly, as if he was a British colonialist trying to communicate with a resident in remotest Africa.

'Ah, habitez. Lyon,' Françoise playfully disclosed.

'I don't know Lyon,' admitted One Ball.

'Lyon is beautiful. Good food,' elaborated Françoise, in fluently accented English.

'Of course,' agreed One Ball ingratiatingly.

'No jam roly poly,' declared Françoise, smiling impudently as she wiped the table.

One Ball laughed. His usual grim mask dropped and there was even a sparkling serenity in his grey eyes.

'What about bread and butter pudding?' proposed One Ball.

'Non, terrible. Crême brulée, soufflé au chocolat, crêpes Suzette, much better,' asserted Françoise proudly, while starting to stack various plates.

'No sticky pudding in Lyon then?' remarked One Ball playfully.

'Certainly not. Ok, sorry, must go,' decided Françoise, as she lifted a pile of plates and made off to the kitchen. 'Au revoir.'

One Ball then moved with the alacrity of an Olympic sprinter to get ahead of Françoise and open the swing door.

'Merci,' responded Françoise casually, before departing into the bowels of the noisy, hectic kitchen.

After feeling like a knight in shining armour, Potts turned round towards the tables and who happened to be gawking at him with a facetious grin but none other than his bloody squit. When One Ball glared at the inquisitive intruder with a glowering gaze, Hayes quickly averted his eyes towards a dining hall painting, as if he was an art connoisseur. One Ball then reacted by walking past the impudent junior with purposeful, militaristic strides.

When tea finished, the boys could make their own way back to their houses. Wandering in the autumnal dark amidst adolescent laughter and shrieks, Hayes accompanied an upset, sulky Sully.

'Barrett took a bloody liberty,' wailed the lumbering Sully.

'He just enjoys an argument,' Hayes replied, trying to pacify his aggrieved friend..

'He insulted my father.'

'He just didn't agree.'

'I think he's a communist. He has some very far out ideas.'

'I don't think so.

'He's likes Nye Bevan. '

'Bevan isn't a communist Sulls, he's a socialist.'

'What's the difference?'

'There's quite a big difference, actually.'

'Maybe, but Barrett always likes being unpatriotic.'

'He just sees things differently. Calm down, Sulls, you'll just have to live with Red Barrett.'

Suddenly Binns ran towards them, clenching his fists and squeezing up his eyes.

'Ah here comes mental,' exclaimed Sully.

'Leave him alone Sulls, he can't help it.'

'Why does he keep doing that?'

'I don't know but just let him be.'

'Boys,' announced Binns somewhat breathlessly, 'did you see One Ball? He was chatting up that French maid. He fancies her.'

'I don't think she'd fancy him,' deduced Sully confidently.

‘No. He’s an arrogant bastard. I don’t know how you put up with him, Tommy,’ commented Binns, sympathising with Hayes’s servile predicament.

‘Sometimes, it is difficult.’ professed Hayes.

‘I can imagine. Personally I would give him a kick in the balls. Sorry. In the ball!’

The boys all laughed at Sully’s semantic correction.

‘He’s a bloody sadist,’ continued Sully. ‘My punishment means I’ve got to run a mile in seven minutes. With my weight, that's going to kill me.’

‘Why don’t you cheat?’ suggested a devious Binns.

‘It’s a possibility. Otherwise, I’m going to have that punishment hanging over me forever. I’m never going to make that time,’ recognised a sullen Sully.

‘Once you clear the Avenue and are past Open Way, you can find a place to hide and stay there for five minutes, then sprint back over the final four hundred yards exhausted but within the time,’ expounded Binns, squeezing his hands excitedly at the thought of his ruse.

‘Binnsy. You’re a mastermind. You should go on The Brains Trust,’ enthused Sully.

‘There you are Sulls. Everything solved,’ cried an optimistic Hayes as the boys made their way into James B.

In the dayroom, those two well-known rockers, Brown and Bunter had taken over the bench next to the radio, listening to the American Forces Network station. Brown, blonde-haired with a big quiff, Bunter, small plump and neat with a cherubically cheeky face and thick dark hair, surreptitiously styled in homage to the ‘Tony Curtis ducktail’. They were seniors but ones with a rebellious streak.

‘The bloody reception has gone again,’ complained Brown, desperately retuning as the sound of rock ‘n’ roll passed into the ether.

‘What was playing Brown?’ asked the ever-curious Sully.

‘Heartbreak Hotel,’ replied the rocker, almost bored at such an inane enquiry.

‘I love Elvis.’ enthused Sully.

‘That reception’s always a problem,’ sighed Bunter. ‘It’s difficult to get anywhere where there’s good music. Just Radio Luxembourg and American Forces Network. When you can hear it.’

‘Ah that’s better,’ said Brown as Elvis’s yearning tones re-emerged.

‘It should be number 1,’ proclaimed Sully.

‘Whack it up Brownie,’ urged Bunter.

Brown obediently obeyed his fellow rocker and Elvis’s resonant voice duly enveloped the whole dayroom.

Immediately, One Ball came thundering out of his study.

‘Turn it down!’ he yelled at Brown and Bunter. ‘And Hayes. Come here, now!’

‘What an idiot,’ whispered Sully.

Every boy in the dayroom was now observing this drama, only to resettle as Hayes cautiously made his way to Potts’s study.

While standing outside the study door, with its four small windowpanes covered by a dark red curtain, Hayes heard the soothing sounds of a string quartet not the usual Wagnerian blitzkreig. He knocked gently on one of the small windows.

‘Come in!’ barked Potts.

Hayes entered and closed the door carefully behind him.

‘Nice music,’ observed Hayes.

‘Yes better than that rubbish on the radio. It’s the Trout Quintet.’

‘Who wrote it?’

‘Schubert. He was only twenty-two?’

‘Sounds good,’ appreciated Hayes chirpily.

‘It’s a development of an earlier piece,’ added One Ball, leaning back on a chair next to his table.

‘I see,’ considered Hayes, unaware of the composer’s precociousness.

‘Anyway Hayes, I didn’t ask you here to discuss the work of Franz Schubert, interesting though that is. I wanted to talk to you about my shoes.’

‘Why? I cleaned them.’

‘No Hayes. You thought that you cleaned them’.

Suddenly, One Ball went across to the cream coloured record player in a corner of the study. He then raised its arm and placed it on its rest. The distant rock 'n' rolling of Elvis in the dayroom replaced Schubert's classical lyricism. One Ball then told Hayes to sit down on a narrow armchair covered by some bizarre celtic patterns. Such decor led Hayes to wonder if One Ball had Scottish or even Irish blood. Before he could assimilate such thoughts, One Ball had extracted a rusty knife from the drawer of his table. He then duly proceeded to turn on his desk lamp and switch off the central light. One Ball then took off his right shoe and held it towards the glare, like a dedicated detective examining incriminating evidence. An area of significant dirt was illuminated. Straight away, an irate One Ball grabbed the knife and launched an aggressive assault on the offending blemish until some of the grime disappeared.

'See, Hayes. You didn't clean it,' accused One Ball, opening the nearby study window to allow the wafting dust to depart from the vicinity.

'I must have missed a bit,' acknowledged Hayes.

'A bit? It's clogged with bloody mud,' thundered One Ball.

Hayes became aggressively silent. What was it about the volatile Potts that one minute he talks to you like a human being and the next he starts being a crazy military commandant. The junior wanted to have a conversation about Schubert, not the cleanliness of his shoes. Although his mother was a classical musician, he'd avoided conversations about her work and retreated into the more obviously male world of sport. After all, hadn't he ambitions to score the winning goal in the FA Cup Final and wave to the crowd from the Oval balcony after winning the Ashes? However, when he heard the captivating sounds of the Trout, he regretted his artistic ignorance.

'What do you think a squit is for, Hayes?' posed One Ball, closing the window, switching off his desk lamp and turning on the main study light.

Hayes abruptly awakened from his cultural musings before answering One Ball, who was now sitting at his desk, staring at his squit.

'To help a monitor.'

'Not help. Serve.'

'You mean like in Victorian times.'

'No, in a modern way. Like a batman does in the army.'

'Batman? I thought he was a character in a comic strip.'

'Not that Batman, idiot. More like the way a soldier is a servant to an officer.'

'But I'm not in the army Potts, but you soon will be.'

'What do you mean?'

'National Service.'

'That's deferred while we study.'

'You're lucky Potts.'

'Lucky, squit?'

'That you're not going to be attacked in the jungle by the Mau Mau.'

'I'll be proud to serve my country, Hayes.'

'Of course, Potts.'

'When the time comes.'

'Or whatever the future brings.'

'That's enough of the philosophical conjecture, squit.'

'Sorry, Potts.'

'I was talking about serving Hayes.'

'Yes, you were.'

'The principle is similar to the army. It's the principle Hayes. The principle.'

'All right, it's the principle,' repeated Hayes unenthusiastically.

'And it's about discipline Hayes. You have to do things thoroughly, efficiently and on time.'

'All right, Potts.'

'And that means making sure that the bloody mud is scraped off my shoes.'

'Ok.'

'Always remember, Hayes. Do better.'

'Yes Potts.'

'Ok. You can go.'

Hayes rose and departed from the study. Once in the noisy and lively dayroom, he forgot about One Ball's pontificating and joined in the general chat before prep. Rice, a senior, who had a small bald patch on his head because of boiling water badly scorching his hair, was enthusing about the merits of the sexy French star, Brigitte Bardot. He had a copy of Picturegoer and a picture of Brigitte in Doctor at Sea. He held it up triumphantly to Brown and Bunter, who were still standing on a bench, listening to Be-Bop-a-Lula blasting forth from AFN.

'Look at that boys,' cried Rice, thrusting Brigitte's picture towards the two rockers.

'Very nice,' agreed an appreciative Brown.

'Not my type,' said Bunter dismissively.

'You must be joking,' exclaimed a bewildered Rice.

'I saw her in that Doctor film,' revealed Bunter.

'She was great,' insisted Rice.

'She was only in it for two minutes,' remembered Bunter.

'Two bloody good minutes,' specified Rice.

'Lovely figure,' noted Brown, gazing at the photo.

'I prefer something more homely. I wouldn't trust Brigitte,' professed Bunter.

'Like what?' demanded Rice?

'Well, you know...,' hesitated Bunter.

'His Mum!' yelled Rice hysterically.

'Shut up Ricey,' bawled Bunter defensively.

'No someone like er... Jean Simmons,' suggested Bunter, struggling to articulate his female taste.

'Too safe,' claimed Rice.

Brown then impulsively rammed up the volume as Gene Vincent and his Blue Caps came to the end of their rockin'. The senior jigged about on the bench with an imitation mike in his hand and was about to throw himself on the dayroom floor and do his imitation of the crouching, leather-clad rocker, when there was a dramatic intervention. Suddenly, Killer Roy entered through the swing door. Killer, a svelte six foot four inches, stared menacingly at the rock 'n' roll miscreant.

'That's enough Brown.'

'Yes sir,' replied Brown, transforming quickly from ecstatic rocker to obsequious schoolboy.

'Nearly time for prep,' announced Killer.

'Right,' conceded Brown, switching off the radio.

'You know what's happened boys?' posed Killer.

'Elvis has got married' whispered Rice.

'What's that Rice?' enquired Killer sharply.

'Nothing sir,' declared Rice innocently.

'Then don't mumble', ordered Killer.

'No sir,' responded Rice obediently.

'The Soviet Union is flexing its muscles in Hungary,' continued Killer.

'What's that sir?' queried the precocious Barrett, advancing towards Killer.

'I was saying that the Soviets have squashed an insurrection in Hungary,' reiterated Killer.

'Have many people died, sir?' questioned Barrett.

'I think, quite a lot. Apparently, it's difficult to judge' replied Killer.

'Stalin's got a lot to answer for,' pronounced Barrett.

'Stalin's dead, thicko,' whispered Rice once again.

'I said stop mumbling Rice,' ordered Killer.

'I was just saying Stalin's dead, sir,' explained Rice, innocently.

'Maybe but his legacy certainly isn't,' maintained Barrett, glaring at Rice.

'This is a dangerous moment boys,' emphasised Killer.

'Let's hope we don't get into any more wars,' stated Brown

'Will the next war be nuclear sir?' asked Barrett.

'Let's hope not, Barrett,' stressed Killer. 'Anyway boys,' he resumed, deliberately changing the subject, 'let's settle down and get ready for prep.'

The boys gradually parted their separate ways. Brown and Bunter, rockers extraordinaire, stepped away from the radio and off the bench. Brown started parting his thick blonde locks with a black comb, making sure that his quiff was secure and settled. Bunter followed him up to the seniors' table, while mumbling a quiet reprise of Be-Bop-A-Lula. Rice had another look at Picturegoer's picture of Brigitte, as he also meandered up to the top of the dayroom. Barrett went to his locker and got out his work for prep. Meticulous in his preparation, he had a small wooden box that contained pens, pencils, rubbers, a ruler and a small notebook. On the top of the box, there was inevitably a picture of Lonnie Donegan. Tonight, Barrett was going to undertake a Latin translation of Caesar's Gallic Wars. This was a task, which he approached with both diligence and alacrity.

He was a scholarship boy with an agile, sceptical radical mind. His thirst for knowledge had come from his father, a bald-headed, genial small man, who always wore corduroy trousers. Mr Barrett was an maths teacher at a primary school in South East London, where apparently he had considerable success in getting his pupils through the dreaded eleven plus exam.

Meanwhile, Killer Roy was walking around the dayroom like a patrolling policeman. Even when, he made a joke he never could fully convince the boys of his sincerity. It didn't help that usually his attempts at humour were facile. You got the feeling that Killer was like an executioner entertaining himself, before dropping a guillotine on his victim's head. He prowled across the dayroom with such intensity that the boys dispersed to their positions with all the haste of civilians fleeing an invading army. While the boys took refuge from the junior housemaster's threatening presence by opening their books and appearing keen, Killer went to the dayroom bell, which was hanging near the swing door, and rang it vigorously. Total quiet descended and the boys were compelled to settle down to prep. After about half a minute, when Hayes looked up to confirm that Killer had actually left the dayroom, a shrill voice interrupted his meditative gaze.

'Get on with it, Hayes,' instructed Pound, looking up from his chemistry studies. He was sitting nearby in his monitor's position, next to a small radiator. Hayes obeyed and got stuck into reading about Disraeli's reforms. When he discovered how the Artisans Dwelling Act helped clear slums, he began to realise that history mattered. It really informed the present.

After prep had concluded, the boys made their way up wooden stairs to the dormitory, while passing various pictures of James B in a previous incarnation. The latter consisted of faded house photos, full of vacuous looking pupils, assembled in lineal formation on a front lawn. There were twenty-five boys in both the senior and junior dormitories. The junior dormitory was on the lower level, the senior on the higher. At each end of a dormitory was a lav end. This consisted of one bath, which was used according to a strict rota, a private toilet and five urinals. There was also a long, elongated basin, where the boys could wash themselves in front of an extended mirror. They used bowls to wash their feet and each boy took it in turn to do lav end duties. This meant that they had to clean the bath and basin as well as mop the floor. They also had to pour bowls of water down all the urinals, because there wasn't a satisfactory flush. In addition, the sleeping accommodation was spartan. The beds were hard as the mattresses lay on brown wooden slats. Every boy had to make his own bed and be ready for breakfast parade at 7 am sharp.

In the junior dormitory, a housemaster on duty oversaw the boys until all of them were in bed. After he left, a monitor stayed at a table with accompanying lamp, where he continued his own work, until it seemed that everybody was fully settled. Tonight, Killer was the master on duty. Thankfully, it wasn't his execution night. That was at the end of the month, when the number of boys to be beaten had accumulated. Killer didn't look forward to it, he just saw it as part of his duties. As far as he was concerned, corporal punishment had a place, like a short sharp shock, a sort of physical reminder not to do something wrong again. He believed it gave the boys a moral compass. His youthful war experience in Burma had convinced him of the need for retribution and that bad behaviour should be severely chastised. After all, he'd seen too much cruelty escape unpunished. Amidst the torturous conditions of extreme heat, heavy rainfall and disease, he believed that it was a miracle that he ever got out of the jungle without being captured. Too many of his fellow soldiers had died or suffered the severe after effects of imprisonment.

Suddenly, some highly animated activity in one of the lav ends interrupted Killer's musings. It looked like there was some kind of aquatic fight and that the boys were flicking water at each other. Killer responded by bestriding the dormitory with intent and marching resolutely towards the scene of the crime.

Inside the lav end, the boys were getting hysterical as they desperately tried to avoid the water spray. Amidst the commotion, Hayes saw the approaching figure of Killer through the lav end's windows, which separated that area from the dormitory.

'KV!' screamed Hayes. 'Killer!'

Immediately, all the boys rushed back to their bowls and self-consciously engaged in an innocent activity. Hayes replete with a blue flannel, started washing his legs with exaggerated emphasis, Barrett cleaned his teeth with incongruous rhythmic aggression and washed his hands as if he was severely contaminated. Binns took cover in the loo and several others went to urinate unnecessarily. Killer was now getting closer as he entered the small corridor, which accommodated laundry hampers. On arriving, he flung open the lav end door so aggressively that it would have swung back and hit him in the face, if his large hand hadn't quickly grabbed the handle.

'Ok. What's going on?' demanded Killer, gathering himself and looking ominously at the boys.

There was an eerie silence.

'Barrett, were you splashing water?'

'Yes sir.'

'Why?'

'We were having some fun.'

'Fun. Fun,' repeated Killer. 'This isn't a time for fun.'

'No sir.'

'This is the time for bed.'

'Yes sir.'

'Is anybody in the loo? yelled Killer, moving stridently towards that part of the lav end.

'Yes sir. Me,' replied a disembodied voice from the toilet.

'Who is me?' pressed Killer.

'Binns,' answered the voice.

'Well come out, Binns,' commanded Killer.

'I haven't quite finished, sir,' continued Binns in a strained voice, obviously in the middle of intimate activity.

'Well, then hurry up. And you boys,' said Killer, referring to those who were huddling strategically by the urinals, 'come out of there.'

Cautiously, they moved towards Killer as did Binns, when he'd finished answering nature's call. Having successfully marshalled all the troops, Killer was ready to make his speech:

'Now look here boys. The lav end is for washing not for a splashing competition. Who else apart from Barrett was involved?'

Gradually, all the boys raised their hands. It seemed that there was solidarity in their disobedience.

'So it was all of you,' discovered Killer. 'Well. Let me say this. Don't think that there's safety in numbers. What you all did was wrong. And if I catch you doing it again, I'll take the slipper to the lot of you!'

With that unpleasant threat, Killer departed the lav end and made his way to talk to One Ball. One Ball was tonight's monitor on duty and had already parked himself at a table, strategically placed to observe any misdemeanours.

'Potts,' said Killer.

'Yes sir,' replied One Ball.

'They've been messing about in the lav end.'

'Doing what sir?'

'Splashing water at each other. Having a sort of competition.'

'A competition, sir?'

'Yes, seeing who can drench the other boy the most.'

'Oh I see.'

'Keep an eye on them. There's a good chap.'

'Of course, sir.'

'Now you're here, I'll go. I've got a lot of marking to do before tomorrow.'

'Ok sir.'

'Goodnight Potts.'

'Goodnight sir.'

In the lav end, Hayes noted that Killer was departing.

'Killer's gone,' shouted Hayes gleefully.

'Thanks,' acknowledged an appreciative Barrett.

'But beloved One Ball is on duty,' observed Sully cynically.

'Still, he'll probably be obsessed with his work,' claimed Hayes optimistically.

'To think that One Ball could be a scientist. Frightening. He could be a new Frankenstein,' proclaimed Sully, as he struggled to bend down and put on his navy blue slippers.

'He does have an interest in other things,' divulged Hayes, as he finished rigorously cleaning his teeth.

'Like what?' queried Sully, while placing his large feet into his slippers.

‘Music. He’s always playing classical pieces,’ confirmed Hayes, concluding his teeth ritual.

‘So did some of the Nazis before committing genocide,’ stressed the studious Barrett, while combing his hair and vainly eyeing himself in the mirror.

‘And he likes The Goon Show,’ added Hayes, before rinsing his mouth in some very cold water.

Barrett responded by singing the chorus of the Ying Tong Song from the popular show.

‘I prefer Educating Archie,’ disclosed Hayes loudly, intruding upon Barrett’s vocal outburst.

‘I’ve heard that Peter Brough is a terrible ventriloquist,’ professed Barrett.

‘But he’s very popular,’ countered Hayes.

‘That’s because he’s on radio,’ explained Barrett earnestly.

‘How do you know that?’ demanded Hayes. He disliked having his illusions destroyed.

‘My Dad’s got a friend who works for the BBC,’ said Barrett proudly.

‘Really?’ questioned Hayes suspiciously.

‘Yes. He says you can see his lips move when he’s doing the Archie voice,’ elaborated Barrett with a mischievous smile.

‘Oh my God, KV! Grim Jim is on the way,’ warned Sully abruptly..

And lo and behold before you could say One Ball, Jim Potts entered the lav end in all his grim glory.

‘Hurry up you lot. It’s time for bed,’ announced One Ball, less grimly than expected.

‘We were talking about The Goon Show, Potts?’ mentioned Barrett, trying to get One Ball to loosen up.

‘Were you? Good. It’s a great show,’ enthused One Ball.

‘What do you like about it, Potts?’ enquired Hayes.

‘The mad, crazy sense of humour, I suppose,’ replied a more amenable One Ball.

‘Prince Charles likes it,’ interjected Sully.

‘That isn’t necessarily a recommendation,’ responded Barrett caustically.

‘You’re not a republican are you, Barrett? queried One Ball distrustfully.

‘No Potts, I’m a socialist,’ declared Barrett defiantly.

‘Oh my God!’ cried Potts.

‘He likes Nye Bevan,’ Sully reminded everybody.

‘Labour are always arguing among themselves and wanting to spend too much money,’ reasoned Potts.

‘But you come from an army family Potts, so you must be Conservative,’ deduced Barrett.

‘Not necessarily, Barrett. Many in the army voted for Attlee. I also respect Bevan. He’s got vision and guts. I just don’t like the state doing everything.’

‘Surely you believe in public services.’

‘Of course, but not in every bloody industry being nationalised.’

‘But surely reconstruction meant that..’

‘Reconstruction doesn’t mean a new Soviet Union, Barrett.’

‘Oh Potts, come off it.’

‘Barrett that’s enough of your Labour Party manifesto. I’ve got to finish my essay and you have to go to bed. So come on. Leave. All of you,’ instructed One Ball, opening the door invitingly wide.

The boys made sure all their belongings were in order and then trudged past the towering figure of a less grim Jim, who seemed almost human tonight.

Barrett, the last to leave, suddenly stopped midway into the corridor and continued his radio probings.

‘Potts, who’s your favourite performer in the Goon Show?’

One Ball was surprised by Barrett’s request. He was about to tell him to get into bed but as a Goon Show obsessive he couldn’t resist answering the question.

‘Peter Sellers. He’s a fantastic mimic. He can do so many voices. And he’s very funny. All right Barrett, tell me your favourite.’

‘Ray Ellington. Great music.’

‘I agree,’ said a softening One Ball.

‘The only black musician appearing on the BBC,’ asserted Barrett boldly. Then he hesitated. ‘Sorry I forgot Edmundo Ros and Winifred Atwell. So let’s say one of the few musicians of colour on the BBC.’

‘Ok Barrett that’s enough, time for bed,’ asserted One Ball, closing the doors behind him and following the junior into the dormitory. Before attending to his studies, he remembered to check the cleaning rota.

‘Whose turn is it to do lav end?’ One Ball asked the boys.

‘Oh mine,’ revealed Sully despondently.

‘Well do it,’ directed One Ball.

Sully was about to get into bed when he was bawled out, so he reluctantly put his slippers on again and strolled casually to the lav end. Cleaning the lav end was a chore. Sully did not intend to fully carry out this arduous task. After all, he was tired and needed a good night’s sleep. In any case, he thought that One Ball will be more interested in his science essay than checking up on lavatorial duties. Sully started mopping the floor while singing the March of the Toreadors. As he sang, he created different shapes on the floor. One of these could be detected as ‘One Ball is a Bastard’ but looking up towards the dormitory and suddenly seeing grim Jim gazing sceptically in his direction, he quickly finished his artistic contours and started to attend to the urinals.

Sully certainly wasn’t going to walk twenty-five times to the piss holes with a full bowl of water. Consequently, after pouring five bowls of water down the first urinal, he conjured up a devious plan to overcome the servile task. He disappeared from One Ball’s eyeline, walking towards the bath with a bowl in his hand. On arrival, he sang another section of the March of the Toreadors to cover the time it took to fill a bowl with water. He then reappeared with an empty bowl and moved to the urinals, while continuing to sing the Bizet song. After all, he had operatic ambitions and intended to get a place at a reputable musical academy. In total, Sully made twenty phantom journeys backwards and forwards to the urinals with an empty bowl. In the process, he exhausted many different approaches to the March of the Toreadors. When Sully had finished his Carmen exploration, he decided to leave. He returned the bowl to the basin, the mop and bucket to a cupboard and made his way back to the dormitory. Sully was just about to get into bed when One Ball whispered menacingly:

‘Sully.’

'Yes', replied an apprehensive Sully.

'Come here.'

Sully walked to One Ball's desk in trepidation.

'Yes, Potts.'

The dormitory was now submerged in darkness, apart from the desk and an Anglepoise light, which seemed like part of an interrogation room. While he spoke, One Ball meticulously continued his work, ignoring the flabby Sully. At the edge of his desk, the meticulous monitor self-consciously paraded his marks for his previous essay about kinetic energy. Sully saw that not only had he received an alpha for his work but also that 'Excellent' was written boldly in red ink at the bottom of the page.

'Have you done lav end properly?' broached One Ball casually, as he continued to write his latest essay on thermal conductivity.

'Yes, Potts,' answered Sully confidently.

There was a pause as One Ball proceeded with his work. Then, while reading what he'd written, he resumed interrogating Sully.

'How many bowls of water did you put down each urinal?'

'Quite a few,' said a vague Sully.

'How many is quite a few?' challenged an irate One Ball.

Sully paused. He thought of lying on a big scale. Surely, One Ball wouldn't check but then he remembered that when he'd completed his ruse, there was still an awful smell in the urinals. Sully's face turned a deep red. What would happen if One Ball discovered the asphyxiating odour? Such was One Ball's propensity for anger, he might even put Sully's head in a urinal. One Ball's love of Schubert and Wagner let alone The Goon Show, certainly didn't erase his demons and Sully was afraid that the monitor's vindictiveness could make his life a continual nightmare. These dark thoughts forced Sully to panic and splutter out:

'About three.'

'What does 'about' mean?' demanded an irritable One Ball.

'I can't remember.'

'Why can't you remember?'

'I had other things on my mind.'

'Like what?'
'The March of the Toreadors.'
'The March of the Toreadors?'
'Yes. I was practising my singing.'
'Sully. There's a time and place for singing practice,' affirmed One Ball authoritatively. Suddenly lifting his eyes away from his work, he stared at the beleaguered junior and shouted, 'but it's not when you're doing the bloody lav end!'
'No Potts,' reacted Sully meekly.
'Go and put ten bowls down each!'
'Oh no, Potts!'
'Do it now.'
'Please.'
'This is an order not a conversation. Go!'
By this time most of the boys were alerted to this exchange and watched a downtrodden Sully return to the lav end. This feud fed growing resentment towards One Ball. Any sympathy he'd earned, because of his unfortunate confrontation with barbed wire, was being eroded. Although as a Goon Show fan, Barrett had a path to a more personal connection with the monitor, it didn't prevent the young socialist from being disgusted by One Ball's lust for power.
Sully made his way back to the lav end sheepishly, like a cricketer returning to the pavilion after being bowled first ball. He felt tired and depressed and when he got the mop out again, he started to feel anger. No, he wasn't going to pour ten bloody bowls of water down each urinal. That would mean there would be fifty journeys. The very thought gave him palpitations. He wouldn't be bullied by such perversity. He would repeat the phantom journeys. Next time, he would be ready for One Ball's sadistic interrogation and if necessary, he would lie. To help him get through the ordeal, he continued to develop his singing, this time with Swing Low Sweet Chariot. Sully's voice wasn't suitable for the song but he loved the way Paul Robeson sang it. The African-American's defiant and resonant bass-baritone voice inspired Sully to do his own version of the spiritual. So up and down the lav end went our aspiring opera singer, pitching his treble voice as low as possible, imitating the celebrated singer. 'Swing low, sweet chariot, comin' for to carry me

home', sang our budding artiste as he laboured with bowl after bowl, occasionally with water but mostly with none. By the time Sully had completed fifty journeys, the song made him feel exhilarated and resolute. He was now ready to escape his bondage and meet his nemesis.

Sully strolled up to One Ball's desk, imagining that he was a proud, exploited worker defying a wealthy and corrupt boss.

'I've done the lav end, Potts.'

Potts didn't reply promptly. He was engrossed in higher things like Fourier's law of heat conduction. He didn't want to be interrupted by the puerile mind of a junior.

'What did you say?' asked a distracted One Ball.

Sully noticed that One Ball's writing was incredibly neat. He wrote with a Parker fountain pen and had a deft way of making his sentences look artistic.

'I said that I've finished the lav end,' reiterated Sully.

'Oh, have you?' queried One Ball, looking up at the junior with disbelief.

'Yes, I have,' verified Sully.

'I hope you have because if you haven't, you'll be receiving another punishment mile, Sully,' warned One Ball.

'I've done it. It's fine,' stated a reinvigorated Sully.

'It'd better be. Go to bed,' ordered One Ball.

'Goodnight Potts,' acknowledged Sully, looking to depart.

'Good night,' answered a preoccupied, dismissive One Ball

Sully then started to make his way to his bed, when One Ball quietly called him back.

'And Sully?'

'Yes Potts? responded Sully nervously.

'Do lose some weight,' suggested One Ball snidely.

'Yes Potts,' replied an aggrieved Sully.

While Sully got into bed and settled into his slumbers, One Ball continued writing his essay. He was confident of understanding the way specific material conducts electricity and now that he was free from Sully and his friends, his writing accelerated with articulacy and verve. One Ball found science a fascinating mixture of the inventive and the logical. He was determined to work his one ball off to get to Cambridge, where he was sure that he would benefit from greater intellectual stimulation. The school had its quota of high-class scientific minds but not as many as in the best universities. In any case, here there were the constant distractions from the likes of Sully and his friends. After half an hour passed, One Ball completed his essay and decided to leave. He put his fountain pen inside his red case, placed his chair under the table, gathered all his belongings, including his books and papers, and switched off the lamp. He then left the dormitory on tiptoe to avoid waking up the little bastards, slowly closing the door.

After One Ball's departure there was a momentary silence. Gradually, out of the darkness, a cacophony of disembodied voices started to emerge.

'Anybody got a radio?'

'I have.'

'Get it out.'

'Let's have Radio Lux'.

After a short pause a sonorous voice emerged from the transistor.

'Good evening friends, I' m Horace Bachelor'

'Oh no!'

'The inventor of the famous Infra-Draw method for the Treble Chance,' announced the avuncular, reassuring Horace.

'Music please!'

'Reception isn't great.'

'Send to Department 1, Keynsham. That's K-E-Y-N-S-H-A-M, Bristol', concluded the Horace advert.

Eventually music returned.

'Ah, that's better.'

'Turn it up.'

The volume increased so that the boys could hear the serene voice and flawless diction of Doris Day singing Que Sera, Sera. It wasn't long before they all became emboldened and joined Doris in a raucous version of the well-known chorus.

Suddenly, one of the dormitory doors swung open and the lights blazed like a searing searchlight zooming in on escaping prisoners. At the entrance was a scowling Killer ready to pounce on warbling, errant pupils. Thankfully, the radio seemed to have disappeared into the ether, but that wasn't going to stop an angry Killer from making his point.

'What the hell is going on here? That racket could be heard everywhere. This is not the time for a concert party. It's time for sleeping. This is a warning to you. If I hear that again, I'll slipper the lot of you. Do you understand?'

A faint chorus of 'yes sir' permeated the whole dormitory. Killer looked around for any further evidence of misbehaviour. He then strode magisterially to the middle of the dormitory, walking slowly like a detective searching for a clue. Several boys had hidden under their bedclothes, so that they could avoid Killer's sinister gaze. Some feigned sleep, others looked apprehensively in a different direction. The thought of Killer 'slippering' everybody was positively homicidal and was to be avoided at all costs, especially as he hit unrepentantly hard. Eventually, when Killer couldn't find any further evidence, he abruptly turned off the lights and departed. He didn't bother to say goodnight.

The next day as the boys went to morning chapel, Hayes wondered how Killer had heard the noise, especially as he entered from the door closer to matron's abode, not from the one nearer his study. It crossed his mind that maybe he fancied matron. 'I wonder,' thought Hayes. Then he thought 'but Killer's married'. Before he could evaluate such suspicions, Binns interrupted his ruminations.

'It's hymn practice with Root after the service.'

'Oh no. Thanks for reminding me.'

The boys attended the School Chapel every morning before lessons. The chapel was at the end of their side of the Avenue, just before the Quadrangle. The congregation faced each other, which gave rise to some bizarre staring, not least at housemasters' families. A long aisle led to the altar and large stained glass windows that depicted events leading to the birth of Christ. Before the altar, on one side of the aisle, there was the pulpit, where various prelates preached too many boring sermons and on the other was the organ, which Mr Sims, the long-suffering Assistant Music Master, played for most of the services. James B sat at the end of the pews, near the main entrance and adjacent to the headmaster and his family, who had especially raised seating. Elaborately carved wooden animals, interspersed with philosophical Latin quotes, surrounded the headmaster's position. Opposite the pews were large classical murals depicting dramatic events in the history of Christianity. Religion was at the heart of the school's ethos, which justified five weekday services and two on Sunday, plus Holy Communion, if you were confirmed.

Both masters and boys made their way to their positions. The Major aka Mr Aizlewood, James B's Senior Housemaster, was placed opposite his house. Genial with a good sense of humour, he was still single at thirty-eight. As a result, the boys were trying to pair him off with all sorts of possible partners, whether it was one of the nurses in the infirmary or the daughter of some ageing housemasters. In fact, the latest betting was on one of the latter, Victoria, the daughter of Wallace, the Senior Classics Master, who wore plus fours and rode around the school on a bicycle. Victoria was working in the town as a secretary for an estate agent but she did appear at chapel during the weekends, which certainly gave the boys a lift. Victoria had pale skin, green eyes, gently tousled chestnut hair and thick red lips, all of which made her a star of Sunday Evening Chapel, as she and her family also sat directly opposite James B.

Regrettably, today was Friday, so the boys had to be content at just looking at the Major, a smart balding man, dressed in a neatly pressed navy suit, with a blue and white gown draped around his shoulders. The Reverend Elwyn, the School Chaplain, was taking the service. The rotund Elwyn's eyes tended to wander upwards, as if he was permanently looking for divine inspiration. The benign chaplain, well upholstered in surplice and cassock, was sincere and committed but somewhat naïve. He lived at one end of the Avenue opposite Wade house, with his wife and three noisy young children. He always appeared shocked by the revelation of any scandal. It was if he was living in a parallel spiritual universe. When Elwyn finished the service, he made his way to the vestry, a location well known to many boys as an anarchic refuge for shenanigans.

Root, the Music Master, was a small squat man of dark complexion, who was always dressed in black and had a short fuse. He got results but wasn't popular with the boys. He'd replaced the well-liked, ruddy-faced Cocks, who was an inventive and imaginative musician. Unfortunately, the convivial, popular Cocks was sacked, when he was discovered drunk, dancing in the Quadrangle fountain singing Handel's Messiah. The boys canvassed the headmaster to try to get the decision overturned but their pleas were ignored. Oliver believed that he'd already tolerated Cocks's volatile behaviour for too long. He was an alcoholic who needed treatment and wasn't capable of fulfilling his duties.

Although Root was in a difficult situation when he was appointed, he didn't endear himself to the choir with his rigid disciplinary methods. When six months after leaving the school, Cocks collapsed in a street and died of a heart attack, the choir's attitude to Root hardened. Various choristers challenged Root, only to be reprimanded and told to be more disciplined. When Root came to oversee the music for Cocks's memorial service, there was a huge row during a rehearsal in the chapel. Francis Ryder, the choir's radical leader, objected to Root disregarding some of Cocks's favourite music, not least the Messiah. Despite this altercation, Root had no intention of programming a work that would remind the school of the former music master's infamous performance in the fountain.

Root ran the weekly school hymn practice as a Nazi rally with him in the role of Führer. After the morning service had finished and all the staff had departed, Root with his black gown swirling behind him, took up his place in the centre of the aisle surrounded by eight hundred boys. Here, he relished the exhilaration of complete power over the massed throng.

'Number 125,' bellowed Root, marching up and down the aisle like a demented sentry.

The boys ritualistically turned the pages of their Hymns Ancient and Modern to the relevant place. The Headmaster, Mr Seymour, nicknamed Oliver because of his Cromwellian puritanism, was the only non-musical member of staff, who remained behind. He wanted to show support for maintaining a high standard of singing at all chapel services. However, while he acknowledged Root's improvement of musical standards, Oliver had become concerned by the music master's more unpredictable behaviour. Meanwhile Sims, while playing the organ, could observe Root's antics through a large mirror. The assistant music master had recently been going out with a nurse from the infirmary. Rumour had it that they were discovered necking under a birch tree near Keats Wood.

'Mr Sims!' screamed the musical Nazi.

Sims obeyed forthwith and played the introduction. The boys then followed, bursting into song:

'Who would true valour see

Let him come hither..'

Suddenly, at the end of the first verse, Root abruptly raised his hand high above his head, which did little to discourage the boys from equating him with the reviled German dictator.

'Mr Sims!' he exclaimed.

The enthusiastic young Sims was so enthralled by John Bunyan's hymn that he didn't heed Root's command. In fact, he revelled in playing his beloved tune, long after the controversial music master's bellowing order.

'Mr Sims! Root reiterated, yelling in desperation.

Eventually, Sims awoke from his musical trance, fearing vengeful retribution from Root.

'Thank you, Mr Sims,' declaimed Root, with an air of cynicism. 'We need to start together and attack the opening lines with gusto. So let's concentrate and sing just the first two lines.'

'Once more, Mr Sims!' shouted the insistent Root. Sims instinctively responded to Root's withering command, by playing with more vivacity.

Sims tolerated Root's public performances with good humour. When they met privately, Root was more of a human being. In fact, the authoritarian music master had already invited his assistant round to his flat to partake of tea and some tasty sultana scones. When Root started talking about Schoenberg, Sims was fearful that his colleague would become doctrinal and boring. Sims wasn't a great admirer of atonal music; he was more of an Elgar and Vaughan Williams man. Nonetheless, such was Root's passion and grasp of the Austrian composer's twelve-tone technique, that he became beguiled. Later, he had an afternoon off and decided to escape the insular bubble of the school and go into the town. While in a local record shop, he espied a Schoenberg LP and became an admirer of the entrancingly poetic Verklärte Nacht. On his return to the school, Sims thanked Root for steering him to Schoenberg's oeuvre. Because of his respect for the troubled music master's commitment and love of music, he tolerated his mood swings. Such oscillation seemed to emanate from an impossible desire for perfection and inner personal demons that he couldn't fully control.

As the hymn practice continued, Root's tendency to use the session as a vehicle to project his own authority irritated the headmaster. Oliver wanted masters to work collaboratively. He disliked 'personality teachers' and believed a little self-effacement wouldn't go amiss. Oliver found Root's attempts at using the school to be a maestro were troublesome. For instance, the music master insisted on taking each hymn two lines at a time. While Oliver admired his attention to detail, he wondered whether it was the best approach, when most of the boys weren't singers.

Oliver had hidden his doubts about Root because of the choir's recent improvement after the cavalier days of Cocks. The boys might have found Cocks's chaotic behaviour entertaining but he did not. The fountain fracas was the climax of a series of embarrassing incidents, including one at a private dinner. After a three-course meal and too many glasses of wine, Cocks raucously declared that the local MP's wife had 'great tits'. Oliver had a dislike of the Conservative politician, who supported hanging but insulting his wife in such an appalling fashion was a major embarrassment and betrayed the ethos of the school, which was about politeness and tolerance. Surprisingly, the wife, a tall, slender woman in a light blue dress with strapless shoulders and a leading light in the local women's institute, remained impressively dignified.

'Thank you,' she replied diplomatically, as Oliver did his best to retrieve the situation.

Regardless of Oliver's efforts, the MP, a former businessman with heavy jowls and a thick girth, took offence and became less enthusiastic in helping to raise funds for a proposed new music school.

Oliver and the school endured Root's deconstruction of hymns 181, God Moves in a Mysterious Way, 352, Nearer My

God to Thee and 483, We Plough the Fields and Scatter. Root then looked to finish the session with a version of hymn 629, Onward Christian Soldiers. Regardless of Root's histrionics, the boys had now warmed up and they eagerly embraced the military beat of the final bombastic hymn. The whole school now sang with a passion and commitment that was both impressive and alarming, as Root waved his arms with metronomic precision. When the voices grew in intensity, a surreptitious smile appeared on Root's face. He thought that this is how the great conductors like Furtwängler and Von Karajan must feel when they're getting a powerful choral response. Root basked in the volume and depth of the sound as it enveloped his whole body, like a tidal wave lapping over a helpless bather. He was in musical ecstasy. Meanwhile, Root's flights of fantasy were increasingly irritating Oliver. Eventually, the martial hymn, which never appealed to the headmaster's more placid instincts, ended with a thundering climax.

After this musical bombardment, Root took out his white handkerchief, with its black RR monogram of his initials, and mopped his brow. He was sweating profusely but as he went towards the vestry to thank Mr Sims, he felt exhilarated. Although he had regrets that he hadn't become a professional conductor, at least this was a very good substitute. The boys then waited for Oliver to depart and once he'd disappeared, they gradually left the chapel. Once back at their house, they collected their books and went to their lessons.

Lessons took place in buildings either side of the imposing Big Hall, which had a large auditorium and presented plays, concerts and a series of Saturday night films. You could access the classroom buildings via the Quadrangle, which lay in front of Big Hall or by the surrounding cloisters, which were particularly useful if it was raining. Inside the buildings were darkly lit corridors, surrounded by dirty white walls, to which were attached a lot of school pictures. These mainly consisted of rugby and cricket teams of yesteryear. There were two levels in each building with eight classrooms on each one.

Hayes was with Sully and Binns, going to a maths class with the dreaded Mrs Hackett. Hackett was the only female teacher in the school. She was married to the head of the modern languages department. They had one daughter Sally, who had a delightfully warm smile and a beauty spot at the bottom of her chin. Sally was studying French at university, so she was often absent, much to the regret of the boys. Most of her appearances were in the summer, when she wore decorative Belle Poque dresses. The boys found it hard to think that she had emerged into this world from the body of Mrs Hackett, who had cold blue eyes, grey-thatched hair and always wore black trousers and check shirts.

'Right boys, settle down' said Mrs H as she entered the class, just as Binns was about to give his paper dart a good fly.

The boys immediately rose and on Mrs Hackett's instruction, they all sat down in their prescribed formation: seven desks in a row, four rows deep.

'We're doing algebra today boys,' announced Mrs H as she hurriedly cleaned the board with a blue duster.

Mrs Hackett then went on to explain various equations. Hayes found that most of this went above his head. In any case, he had an instant dislike of Mrs Hackett. Equally, Mrs Hackett couldn't stand Hayes. The indomitable maths teacher thought he was a lazy, arrogant London boy. Unhappily, for Hayes, Mrs Hackett didn't have a high level of tolerance for perceived stupidity. Sensing that Hayes had dozed off, the redoubtable maths teacher pounced:

'Do you know the answer to this equation, Hayes?' asked an irritated Mrs Hackett, pointing at the blackboard.

'No, miss,' replied a confused Hayes.

'There's no need to call me miss. For a start I'm not a miss but more importantly as I'm the only female teacher here, it's easier to call me sir, then there's less confusion.'

'But you're not a man, miss.'

'Sir, Hayes!'

'Ok miss, I mean sir.'

'Hayes, please stop it.'

'Don't you want to be addressed as a woman?'

'Hayes. I told you before. It's easier and more practical to say sir.'

'Right.'

'Now, who knows the answer?'

'Sir! Sir! Sir!' exclaimed Sully in an outburst of false ardour.

'Yes Sully?'

Sully then went on to give the right answer. Mrs H was delighted and revelled in Sully's triumph.

'Well done, Sully. You see. Enthusiasm. Enthusiasm everybody. Note Hayes.'

'Yes. Enthusiasm.'

'Negativity gets you nowhere, Hayes. Now watch the board while I go through it.'

Mrs Hackett then proceeded to start writing so aggressively that her chalk broke. Inevitably, Sully rushed over and picked it up, like a medieval knight aiding a damsel in distress.

'Oh thank you, Sully. That's so kind of you,' appreciated Mrs H, smiling benignly at her revered pupil.

'Now watch the board boys and I'll teach you how to multiply!' screeched Mrs H, as she relished explaining how the answer to the equation was realised.

Hayes found it difficult to make head or tail of Mrs H's maths lessons. It wasn't helped by Mrs Hackett looking at him was as if he was some sort of low life, who should be shot. With her glacial eyes and bellicose demeanour, Hayes felt as if an alien prosecutor bent on causing pain, had interned him for interrogation. Consequently, when the bell sounded he felt like a prisoner freed from captivity.

'You suck up to her every lesson,' said Hayes accusingly to a bulky, swaggering Sully, as he sauntered confidently through the classroom corridors.

'That's the way to deal with her,' remarked Sully.

'But I'm useless at maths,' admitted an upset Hayes.

'It's not that hard,' asserted Sully. 'Just get the basics right.'

'Maybe you're right,' acknowledged Hayes reluctantly.

'You know your trouble?' questioned Sully.

'What?' queried a defensive Hayes.

'You're oversensitive,' claimed Sully.

'So would be you dealing with the likes of One Ball and Mrs Bloody Hackett. I'm lumbered with a combination of an SS guard and Lady Macbeth,' retorted Hayes in passionate self-justification.

Suddenly, Sully's confident aura diminished once he remembered that his day of reckoning was nigh.

'Oh, I nearly forgot. Today's my punishment day.'

'For rank insubordination?' enquired Hayes, looking for corroboration.

'For rank nothing,' confirmed Sully bitterly.

The boys walked briskly through the cloisters and into the crowded avenue back to James B. It was now time for PE, which meant they had to change into their sports gear and do exercises on the asphalt, at the back of the house. Today, Staines was going to supervise the session. Staines was an able gymnast, Hayes had observed him transcending the vaulting horse like a flying meteor. Witnessing such dextrous aplomb, Hayes could only admire his sense of timing and athleticism. Staines wanted to go to Sandhurst rather than university but he also had an interest in acting. However, as he had light blonde hair and a fair complexion, he was always playing women in school productions, much to his chagrin. Staines started the PE session with various stretching exercises that severely strained Sully's huge frame. The demands of press ups forced the bulky junior to collapse but he recovered gallantly. Meanwhile, Hayes, with his slim physique, found the workout less troublesome. Staines ran the session with tact. He wasn't a monitor but a senior, who was given the task because of his physical skills. He ended the session with 'the highland fling', that involved a series of strenuous movements based on the Scottish dance. Staines called out the changes but initially there was muddled chaos. Fortunately, when he went through the routine slowly, even Sully managed to do it.

'I'm knackered,' complained Sully after the session.

'You'll feel better after a shower,' reassured Hayes.

The boys made their way into the changing rooms, where they had hung their school uniforms. They then stripped and with a towel around the waist queued for the shower, which was placed between the senior and junior changing rooms. There were always too many people waiting to wash themselves. Still, as everybody knew that the amount of time to get to the next lesson was ludicrously short, each boy showered quickly. Hayes allowed the warm water to pour all over his thin, undeveloped body, then he soaped himself with a suitably quick lather, got out of the shower trough, grabbed his towel, dried himself, put on his uniform, went to his locker, grabbed his Latin books and finally cantered to Mr Collins's class.

Collins, an amiable man with a reddish face, wandered down the classroom aisles with his hand clutched lightly to his heart, giving his Latin dictation. Hayes found being in Collins's class a relief after Hackett's brutal regime. He enjoyed Latin because of both its link to other languages and its fascinating historical roots. As Collins wondered around the room reciting the archaic language, his mournful eyes looked towards the murky white ceiling. Occasionally, he looked forlornly out of the window, despite an unprepossessing red brick building blocking his view. Hayes wondered whether Collins was happy. To the boys, he seemed a rather isolated, lonely figure. He wasn't a housemaster and he didn't partake much in the schools' social activities, although he occasionally assisted in some sports coaching. Hayes wondered whether he was in good health. Maybe the constant rubbing of his heart was a symptom of something more serious. Hayes hoped not, as he regarded Collins as a good teacher who treated pupils with respect. He'd heard rumours that he was a good friend of Smallman's. Apparently, they went on holidays together to the Norfolk Broads. On some occasions, several boys joined them there and they all went sailing.

After the dictation was completed, Collins went round the class and collected the boys' efforts. The bell went and Hayes left with a feeling of satisfaction. His Latin may not have been perfect but he enjoyed trying to improve it.

In the Avenue, as he made his way back to house, Hayes met Sully who had been attending a biology class.

'God. Mr Endersby is boring teacher,' testified a frustrated Sully.

'Not a good class?' enquired Hayes.

‘I’ve never heard anybody make the human body seem so uninteresting.’

‘Do you remember him in the masters’ play?’

‘Yes. His Freddy Eynsford-Hill was terrible.’

‘He kept forgetting his lines.’

‘And the whole school laughed as he got prompt after prompt.’

‘Actually I rather like Endersby.’

‘Trouble is he can’t teach.’

‘And he’s an even worse actor.’

‘Endersby put me off Pygmalion for life.’

‘Mind you, Victoria Wallace was a dishy Eliza.’

‘Trouble was she kept dropping her cockney accent.’

‘Yes. I suppose it was an entertaining disaster.’

The two boys now turned off the Avenue to James B. Suddenly, Sully stopped.

‘Now I’ve got to do my punishment.’

‘Rank insubordination?’ queried Hayes, looking for confirmation.

‘Yes. I’ve got to cheat. Like Binnsy mentioned.’

‘Hide behind one of the bushes near the colts’ rugger pitch.’

‘I’ve got to do something, otherwise I’ll never make the time limit.’

‘I’ll keep KV for you.’

‘Will you?’

‘Yes. I’ll go for a walk on Open Way, near those bushes.’

‘Thanks Hayesy.’

On arriving at James B, Sully went to change while Hayes meandered around the dayroom, reading the morning papers that lay on various tables. Most of the headlines were about the Suez crisis. The Middle East seemed far away and Hayes couldn’t really understand why we were getting involved in such places. He swiftly moved to the back pages of the News Chronicle, where he looked at the latest football news. Hayes enjoyed his rugby but like a lot of the boys he had a greater passion for football and in particular Charlton FC, even though they languished at the bottom of the first division. Unfortunately, he couldn’t get much news about the south

London club as the Chronicle was full of John Charles and the Leeds United star's possible move to Juventus. Therefore, the disenchanted football supporter unwillingly turned to the news pages, where there was an article on China. He remembered his mother mentioning the Korean War in the family drawing room after a Sunday lunch but there was never a conversation about China. All Hayes knew about that country was that it was a communist state. As he started reading an extensive article by somebody called James Cameron, Hayes was beginning to get a wider appreciation of that far-off nation, only to be interrupted by Sully, all togged up in James B's black and white hooped shirt and black shorts. He was ready for action, or to be more precise, subterfuge.

'Ok Sulls. I'll go for a walk on Open Way. I'll get my scarf,' announced Hayes.

'Ok. I'll see One Ball,' replied a tentative Sully.

'Remember. The bushes by the colts' pitch.'

'Yes'

'Have you got your watch on?'

'Oh hells, bloody bells.'

'Where is it?'

'In the changing room, I think.'

'You need it Sulls, to synchronise your leaving time with One Ball.'

'Right,' said Sully nervously.

'Ok let's go and find the watch,' decided Hayes as the two boys made their way into the changing room. On their arrival, Hayes picked up his black scarf and swung it precariously around his neck. In contrast, Sully rummaged neurotically in his coat and breeches.

'I can't find the watch, Hayesy.'

'It must be there somewhere.'

'It's not in my pockets.'

'Then where else could it be? Retrace your steps.'

'I just came in here to change.'

'But when did you last see the watch?'

Sully paused and contemplated.

'Ah, let's see. Before I took off my shirt.'

'You must have put it somewhere else Sulls?'

'Right.'

'Think. What did you do before you took off your shirt?'

There was a tense pause. Then suddenly Sully remembered.

'I put it in my gym shoe.'

'Good. Fish it out then.'

Sully proceeded to look under the long narrow bench, which lay next to where the boys hung their clothes. He ceremoniously brought out his gym shoes, rummaged and then stared vacantly.

'It's not there.'

'Where else did you go?'

'To the bog.'

'Ok, let's look there.'

The two boys then left the changing room and went towards the lavatory, which was behind the changing rooms at the rear of the building. They crossed a narrow outdoor corridor and stepped into the toilets.

'They don't seem to be here' said Hayes looking at the windowsills.

'I was shitting,' revealed Sully.

'Where?' challenged Hayes urgently.

'Over there,' replied Sully, pointing to the far end of the lavatory.

When Sully and Hayes approached the relevant cubicle, the 'engaged' sign greeted them.

'I'm already late reporting to One Ball,' cried a flustered Sully. The brazen confidence of Mrs Hackett's favourite pupil seemed a remote memory.

'Let's deal with the watch first,' suggested Hayes, as he went over to knock on the cubicle door.

'Hello. Who's there?'

'Me,' responded a disembodied voice.

'Who are you?' pursued Hayes.

'Binns. Who is it?'

'Hayes.'

'What the hell do you want? I'm having a crap,' yelled an inconvenienced Binns.

'Has Sully left a watch in there?' asked Hayes insistently.

'Wait a moment,' insisted an irritated Binns.

There was a pause while Binns finished his business and pulled the chain.

Suddenly, a hopeful voice emanated from the cubicle.

'Oh yes. A Timex watch is here. On the windowsill.'

'Hurry up Binnsy. Sully has got to do his punishment mile and he's late,' Hayes reminded him sternly.

'Ok. I'm coming,' reacted the harassed Binns.

After another pause ensued, Binns howled in frustration:

'Oh shit!'

'What's up Binnsy?'enquired a concerned Hayes.

'I've dropped the watch in the loo,' confessed an apologetic Binns.

'Well bloody well get it out!' shouted Hayes.

After a yell of disgust, Binns emerged from the toilet with a sodden watch.

'Give it to me,' demanded Sully, going into the cubicle and tearing off some loo paper, with which he started to dry the watch.

'Sorry,' said a chastened Binns.

'Thank God, it's waterproof. My father gave it to me. He bought it in Singapore,' divulged a relieved Sully.

'Ok Sulls, no more about your father, please. You need to go and see One Ball pronto,' emphasised Hayes, trying to get Sully focused on the plan.

'Ok. I'm going,' maintained Sully.

'I'm off to Open Way. Remember the bushes at the..?' quizzed Hayes, testing Sully's strategic memory.

'Colts' pitch,' answered Sully determinedly.

'Exactly,' confirmed Hayes, striding out of the lavatory, his scarf trailing in the breeze as he proceeded to Open Way.

'Sorry,' repeated an embarrassed Binns, while washing his hands as Sully nervously departed towards the dayroom.

One Ball was lounging in his study armchair like some deluded Caligula waiting for his minions to serve his every whim.

'You're late,' he accused Sully disdainfully.

'Sorry, Potts,' apologised the apprehensive junior.

'I've told you before, Sully. Sorry isn't good enough.'

'I couldn't find my watch.'

'Why didn't you put it in a safe place, you idiot?'

'I thought I did.'

'You need to be organised Sully. Otherwise you won't get anywhere.'

'I left it in the bog.'

'I don't care where you bloody left it, just be on time.'

'Yes Potts.'

One Ball then collected himself and looked at his watch.

'Right. Let's synchronise. It's 12:20 pm and 15 seconds, ok.'

'Is it?'

'I wouldn't say it is, if it isn't would I?

'No, I suppose not.'

'There's no suppose about it.'

'It's just that..'

'You've got to complete the mile in seven minutes.'

'Ok.'

One Ball then moved to his bookshelf, where he gathered a silver stopwatch.

'Are you ready Sully?'

'I think so.'

'Don't think, you either are or you aren't.'

'Then I am.'

'Good. Ready. Steady. Go!' shouted One Ball as he firmly released the handle of the watch.

Sully clumsily opened the study door and manoeuvred his flabby bulk through the dayroom, much to the surprise of the other pupils diligently doing their studies. He then floundered through the corridor and porch onto the exterior asphalt, crossed the Avenue and sauntered down Copse Drive to Open Way. On his way, to the right, he saw Killer's house. In fact, he thought he detected Mrs Killer putting out some washing in her garden. On his left, there was the house of Percival, a history master, who seemed to be more interested in being a rugby referee than the causes of Italian unification. Sully then left the darkness of the leafy foliage surrounding Copse Drive and emerged into the harsh light of Open Way. It was a chill autumn day and the expansive sports field made Sully feel vulnerable and exposed.

He needed to find the bushes as soon as possible so he ran intensely down the path to the colts' pitch. Eventually, he arrived at suitable shrubbery. Such was his haste to find some camouflage, that he pricked himself on a gooseberry bush. Thankfully, he managed to stifle his painful cry and crouch behind some of the taller undergrowth. As he revelled in his subversive hideaway, he felt like Fidel Castro, a guerrilla fighter combatting the corrupt reign of a dastardly dictator. While One Ball reigned supreme in his comfortable study, backed by a powerful establishment complex, he was a revolutionary looking to overthrow a vile, despotic regime. Unfortunately, a glance at his watch dispelled Sully's heroic fantasy. Despite Binns's best efforts to destroy it, it seemed to be working. He checked the time: he'd taken 2 minutes 30 seconds to get to the bushes, so he had some leeway to gather his breath. As he did so, he started panicking that Hayes hadn't appeared. Then, just when he'd given up on his traitorous comrade, he suddenly heard a voice yelling urgently:

'Sully. Where are you?'

'Over here!' replied Sully desperately.

'Where?' insisted Hayes.

'By the gooseberry bush.'

'For God's sake Sulls, there's a lot of them.'

Intuitively, Sully got hold of a stone and threw it vigorously, while shouting 'here! He released the missile with such careless abandon that it hit Hayes's foot with an unerring thud.

'Ow!' screamed Hayes. 'That hurt.'

'Sorry!' shouted Sully.

'Thank God you weren't in the war, Sulls' said Hayes, finally discovering the crouching bulbous figure of his friend.

'Why do say that? My father thinks…'

'You would have killed your own side.'

'No I wouldn't. I'd have been a hero like my father.'

'Oh shut up, Sulls,' cried Hayes, while feeling the pain from his foot. 'There's bad news.'

'What?'

'One Ball has got a spy patrolling Open Way.'

'Who?'

'Gregory Pound.'

'Gregory isn't the worst.'

'No, he's hardly the Gestapo.'

'Mind you, he'll still report back to One Ball.'

'Exactly. Let's give him the slip. Wait here and I'll tell you when to start running back,' instructed Hayes.

Just as he left Sully's hideout, a gooseberry bush ensnared his school scarf.

'Bloody hell!' screamed a frustrated Hayes.

'What's up?' cried Sully.

'There's a bloody hole in my scarf. Damn. I hate sewing.'

Hayes then rapidly disappeared onto the nearby path. As the pain from Sully's careless stone throw was diminishing, he was able to walk freely with incongruously feigned innocence, like an incompetent secret agent. Seeing that the coast was clear, he leaned discreetly towards the bushes and yelled hoarsely.

'Go Sulls!'

Sully then came out of the bushes and started running back towards James B.

'See you back at house,' shouted Hayes, mimicking one of One Ball's favourite commands, as Sully went lumbering past him with spots of blood from thorns discernible on his thick legs.

Sully knocked on One Ball's study door.

'Who is it?' projected Potts disinterestedly.

'Sully,' declared a supposedly exhausted runner in a fatigued voice.

'Wait Sully,' ordered One Ball

'I'd better go, Jim,' said Pound, inside the study. He was keen to be relieved of his uncomfortable duties, having observed Sully's deception and dutifully reported it to his fellow monitor.

'Ok,' replied One Ball dismissively, accepting that Pound had served his purpose.

Pound opened the door and discovered a heavily panting Sully. Sully's efforts to portray exhaustion were as absurd as a melodramatic actor overplaying a death scene. On confronting his grotesque performance, Pound feared the worst for Master

Sully. Accordingly, he made a diplomatic departure and crept into the dayroom, closing the door firmly behind him.

'I'm on time, aren't I, Potts?' said Sully optimistically.

One Ball rose from the seat by his desk to get the stopwatch.

'Yes,' agreed One Ball,' stopping the timer, 'just.'

'Good. Can I go then?'

'No, you can't.'

'Why?'

'Sit down, Sully.'

Sully apprehensively sank into Potts's armchair. He feared what was coming. One Ball's order had the feeling of a death knell.

'I've been talking to Pound,' disclosed One Ball, pacing the study.

'I realised that. How is he?' enquired Sully impudently.

'He's fine, Sully. Thank you.'

'I'm glad,'

'Pound was cycling around Open Way and he saw you coming out of shrubbery near the colts' rugger pitch.'

'It was part of my run.'

'Do you think I'm stupid, Sully? Going into shrubbery isn't part of a run.'

'I needed a pee.'

'You were there a long time before coming out.'

'It was a long piss

'It wasn't a long piss. In fact, it wasn't a real piss at all. More like a piss-take!'

'I forgot to go before I left the house.'

'Stop lying Sully,' demanded One Ball. 'You came out of the shrubbery like an escaping convict. It was manifestly clear that you were hiding there for some time, to cut down the running time.'

'I told you. I was just having a pee.'

'Stop this pee and pissing nonsense. You were hiding weren't you?'

'No.'

'You were cheating.'

'I wasn't.'

‘You‘re lying.’

‘No I’m not.’

‘Yes you are. You couldn’t face running to the time. So you cheated.’

‘I didn’t.’

One Ball looked down at Sully with a disdainful glare.

‘As a result of your stupidity, you will not only have to redo your punishment mile but also do another one.’

‘Oh no Potts,’ screeched a desperate Sully.

‘Yes, Sully. Only this time it will be for outright duplicity.’

‘Outright what?’

‘Duplicity. Deceitfulness, Sully.’

Sully was now crestfallen and silent. He foresaw a torturous future.

‘Both to be completed within the next month. I’ll put it in the book.’

Sully felt so upset that he refused to look at One Ball. Instead, he stared at the poster on the wall of a stern looking man with a neatly tied cravat, a jacket with velvet collars and a beret slanting across his head.

‘That’s Wagner, Sully,’ pronounced One Ball emphatically to the beleaguered junior.

‘I didn’t recognise him,’ admitted Sully.

‘That’s because you’re ignorant,’ retorted One Ball.

‘Why am I?’ queried Sully defiantly.

‘Because he’s a genius,’ proclaimed One Ball.

Sully was exhausted and nonplussed. He felt beaten down by One Ball’s aggressive interrogation. Maybe he shouldn’t have cheated but it was worth a try. In his current physical condition, he was never going to run a mile in that time so deception was an attractive alternative. Alas, his plan had failed and now he had two punishments hanging over him. Although he felt distressed, he was also angry at such injustice. He believed that One Ball’s authoritarian regime had to be defied.

‘You’re dismissed Sully. You can go,’ announced a triumphant One Ball.

Sully got up slowly and left the study. One Ball then put on his record of the Tannhäuser Overture. As he lay back in the vacated armchair and allowed the magnificent power of the music to wash over him, One Ball thought to himself, 'that boy Sully will never get anywhere.'

After having a shower and getting changed, Sully sat on a bench next to an assortment of hanging clothes. He looked like a shattered sportsman after a humiliating defeat. As he started to feel tears well up in his eyes, Hayes suddenly emerged, replete with his torn scarf dangling untidily from his neck.

'Sulls. I've been looking for you,'

'The bastard found out. I've now got another mile.'

'Blimey. I'm sorry but I didn't catch Pound.'

'He would have told him anyway.'

'Bloody One Ball's power mad.'

'Something's got to be done.'

'Maybe we should report him.'

At that moment, Barrett purposefully entered the changing room.

'Ready for lunch boys,' exclaimed a cheery Barrett, gathering his shoe cleaning equipment from a hanging blue bag.

'Not really,' replied Sully.

'Sulls has got another punishment. Our plan didn't work,' confessed Hayes.

Barrett was now carefully distributing black polish on his shoes and looking at his own work like a painter observing a preliminary sketch.

'Maybe we should report One Ball for bullying,' thought Hayes.

'I think we might need more evidence for that,' argued Barrett, while spitting on his shoes.

'Would the Major side with me?' questioned Sully.

'He might, but there could be unpleasant consequences,' said Barrett as he brushed his shoes with intense alacrity. 'He could discipline One Ball and that could make him very resentful.'

'And look for revenge?' suggested Hayes.

'Exactly,' agreed Barrett, brushing his shoes once again.

'But surely, he'd then risk being demoted?' queried Hayes.

'And would a demoted One Ball improve the situation?' posed Barrett, as he put his brush and polish into his bag and brought out an immaculate yellow duster. 'He'd be even more vengeful and on the loose, which could make him very lethal indeed.'

Barrett started shining his shoes with his duster. He believed that he should look smart before every meal, so he kept up a rigorous cleaning regime.

'Then what can I do?' pleaded a desperate Sully.

'Do the punishments at the last moment. Meanwhile, we should mobilise more support against One Ball,' proposed a strategic Barrett.

'But how?' wailed Sully.

'By getting others' opinions,' stated the judicious Barrett, continuing to fanatically shine his shoes. 'We need to get help to combat One Ball. Do you know Ryder?'

'Yes. A senior monitor from Wade B. He's leader of the choir. I've always been a bit daunted by him,' divulged a calmer Sully.

'Don't worry. I'll talk to him,' asserted Barrett, completing his obsessional shoe cleaning. 'I've heard that he's good at mobilising dissent.'

'Thanks Barrett,' acknowledged Sully, who didn't feel at all confident dabbling in school politics.

'Brilliant,' enthused Hayes.

'Thanks boys. You've made me feel a bit better,' confessed a relieved Sully.

Barrett thought that his shoes were now immaculate. He carefully folded his yellow duster and placed it in his blue bag. Then he turned to his two friends and claimed:

'By the time we've finished with him, James Potts will have no balls!'

As Hayes and Sully responded with gleeful laughter, the school bell rang. In response, they all got ready for parade. They then marched to lunch accompanied by the school band playing The British Grenadiers.

Françoise found the English strange. She realised that it was a peculiar country when she saw people putting a hat on their boiled eggs. Why would you put a hat on an egg? And why would you call it a 'cosy'? Then, there was their attitude towards sex. On a stroll around the town, she was surprised to see crude postcards full of grotesque pouting, fat women and lecherous men, as if sex was something dirty rather than natural. Françoise wasn't a virgin. One night just after leaving school, she went to the cinema with her English teacher and following a coffee and a discussion on the films of Jean Renoir, she ended up in his bed. It wasn't an unpleasant experience: exciting, a bit painful, yet still pleasurable. In fact, her teacher was married and didn't want to leave his wife, especially as they had two young children. Occasionally, she met them both in the street and his wife, a small woman with a childlike oval face, smiled at her so serenely that it was clear she hadn't any knowledge of her husband's infidelity. Françoise continued to see her lover but eventually she but found his domestic situation a strain. Consequently, she decided to look for work abroad to improve her spoken English before going to university.

Menial tasks in the kitchen of a boys' boarding school weren't exactly what she had in mind but it was still good living experience. Some of her colleagues were rough and temperamental but she'd made friends with another French girl, Yvette, and they shared a cottage by the school's station. Yvette was also determined to refine her oral anglaise during her year out. Therefore, the two women agreed to talk in the language of their employer as much as possible.

Tonight, on a mild autumn Saturday evening, Françoise was going to meet Arthur Rutter in the cricket pavilion. An eccentric venue for their assignation but more secure than her rented cottage, which was surrounded by prying neighbours. She knew nothing about cricket but discovered that Rutter was the rugby captain. Apparently, that meant that he had a key to the building. She was going to bring something to eat and he was supplying the drink. She was excited by her amorous adventure. Rutter wasn't an oil painting but she found him rather sexy. He was very small and fun. You felt that you could put him in your pocket. He also kissed rather well, slowly and intensely. He wasn't in any hurry. It was as if you were the only person in the world at that moment. So far, they hadn't had sex as they wanted to be careful. Although they were cautious, they certainly planned to do so and Rutter said that he'd bring some

Johnnies. She hadn't a clue what he meant until he explained that it was a nickname that came from a man named John, a medicine salesman, who was the first person to sell contraceptives. After these studious revelations, Rutter enlightened her further by telling her why a penis is sometimes called a John Thomas. Yes, thought Françoise, the English were not only eccentric but also funny.

She wasn't going to overdress to go out to a cricket pavilion, so she wore a brown woollen coat and boots with a red beret. Yvette kept telling her to be careful. She was worried that Françoise would be caught and lose her job. Yvette was more conservative, which was another reason why Françoise didn't contemplate inviting Monsieur Rutter to their abode. Yvette was a practising catholic, who went to mass every Sunday, much to the frustration of rampantly randy Barrel, whom she met secretly on occasions. Barrel just about managed to keep his feelings under control, by concentrating on their mutual love of Molière.

Françoise usually used her bicycle to get around the school grounds but tonight she decided to walk, because she had to carry the food. She'd arranged to meet Rutter at 7:30 and as it was now dark, she'd brought a torch to supplement the inadequate school lighting. At the same time, Yvette had gone into town to see Around the World in 80 Days with one of the Spanish women, who worked in the kitchen. She'd read the Jules Verne story at school but she was intrigued as to how it would transfer to the screen. In any case, she was sure that there would be enough action to compensate for any dialogue that she couldn't understand. So, while Yvette and her friend set out to embrace the worldly travails of Phileas Fogg, Françoise started her journey to the pavilion.

She moved briskly to give the illusion of an official meeting. She proceeded uphill from the cottages, towards the gymnasium and swimming pool. She enjoyed using those facilities where she could relax and keep fit.

As she went towards the school, she decided to use the main road that led to the Avenue rather than the path in front of her, which bisected various rugby pitches. Even though it was dark, she thought that she'd be more conspicuous in the middle of such open land. Hence, she turned right and kept close to the verge as there wasn't a formal pavement. Thankfully, no traffic passed and she made her way safely to the Avenue, where she suddenly saw a murky figure coming towards her. She discovered that it was Smallman, in a stylish trilby hat and a blue cashmere coat. Immediately, she was nervous as not only was Smallman Rutter's housemaster but he also could converse in fluent French. What's more, Rutter had told her that he'd been an intelligence officer in the war, so she was concerned that he might be suspicious of her large canvas bag. As Smallman approached, Françoise took a deep breath and made an immediate decision to charm him.

'Bonsoir,' said Smallman , raising his trilby in respect.

'Bonsoir monsieur,' replied Françoise smiling pleasantly.

'Comment allez-vous?'

'Je vais rendre visite à une amie.'

'Bien. Passe une bonne soirée.'

'Merci.'

'Bonsoir,' repeated Smallman, giving a lingering glance at her bag, before once more tipping his navy trilby and making his way down the Avenue.

Françoise wasn't sure whether Smallman believed her, so she decided to proceed as if she was going to visit one of the nurses in the infirmary. She didn't dare to look behind but moved towards the Quadrangle. Only when she'd crossed to the other side of the Avenue did she look back. Luckily, Smallman had disappeared. Rutter had told her that he was friendly with Collins, who lived at that end of the Avenue. As Smallman was walking steadfastly in the same direction, Françoise became more reassured when she remembered the warden's emotional needs. She turned round, went back to the Quadrangle, walked sedately through the nearest cloister and turned right towards Big Hall. She then made her way past that imposing building towards the Music School. Occasionally, she glanced cautiously over her shoulder but mercifully Smallman was still nowhere to be seen. Relieved that she was free from suspicion, she advanced around Open Way as quickly as she could. She looked at her watch. She was going to be late. Maybe that was a good thing. It will test Rutter and remind him that she wasn't at his beck and call. Eventually she passed the colts' rugger pitch opposite the railway line, where she'd seen young boys hurling themselves after an oval ball as if they were rigorously pursuing some illusive dream. She then had to turn left towards the pavilion, which meant she had to walk on the grass. Gingerly, she made her way amidst the enveloping dark. At first, she couldn't see Rutter but when she shone her torch, she discovered the back of a small hunched figure sitting on a bench, who impulsively shouted 'switch it off!'

Françoise did so and went up to the bench.

'Sorry,' said Rutter, 'but we don't want to get caught. Did you get the food?' continued the school rugby captain earnestly.

'Yes it's here in the bag.'

'Ok let's go in.'

Rutter looked around him and moved towards the pavilion door. He got the key out of his neatly pressed breeches and turned the lock.

'Bloody hell. I think it's jammed.'

'Jammed?'

'Stuck.'

'Oh. Maybe more gently.'

'Ok.'

Rutter tried again, taking Françoise's advice.

'Ah that's better.'

Gradually the ancient door opened to the accompaniment of its creaky hinges. Hesitantly, Rutter and Françoise entered its dark portals.

'Have you got the candle?' asked Rutter. 'We can't turn on the lights, otherwise it'll arouse suspicion.'

Françoise started calmly looking through her bag. There was the wine, the cake and the sandwiches but no candle.

'Ah merde!' she cried frustratedly.

She then decided to search more methodically and discovered that the numerous sandwiches had concealed both the candle and some matches.

'It's here,' discovered a relieved Françoise.

'Terrific,' replied a grateful Rutter.

Rutter then led her into the cricket team's changing room. He took the candle, which he placed in a nearby cup. He then moved it to the windowsill and lit it. Fortunately, it gave off enough light.

'Is there a table?' enquired Françoise.

After leaving the room and looking around, Rutter admitted defeat.

'They must have taken them out.'

'Tant pis. I've got a rug.'

'It'll get very dirty.'

'That's ok. I'll give it a good clean afterwards.'

Françoise then proceeded to unfurl a large, white woollen rug with blue stripes.

'Someone told me it was Moroccan.'

'It looks great. It'll do the job,' said Rutter.

Françoise took off her swing coat, which she placed on some nearby pegs. She then brought out a bottle of Muscadet from her bag and put it on the rug. This was followed by two wine glasses, a corkscrew, some plates and a golden tin

'Would you like to open the wine?' requested Françoise as she handed Rutter the corkscrew.

'Ok,' complied Rutter boldly. In fact, he wasn't very good at extracting corks. The last time he tried to do it, the cork sank dramatically into the bottle, much to his embarrassment. It was at the reception for his elder sister's wedding and all the guests thought it was hilarious. Ever since, Rutter had been suspicious of some suburban humour. It was as if the Purley neighbourhood relished someone's failure.

'This cork is bloody useless,' Rutter murmured to himself as he struggled to get the corkscrew solidly embedded. Eventually, he decided to risk it and go for lift off. He put the bottle of Muscadet between his legs, pulled and 'pop', the corkscrew came flying out. Rutter then poured two glasses and sat opposite Françoise, who was now kneeling on the rug.

'Cheers,' declared Rutter.

'Santé,' replied Françoise

The two young people went on to discuss the respective merits of their country's culinary status, while drinking and munching away at some ham and cheese sandwiches. Despite Rutter's efforts to defend toad in the hole, bubble and squeak and spotted dick, he made little headway in persuading

Françoise, who burst out in hysterical laughter when she understood the innuendo related to the latter name, almost spilling her wine on the stylish rug. Recovering her poise, Françoise rigorously defended Le Cordon Bleu and listed ratatouille, foie gras, cassoulet and duck confit in a spasm of national pride, which Rutter thought best not to counter. As they continued to eat and drink, Françoise mentioned that she'd met Smallman on her way to their rendezvous. Rutter looked concerned but Françoise reassured him that he was very polite and didn't follow her. Rutter was relieved, given Smallman's detection expertise.

While they enjoyed their repast, Françoise divulged what went on in the kitchens. There was a whole subculture there, of which Rutter was ignorant. The French were in the minority as the main employees were Spanish workers, many of them from rural areas. Apparently, there were some fights, mainly over women but Françoise hadn't witnessed them, as she and Yvette kept to themselves. However, sometimes these animosities spilled over into the workplace, which made for a bad atmosphere. Happily, the redoubtable Miss Pollard, the Kitchen Supervisor, managed to control those tensions. Miss Pollard was a severe, single woman in her thirties, whom the boys nicknamed Mrs Danvers after the macabre housekeeper in Daphne du Maurier's Rebecca. The supervisor's chilly disposition discouraged even the most hot-headed Iberian from allowing their resentment to manifest itself for too long.

When they'd finished eating Françoise's tasty food, an animated discussion about the merits of French singers developed. Rutter found les chanteurs old fashioned and stale compared to Little Richard and Elvis but Françoise defiantly defended the likes of Edith Piaf and Juliette Gréco. After talking to her for an hour about a myriad of subjects, Rutter felt an urgent desire to touch Françoise. Consequently, he recommended that they finish the remnants of the wine and clear up. After they'd gathered everything together and placed them in the bag, only the Moroccan rug was left.

'I think we'll leave that,' ordered Françoise smiling with a twinkle in her eye.

Françoise stared directly into Rutter's eyes. At once, he felt confident and reassured. He moved towards her, accepting her enticement with a long kiss, during which their tongues danced together in exciting harmony. This went on for such a long time that Rutter could feel himself getting seriously aroused. As a result, he gently took off Françoise's red beret, put it to one side and was about to remove her red sweater, when Françoise intervened. 'Un moment monsieur,' she said quietly as she lifted her arms to make the operation easier. Rutter then lost no time in obliging and discovering her brown-striped blouse. Firmly and gently, he started unbuttoning it until he discovered her black laced brassiere and white stomach. Rutter kissed her gently, and then allowed his arms to go behind her back and start unbuttoning the bra. Rutter regarded himself a master of this particular art but on this particular occasion he started to have problems. Initially, he dealt with the challenge calmly but the more he got excited, the more he began to lose control and unsuccessfully force the issue

'Does Monsieur want some help?' suggested Françoise, who then casually unbuttoned her bra and exposed her breasts. While Rutter observed this vision, Françoise questioned his hesitancy.

'Don't you like what's on offer Monsieur Rugby Captain?'

'Yes of course I do,' replied Rutter.

Rutter then started to unbutton her blue jeans.

'Boots first,' directed Françoise as she lay on the rug, one foot after another pointed in the air while Rutter pulled off her footwear.

Rutter then took off her socks and resumed his efforts on Françoise's jeans, only to be interrupted again.

'Have you got your Johnnies?' Françoise reminded him with a humorous smile.

Rutter pulled away and checked his pockets. He suddenly realised that they weren't there. While he searched for the durex, Françoise lay patiently on the rug in her knickers. Rutter was becoming increasingly frustrated and feared the whole evening was going to end disastrously. Finally, he came to the last pocket of his breeches and lo and behold he felt the indispensable packet, which he'd wrapped with Cassandra's column in the Daily Mirror.

'My Johnnies!' he yelled in celebratory relief.

After joyfully discarding his tabloid camouflage, Rutter extracted one Johnny from the packet and placed it on an accessible table. He then calmly took off his school uniform and lay in his pants on the rug with Françoise. Within seconds, they started kissing. When their arduous foreplay reached a satisfactory state of mutual arousal and Rutter started to put on his Johnny, somebody knocked on the pavilion door.

'Bloody hell!' muttered a frustrated Rutter, the Johnny dangling precariously in his hand. Hastily, he stuffed the unused durex into the packet, wrapped it with the remains of the Mirror and placed it under a nearby flower pot. While periodically calling 'coming!' he then put his pants on over his decreasing member and started dressing hurriedly. In contrast, a disappointed Françoise reluctantly put on some clothes, disdainful of such farcical antics.

Eventually, Rutter, patting down his ruffled hair into a semblance of order, arrived at the pavilion door.

'Who is it?' he whispered.

'Me, Fred.'

Fred Ord was the cricket coach and head groundsman. A genial man with a ripe midlands accent and a cherubic face, who'd played county cricket for Worcester.

Rutter gathered his composure and unlocked the creaky door.

'Hello Fred,' said Rutter with a nervous, genial smile.

'Ah it's you, Rutter,' replied Fred, relieved to see a familiar face.

'Yes, just relaxing,' stated Rutter innocently.

'Ok. I don't want to know how you're relaxing. It's just that when I saw that light in the pavilion, I wondered what the hell was going on as it's getting late. I was just taking the dog for a walk,' explained Fred, pointing to a bemused grey and white coated canine on a lead.

'What a lovely dog,' remarked Rutter, delighted that the visitor wasn't Smallman or that fool One Ball, who had designs on Françoise.

‘The wife loves him. Thinks he’s almost human,’ added Fred.

‘I can see that’, confirmed Rutter, looking towards the appealing dog.

‘I thought we might enter him for one of those dog shows but the Mrs wasn’t having it. She thinks they’re demeaning and cruel. Still he’s good to have in the home. Especially, when the Mrs can’t have kids.’

‘I can imagine. What’s his name?’ asked Rutter.

‘Ollie. He’s a very friendly dog. Is that a candle you’re using?’ probed Fred, abruptly changing the subject.

‘Yes,’ answered a nervous Rutter.

‘Now come on Rutter, douse that. We don’t want the whole bloody place to go on fire.’

‘Ok Fred. I’ll deal with it.’

‘You know you shouldn’t be here, Rutter. I’m not coming in because there will be things I shouldn’t see. I heard two voices in there and one of them was female. Now I know such things happen, not least when Worcester we were on the road in the old days, but be careful.’

‘I will Fred. Don’t worry.’

‘You’re lucky it’s me and not one of those stuffy masters. So just promise me one thing: that you’ll clear up and not leave any mess. I don’t want to discover any unpleasant surprises when I go into the dressing room.’

‘That’s ok Fred I’ll get rid of the fag ends.’

‘It wasn’t exactly fag ends that I was thinking about.’

‘Ok Fred. Don’t worry. I’ll leave it as clean as in the Persil ad.’

‘I don’t trust adverts. Mind you, the Murray Mints one is good. Very funny.’

‘Yes. With the guardsmen all marching and singing.’

Suddenly the schnauzer started barking, looking up at Fred with imploring eyes.

‘I’d better go. He wants to get some exercise,’ said Fred starting to leave, before turning round and imparting further advice. ‘And by the way, when we get to the cricket, do stop playing across the line with the moving ball. Play late and straight, Rutter.’

‘I’ll work on that, Fred’

‘Good’ said Fred. ‘And don’t do anything I wouldn’t do?’ he chortled with an infectiously manic laugh, as he and Ollie started to walk across Open Way.

Rutter came back into the changing room to see Françoise sprawled on the Moroccan rug.

‘Now what was I doing before I was interrupted?’ he recollected playfully.

Françoise laughed as Rutter knelt down, joining her on the rug. They then proceeded to kiss each other intensely.

As the term progressed, Root’s relationship with the choir didn’t improve as he prepared Prince Igor for an end of term concert. One evening during a rehearsal at the Music School, the music master became so exasperated with the choir’s lack of progress, that he hit his baton aggressively on a music stand and demanded them to reach a higher level of performance.

‘We’ve been practising Borodin’s great work for weeks now and still some people can’t hold their notes. I’ll be blunt with you. If you’re unable to do so, you shouldn’t be in this choir. The school has a reputation for high standards and you have to reach and develop them, not just sloppily accept second best. We’re not about doing easy things, I grant you, but we’re about aspiring to be better, to meet challenges, to do great things. Yet what do I get from the trebles but a shrill, out of tune whine, which sounds like screeching hyenas. In short, it’s not good enough. And I for one don’t want to present a comedy act at the end of term concert with Big Hall full of the great and the good.’

‘The great and the good, who’s that, sir? questioned Ryder, the choir’s leader and the school’s Lenin.

‘It’s a phrase Ryder, meaning powerful people of importance who’ve achieved something in their life.’

‘Or people, who’ve just got money?’ suggested the suave Ryder provocatively.

‘Funnily enough Ryder, you can both have money and achieve good outcomes.’

Ryder didn’t look convinced as he stood proud and upright at the head of the tenor section, turning his eyes away from the manic music master. Nonetheless, Root ignored his cynicism and continued his tirade.

'This concert will be a shop window for the school and for your own talents. You need to respect that. It will also be a suitable occasion for Borodin's rousing nationalist opera. We need to attack the piece with passion and control. Embrace the emotional heart of its Russian folk roots, not sing like Home Counties suburbanites. Use your imagination. We are singing about a medieval war here, not a parish council meeting. You need to do more preparation and come to rehearsal ready to deliver not dither. I repeat. There's slovenliness in the trebles. Yes slovenliness. You're going out of tune on the high notes. I've told you before, watch my baton. Then you will keep time and have control. And they're not the only ones. There's lethargy in the tenors as well. Sloppy articulation and lack of clarity. And yes, it would be helpful if the basses could come in on time, if it's not too much trouble. It's just not good enough. I have standards and if they're not reached, I don't beat around the bush with the soothing words of phony diplomacy, I tell you straight. Work and get better. Quickly. I'll see you in three days' time. Good night gentleman.'

No one in the choir replied to Root's harangue. Instead, the boys rapidly left the room until only Mr Sims, who was accompanying on the piano, and a vigilant Ryder remained.

'Thanks Reg. I'll see you tomorrow. Beth's got a night off from the infirmary, so we thought of going out for a meal,' divulged Sims, looking to depart swiftly.

'Ok Tim. Have a nice evening.'

'Goodnight Ryder,' said Sims as he passed the choir leader on his way out.

'Goodnight sir,' acknowledged Ryder, who liked Sims but thought he was weak, because he never challenged the venomous Root.

'What is it, Ryder?' enquired Root as soon as Sims had closed the door. The music master was now starting to pack away his musical score into his case.

'Why do you have to be confrontational?' protested Ryder.

'Sometimes you need to be direct and honest Ryder.'

'Why can't you work collaboratively?'

'Because I know more about the work than you do.'

'Maybe, but can't you share that knowledge?'

'I do share it, but not in your way.'

'No you don't sir. Instead of nurturing us to get better, you do your best to destroy confidence.'

'Nurturing Ryder? I'm not a social worker.'

'We're not professional singers.'

'But some of you want to be.'

'Maybe but most don't, so can't you encourage them?'

'A choir isn't a commune, Ryder.'

'Well in a way it is. After all, it's a group of people sharing a creative experience.'

'I'm not in the business of social engineering, Ryder, I'm running a choir.'

'I know that, but if you're too dogmatic you obstruct talent.'

'They weren't prepared Ryder.'

'Because they were scared.'

'No, Ryder, they weren't scared. They were lazy. They lacked discipline. Discipline gives you freedom.'

'It can also oppress you, sir.'

'No it won't, it will make you a better artist. Last summer I was in Germany and heard a talk by Herbert Von Karajan. He spoke so inspiringly of his commitment to work and discipline, his total absorption in the music.'

'I think Von Karajan was a member of the Nazi Party, sir.'

'That's irrelevant.'

'No it's not.'

'Yes it is. I'm talking about his talent, commitment, and work ethic, which has made him become the conductor of the Berlin Philharmonic, one of the greatest orchestras in the world.'

'They played for the Nazis as well,'

'Ryder stop going on about the Nazis and the war. It seems to be an obsession with you. The war is over and we're trying to get you boys ready for a new world.'

'A more cooperative one?'

'Whatever world it is, Ryder, there's going to be competition, that's human nature. So you'd better be ready for it. Politicians can dress it up in any way they want but it's a tough old world out there and I'm preparing you all for it.'

'Can't you prepare us to change the world?'

'The artist can't change the world but he can make it better by working hard and giving good performances of works like Prince Igor.'

'We are working hard.'

'Not hard enough.'

'We also have our lessons and homework to do.'

'That's no excuse for not preparing properly.'

'You're too hard on us. People are terrified to make a mistake, so they get worse.'

'Then do things better.'

'Ok sir,' said Ryder, reluctantly accepting that he'd reached an impasse.

'Ryder. You're a good singer and choir leader. Together we can do great things,' insisted Root, reverting to seductive flattery.

'Yes sir,' responded Ryder plaintively.

'I think we've had a frank conversation Ryder. Now maybe we can understand each other better,' concluded Root, disappointed that his attempts at reconciliation had failed.

'Yes sir,' added Ryder flatly, as he departed from the room.

Root watched him leave, then he gathered his music case and switched off the lights, before making his way into the dark night.

One Ball awaited the visit of his mother with trepidation. After his father died in the war, she'd become an isolated figure. She had her interests like the local dramatic society and was a regular parishioner at the nearby church but these activities weren't a substitute for her relationship with Julian Potts. A portrait of Julian in uniform hung in her dining room. He looked handsome and smart but there was a vacant sadness in his eyes. A local artist, who knew him, had painted it and caught a profound vulnerability in the soldier's nature. Sometimes, at night when Martha went into the dining room, it seemed like a ghost was hovering over her.

Although Julian Potts had been more comfortable in the company of men, he was always respectful and polite to women. Not only did he always raise his hat but he also opened doors for them and when he was on a bus, he would instinctively rise to offer his seat. Julian Potts was a gentleman and Martha appreciated his courtesy. They met at a ball and married six months later at St Luke's Church. She found him good looking, sensitive and dashing. At that time, he lived in London at Fawcett St, near the Fulham Rd, while Martha was sharing a flat with some girl friends in Beaufort St, off the Kings Rd. After they married, they lived at his place. They had a lively social life full of dancing, dinner parties and tennis matches at the Hurlingham Club. When Julian's parents both died in rapid succession before the war, they moved into his family's house in Farnham. They now had a son and after only being in their Surrey home for a few years, Julian went to North Africa. After the victory at El Alamein, he returned home before going to Italy. He never came back.

Martha tried to restart her life but she found it difficult. Although she had some help from her parents, bringing up James was difficult, especially as he was a bundle of unruly energy. Still, he proved to be a bright young boy, who did well at the local primary school. The only blemish was when he had an accident while impetuously climbing a fence. When Martha discovered that his testicles had been badly cut by barbed wire, she panicked. Initially, she feared that her son wasn't going to have any testicles at all, but such was the skill of the surgeon that at least one survived and apparently his sexual and reproductive capacity weren't impaired. Martha was relieved and just hoped that her son wouldn't have a complex about such a traumatic experience. She was proud that he'd recovered, done well academically and had got a conditional place to go to Cambridge next autumn. Such thoughts permeated Martha's mind as she stepped off the train at the school station.

Dutifully, One Ball was there on the platform in his school uniform to meet his mother. Martha Potts was wearing a dark brown coat with fur on its lapels and carrying a green carrier bag in one hand, while her leather handbag was dangling over her other arm.

‘Let me take that, mother,’ said One Ball, relieving her of the carrier bag. ‘Lovely to see you,’ he added, kissing his mother on the cheek.

‘And you darling. There are various things for you in the bag,’ replied Martha enthusiastically.

‘Oh thanks.’

‘Home made jam and a pineapple. You like them don’t you?’

‘Yes. What a good choice.’

‘We’d better drop these off before we go into the town’

While One Ball left the pineapple and the jam in his study, Martha waited outside the dayroom watching the coming and going of various boys. Although she had been to a girls boarding school herself, she still found the atmosphere strange. To have so little contact with the opposite sex seemed unnatural. She had suffered from that herself. She didn’t really know a lot about men when she left school. Still, these boys seemed happy enough as they rushed into the dayroom and James was doing well, so she had no reason to complain. After a few minutes, One Ball appeared and they set off back to the station to go into town.

When they arrived, they went to a Chinese restaurant for lunch.

‘This is unusual darling,’ remarked Martha while surveying the menu.

‘Yes, full of dragons,’ observed One Ball looking at the design on walls.

‘I don’t know any of these dishes, do you?’

‘Sweet and sour pork is good.’

‘Oh, you’ve been to a Chinese restaurant before?’

‘Yes. In London.’

‘Soho?’

‘Yes.’

‘What were you doing there, darling?

‘Going to the Sunset Club.’

‘The Sunset Club?’

‘Yes, it’s a jazz club.’

‘I didn’t know you liked jazz, James?’

‘Of course, I prefer classical but some boys from my class wanted to go.’

‘Your father liked Harry Roy and Geraldo.’

‘They’re not jazz mother.’

‘What are they then, darling?’

‘Dance music.’

‘Oh, I see. Yes, your father certainly liked to dance to them.’

Suddenly a small Chinese woman approached their table.

‘Are you ready to order?’ she enquired in a thick accent.

‘I beg your pardon? queried Martha abruptly.

‘Are you ready to order?’ the waitress repeated with greater emphasis and a little more clarity.

‘Thank you. We need more time. Ok?’ requested Martha.

‘Ok,’ replied the waitress, sulkily replacing her notebook and pen into a large pocket.

‘I couldn’t understand a word she was saying, darling,’ complained Martha.

‘Yes it was a bit difficult,’ agreed One Ball.

‘If they’re running a business, they should speak English properly.’

‘Ok, mother. What would you like?’

‘I don’t know. None of it makes sense to me.’

‘Shall I choose for you then?’

‘All right. That’ll be fun. Do.’

‘Chicken chop suey with rice. You’ll like that.’

‘Ok. I’ll try it. It certainly sounds strange.’

‘It’s a very common Chinese dish mother.’

‘Oh really, I’ve never heard of it.’

‘I’m going to have char chi har yen.’

‘Good God. What’s that?’

‘Prawns in batter.’

‘There’s an English translation in small print.’

‘Oh so there is,’ said Martha, getting her reading glasses out of her handbag and looking intently at the menu again. ‘But surely it should be clearer,’ she complained. ‘After all, we’re in Sussex not Beijing!’

‘Let’s get on with the meal mother,’ pressed One Ball. ‘Waitress,’ he called, summoning the young Chinese woman, who was now huddling by the small bar with her sullen compatriots. Eventually, Martha and One Ball ordered their meals and the waitress diligently wrote them down.

'Anything else?' she added.

'Not at the moment, thanks,' replied One Ball.

The waitress took up the menu and was about to leave when Martha called her back.

'Excuse me dear.'

'Yes,' responded the waitress, who had short, swept-back black hair.

'Where do you come from?'

'Hong Kong.'

'Which part?'

'Kowloon.'

'Ah my late husband went to Hong Kong. But not Kowloon.'

'It's in the south.'

'Ah I see. Thank you.'

The waitress swiftly departed and went directly past the dimly lit oriental bar and disappeared through the red swing doors into the kitchen.

'I wonder why they came here,' pondered Martha.

'The communist regime probably,' suggested One Ball.

'But Hong Kong's independent?'

'Maybe they don't think it will be for long.'

Mother and son paused to absorb the possibility of such an alarming development.

'I didn't know father went to Hong Kong,' mentioned One Ball, resuming the conversation with a hint of resentment.

'He was invited to a conference just before the war,' explained Martha.

'A conference?'

'British troops were out there in China Command. Julian was advising them about security. They were worried about the Japanese as well as the communists. Unfortunately, their fears became a reality.'

'I see. I think there's quite a lot I don't know about my father.'

'Why do you say that?'

‘Well. He was emotionally reticent. He didn’t talk to me much. His work seemed more important.’

‘No, Julian wasn’t the best with young children; he was hardly one of nature’s nappy changers.’

‘He did read stories to me.’

‘Winnie the Pooh. Yes I remember.’

‘He’d gone before I progressed to the Jennings books.’

‘I’m sorry about that.’

‘It’s not your fault mother. Anyway, he would have found Jennings too anarchic.’

‘Anarchic, darling? That’s an extreme word for a children’s book.’

‘Well he was concerned about discipline.’

‘Too much so.’

‘But it’s necessary mother.’

‘Sometimes.’

One Ball and his mother continued to talk about Julian. One Ball found his father remote and intimidating but then he only knew him when he was very young. Certainly, his father always looked immaculately well groomed. One Ball noticed that he always spent a lot of time looking in the mirror. Sometimes, when he reluctantly left the reflection of himself, he couldn’t resist popping back for a further gaze, just to check that his original perception was satisfactory. One Ball remembered his father as both a warm and intimidating presence. Julian loved his son but on his own terms.

Julian wasn’t particularly artistic but he did like music. Beethoven was a particular favourite. However, when Hitler rose to power, he couldn’t believe that a nation that could produce such beauty yet descend into evil barbarism. At once, he attempted to subdue his enthusiasm for anything German. One Ball saw a manifestation of this, when he witnessed his father throwing a record of Beethoven’s fifth symphony on the floor and crushing it with his shoe. The great composer’s artistry scattered into fragments across their drawing room. This so alarmed Lucky, the Potts’ black cat, that she urinated all over Furtwängler’s classic recording. Apparently, Lucky also wasn’t keen on the Nazis.

Martha also recalled Julian being so angry about Chamberlain's appeasement policy that at a sherry party he had an argument with the Kirwins, who came from Manchester and had Irish roots. Leonard Kirwin, a pugnacious journalist, took offence at Julian's support for Churchill. He saw him as a warmonger, who had sent the murderous Black and Tans to fight the Irish during the War of Independence. Tom stormed out of the Potts's party, leaving Angie, his freckled, flame-haired young wife, trailing in his wake. Immediately, Julian followed the couple out of the front door, trying to pacify his swarthy neighbour.

'Oh, for God's sake, Len. Don't take it so personally.'

'We colonised half the world and made a balls up of that. Now we want to create more bloody chaos. When will we ever learn?'

'Hitler's a dictator, Len.'

'Churchill butchered Ireland.'

'Tom, stop. Let's go home. Sorry,' said Angie, apologetically turning towards Julian, 'he had a few before coming, it's the drink talking.'

'No it isn't the bloody drink talking Angie. We've exploited Ireland for eight hundred years and that fat clown with the cigar and his Black and Tans were part of it.'

'I do hope we can still be friends, Len,' replied a placating Julian.

'He'll be different in the morning,' maintained Angela.

'Stop bloody excusing me, Angie,' reprimanded Kirwin. 'I needed a lining. Sherry? That's for old ladies.'

'I do hope we can see you soon,' pleaded Julian desperately.

'Thanks for the party,' cried Angie, while trying to prevent Len from falling into Martha's roses in the front garden.

As Julian stood at the doorway, upset and bewildered, the Mancunian couple departed. He could hear Len Kirwin defiantly singing some rebellious ditty as the couple sauntered back home.

One Ball and Martha enjoyed their Chinese meal. In fact, the chop suey went down so well with Martha that she also ordered a pumpkin pancake for her dessert, while One Ball went for a sweet egg bun. Mother and son followed this by sampling some

Chinese green tea, which they found strange after regularly drinking Brooke Bond or Typhoo.

'I missed the milk in my tea,' confessed One Ball.

'Yes, I could have also done with some sugar. Still it's been a bit of an adventure,' declared Martha, smiling warmly at her son.

'I'm so glad you liked it mother.'

'Yes I did. We must come here again darling.'

'Is there any tea left?'

Martha looked inside a white teapot decorated with a variety of coloured flowers.

'Yes enough for two. Let's finish it off.'

Martha poured from the teapot into two similarly designed cups.

After they both drank and again absorbed the new taste of the green tea, Martha looked directly at her son.

'Is everything ok at the school, James?'

'It's ok, mother.'

'What does that mean?'

'I'm working hard and feel confident about going to university.'

'Good.'

'But what about other things?

'Like what?'

'Hobbies.'

'Well. I'm listening to music, playing rugby.'

'You take after your father.'

'Really?'

'Same interests.'

'I suppose so.'

They continued to drink in silence, while much to their surprise, laughter emanated from the bar. Apparently, the Chinese family were sharing a humorous recollection. Martha then gently put down her cup on its saucer.

'I didn't really know your father that well.'

'Why did you say that mother?'

'Everything went so quickly. Our courtship, marriage, your birth, the war.'

'You loved him didn't you mother?'

‘Of course but his death was like lightning striking.’

‘I know.’

‘I loved somebody I didn’t really know and now he’s gone.’

‘You’re coping with it though.’

‘Yes. Sort of.’

Martha looked blankly around the restaurant. At the far end, there was a middle-aged man with a handlebar moustache, eating on his own. He had a parting in the middle of his grey hair and wore a smart dark suit, white shirt and a tightly knotted blue tie. After eating portions of food, he took up a napkin to wipe his lips. Martha thought that he looked lonely. Suddenly, the man caught her eye and she averted her gaze. When she finished drinking her tea, she looked intently at One Ball.

‘How’s the monitoring going?’

‘Ok.’

‘I hope you’re not too hard on the younger boys.’

‘Not really.’

‘They’re just children.’

‘They still have to learn.’

‘What exactly?’

‘Discipline. Responsibility.’

‘Yes, but they’re not in the army.’

‘Maybe not but those principles still apply.’

‘You sound like your father.’

‘That’s the example he gave me.’

‘And look where it got him!’

Martha’s emotional outpouring disturbed the sleepy demeanour of the restaurant. The man with the handlebar moustache looked up irritably, as if he was inconveniently disturbed. To the left of the Potts family, a woman in a pink hat wearing tortoiseshell spectacles, peered above her Times with a thunderous demeanour. The squat Chinese waitress, sensing general discomfort, made her way across to Martha and One Ball’s table.

‘Anything wrong?’ she asked.

‘No, not at all,’ replied a flustered One Ball, ‘please give us the bill.’

The waitress responded by moving to the till, which lay at the far end of the bar.

Martha then stretched towards the floor and lifted her handbag onto the table. She got out her compact, stared at a small mirror and briefly powdered her face.

'That's better,' she reassured herself, taking a deep breath and putting the compact back into her bag. 'Sorry but your father could be reckless.'

'That's not the father, I remember,' said a bewildered One Ball.

'But you were very young. You idealised him.'

'He was a good man, mother.'

'He got obsessed with war.'

'Obsessed?'

'Yes. He started to bend strategy. Take risks.'

'Maybe he was under orders.'

'He enjoyed war. He saw it as a game.'

'Really?'

'Fighting an evil enemy, gave him the excuse, he wanted.'

'Mother. Father was principled and disciplined.'

'Yes, he was, but in that last campaign he changed.'

'How do you know this mother, you weren't there.'

'Members of his regiment told me.'

'I find it hard to believe.'

'He told me that war is a terrible thing but when it starts, it's exciting.'

'But how did he change, mother?

'Apparently, he had bad dreams. He couldn't sleep.'

'Bad dreams?'

'Yes. That's when he started pursuing the enemy recklessly.'

'He must have been ill. '

'He probably was. He started exposing his position.'

'And that's why he died?'

'Yes, apparently. Others did too. They were an easy target.'

One Ball paused before replying.

'This isn't the father I knew.'

'It isn't the man I married. The war changed everything.'

Laughter emanated from the dimly lit bar, the Chinese family were sharing another joke. While indulging in this mirth, the waitress caught Martha's eye and brought over the bill, which was on a white saucer with two mints.

‘Thank you very much,’ stated the waitress.

‘Thank you. I’ve rather taken to Chinese food,’ divulged Martha, smiling tensely.

The waitress acknowledged Martha hesitantly and made her way back to her refuge at the bar.

‘How much is it, mother?’ enquired One Ball.

‘2 pounds, 5 shillings,’ replied Martha, looking attentively at the bill. ‘Quite decent value,’ she conceded.

‘That’s very good mother,’ mentioned One Ball. ‘They’re only starting so they’ve got attractive prices. Look here,’ remarked One Ball, discovering another section of the menu. ‘They’ve also got English food. Like mixed grill. They must be looking to wean us on to Chinese dishes gradually.’

‘Well they’ve done a pretty good job, I must confess,’ admitted Martha.

There was then a pause as both mother and son exhausted their conversation about Chinese food. The ghost of Julian seemed to fill the silence.

‘I never knew that about father,’ confessed a contemplative One Ball. ‘Why didn’t you tell me before?’ he demanded indignantly.

‘I only heard about it recently. I was a guest at a reunion dinner,’ said Martha defensively.

‘Really?’

‘I don’t think they wanted it to be official.’

‘I see’

‘His friends apologised.’

‘Apologised?’

‘For going along with the lie.’

‘Guilt? Misplaced loyalty?’

‘Yes, they were very emotional.’

‘I can imagine.’

‘Still. It’s best you know’.

Mother and son were still and silent, locked in their memories. Eventually, another confession broke the tranquillity.

‘I didn’t really know him either,’ confessed One Ball.

‘He loved you James,’ vowed Martha.

‘Yes, I suppose so.’

‘No darling, he really did.’

‘But he didn’t show it very easily.’

‘Yes, he could be emotionally reticent.’

‘Reticent? I don’t remember him even touching me.’

‘I’m sorry about that.’

‘It’s not your fault.’

‘Maybe I shouldn’t have told you about his death.’

‘No, it’s best to be honest.’

‘It was an unnecessary advanced sortie, apparently.’

‘That’s so unlike him.’

‘His battalion got bogged down in the hills.’

‘Where?’

‘Monte Cassino.’

‘Where’s that?’

‘About a hundred or so miles, south of Rome. It was a hard slog there, apparently. He must have got frustrated. He tried to break enemy lines.’

‘I suppose he wanted to be some kind of English hero.’

‘Maybe.’

The man with the handlebar moustache was now relishing his dessert. The woman in the pink raffia hat was drinking a coffee. The Chinese family continued to talk earnestly to each other. Beyond the bar, two of their older members were playing cards on a small table. Outside, grey clouds hovered over an increasingly overcast afternoon. As One Ball looked towards the street and saw the Saturday afternoon shoppers gliding by, he gathered his thoughts. He now realised that the father he admired, who had taught him how to walk, had become ill and had a brainstorm. He was upset and disappointed that he’d died in such an impetuous manner He always thought that he was a very able strategist. Something in him must have snapped like those deserters who went AWOL. Maybe, a rush for glory seduced him. Whatever it was, One Ball felt angered by his recklessness and the distraught legacy he’d left behind. In that moment, he decided to no longer idealise him, just remember the good things and understand the bad. He had his own life to live and so did his mother. As he observed Martha looking forlornly out of the window, watching some unruly teenage girls sucking lollipops, One Ball reined in his feelings. They needed to move forward into the future and not be victims of the past.

When the raucous girls departed across the road to share a cigarette with some rebellious boys, One Ball looked directly at his mother. He smiled benignly and encouraged her to start life anew.

'You know mother, you need to work again'

'I do have a house and garden to maintain.'

'You used to work.'

'Before I met your father. In a boring office with boring people.'

'You should teach young children, mother.'

'I'm not trained for that.'

'You could get trained. A whole new generation needs people like you. You can't just be watering the roses and thinking of father.'

'I loved your father, James. Love isn't rational.'

'I know but you need to start a new life.'

'I'll think about it.'

'Who knows you might even fall in love again?'

'I doubt it,'

'You won't if you just live on memories.'

'It isn't as easy as that.'

'Whatever he did in the war, father is dead. He won't come back.

'I know that.'

'Then live for the future mother, please.'

'I'll try James. I'll try.'

Martha and her son then got their coats and went up to the till. Martha got out her red purse and produced crisp 5 pound and 10 shilling notes. The waitress accepted the money and placed it carefully in the till.

'Goodbye,' said the waitress as her family's card players all smiled in unison.

'Goodbye' replied Martha.

'Thanks,' added One Ball. As they both moved towards the door, he suddenly stopped.

'Mother. A tip.'

'Ok. I'll see what I've got'

Martha took a florin piece out of her purse and laid it out on the table. Seeing the money, the waitress thanked them and mother and son departed into the chilly autumn air.

'Thanks so much, darling,' enthused Martha, once outside the restaurant. 'And you're quite right. I must live.'

Immediately, Martha put her arm through her son's. One Ball appreciated her warmth. It made him feel wanted.

'Let's go and explore some shops' Martha enthused.

A good idea mother,' agreed One Ball as they walked further into the town.

Hayes glowed with happiness when he saw his mother Hannah, and his sister Poppy coming down the centre path. In the distance, they appeared an odd couple with Poppy rushing ahead doing periodic hopscotch while Hannah, walking serenely with a large raffia bag, smiled at her daughter's antics. Hannah had been divorced for four years and since then Hayes often felt like a shuttlecock struck by badminton players, as he moved between home and boarding school, his father and his mother. Hayes got particularly upset when one Sunday in their Battersea flat, Hannah broke down and cried, trying to carve the Sunday joint. To Hayes, it was as if the tears had spilt onto the roast lamb. It wasn't the effort of the cooking that had upset Hannah. It was the pain of the break-up with Phil while managing two young children. There was also the social stigma of divorce. Hannah was a Christian and believed in marriage so she felt a sense of failure.

Like many couples, Hannah and Phil struggled after the war. They met in the RAF. She was in the WRAF from a middle class background in Godalming; he was a flight lieutenant from a humble background in the East End. Both were artists, Hannah was a pianist, who'd graduated to giving concerts at Wigmore Hall, Phil was a jazz musician who played in various groups and got further income doing session work. After the war, Hannah gave up her career to be a mother and Phil couldn't get enough employment. The realities of civilian life began to tear them apart. There were rows. Hayes remembered one in particular, when his father was inebriated. He left the flat shouting incoherently, slammed the front door and threw a coin, which shattered a pane of glass. Hayes remembered that splintered image as summing up the end of their marriage. However, regardless of such emotional turmoil, Hannah had returned to her musical career. She had recently acquired a job teaching the piano at a convent school in Guildford. This had not only given her a sense of being part of a new community but also a renewed interest in performing. In fact, she'd already started playing chamber music with professional friends.

Hayes came out of back of James B, cut across the athletics track and moved towards his family. Suddenly, Poppy, who was slightly younger than Hayes, ran down the path and embraced her brother, clasping her arms around his chest.

'How are you Tommy?' asked Poppy.

'I'm fine, Poppy. Lovely to see you,' replied Hayes, kissing his sister on the cheek.

Gradually Hannah caught up with the children and hugged her son.

'I thought we'd drop into James B before going into the town,' advocated Hayes, while extricating himself from his mother's arms. 'You can leave stuff there, if you want.'

'Ok. that's fine, Tommy,' agreed Hannah.

'Let's get some sweets first,' stipulated Poppy.

'Ok. We can go to the tuck shop, it's on the way,' accepted Hayes.

In the tuck shop, Poppy surveyed the sweets with considerable vigilance. She always took hours to decide whether to buy dolly mixtures or jelly babies. Mrs Butcher, The Tuck Shop Manager, stood behind the counter with weary patience. A tall, big woman with a fearsome voice, she was always complaining that boys stole various items from her shop without revealing any proof. This formidable boss was married to Frederick Butcher, The Stationmaster. Frederick was a mild mannered man, who was softly spoken and courteous. In contrast, Mrs Butcher could be raucous and vulgar. Rumours had it that when she got drunk in the town, she'd start getting outrageously flirtatious, much to the annoyance of her long suffering husband. She also fancied herself as a singer and sometimes at her most inebriate, she would sing You'll Never Walk Alone. Her rendition was rumoured to be one of the most hilarious you could ever witness, as she had a tendency to go wildly out of tune. This didn't perturb the redoubtable Mrs Butcher from developing her erratic performing skills and in the staff's infamous production of Pygmalion, she played a booming Mrs Pearce. Unfortunately, at one performance, she was late for one of her entrances as she was 'at the toilet'. The consequent ad-libbing was so inappropriately modern and farcical that the boys were in stitches. Despite these artistic hiccups, Mrs Butcher was very much her own woman in the tuck shop and ruled it with a rod of iron. The boys always approached her with cautious respect. That didn't stop her keeping her two lively teenage daughters well away from the school.

'Have you chosen yet?' enquired Mrs Butcher wearily.

'I think so,' replied Poppy.

'Take your time,' suggested a cynical Mrs Butcher.

'Oh Mrs Butcher,' intervened Hayes 'this is my mother.'

'Pleased to meet you,' announced Hannah, stretching her hand across the counter.

Mrs Butcher shook Hannah's hand courteously but without enthusiasm.

'She's a slow one,' observed Mrs B.

'Yes, she's very meticulous about sweets,' revealed Hannah.

Eventually, Poppy chose a Mars Bar and some Strawberry Bon Bons. Mrs Butcher took the money from Hannah and the Hayes family left the formidable tuck shop manager to her considerable devices.

'Guess what I've brought for you, Tommy?' Hannah tested Hayes as they strolled towards James B.

'Tomatoes? answered a hopeful Hayes.

'Yes, of course,' verified Poppy as she demolished a Bon Bon.

'Tommy loves tomatoes,' regaled Poppy.

'Why?' quizzed Tommy, expecting the answer.

'Because when Mum was pregnant she ate a lot of tomatoes,' chanted Poppy as if it was part of a family ritual.

'Who told you that?' questioned Hannah with a grin on her face.

'Dad,' replied Poppy, while relishing another Bon Bon.

‘Oh, I see,’ said Hannah hesitantly, suspicious of such old wives tales. ‘Anyway,’ she added ‘you like them darling, don’t you?’

‘Yes, I certainly do. Thanks,’ confirmed Hayes emphatically.

‘I’ve also got you something else. Guess what?’ challenged Hannah.

‘Pineapple?’ judged Hayes.

‘No,’ answered Hannah with a warm smile.

‘Good. Dad already sends them to me through International Stores,’ a relieved Hayes reminded everybody.

‘Come on Tommy,’ urged Poppy.

‘Oranges?’ guessed Hayes.

‘No,’ asserted Poppy like a quizmaster rejecting a contestant’s answer.

‘Bananas?’ blurted out Hayes intuitively.

‘No,’ maintained Poppy, continuing like Jerry Desmonde compering the 64,000 Question.

‘Something even more delicious,’ prompted Hannah, giving her son a clue.

‘Grapes,’ proposed a desperate Hayes.

‘Well done,’ applauded Hannah. ‘Also, some crunchy peanut butter.’

‘You’re spoiling me, Mum,’ uttered Hayes with a widespread grin.

‘Congratulations. Would you like a Bon Bon?’ offered Poppy, holding out her confectionary bag.

‘I was wondering when you were going to ask,’ replied Hayes, gleefully accepting the raspberry sweet.

Eventually the Hayes family arrived at James B and Hayes put the food in his locker. When he returned to his mother and sister, they were standing in the corridor outside the dayroom, where Barrett was renewing his acquaintance with Poppy.

‘Hello Barrett.’

‘Hello Hayesy.’ I was just telling Poppy that I’m going to watch the 1st XV play Cranleigh,’ explained Barrett. ‘A sort of derby, I suppose.’

‘We’re going into the town,’ said Hayes.

‘To visit a few places,’ interjected Hannah.

‘So we’d better go,’ decided Hayes, eager to get away from the confines of the school.

‘Good to see you again Poppy, Do tell me about any marches against the bomb,’ requested Barrett with enthusiastic commitment.

‘I will. It’s a serious matter,’ stated Poppy earnestly.

‘It certainly is,’ acknowledged Barrett with equal youthful zeal.

With that emphatic meeting of minds, the Hayes family left James B. They all walked to the station where Mr Butcher, The Stationmaster, was significantly absent. According to Mr Dodds, the bespectacled booking clerk, who had a parting in the middle of his greying hair, it was his afternoon off.

Later, on the train, Hayes’s first thought was to go to one of the town’s record shops.

‘Mum, can we go to Sussex Rockers?’ pleaded Hayes.

‘What’s that? queried Hannah.

‘A record shop,’ illuminated Hayes enthusiastically.

‘Sounds good,’ agreed Poppy.

‘Have you eaten, Tommy?’ asked Hannah.

‘Yes, I had lunch at school,’ Hayes reassured his mother.

‘We had sandwiches coming down on the train,’ disclosed Hannah.

‘Cheese and pickle,’ prompted Poppy.

‘All right. Sussex Rockers it is,’ conceded Hannah.

‘Sorry Mum. There’s not much classical there,’ confessed Hayes.

‘That’s ok,’ accepted a resigned Hannah.

‘This way,’ directed Hayes as he led the family off the train.

After they left the town’s station, Hayes led Hannah and Poppy to the rear exit, which led to a series of narrow streets and alleyways. After walking through a veritable maze, they arrived at the colourful record shop. ‘Sussex Rockers’ was emblazoned across the front of the building in gold letters. In the window was a huge cut-out of Elvis Presley.

‘Who’s that? mentioned Hannah.

‘Elvis,’ verified Hayes.

‘Who?’ said a bemused Hannah?

‘Elvis Presley,’ elaborated Hayes as if he was trying to educate an ignorant child.

‘He looks like something that has crawled from underneath a stone,’ alleged Hannah.

‘Oh Mum. He’s sexy,’ proclaimed Poppy.

‘Sexy? Good God!’ exclaimed Hannah incredulously.

‘Let’s go in,’ urged Hayes.

Inside the shop, LP covers were stacked alphabetically. On the walls were pictures of current stars, with the emphasis on rockers like Elvis and Bill Haley. By the counter, there were young boys all wearing black leather jackets decorated with various badges, tight matching trousers and tall boots. They were laughing with two similarly dressed girls, who had bandanas around their necks. To the side of the counter were turntables where you could listen to the latest records with headphones. Hayes started looking at the LP covers in the various boxes as Bill Haley’s Rockin’ through the Rye blasted through the speakers. Poppy smiled nervously at some much older bobby soxers, who were browsing near her. They wore poodle skirts embellished with flamingos and flowers, light saddle shoes and short white socks. One of them had a bracelet around her hand with the name ‘Lisa’ on it. The grotesque bobby soxers smiled back at Poppy as they devoured the LPs under S. It was obvious that they were big Sinatra fans and were paying homage to his 40s fan base. Consequently, the leather boys and girls looked at them with contempt and thought ‘Daddy-O, they certainly aren’t cool cats!’

Hannah observed this tension and felt like bursting into laughter. It was like a modern pantomime, full of contrasting cultures and dress codes. What’s more, she found it strange that Mr Haley, the fashionable rocker with the kiss curl, who had made scandalous headlines because he’d inspired couples to dance in the aisles of cinemas during Rock Around The Clock, seemed rather old to arouse youthful adulation. As someone taught by a great classical pianist like Solomon, she could never take pop music seriously. She found a lot of it very simple, repetitive, and predictable. She thought that music should strive for something higher, but she wouldn’t mention that to Tommy and Poppy as they rummaged through the LPs.

'Mum, could I buy a record?' entreated Hayes.

'Yes all right. But where are you going to play it?'

'I'll play it in the holidays. They're not far away.'

Poppy, overhearing this offer while exploring the oeuvre of Dickie Valentine, decided to make her own pitch.

'Can I buy one as well, Mum?'

'Yes, all right, Poppy.'

'But just a single one.'

'Ok.'

Tommy and Poppy then started looking at the charts above the counter. For Tommy, it was Hound Dog all the way. Poppy was in her usual state of Hamletian indecision but eventually chose Sixteen Tons by Tennessee Ernie Ford. Tommy put his sample Elvis disc on the turntable and jiggled about as if he was a mature rocker, much to the amusement of the real ones up at the counter. Poppy followed suit, incongruously miming to Sixteen Tons as if she was a coalminer in Kentucky. When they had finished listening, the leather boys and girls self-consciously made way for them at the counter.

'I'd like Sixteen Tons, please,' said Poppy.

'Of coal, love?' replied the cheeky assistant behind the counter, bursting into laughter at his own joke, just like Norman Wisdom in his films.

This was obviously the highlight of the day for the assistant, who deliriously strutted around the counter. His large Brylcreem quiff, dark black shirt and protruding white tie gave him an imposing sense of his own importance.

'And what's yours mate?' he asked Hayes.

'Hound Dog,' answered Hayes nervously.

'A lad with taste,' observed the rocker with long sideburns and a pompadour hairstyle. He had his arm around a leather-clad blonde girl. 'Like the uniform,' he added, surveying Hayes's attire.

'You're at the school then?' remarked the rocker.

'Yes, he is' interrupted Hannah.

'Bit posh isn't it?' challenged the rocker.

'Not really. All types go there,' clarified Hannah.

'But it's a public school and they're posh,' persisted the rocker.

'You can get grants,' indicated Hannah.

This revelation made the rocker indignant.

'My Mum and Dad never told me that. I ended up in a secondary modern. We were treated like rubbish.'

'You do have to fulfil certain criteria,' elucidated Hannah.

'What about 'ignorant rocker'?' suggested the rocker.

All the other rockers started getting hysterical at the unique public school application. Only when their mirth had sufficiently subsided did Hannah look to respond.

'I'm not sure about that particular one but it does cater for the less well off,' resumed Hannah with a warm smile.

'It's a gorgeous uniform. I love the knickers,' observed the blonde girl looking intensely at the Hayes's breeches.

'Thanks,' responded a blushing Hayes.

'I'd like to wear schoolboy clothes,' fantasised the blonde girl.

'So would I. Yeah. Good for a laugh,' thought the small girl in the leather suit. She had dark cropped hair and seemed to Hayes like a tomboy.

'Mind you, it wouldn't be easy going on the bike with that coat on,' warned the blonde girl.

'Naw, you need to get a jacket,' insisted the tomboy.

'You could bundle it up?' suggested Hayes.

'It'd have to be a bloody big bundle!' screeched the tomboy deliriously.

'Otherwise you'd end up like that weird one. What's her name? Her scarf got caught in a wheel and it did her in,' elaborated the blonde girl.

'Do you mean Isadora Duncan?' submitted Hannah tactfully.

'Yeah. That's her. Isadora,' remembered the blonde. 'I ask you. You wouldn't call your worst enemy a name like that.'

'Sometimes, you chicks are weird,' interrupted the rocker impatiently.

'Not as weird as you. Didn't you go to a party recently as Marlene, what's her name? quizzed the tomboy.

'Dietrich,' prompted the blonde girl, reminding her friend of the androgynous star.

‘Anyway, who’s paying for this?’ interrupted the shop assistant, before the rocker could articulate his attachment to the German icon. He was frustrated that he had no longer been the centre of attention.

‘Me,’ volunteered Hannah.

‘That’ll be 13 shillings and 6 pence,’ concluded the assistant abruptly.

Hannah gathered the money from her blue purse, paid the shop assistant, gave the records to Hayes and Poppy and moved towards the door. Her two children followed, clinging on to their newly acquired purchases as if they had just won a lottery.

As they were about to leave, the rocker called out defiantly:

‘Don’t forget a revolution is around the corner but it’s not in schools, it’s in rock ‘n’ roll. Elvis is only the start.’

‘Thanks for the warning,’ replied Hannah, hastily ushering her two children out of the rockers’ lair.

The Hayes family wandered around the town looking at the various shops. Poppy pestered Hannah to buy her a pair of shoes. After a prolonged discussion about the necessity of such a purchase, Hannah relented and got her some mid heel red footwear. Poppy said that she wanted them for parties. Certainly, Miss Hayes seemed to be a very social animal. While Hayes was stuck going to the tuck shop for One Ball, Poppy was not only living it up with her anti-nuclear friends but also attending meetings and hearing Bertrand Russell speak. He felt resentful that he didn’t have that kind of social life. Going to a day school certainly had some advantages.

Hayes, Hannah and Poppy continued to drift through the town, making a quick trip to a crowded Woolworths, where Hannah bought some dark buttons for her sewing box. As they meandered around, they came to a bandstand where a crowd had gathered to hear a squat, bald man in a grey suit, shouting into a microphone about what was happening about the Suez Canal. He believed that Britain had no right to be threatening Egypt, that Nasser wasn’t a dictator and our troops shouldn’t get involved. To the side of the speaker, there were three men and an older woman, all looking suitably serious. At the rear of the bandstand, there was a banner saying ‘No War Over Suez. Eden

Must Go.' The speaker was working himself into a lather, berating Churchill's successor for his bellicose stance. After dealing with the Prime Minister, he started attacking the Conservative party as a whole. He denounced it as a corrupt institution, mired in class privilege and empire building, which protected their own financial interests and exploited workers. Towards the end of this political aria, a man in the crowd wearing a green felt hat shouted out:

'And how much is the union paying you?'

This heckle was greeted by a cacophony of boos from the rest of the crowd. Despite this aggressive protest, the man in the green hat didn't stop pursuing the speaker.

'Come on. Answer the question. How much are you getting?'

The speaker blithely ignored his question and continued.

'Our Tory friend,' said the speaker 'wants to divert us so he can ignore the ignominy of this government, who are being aggressive imperialists.'

'Rubbish!' shouted the man in the green hat. 'Nasser has an arms deal with the Soviets. He wants to destroy the West.'

'Nasser is defending his people, my friend and he's got a right to do so,' replied the speaker forcefully.

While the speaker listed his litany of grievances against the government, a couple of students from the local university with their red and yellow striped scarfs blowing in the wind, approached the man in the green hat.

'Why don't you shut up?' insisted the bigger of the students. He was an imposing presence, about six foot five, a good man for a rugby lineout. 'We don't like your war sentiments,' continued the burly giant with the face of a bulldog.

'I don't want to go to war,' stressed the man.

'Why are you defending Eden then?' demanded the giant.

'Because Nasser nationalised the canal,' reasoned the man.

'We can negotiate,' maintained the giant.

'You can't with dictators. The war taught us that,' answered the man resolutely.

'He's not Hitler,' interjected the smaller student derisively.

'He's not Santa Claus either,' countered the man.

‘Are you trying to be funny?’ threatened the giant menacingly.

‘No I’m not. What he did was illegal, he broke an international agreement,’ upheld the man, outstaring the bellicose, canine-looking student.

‘That makes war all right then?’ questioned the smaller student, who seemed to have considerable amount of dandruff nestling on the shoulders of his sheepskin jacket.

‘It certainly makes it justified,’ responded the man haughtily.

The Hayes family observed this conversation from a safe distance. The altercation fascinated Hayes and he was certainly going to tell Barrett about it. Meanwhile, Poppy was just about to shout out wild imprecations at the man like ‘fascist’ or some such epithet but Hannah, knowing Poppy’s emotional stand on such matters, quickly applied the full force of her hand across her mouth. It was just as well, because two nearby policemen were now approaching the two students with strident intent.

‘So what’s going on here?’ demanded one of the Bobbies.

‘Ah, here comes Dixon of Dock Green,’ chimed the giant.

‘Very funny. You‘ll be laughing on the other side of your face in a minute,’ warned one of the policeman, a middle aged man with a florid face and a thin, pencil moustache. ‘Now calm down both of you and listen to the speeches. We don’t want any trouble now, do we?’ uttered the policeman benignly.

‘Of course not, officer,’ agreed the man in the green hat.

‘We weren’t doing anything,’ implored the smaller student, who had his hair parted to the side of his forehead and wore brown-rimmed spectacles.

‘You were potentially endangering the peace,’ warned the policeman.

‘Just behave yourself,’ elaborated the second, younger, fresh-faced policeman.

‘Stay here and keep your nose clean or leave,’ ordered the older policeman.

‘Ok officer,’ said the man.

‘People get passionate over politics,’ contended the giant.

‘Some people,’ replied the younger policeman curtly.

‘Never talk about religion or politics. That’s what my mum told me,’ divulged the older policeman.’

Just as the two Bobbies were about to move back to their original position at the back of the crowd, the older one turned round and made a confession.

‘Dixon isn’t my favourite show. Policing isn’t like that. I prefer The Grove Family.’

Hannah decided that this was a good time to get the children away from the meeting. She felt that something unpleasant could still emerge, so she grabbed hold of her progeny and steered them away from the bandstand and ubiquitous political passions.

‘Oh Mum. That was fun, why do we have to leave?’ cried Poppy.

‘Poppy’s right, Mum. It was just getting interesting,’ protested Hayes.

‘Exactly, that’s why we should now have some tea,’ decided Hannah resolutely.

They all moved towards the centre of the town, the two children straggling behind their mother, still wondering what was happening at the meeting.

‘Come on darlings,’ implored Hannah.

Hayes and Poppy reluctantly increased their pace and got closer to their mother.

‘Wasn’t that Tory awful?’ remarked Poppy.

‘Yes, he looked as if he’d just come off a huge country estate,’ added Hayes.

‘He had his own point of view.’ said Hannah, trying to achieve some balance.

‘But he was so high and mighty,’ thought Poppy.

‘But maybe he was honest?’ suggested Hannah.

‘Honest?’ Poppy looked appalled.

‘To make his views public at such a meeting,’ explained Hannah.

‘But his views were terrible,’ asserted Poppy.

‘But he did challenge people,’ claimed Hannah.

‘With what?’ queried Hayes.

‘He knew what he’d say would be unpopular but he went ahead because he believed in what he was saying,’ contended Hannah.

‘And I didn’t like his hat,’ commented Poppy as a bitter afterthought.

‘Yes, he did look like somebody who shoots grouse,’ conceded Hannah. ‘Ah, here we are. Lyons,’ she indicated, pointing to the renowned British institution. ‘Let’s go for a cuppa.’

The tearoom was packed. Tables and chairs were massed together to maximise the space. A cacophony of diverse voices created an infectious energy. Waitresses with their white mitre-styled caps navigated these obstacles like cyclists weaving their way around cars in a traffic jam. One of them steered Hannah and the children to a scarce empty table at the back of the room. Immediately, Hayes grabbed the menu and shared it with Poppy.

‘Let’s have a pot of tea shall we?’ proposed Hannah.

‘Ok but I’d like a toasted muffin. Only tuppence,’ noted Poppy.

‘Pancake for me. It’s fourpence,’ chimed Hayes

‘Double your money!’ exclaimed Poppy in a strangulated North American drawl, imitating Hughie Green, the popular game show’s host.

In fact, Hannah had only recently acquired a television at the request of the children. Previously, what she’d seen was at her mother’s house. While viewing the coronation there, her niece danced chaotically in front of the TV, which led to the image of the Queen constantly going up and down like a seesaw. Personally, she preferred the radio and in particular, the classical music of The Third Programme. Nonetheless, even she found some of that station’s announcers insufferably pompous, as if they alone were the arbiters of the nation’s culture. She feared their arrogant tone was unlikely to attract a wider audience to the music that she loved

A waitress came to take their order. As well as her distinctive cap, she was wearing a black dress with a JL badge on its bodice, a white collar and cuffs, supplemented by a matching apron. Even with an absence of make-up, Hayes still found her pretty. He liked her warm smile, friendly face and the way her hair came down neatly over her ears. As she departed with the order towards the kitchen, Hayes also noted her slim figure and black stockings. As he turned back to his family, at a table near the entrance, he suddenly saw the dreaded visage of One Ball. Grim Jim was talking to a woman that he took to be his mother.

'What's the matter, darling?' mentioned Hannah.

'Nothing,' replied Hayes, nervously gazing at the table.

'You look as if you've seen a ghost,' observed Hannah.

'I was looking at the waitress,' said Hayes.

'We know that,' confirmed a giggling Poppy.

'But it was after she'd gone,' observed Hannah.

'I was thinking about her,' insisted Hayes, fiddling with a napkin.

'You're not very convincing, darling,' noted Hannah.

'I told you I was admiring the waitress,' reiterated Hayes adamantly.

'Admiring. You mean fancying,' corrected Poppy.

'Oh shut up, Poppy,' snapped Hayes, glaring angrily at his sister.

'Ok that's enough,' interrupted Hannah firmly.

'I think you saw someone from the school,' pursued Poppy teasingly.

'What makes you think that?' challenged Hayes defensively.

'I don't know. Instinct,' admitted Poppy casually.

Hayes now felt cornered. He couldn't bluff any longer. He had to tell them.

'Ok, Poppy, you win. It was One Ball,' confessed Hayes grudgingly.

Poppy started to get hysterical. Even the serene Hannah started to laugh.

'Who darling?' queried his mother, taken aback by the nickname.

'One Ball,' repeated Hayes emphatically.

'Who's that?' asked Hannah.

'He's a monitor, I'm his squit,' disclosed Hayes.

'Squit?' probed a bewildered Hannah.

‘Well, it’s a kind of a batman,’ elaborated Hayes.

‘Who’s Robin?’ quizzed Poppy deliriously.

‘Thank you, Poppy,’ remarked Hayes brusquely.

‘So what’s a squit, darling?’ pleaded Hannah.

‘I do things for him,’ continued Hayes.

‘Like what?’ pursued Hannah.

‘Clean his shoes and coat, go to the tuck shop, things like that,’ clarified Hayes.

‘Sounds medieval,’ observed Hannah.

‘I suppose it is,’ acknowledged Hayes.

‘Although they were called serfs,’ Hannah reminded herself.

‘Being a squit sounds awful,’ thought Poppy.

‘It does seem rather abusive,’ agreed Hannah.

‘Why is he called One Ball?’ pursued Poppy, trying to suppress her giggles.

Hayes then started to tell the story of One Ball but just as he was about to get to the climax of the barbed wire, the waitress reappeared with their order on a silver tray. She placed a white teapot with three matching cups, saucers and side plates on the Formica table. She then added a small stand with their selected cakes and pastries.

‘Thank you very much,’ said Hayes.

‘It’s a pleasure,’ replied the waitress, smiling back at the young boy.

Hayes blushed and looked away in embarrassment.

‘Is there anything else?’ enquired the waitress.

‘No, not for the moment,’ responded Hannah politely.

As the waitress departed, she had a mischievous grin on her face. Perhaps, she’d heard part of the One Ball conversation.

Hannah then started to pour the tea while Poppy continued her investigation.

‘So what happened to One Ball?’ she pursued excitedly, longing to hear the rest of the narrative.

Hayes resumed the story of the barbed wire, Sully’s problem with his punishment for ‘rank insubordination’ and One Ball’s unhealthy pursuit of discipline.

‘This One Ball was unfortunate,’ said Poppy sympathetically.

‘Well yes but…’ started Hayes.

‘He still sounds like an awful bully,’ interrupted Poppy.

‘I should talk to Mr Aizlewood about this,’ declared Hannah.

‘No. Please don’t do that,’ cried Hayes abruptly.

‘Why not?’ demanded his mother.

‘Because it’ll make things worse,’ alleged Hayes.

‘What will be worse?’ continued Hannah defiantly.

‘My relationship with One Ball,’ pointed out Hayes, fearful of the consequences.

‘Can we stop calling him One Ball? What’s his proper name? insisted a frustrated Hannah.

‘Potts. James Potts,’ revealed Hayes flatly.

‘Ok. Let me have a word with Mrs Potts over there,’ decided Hannah.

‘You don’t understand Mum. When you all leave, he’ll make me pay for any indiscretion,’ implored Hayes.

‘Indiscretion? Defending your son,’ proclaimed an incredulous Hannah.

‘He’ll be annoyed and take it out on me,’ countered Hayes anxiously.

‘I’ve got to see Mr Aizlewood,’ repeated Hannah.

‘The Major can’t protect me, Mum,’ emphasised Hayes.

‘Surely that’s his job,’ stressed Hannah.

‘He can’t be around everywhere all of the time,’ remarked Hayes.

‘Maybe not but he should be informed,’ continued Hannah.

‘It won’t help,’ asserted Hayes.

‘I don’t want my son living out a version of Tom Brown’s Schooldays,’ affirmed Hannah forcefully.

‘It’s not as bad as that, Mum,’ implored Hayes, trying to mollify his mother’s concern.

‘It sounds terrible,’ claimed Poppy.

The family then started to drink their tea and eat their cakes and pastries. Eventually, Hayes persuaded his mother not to tell the Major about One Ball. However, Hannah insisted that Tommy kept her informed of any further abuse. She was still determined to take action if necessary, whether her son liked it or not. She hated injustice, abhorred cruelty and would do anything to protect her child. In an effort to divert the conversation away from One Ball's tyrannical regime, Hayes purposely mentioned his father.

'He took Poppy on the Big Dipper.'

'At the fun fair?' queried Hannah.

'Yes,' replied Hayes.

'It's really scary,' said Poppy with gleeful relish.

'Maybe Dad shouldn't have taken you,' thought Hannah.

'Oh no, I loved it,' enthused Poppy.

'I went once,' remembered Hayes.

'Only once?' responded a mocking Poppy.

'I was in one of those cars with Dad,' recalled Hayes. 'It seemed like the whole train was going to go off the rails. Then suddenly, just as we came to the edge of the track, it lurched violently back on course. People were screaming hysterically. It was scary.'

'It's meant to be scary. I loved it,' reiterated Poppy.

'There'll be an accident on the Big Dipper,' prophesied Hayes gloomily.

'It must have been checked surely?' argued Hannah.

'Exactly!' blurted out Poppy.

'I think it was built for the Festival of Britain,' added Hannah.

'That's no guarantee of safety,' claimed Hayes cynically.

'There's a risk in everything,' retorted Poppy.

'Anyway, darling how was Dad?' interrupted Hannah.

Hannah found out about Phil, her ex-husband, through her children. Despite, their difficulties, she couldn't resist wondering how he was getting on. In some irrational way, she missed him. Theirs was a passionate love affair during difficult times. As soon as the war ended and they had to deal with the practicalities of civvy street, it was as if they didn't know each other. Suddenly, she was a mother and he was a jazzman. This meant Phil indulged in late nights, drink and the allure of other women. Although he took session work, he couldn't find enough employment to make ends meet. There was just never enough money to keep pace with the outgoings. He tried being in the pit for musicals but it drove him crazy, playing the same score monotonously every night. What really inspired him was the bebop music instigated by Charlie Parker. The fast playing, the challenging chord changes, the dynamic shifts of key and the sublime virtuoso improvisation. This new musical language inspired Phil and led others to create their own British version. Initially, there wasn't a big demand for bebop but Phil felt the inspiration of an emerging musical landscape. Musicians were meeting in old derelict buildings to play this new, dynamic music. New idiosyncratic venues were emerging. Change was definitely in the air and Phil wanted to be part of it.

Darkly handsome, charming and spoilt by women, he didn't take to married life, especially after his career had missed out on six years because of the war. He felt cheated and wanted to make up for lost time. Hannah was interested in bebop. She found it musically challenging and liked the way that Phil played. Still, as the years went by, she felt that he showed increasingly less appreciation for her own musical talents. At first, Phil liked Hannah working as a pianist but as soon as the children came along, she was relegated to permanent mother and couldn't develop her career. Hannah wasn't madly ambitious but she did miss the creative energy of music making. It was only after she was divorced that she gained a new artistic confidence.

'Dad was in good form. Although he looked tired,' thought Poppy.

'Too many late nights,' said Hannah.

'Probably,' agreed Poppy.

'Dad took me to football last season,' declared Hayes, asserting his own relationship with his father.

'You didn't tell me that. Where?' probed Hannah.

'Charlton,' announced Hayes proudly.

'I didn't know he supported Charlton,' divulged a surprised Poppy.

'He doesn't. It's just because he's living in south east London,' elucidated Hayes.

'In Woolwich,' Poppy reminded everybody.

'He came with a friend of his called Bob, who kept on saying 'old boy',' continued Hayes.

'Who's Bob?' asked Poppy.

'A bachelor type in a cheese cutter cap and khaki mackintosh,' disclosed Hayes. In fact, he'd overheard that Bob always had a hot bath before he made love but Hayes thought that he'd omit that revelation.

'I suppose he lives near Dad.' surmised an intrigued Poppy.

'Yes I think so. He runs a booking agency,' mentioned Hayes.

'Did you have a nice time?' enquired Hannah.

'I hate football,' stated Poppy unrepentantly.

'It was dramatic,' recalled Hayes. We went to the terraces but the crowd was heaving. The force of so many people pushed Dad and Bob away from me. I was very frightened being left on my own.'

'You didn't tell me this,' interrupted an offended Poppy.

'I can't share everything with you and Mum,' insisted Hayes. 'I have to have some things that just remain with Dad,' he remarked, taking a further sip of his Brooke Bond tea. 'Anyway, Dad was like a drowning man being submerged by waves. Luckily, this bloke behind me, seeing Dad's predicament, helped me sit on the stanchion so I could see properly.'

'The what?' questioned a perplexed Poppy?

'The bar that holds the barrier on the terraces silly,' explained Hayes, rebuking his sister for being so ignorant of the beautiful game.

'Oh, right,' said a bemused Poppy

'Who won, darling?' responded Hannah.

'Charlton lost two-nil, conceded Hayes unhappily. 'The Charlton goalie had no chance of stopping the goals. He's a sandy-haired chap called Sam Bartram, a cult figure down there. He's got a shop near the ground.'

As the Hayes family munched the remains of their food and sipped their tea, Hayes decided to broach a more sensitive subject.

'I met Amy,' revealed Hayes.

'When?' quizzed Hannah, somewhat taken aback.

'After the game,' replied Hayes.

'What was she like?' pursued Hannah, curious to get her son's reaction.

'Ok. She's a singer,' imparted a non-committal Hayes.

'How glamorous,' proclaimed Hannah ruefully.

'Not really. She isn't getting much work,' reported Hayes.

Hannah drank the remains of her tea. Although she accepted that the children would eventually meet their father's girlfriend, Hannah found it hard to hide her resentment, especially when Amy was very different to herself, being more pragmatic and less idealistic. She also thought that Amy was an able performer without being distinctive. It seemed to Hannah that she was copying American singers without adding anything original. However, while admitting that Amy's practicality was more suitable for dealing with Phil's hedonistic lifestyle, Hannah reminded herself that the jazz singer didn't have to look after two young children.

'All right darlings, let's go!' decided Hannah abruptly.

Hayes and Poppy swigged the remains of their tea and quickly ate what was left of their Swiss rolls. When the Hayes family made their way towards the exit, the waitress in black stockings gave Hayes a warm smile. Hayes blushed again but it didn't stop his sense of exhilaration. Then unexpectedly, Hannah stopped by the Potts' table and introduced herself.

'Hello. I'm Hannah Hayes.'

'Oh no!' muttered Hayes under his breath.

'Martha Potts. This is my son, James.'

'Oh yes, Tommy has been telling me all about him,' substantiated Hannah.

'Really?' reacted Martha quizzically.

'Yes, apparently he's James's squit,' mentioned Hannah.

'His what?' reacted Martha incredulously.

'Squit,' repeated Hannah.

'I don't understand,' said a perplexed Martha.

'I believe it's a description of a helper, like a batman in the army,' explained Hannah.

'Is that right James?' Martha challenged her son.

'Yes, that's about it,' endorsed One Ball perfunctorily.

'But you're not in the military,' reasoned Martha.

'It's a way of taking responsibility,' contended One Ball.

'Seems more like subservience,' remarked Martha.

'Not really. You see the more you do things for others, the more you'll do them for yourself,' propounded an earnest One Ball.

‘Do you mean ‘others’ or ‘superiors,’ darling?’ commented Martha cynically.

‘Well both, I think,’ articulated One Ball hesitantly.

I didn’t know that my son was signing up for something so bizarre,’ confessed Martha.

‘Nor did I. It’s alarming. Why can’t men see that such traditions will soon become obsolete?’ stressed Hannah.

‘Perhaps they should allow women at the school,’ suggested Poppy.

‘Now that would be a very welcome revolution,’ agreed an excitable Hayes.

‘I think that could create chaos,’ insisted One Ball.

‘Oh don’t be so old fashioned darling,’ affirmed Martha, chastising her son.

‘You’ve got to have structure,’ continued a dogmatic One Ball.

‘Not if it’s the wrong one surely?’ queried Hayes.

One Ball glared at Hayes with intense anger. He hated the idea of his squit contradicting him in public.

Suddenly, the smiling waitress in black stockings moved hurriedly towards the Hayeses.

‘Excuse me!’ she cried as she went to the kitchen, precariously balancing a full tray.

‘Oh certainly,’ reacted Hannah, moving out of the way of the harassed waitress. ‘I suppose we’d better go,’ she decided with a flustered smile. ‘Well very nice to meet you.’

‘And you,’ acknowledged Martha, instantly diving into her handbag and producing a card. ‘Do take this, it’d be good to keep in touch.’

‘Thanks,’ said Hannah, taking the card and examining it. ‘Farnham?’

‘Yes,’ replied Martha.

‘William Cobbett land,’ remembered Hannah with a friendly smile.

‘Indeed,’ confirmed Martha, surprised that Hannah knew of the celebrated advocate for rural England.

‘Well, let’s keep in touch,’ suggested Hannah. ‘We need to keep an eye on these boys, after all.’

‘In any case, I hope to see you next term,’ concluded Martha, cautiously avoiding making a specific commitment. She disliked people making promises that they might not keep.

‘I’d forgotten they’re breaking up soon,’ revealed Hannah, realising that the chaos of the holidays would soon be upon her.

‘Four weeks Mum,’ highlighted Hayes like a prisoner counting the days before his release.

‘Goodness me, I’d better get prepared!’ exclaimed Hannah with a giggle.

‘And so should I!’ responded Poppy with mock ferocity.

They all laughed and made their way to the exit. It was beginning to get dark. The Hayes family left Lyons and trudged along to the station. It wasn’t long before the Pottses followed them. Despite the tense exchanges, both mothers had enjoyed their afternoon with their sons. Eventually, they caught the same train back to the school and deposited their boys back into their strange male world.

A few days later, just before tea, Brown and Bunter, rockers extraordinaire, were by the radio dancing away to Elvis’s Blue Suede Shoes. Just as their gyrations came to a climax, an animated Rice confronted them, insisting that they tune in to the Home Service.

‘What’s up?’ said Brown.

‘We need to hear the latest about Suez,’ demanded Rice.

‘Oh all right, I suppose we’d better,’ conceded Bunter reluctantly.

Brown slowly started moving the dial away from AFN. While they heard the squeaky frequency sounds, the boys remained silent and looked apprehensive. Eventually, Brown tuned into the Home Service and they heard a newsflash read in highly articulated Queen’s English by Alvar Lidell. As the boys listened attentively to the report of the seizure of two ports in the Suez Canal, the Major, who was on one of his occasional patrols, entered the dayroom. As he absorbed the news, he just hoped that Eden could deal with the crisis by defending British interests. When Mr Liddell moved on to the aftermath of the Hungarian Uprising, the Major instructed Brown to turn off the radio. He then proceeded to start a debate.

‘So what did you think of that boys?’ asked the Major, looking for an informed response.

‘Looks like we could be moving to war, sir,’ feared Rice.

‘I don’t think so, Rice. This will be just a shot across Nasser’s bows,’ insisted the Major.

‘A pretty big shot, sir,’ feared an apprehensive Rice.

‘Maybe. But it’s necessary,’ upheld the Major.

‘Why sir?’ doubted Rice.

‘Because Nasser is a dangerous man, who threatens our interests,’ accentuated the Major.

‘Is he really that dangerous?’ questioned Rice.

‘I think he is, Rice. He’s a dictator, who has ambitions to reignite the conquests of Islam,’ continued the Major determinedly.

‘But he sees it differently sir,’ disputed Barrett, who’d speedily gathered around the radio.

‘In what way, Barrett?’ probed the Major, noting Barrett’s fervour.

‘Well sir, he regards us as imperialists continuing our colonial legacy,’ answered Barrett.

‘But he’s wrong. We couldn’t stand idly by,’ countered the Major.

‘But why do we control a canal thousands of miles away?’ declared Barrett

‘There’s an international treaty to protect trade. We were part of it. Nasser has violated it. All parties agree on that,’ clarified the Major.

‘Surely, it’s just a way of international oil companies exploiting a national asset and now the Arabs want it back,’ articulated Barrett.

‘Nasser is flirting with the Soviets and there is a cold war going on,’ argued the Major. ‘What’s more, the Middle East is a very unstable region, Barrett.’

‘Exactly sir,’ agreed One Ball, who had now joined the group intending to impress, ‘and look at what the Soviets have done in Budapest.’

‘Oh really Potts,’ that’s different,’ claimed Rice re-entering the debate.

‘Suez is a major international waterway. Nasser wants to throw us to the dogs and look for new friends,’ maintained One Ball.

‘It doesn’t help that Eden looks sick,’ said Bunter ‘like a pale ghost.’

‘His secretary lives in our block of flats in Battersea,’ disclosed Hayes, suddenly joining the conversation.

‘Really Hayes?’ challenged an incredulous Major.

‘Any scandal? enquired Brown voyeuristically.

‘Not really, she adores him. ‘She did tell me that he likes art. Apparently, Cézanne is one of his favourite painters. And, oh yes, he speaks some Arabic,’ added an enthused Hayes.

‘Really?’ reacted the Major with an air of surprise.

‘Studied it at Oxford apparently, sir. And Persian,’ revealed Hayes, relishing his authority on such matters.

‘You’re quite a fount of knowledge regarding our Prime Minister, Hayes,’ observed the Major.

‘Not really, sir. Just overhear stuff, sir,’ replied Hayes modestly. ‘I take Mrs Osborne’s dog out for walks.’

‘Mrs Osborne?’ queried a confused Major.

‘Eden’s secretary. The dog’s a bit of a handful, sir. He likes chasing motorcyclists,’ divulged Hayes with a wry smile.

‘Given his studies, you’d think that Eden would have understood Nasser better, not stitch up a deal to invade with just the French and the Israelis. Especially, when there was such a lack of substantial international support,’ said Barrett, chiming in and interrupting the canine interlude.

‘Well he saw through Hitler before others did, so let’s hope he’s got this right as well,’ asserted the Major defensively.

‘Nasser isn’t Hitler, sir,’ claimed Barrett.

‘Maybe not but he’s of the same disposition,’ believed the Major.

‘Really sir?’ queried the ever persistent Barrett.

‘Yes I think so. He’s of a totalitarian tendency,’ affirmed the Major.

‘It’s enough dealing with the atomic bomb without more wars sir,’ disputed the inexorable Barrett.

‘Sometimes there are just wars, Barrett,’ upheld the Major.

‘What’s a just war, sir?’ challenged Rice.

'The Second World War is a good example,' suggested the Major.

'I suppose so but all wars are a failure, sir,' reflected Rice.

'World War two wasn't a failure, Rice,' responded the Major stubbornly.

'No. We were on the winning side against an evil adversary. But the very fact that there had to be a war that killed a lot of people. That's a failure,' disputed Rice.

'We tried to negotiate with Hitler and look what happened,' deduced the Major.

'You're not a pacifist are you, Rice?' accused One Ball.

'No. I'm not,' emphasised Rice with idealistic fervour, 'but maybe if people, the German people, us, everybody, could have seen through and dealt with an angry Austrian art school reject earlier, things could have been different. As well as all the Nazi atrocities, we wouldn't have had Hiroshima and Dresden.'

The Major, noting the time on the dayroom clock, realised that this conversation needed to come to a halt, as he had to mark some geography essays. A task he found tiring and at times very trying. In any case, although the Major thought that Eden needed to be resolute, he wasn't his greatest admirer. After all, he was Churchill's Foreign Secretary and he believed that Churchill had prevented his boss, Commander-in-Chief Archibald Wavell, from having sufficient resources to relieve Tobruk.

'Ok, boys, it's been good to talk to you but I've now got to do some work and you've got to go to tea,' concluded the Major. 'We may not have saved the world but we've had a damn good try. I'll see you later.'

After the Major departed, the boys dispersed and got ready to march up to the Dining Hall. They went to the lavatory, washed their hands and combed their hair, before they assembled on the forecourt outside James B. When everybody seemed to be present, One Ball came out ready to give the marching orders, a ritual he increasingly relished. Just as he was about to go into full vocal throttle, he was interrupted by a cry from Sully rushing out from the lavatory.

'Sorry, Potts,' said Sully hurriedly buttoning up his coat.

‘Come on Sully,’ replied One Ball, wearily but with unusual tolerance.

Since his mother’s visit, One Ball hadn’t erased Sully’s punishments but had paused for contemplation. During this period, he pretended to forget about Sully’s indiscretions. His mother’s shock at some of the school’s rituals had certainly made him think more deeply. However, after this period of cogitation, he concluded that he still didn’t agree with her criticism. There had to be consequences for bad actions, otherwise nobody would learn anything. What’s more, he wasn’t afraid of being unpopular if he stuck to his principles. He’d summon the overweight junior again shortly. Eventually, after what seemed an age, Sully had fastened his coat and One Ball went into military mode.

‘ATTENTION! LEFT TURN. BY THE LEFT, QUICK MARCH!

On a frosty November evening, James B was away, marching to tea with regimented rigour. One Ball was delighted as they progressed briskly down the Avenue, in time and at an even pace while keeping the dressing.

‘It’s almost balletic,’ reflected One Ball triumphantly.

In the Dining Hall, Rutter read grace in the manner of Marlon Brando in On the Waterfront, while Smallman observed his antics with disapproval. Smallman liked drama and on occasions directed house plays, usually old-fashioned ones from the pre-war period like The Holly and the Ivy. Unsurprisingly, he wasn’t an admirer of the method. He just couldn’t understand why an acting style which lacked such clarity of diction could be taken seriously. Still, Smallman accepted that things were changing, what with those angry young men at the Royal Court Theatre. Although he observed an energy and commitment in the new plays, he felt uncomfortable about their extreme criticism of British society. He didn’t go through a tough war to be told that he was fighting for an unjust country. Still, he decided that he wouldn’t reprimand his senior monitor too heavily. After all, as manager of the 1st X1, Smallman needed Rutter’s indispensable wicket-keeping, so he didn’t want to create any friction that could undermine his form.

Consequently, he decided not to mention the 'Brando grace' until a suitably diplomatic opportunity emerged. Nevertheless, such a concession didn't alleviate his irritation at the exploitation of a prayer for such parodies. Despite such concerns, Smallman put his personal feelings aside, stuck to his decision and deliberately bestrode the hall, making sure that everything was in order.

Meanwhile, Françoise was serving food with Yvette. Apparently, there had been in a rare mistake in Miss Pollard's rigorous scheduling and Yvette wasn't actually needed in the kitchens. Accordingly, much to the kitchen supervisor's frustration, she transferred her to ladling duty. This made the queue move faster but was manifestly an inefficient use of resources, of which Madame Danvers was ashamed. Delighted to work together, the two young women giggled away at Rutter's reading of grace. They weren't quite sure whom he was imitating but they still found it very funny. As they poured big dollops of Irish stew out of a huge iron urn, their laughter became unabated. Their shared hilarity was so intense that they couldn't help themselves breaking their promise of not speaking in French. One Ball, who was about to be served, became frustrated by this sudden foreign outburst. He desperately wanted Françoise's attention and couldn't tolerate their exuberant alien merriment being so prolonged.

'What's so funny?' enquired One Ball, purposefully moving his bowl towards Françoise.

'Rutter,' replied Françoise.

'Oh him,' lamented One Ball.

'He was imitating someone doing grace,' continued Françoise.

'An American,' added Yvette giggling.

'He's always playing the fool,' said One Ball severely.

'Didn't you find it funny?' asked Françoise.

'No, not really,' admitted One Ball. He was depressed. He was never going to get anywhere with Françoise while Rutter was around. She seemed to be obsessed with the profane midget. Increasingly, One Ball feared that his packet of Johnnies could become redundant.

'Why is it Irish stew?' queried Françoise.

‘What do you mean?’ responded One Ball peremptorily.

‘Why is it Irish, not Scottish, for instance?’

‘Good question.’

‘Maybe tradition?’

‘Probably because they were poorer and could get mutton cheaply.’

‘Mutton?’

‘From the sheep, especially those who weren’t any use for wool or milk.‘

‘Ah. It’s because the sheep is in the stew.’

‘Well yes, plus the other ingredients.’

‘Like cabbage, carrots and potatoes?’

‘Yes. And years ago during needy times it was just easy to cook stew on an open fire.’

‘I thought the Irish were starved out of potatoes.’

‘That was just one unfortunate period of history.’

‘Unfortunate?’ questioned Françoise.

‘Tragic would probably be a better word,’ conceded One Ball.

‘That’s better. You should say what you mean,’ stated Françoise.

One Ball felt admonished. He only knew a bit about Ireland through Len Kirwin’s rants and he had no desire to discuss the merits of Rutter’s mimicry. He wanted to chat about personal things with Françoise: her life in France, her studies and how she was going to use her knowledge of English. Unfortunately, his time had run out, as he construed from the multitude of disapproving looks he was getting from those waiting in the queue. He casually acknowledged their concerns and departed disheartened with his solitary green bowl.

The boys eagerly attacked the Irish stew and the accompanying crig in wicker baskets. One Ball sulked as Boring Beckett tried to cheer him up. Not even the knowledge that James B were progressing well in the house rugby cup, could stop him thinking about Françoise’s obsession with Rutter.

Later, further down the long table, Sully was again pontificating on his father’s war experiences. It seemed as if Biggles, Bulldog Drummond and Dan Dare were rolled into one as far as Sully's father was concerned. Blithely ignoring previous ridicule, Sully proceeded to give long lectures about the merits of Singapore, his father's wartime role and his many triumphs. Being constantly undermined with harsh facts, still didn't seem to hinder him. On the contrary, it gave him inspiration to fantasise further. Barrett, in his own inscrutable way, pointed out some of the tensions over Singapore's desire for independence, but it was an aria that couldn't be stopped. It had the constancy of the outpouring of a waterfall.

Thankfully, the effusive, golden-haired Boot, sauntering down the aisle with a humorous swagger, halted Sully's historical revisionism. He looked at Hayes from the other side of the table and immediately imitated the Japanese POW commander in The Bridge on the River Kwai declaring, 'do not speak to me of rules. This is war. This is not a game of cricket'. Such was the absurdity of Boot's characterisation that the boys revelled in the fortuitous diversion. Now, Boot wasn't the brightest but he was a good seam bowler, who was in both the colts and house cricket team. One of his hobbies was films and Kwai was a favourite. In fact, the school had shown the war adventure recently in the appallingly draughty Big Hall. It was so freezing there that the boys had to wrap themselves in blankets, while incongruously watching a film set in the sweltering heat of Burma. Nonetheless, Boot and Hayes bonded over the film, which conveniently stopped Sully's never-ending homage to his foreign paradise and his father's military accomplishments. Fortunately, the self-proclaimed Singapore marketing executive and war historian withdrew into a silent retreat.

'Hello Booty!' hailed Hayes.

'Hayesy!' cried Boot

'We'd better win the rugger.'

'We're still in the cup.'

'Is there another film this term?'

'20,000 League Under the Sea.'

'That'll be good.'

'Kirk Douglas sings in it.'

'But it's not a musical.'

'Dimple chin only sings one sea song.'

‘Thank God for that.’

‘Hello boys,’ said Boot, leaning his tall gangly frame over the table to acknowledge Barrett and Sully, who muttered a muted response.

‘Well. Better go over and chat up Yvette and take advantage of more leftover desserts,’ announced Boot mischievously.

‘I’ll follow you,’ responded Hayes.

Although Yvette was more conservative than Françoise, she had a good sense of humour. She found Boot an amusing, innocuous pest. In any case, she had taken care not to get too emotionally involved with anyone. Certainly not Barrel, that ever-persistent Welsh boy. She wasn’t judgemental about others; it was just that she believed that sex was for marriage, not for casual pleasure. Her family had brought her up that way. It was part of her faith. Although Françoise, disagreed with these views, the two women still enjoyed each other’s company, cooking together and going on adventurous sojourns into the Sussex countryside. Yvette came from Magalas, a village in the south of France known for its medieval architecture. Her father ran the local post office with her mother and her younger sister was still at school. Yvette had studied hard and like Françoise she was taking a year out before going to study English at the University of Paris.

‘What’s French for apple pie and custard?’ mentioned Boot, holding out his plate for his dessert.

‘Aren’t you studying French?’ challenged Yvette, surprised at his basic lack of knowledge.

‘Well. Yes but er we haven’t done meals.’

‘You’re meant to be at a good school.’

‘I know. To be honest, Yvette. French isn’t my strongest subject.’

‘What is Maître Boot?’

‘That would be difficult.’

‘There must be one.’

‘Cricket?’ claimed Boot with a broad grin.

‘Cricket isn’t a subject.’

‘I know. I like history though.’

‘You’d better get going, you’re holding up the queue.’

'Ok, Yvette, here's your 64,000 question. What date was the battle of Waterloo?'

'1815.'

'You have won sixty 4000 shillings!' exclaimed Boot, doing his game show act.

'Go away Maître Boot, I've got work to do,' said a preoccupied Yvette.

'Bye Yvette, see you soon,' responded a cheery Boot as he departed with his stodgy apple pie and thick custard.

'Tarte aux pommes et crème anglaise,' called Yvette as Boot moved away.

'What's that?' projected Boot, before sauntering back to Yvette, who was wearing a big white apron.

'Apple pie and custard, Maître Boot,' explained Yvette.

'Thank you Yvette. Can you give me more French lessons?' requested the impudent, beanpole Boot.

'No. Go away Boot!' ordered a defiant Yvette.

Boot went back to his seat laughing uproariously. If only he was a little older, he thought that he might have a chance with Yvette, notwithstanding the claims of horny Barrel, who was staring aggressively at him from the furthest end of the tables. Boot quickly averted his eyes from the angry Welsh senior and dug into his apple pie. The cheeky junior still contemplated giving it a go with Yvette, despite Barrel's angry protestations. Meanwhile, the rest of the James B boys eventually got served, after becoming frustrated by the loquacious Boot's incongruous shenanigans.

Gradually, everybody settled down to enjoy their dessert. While finishing eating, Barrett and Sully were in the middle of an ardent discussion about the merits of Michael Holliday, 'the British Bing Crosby', when a note was passed down from the top table. It said that 'tonight at chapel, miss out verses 2 4, 6 and 8 of hymn number 250.'

'I think Ryder is behind this,' sensed Barrett.

'What do you mean?' asked Sully, spooning a large dollop of custard into his mouth.

'I think it's a form of rebellion against Root,' revealed Barrett excitedly.

'Missing out the verses?' suspected Hayes.

‘Exactly,’ this is his way of challenging Root’s autocratic rule,’ insisted Barrett.

‘Is any good going to come from it?’ queried a sceptical Binns.

‘Of course it will. It’ll send a message to Oliver that Root must go and that the old order is finished,’ declared Barrett.

‘You’re talking like a revolutionary, Barrett,’ observed an alarmed Binns.

‘Let’s just say change could be on its way,’ continued Barrett unrepentantly.

‘It’s certainly going to make chapel exciting,’ enthused Sully, greedily relishing his remaining rhubarb crumble.

‘That’ll be a change,’ remarked Hayes cynically.

The boys ate the remnants of their desserts with ruminative enjoyment, anticipating an evening’s drama.

Later, in the chapel, the boys from James B were in their usual place near the entrance. From that position, they observed the staff solemnly entering the sacred building. The masters were dressed in their Sunday best and wearing their variously coloured academic gowns. Their families traipsed somewhat reluctantly behind them, ignoring eye contact with the boys. Observing this procession, Hayes noted the presence of the incandescent Victoria Wallace. She wore a black crescent hat with a red rose, perkily placed at an angle. She was sitting close to Wallace, who was dressed soberly in a black jacket and trousers, rather than his usual plus fours. His cheery silver-haired wife sat next to him, wearing a matching tweed jacket and skirt. While Hayes was admiring the pale beauty of Victoria Wallace, his bête noir the formidable Mrs Hackett, entered in a smart two-piece blue suit, not her trademark black pants. Hayes had to confess that she almost appeared human. Her husband J.E.T. Hackett, unsurprisingly known as Jet, accompanied her. In his stale grey outfit, he looked bored by the whole proceedings. Hayes’s interest in the elderly Hacketts was soon broken by the arrival of their daughter, Sally, the lady with the beauty spot on her chin. Hayes thought that she must be down for the weekend from York University. Sally’s black dress left her arms bare from the elbow. A dark blue velvet pillbox hat, with a light veil discreetly pulled over her face, gave her a stylish presence. An entranced Hayes concluded privately, 'Audrey Hepburn move over!'

The Hacketts made their way further up the chapel, where most of the other masters and their families had congregated. Hayes wondered how this well dressed establishment were going to deal with the protest. Barrett, who was sitting beside him, waited in excitable anticipation for the insurrection. At the far end of the chapel, Sully was by now no doubt privy to the intimate details of the devious strategy concocted by Ryder, his redoubtable choir leader.

Suddenly, the entrance of the blackly clad Root walking eerily to his place, interrupted Hayes's musings. The music master didn't appear to be fearing any forthcoming rebellion. In fact, as he passed down the aisle, he smiled broadly at the Major, who was once again sitting next to the Wallaces. Hayes was sure that the Major was seriously interested in Victoria but the housemaster didn't give anything away, as he sat in his pew with a neutral, straight-backed military air. Hayes also noted that he was looking even smarter than usual. He'd had a haircut and his shaggier locks had been severely shorn. What's more, he was wearing what looked like a newly acquired charcoal grey Burton suit. This made Hayes even more convinced that his housemaster wanted to impress the elusive Victoria. Hayes wondered what Wallace would think of that, given the age gap. Maybe, thought Hayes, the Major had already asked Wallace's permission to court his daughter. After all, it would be inadvisable to cross Victoria's volatile Scottish father.

Gradually, the chapel filled. Hayes thought it was good that there was going to be a full house to participate in the forthcoming act of sabotage. The boys may not have been Maoists inspiring the people to rise up against a corrupt nationalist government, yet they still felt a distinct rush of revolutionary adrenaline in middle class Sussex, as they awaited the call to action.

Hayes then noticed Barrel arriving late as he discreetly made his way to the end of a pew. He wondered what he was doing. Maybe he was having serious words with Yvette about her messing around with the flirtatious Boot. Finally, all the staff assembled in the chapel including a chirpy Leslie 'we're joining the Common Market, chaps' Le Mesurier, a beaming Smallman, the dastardly, complacent Mr 'I hate dreamers' Sykes, a breathless Long John wooden-legged Carson, Killer Roy and Mrs Killer. In contrast, their pupils all kept as tight lipped as cold war spies awaiting insurgent action.

Evensong progressed along the usual lines of lessons from the Bible, prayers, a psalm, the Magnificat and the Nunc dimittis, interspersed with hymns. The service started well, the school were in splendid voice and the darkly attired Root beamed with smug satisfaction. The first lesson was read sincerely by a Wade A senior and the responses to the prayers were fulsome. As Oliver looked on benignly with his family, he felt happy seeing a community so energised and at one with itself.

As the time for the rebellion approached, Hayes gave Barrett furtive, knowing glances. There was now just the second lesson before the hymn that was to be mutilated. A senior monitor from Tickle B, was reading a section of Corinthians 2. However, none of the boys were listening. The scriptural wisdom flew over their heads. They were like terrorists waiting nervously to execute their plan. Eventually, the lesson finished and the music started for the school's very own fateful hymn, number 250. The time for the action was nigh.

'Praise the Lord for our great school, praise it for its glorious past' sang the boys and staff enthusiastically. However, when it came to the second verse, there was absolute silence apart from the staff and their families as the Major, Le Mesurier, Smallman, Long John, Sykes, Killer and Mrs Killer led the way, even though several of them were wildly out of tune. Halfway through the verse, they looked bewildered as they realised that none of the boys were singing. Their confusion only increased when eight hundred boys gave a hearty rendition of the next verse in a loud, exaggerated declamatory vein, in comic contrast to the reedy voices of forty masters and their relatives. As the hymn progressed and the choir and school didn't sing verse four, Root started to get angry. He detected the hand of Ryder in such subversion. This was an act of defiance that he took personally. He wasn't going to let all the good work he'd done with his choir be ruined by such a devious political operator. 'Bloody Ryder must be stopped. He must be stopped now,' murmured the affronted music master.

Root felt like a helpless theatre director who becomes impotent when an actor deliberately does the opposite to what was rehearsed. 'Well,' thought Root, 'maybe, in such circumstances, a director would find it hard to bring the curtain down, but in this case the service will cease.' When the whole school sang verse five very raucously and only the dreadful discordant singing of the beleaguered staff proceeded with the next verse, a raging Root decided to consult the Major. He brusquely squeezed past the bulbous Mr Endersby and nearly tripped over Long John's wooden leg as he descended into the aisle. He then bowed cursorily towards the altar, walked towards the Major and ascended steps that led him to the neatly attired housemaster at the end of the row. On his arrival, he whispered angrily.

'It's revolutionary Ryder, Bill. This is deliberate sabotage.'

'Calm down, Reg,'implored the Major with quiet intensity.

'He's ruining my work,' raged the incensed music master.

James B and the rest of the school were enjoying Root's discomfort. They believed that it was appropriate revenge for his musical Nazi rallies. In contrast, Oliver was concerned about Root's disruptive behaviour and stared angrily at both the music master and the Major.

'It's just a schoolboy prank,' implored the Major.

The school were now singing verse seven in an increasingly false, hearty tone, encouraged by Root's manifest unease.

'Just go back to your place, Reg, and forget it.'

'I want Ryder exposed and expelled.'

'That's a bit extreme, Reg. Look Oliver is getting exasperated,' warned the Major, becoming aware of the headmaster's icy gaze. After all, Oliver had previously experienced an infamous chapel incident. This was during a service, when wafts of smoke appeared through a large grille in the middle of the chapel's aisle, because several boys were puffing on cigarettes in the tube below. Now, he was witnessing further desecration.

'It's best that you return to your place respectfully,' said the Major insistently.

Root finally realised this was a serious warning. Consequently, he went back in slow, reverent mode, complete with pronounced bows to the altar, while a weary voiced staff and their increasingly bewildered families were musically mauling the final verse. By the time hymn 250 finally ended, Rev Elwyn had ascended the pulpit with his eyes inevitably fluttering towards the heavens. Whether this was because of the rendition of the hymn or just another plea for spiritual strength, wasn't clear. In any case, Elwyn's sermon seemed a minor event compared to the preceding sabotage.

Given that the seating arrangements in the chapel meant that the staff faced the boys, Hayes and Barrett did their best to avoid eye contact. In the choir, Ryder had a smirk on his face while Sully was worried that his relationship with Root would be seriously impaired. After all, he was hopeful that the music master's contacts could help him get a place at a college that specialised in singing. Although, he enjoyed the excitement of the insurgency, he feared the inevitable repercussions. Ryder, on the other hand, was willing to take whatever consequences ensued. He believed that insurrectionary action was necessary to combat Root's appalling behaviour. Ruling by fear and shouting every time something was wrong was never going to help young boys. He was not a maestro and he needed reminding of the fact. As far as Ryder was concerned, the school was a community and everybody needed to help each other.

In fact, the Reverend Elwyn's sermon centred on this very subject. He didn't refer directly to the shenanigans around hymn 250 but stressed the importance of tolerance and forbearing. He called on all those in society to try and settle their differences through mutual respect and resist aggression and violence. Elwyn was sincere and supported his thesis with various scriptural quotes. Unfortunately, he undermined his sermons by his inability to resist mentioning popular figures. In this case, it was Mahatma Gandhi and Martin Luther King. As Elwyn mentioned these appropriate but predictable emerging luminaries, Barrett gently nudged Hayes and under his breath whispered:

‘Next week, it’ll be Elvis and Jerry Lee Lewis.’

‘Not Lonnie?’ replied Hayes quietly.

‘Could be. You never know,’ said a giggly Barrett, who was immediately confronted by the Major staring at him intensely. Barrett instantly pulled himself together and looked round to the pulpit, pretending to respect Elwyn’s efforts to be fashionable. Although the chaplain tried earnestly to get his points across, he’d now lost the boys attention. They were either thinking of the consequences of the rebellion or what fun and games they were going to get up to after the service. Eventually, Elwyn concluded his plea for forbearance and everybody stood up for the final hymn, number 27 Abide with Me, which ironically the boys sang with clarity and passion. Hayes particularly liked it as it reminded him of the FA Cup Final when it was sung annually as a community hymn. As his voice attacked it with heartfelt ardour, Hayes’s thoughts drifted into believing that he had scored the final’s winner in the last minute with a header at the far post, and that his teammates were mobbing him. During the last verse, he saw himself shaking hands with the Queen and running around Wembley grubby-kneed, socks at his ankles, holding the cup aloft with his teammates. Suddenly, harsh reality shattered such transformative thoughts. There, directly in his eyeline towards the end of the final verse, was the severe countenance of Mrs Hackett, glaring at him witheringly. To Hayes, she now looked like a Gestapo interrogator, with her glacial blue eyes only adding to her apparent lack of empathy. Hayes quickly averted his gaze from Frau Hackett, only to discover Root looking around murderously at everybody. He obviously hated the boys for singing Abide with Me so vigorously, after the previous musical atrocity. Root took things very personally and he was not going to let the incident go unpunished. He would insist that Oliver exact retribution.

In fact, Oliver had already decided that there was going to be an investigation into such a public show of indiscipline. Not since the ‘smoke arising’ incident, during one of the local Bishop’s more bombastic sermons about sin, had Oliver felt so embarrassed. Although in that particular case, the compromised

Bishop joked that the smoke might have been just a suitable spiritual accompaniment to his sermon's theme, Oliver didn't find the incident amusing. Consequently, the perpetrators had to attend several exacting punishment parades with the Combined Cadet Force's demonic Sergeant Thatcher. Meanwhile, Oliver regarded the current hymn fracas with even greater seriousness than the smoking escapade. He believed that it was more organised, threatening and obviously the work of an inventive strategist.

After several weeks, the school's Disciplinary Committee, consisting of various masters and chaired by Mr Le Mesurier, concluded that it was Ryder who planned the omission of the verses. They accused the school's Lenin of being the catalyst that incited the rest of the school to follow his incorrigible dictate. Given that the term was ending shortly, they recommended that Ryder went home early for 'a serious period of reflection' and that every boy should be warned that further behaviour of that kind would lead to severe punishment.

Having digested the report, Oliver decided to tell Ryder himself of the Disciplinary Committee's counsel. He'd told him to come to his home next to the chapel, where he was ushered into the living room by his wife, a quiet, self-effacing woman in a plain grey dress. Her hair was neatly plaited around her head and she wore little make up, which made her look puritanically austere. Mrs Seymour or Mrs O as the boys called her, liked to keep in the background and only get involved in the school on a social level.

'Please do sit down, Ryder,' entreated Mrs O as they entered the room.

'Thank you,' replied Ryder who sank into a decorous high-back chair.

'Would you like a cup of tea?'

'I'd love one.'

'Sugar?'

'Yes please. Two.'

'Milk?'

'Thank you.'

'Good. I'll be back in a moment. Please excuse me.'

In the interim, Ryder took the opportunity to look around the living room, which was at the front of the house. In the corner was a Bechstein grand piano with a musical score on a wooden stand above the keys. On top of the piano were pictures of Oliver's family. A red curved sofa, a wingback brown armchair and an elegantly tiled fireplace gave the room a cosy ambience. On the walls were various paintings depicting various rural English settings: a farm, a garden and one of a coastal resort, which was full of seagulls. They looked amateur yet beguiling. After Ryder had contemplated Oliver's decor for several minutes, Mrs Oliver suddenly interrupted his visual ruminations.

'Here we are,' she said, placing the china cup and saucer on a small side table next to his chair.

'My husband will be with you very shortly.'

'Thanks.'

Just as she was about to leave the room, Mrs O turned and remarked:

'I do hope you stay with us.'

'Thank you.'

Mrs O's personal comment surprised Ryder as it was at odds with her usual detachment. In fact, she stayed at the threshold of the door and with an effusive smile continued to talk benignly.

'Enjoy your tea.'

'I will. Thanks for bringing it.'

'It's a pleasure.'

After listening to Mrs O's encouraging words, Ryder felt more confident of dealing with Oliver. He leant back in the chair and enjoyed an impressive cup of tea. He thought that so many people make tea carelessly, but Mrs O had brewed a perfect cuppa, neither too strong nor too weak. As he drank away, he thought about what he was going to say to Oliver. After a few minutes of deliberation, the headmaster entered and Ryder put down his tea and rose from his chair.

'Do sit down, Ryder,' insisted Oliver as he parked himself on the sofa. 'Sorry about the delay. One of the council members on the phone.'

'Nothing serious, I hope,' replied Ryder tactfully.

‘Just the usual money worries.’

‘Sorry to hear that, sir.’

Oliver made himself comfortable and then held up some papers.

‘Now Ryder, I thought I should explain the conclusion of the Disciplinary Committee’s report.’

‘Yes sir.’

‘Well we.. I mean, I think you should have a cooling off period?’

‘Cooling off?’

‘Yes. We, I mean I, feel that you should go home early.’

‘I see.’

‘This is what the Disciplinary Committee have advised and I agree with them.’

‘As a punishment?’

‘Yes. Term is coming to an end in a few weeks so you can be given work to do from home during that period. If you’d been less senior Ryder, you probably would have had to endure Sergeant Thatcher’s punishment regime.’

‘I see.’

‘I understand that Mr Root is quite a frustrating character. Indeed, he frustrates me but we can’t have pupils staging stunts every time they feel unhappy.’

‘It wasn’t a stunt sir, it was a protest.’

‘All right, a protest.’

Ryder sipped his tea and gathered his thoughts. He still wanted some form of change in the behaviour of the authoritarian music master. He replaced his teacup on its saucer and then started to probe.

‘Have you talked to Mr Root, sir?’

‘I have.’

‘And what did he say?’

‘That’s in confidence Ryder.’

‘Maybe, but our protest didn’t come out of nowhere.’

‘Your protest was uncivil and unnecessary,’

‘It was necessary, sir. Mr Root is an unacceptable authoritarian.’

‘All right, Ryder, I will reveal this much. I did tell Mr Root that he has to listen more.’

'What did he say?'

'He said he would.'

'And what about his shouting and screaming?'

'I've told him that he has to be calmer to bring the best out of all his pupils.'

'Did he agree?'

'Yes, he did.'

Oliver paused and composed himself before deciding to substantiate Root's path to enlightenment.

'In fact, he's going to take yoga lessons,' announced Oliver in his most ethereal voice.

'I don't believe it,' exclaimed Ryder in amazement.

'Apparently Yehudi Menuhin does it?'

'What?'

'Yoga.'

'I see.'

'Root admires Menuhin.'

'That's a change. He's not German.'

'Ryder I don't want to get into an assessment of Mr Root' s Teutonic taste as it's not relevant.'

'Let's hope not.'

'What do you mean by that?'

'Nothing, sir.'

'I sincerely hope so.'

Oliver watched Ryder superciliously drinking his tea for a few moments. He then decided to be firm with the radical reprobate.

Now listen Ryder, you're talented and this school will do everything to support you getting to Oxford.'

'Thank you, sir.'

'But it won't tolerate uprisings.'

'We were all frustrated because Mr Root wouldn't listen.'

'He'll listen now.'

Suddenly there were the loud sounds of a dog barking from the other side of the house.

'There you are Ryder, Hamlet agrees with me.'

'Hamlet?'

'Our golden retriever. We always need a reminder of England's greatest.'

‘Oh, I see,’ said Ryder, bewildered by Hamlet’s interruption, ‘but sir but what happens if yoga doesn’t calm Root down.’

‘Come to me and we’ll try to resolve it.’

‘All right sir.’

‘And what if that doesn’t work?’

‘We’ll have to send him to Germany!’ declared Oliver with an impish grin.

During Ryder’s absence, the term dawdled to a close. Mrs Hackett continued to berate Hayes as Sully sycophantically basked in her praise. Barrett felt that revolution was in the air after the chapel rebellion. One Ball didn’t press Sully to do his punishments. Brown and Bunter kept rockin’ to AFN. Rutter still met Françoise in the pavilion. Yvette devotedly attended the Catholic Church in a nearby village, while keeping the randy Barrel and the frisky Boot at bay.

As for the staff, they couldn’t wait for the break. The Major yearned to see more of Victoria Wallace, without a mob of boys watching every move he made with voyeuristic delight. Smallman looked forward to getting away from the juvenile posturings at grace and go on holiday with Collins, his devoted colleague. Long John couldn’t wait to meet up with his friend, Cathal Larkin in Dublin where he hoped to learn more about John Millington Synge. The red-haired Mr Sykes wanted a break from the intolerable insolence of Binns and his friends, so that he could spend time with his mother in Andover. Le Mesurier was going to visit Madame Defarge, a Parisian friend, who intended to take him to the Comédie-Française.

At an end of term concert, Root managed to conjure up an acceptable performance of Prince Igor without the presence of the radical choir leader. He was only too happy to forget the nefarious, reptilian Ryder and his revolutionary antics. The music master was now eager to retreat to his Indian yoga teacher in Birmingham and explore alternative states. Meanwhile, Mr Sims was eager to escape from Root’s dramas and depart with Beth to the Lake District . Oliver and his family were just looking forward to having the school to themselves, so that the children weren’t put on such a tight leash. Only

Killer had to administer one final duty, the term's punishment beatings, known colloquially as Killer's floggings.

Killer's floggings took place on the last Friday of term. On this particular occasion there were three thrashings: Rice for defacing a library book by replacing the picture of an esteemed general with that of a baboon, Boot for consistently putting sugar in matron's bed and Binns for calling Mr Sykes 'a fascist'. In fact, Rice was the only senior flogging, so it was more practical for him to take his punishment with the juniors. Before the floggings Killer appeared in a genial mood, chatting amiably with the boys as if his brutal battering wasn't going to take place. On this occasion, Killer was regaling the boys about his misadventures during a camping holiday. Although his altercation with an unaccommodating cow was amusing, there was still a menacing threat lurking behind the veneer of Killer's idle chat.

After he'd exhausted his holiday tales and the boys had left the lav end, Killer told One Ball, who was the monitor on duty, to go upstairs to the senior dormitory and get Rice. Eventually the boys nestled in their beds, anticipating the floggings like an ancient crowd preparing for a hanging. A few minutes later, Rice entered through the dormitory door, followed by One Ball, who appeared like a compliant jailer to Killer's hangman. Meanwhile, Killer went to get his 'special slipper', which was perched on a nearby radiator. One Ball then proceeded to lower a central hanging light and turn off all other illumination. The preparation completed, Killer strode dramatically into the luminous pool of light, gathered himself and called out the first name.

'Rice,' ordered Killer in a flat, commanding tone.

Some of the boys now hid under their bedclothes.

Rice came over to the light in his flimsy, blue-striped pyjamas, through which Killer was confident of penetrating.

'Bend over,' directed Killer.

As Rice did so, his bald patch shone brightly in the descending light. He hadn't been beaten before but he was determined to keep mentally strong while the thrashing took place. He decided that Brigitte would help him in his task. He thought of her body as displayed in Picture Show: the fishnet stockings, the long stylish gloves and the short inviting negligee.

'One!' counted Killer as he flogged.

Rice started to expand his sexual thoughts after his posterior stung in pain. 'I'll take it from you, BB,' he murmured to himself.

'Two,' cried Killer as he thrashed away.

Perversely, Rice was finding the flogging rather exciting. While he thought of BB beating him, he felt increasing pleasure as his buttocks went on fire.

'And three,' fulminated Killer, putting everything into the climax.

'Thanks BB,' whispered Rice to himself, as the full brutality of the final beating left his rear raw, yet feeling curiously fulfilled.

His flogging concluded, Rice made his way back to the senior dormitory, passing the stern visage of One Ball, the executioner's accomplice, on the way. As he opened the door and turned to Killer, he said with the hint of a cynical smile:

'Thank you sir,' before leaving quickly and going upstairs.

Killer was perplexed as to why Rice was pleased to be beaten.

'He couldn't of enjoyed it could he? That defeats the whole purpose of the exercise,' surmised a bewildered Killer.

Anyway, he reassured himself that it wasn't for him to reason why and plumb the depths of Rice's eccentric soul. He had a job to do and like any good torturer, he would carry his task out with efficiency and detachment. Hence, he promptly took his mind away from Rice's bizarre behaviour by screaming for the next victim.

'Boot!'

Boot, in his red and white striped pyjamas, strolled defiantly towards the hanging light where Killer waited for him. By this time, most of the boys had sat up in their beds vicariously watching the violent performance. Although Killer's robust actions had made them apprehensive of experiencing such punishment themselves, they were still compelled to look at the grisly ritual.

'Bend over,' instructed Killer.

As the elongated Boot bent his tall, gangly frame, he was determined to hold on to the power of song. In his particular case, an old English nursery rhyme that appealed to his impish sense of fun.

'One,' spluttered Killer as his slipper clattered Boot's bottom.

'Hickory dickory dock,' sang Boot to himself.

'Two,' ejaculated Killer as he gave him another thrashing.

'The mouse ran up the clock,' continued Boot.

'Three,' thundered Killer with another whack.

'The clock struck one,' added Boot painfully.

'What were you mumbling Boot?' demanded a disturbed Killer as Boot rose to his full height.

'Nothing sir,' answered Boot.

'Well it must have been something Boot,' insisted Killer

Boot eventually decided that he had better confront Killer rather than not reveal his defence mechanism. In doing so, he thought that he'd earn more respect from the flogger-in-chief.

'It was Hickory Dickory Dock.'

Muffled sniggers emanated from around the dormitory before Killer exclaimed:

'The nursery rhyme!'

'Yes sir. I just love the words.'

'This isn't the time for literary appreciation, Boot.'

'No sir.'

'Go to your bed immediately,' instructed Killer.

Boot then moved slowly but defiantly to the far end of the dormitory. As he sauntered along he mumbled, 'the mouse ran down, hickory dickory dock,' to conclude his poetic resistance. His derriere hurt but the discomfort was bearable. Boot thought that brutal Killer was beginning to tire as the slipper didn't always land with its fullest force. Anyway, he was sick of bloody matron. 'She deserved to have Demerara sugar in her bed. That Witch of Wigan never stops nagging,' he justified to himself. 'Next time, I'll add some honey for lubrication.' Boot had now reached his bed and lay down in a vengeful but rascally mood. Ryder's recent coup at Evensong had given him extra inspiration to be insolent.

‘Binns,’ shouted Killer, mopping some beads of sweat from his brow with a large maroon handkerchief.

Binns made his was way solemnly towards the dormitory’s gallows. He was nervous but he still didn’t regret making comments about the odious Sykes. Binns found his jingoistic nationalistic views particularly offensive. So, despite his apprehension of the ensuing violence, he was glad that he had been abusive to such a red-haired loon.

Whatever Killer threw at him, Binns was going to hold on to his views about the Common Market and practise his languages.

‘Bend over,’ decreed a hoarse Killer.

Binns reluctantly obeyed the lean, towering figure before him.

‘One,’ shouted Killer, ramming the slipper into Binns’s buttocks.

‘Charles De Gaulle. Vive La France!’ muttered Binns passionately to counter the pain.

‘Two,’ screamed Killer, taking a run-up to clatter Binns’s rump.

‘Konrad Ardenauer. Es Liebe Deutschland!’ murmured Binns, rebelliously revelling in his minimal German.

‘And three,’ howled an exhausted Killer, hurling the slipper at Binns’s posterior.

‘The Common Market forever!’ droned Binns in muffled defiance.

Binns’s backside was sore but as Killer was undoubtedly tiring, the junior thought that it could have been worse. Binns regarded Killer as an unwitting accomplice, a science teacher of average ability, who lacked imagination. Nonetheless, his war service made Killer more aware of moral and political complexity than most at the school. Something, on occasions, he was happy to impart to the boys. However, too often he buried the pain of the violence and injustice he’d experienced, in favour of assimilating a mask of conformity to accommodate a comfortable life. In any case, Killer believed in doing a job well and his army training made sure that he didn’t look too deeply into the reasons for corporal punishment. Anyway, he didn’t think such beatings would leave permanent scars. If administered with controlled violence, they acted as a deterrent, which stopped pupils from embarking on such an activity ever again. In fact, Killer regarded it as a form of redemption.

Binns looked up at his torturer blankly.

'You were mumbling as well, Binns.'

'Was I?'

'Yes you were.'

'Must have been my subconscious, sir.'

Subdued giggles percolated around the dormitory, inciting One Ball, the executioner's accomplice, to glower at the areas of levity. Hayes, Sully and Barrett all caught his eye and hastily looked another way. In fact, One Ball secretly admired the tactics of those who'd been beaten. If you're going to be flogged, you needed such endurance defences. Still, he hated any loss of respect. After all, surely that was the basis of a civilised society.

Killer continued to look at Binns querulously:

'Your subconscious, Binns?'

'Yes.'

'I think I heard the words Common Market.'

'That's right.'

'Well, what was that about?'

'I was dreaming of us in a new Europe.'

'Good God!'

'You see sir when..'

'That's enough Binns,' said Killer, interrupting before Binns could expound on his European vision. 'Your dreams sound more like nightmares. Get into bed,' he ordered. After all, Killer firmly believed in an independent Britain, not being part of a bureaucratic European block run by dubious foreigners. Binns made his way back to bed, rubbing his hands together and squeezing his eyes into peculiar contortions, as was his won't. A chorus of 'mental' came from various quarters of the dormitory but One Ball's harsh intervention stopped the cacophony in its tracks.

'Keep quiet!' yelled One Ball at his minions.

A grinning Killer then approached One Ball.

'Thank you Potts,' expressed Killer respectfully. 'The troops have to be kept in order.'

'Yes indeed, sir.'

'Well, I think I'll call it a day.'

'All right. Good night sir.'

'Good night.'

As Killer made towards the door, One Ball discovered the infamous slipper on the floor.

'Sir.'

'Yes Potts.'

'Your slipper.'

'Oh, thank you Potts,' replied Killer, picking up the flogging implement and moving back towards One Ball.

'I wouldn't want to leave my instrument of torture here, I could well need it again,' declared Killer, laughing nervously.

'Let's hope not,' responded One Ball warily.

'Indeed, but remember Potts, before my time beatings were done by monitors, people like you.'

'I'd heard that.'

'What do you think of that?

'What, sir?'

'You doing the beatings.'

Sully looked up over his bedclothes to hear the conversation more clearly. The thought of One Ball being in charge of floggings made him shiver nervously.

'I would have done my duty sir,' proclaimed One Ball righteously.

'That's what I like to hear, Potts,' affirmed Killer

Killer turned to leave but One Ball suddenly stopped him from departing.

'But why was that system stopped, sir?'

'Because there were cases of uncontrolled violence,' answered Killer, moving closer to One Ball and lowering his voice. 'It was some years ago but apparently, James B had a senior monitor called Sharp. He was six foot six inches tall and intimidating. He was captain of the 1st XV. Unfortunately, he got carried away. He beat one boy so hard that the chap fell unconscious on the floor. He had to go to hospital. After that unfortunate incident, the system changed.'

'What happened to Sharp?' enquired an alarmed One Ball.

‘Nothing of any immediate consequence. He went on to become a judge,’ revealed Killer cheerily.’

‘And the other boy?’

‘Thankfully, he recovered and became an MP.’

‘Really?’

‘Yes. In some obscure Welsh constituency,’ affirmed Killer. ‘Goodnight Potts,’ he concluded, ‘and thanks for the slipper.’

‘A pleasure sir.’

Killer then said goodnight to the boys, to which he got a lukewarm reply. He wasn’t surprised but it didn’t worry him. Being slaughterer-in-chief meant that he wasn’t exactly on their Christmas card list. In any case, Killer didn’t regard being a schoolmaster as a popularity contest. He turned out the main light and left with his flogging equipment. He could now concentrate on tying up various loose ends before the term finished.

One Ball was now sitting at the desk, isolated in his Anglepoise light. He looked forward to the term finishing in two days’ time. Of course, he’ll have to cope with his mother and her obsession with the garden as well as inquisitive neighbours, but he’d manage. He just hoped that the memory of his father’s ignominious end had faded from Martha’s mind.

Hayes couldn’t get to sleep. He was so excited by the thought of seeing Hannah and Poppy again that he became restless. He wondered if his sister had any Christmas parties lined up. She had so many connections that she was bound to have something arranged. He also hoped to see his father and watch Charlton again.

Sully was worried that if he didn’t complete his punishments, Killer would flog him. Still, he was determined to put such thoughts to the back of his mind. He couldn’t wait to see his family, not least his all-conquering father. Yet he realised that he needed to check his facts about the war, so that he could prevent other boys ridiculing him. The praise of Mrs Hackett meant nothing if your friends thought that you were a fool.

Barrett couldn’t wait to play his Lonnie Donegan records and hear how his Dad was getting on at his school. He anticipated a simple, homely Christmas with no frills. He loved the way his mother organised that. He just hoped that Ryder’s chapel coup would lead to greater justice, not least in dealing with One Ball. Although he revelled in the school's academic opportunities, he intensely disliked its ethos.

The dormitory became silent as One Ball scribbled away. Most of the boys fell asleep quickly, maybe as an antidote to the brutality they had been forced to witness or perhaps because they preferred to dream of going home. Whatever the reason, it had certainly been a long term with its inevitable oscillations. In a few days, they would be departing to many different areas of the country to have Christmas with their families. When One Ball completed his last essay of term about the comparison of liquid densities, he turned off his light. He then took his belongings, tiptoed across the floor, so as not to awaken the juniors from their slumbers and closed the dormitory door.

Lent Term

'You told nobody about my Johnnies?' asked One Ball severely.

'No Potts,' confirmed a reticent Hayes.

'Not even your mother?'

'Certainly not.'

'Where's my coat?'

'I'm still cleaning it.'

'Well hurry up.'

'All right.'

Hayes deposited the obligatory Tizer on Potts's settle, accompanied by the inevitable Mars bar, and left the senior dormitory.

One Ball lay back in his bath revelling in the house rugby cup victory against Tickle A, not least his own contribution to the conquest. With the scores level in the quarter final, One Ball heroically inspired a pushover try to win the game. He wasn't able to produce a moment of invention or skill as he was too slow and clumsy. He didn't have a good spring so he was useless at catching the ball in lineouts. He wasn't the man to miraculously open up play with a dummy pass or produce a drop kick out of nowhere. He was a warrior who embraced the physical battle. He had the size and weight to be good in the scrum especially against more undeveloped boys. This was how he triumphed, pummelling the opposition by brute strength.

After the victory, One Ball decided to treat himself. He stretched across to get hold of his Matey Bubble Bath, which was perched on the side of the tub. On the bottle was a cartoon drawing of a desultory man with yellow cheeks and lips, who looked sad and sullen. One Ball looked at the picture disdainfully and then poured the liquid into the bath with his particular diligence. He soaked his big frame into the scented water: his wide thick shoulders, his strong arms and his thick muscular legs all submitted to the soapy lather. One Ball relished a sense of achievement, a moment of success that went beyond mere academic attainment.

Hovever, there was still an emotional hole in his life. That's why he needed to meet Françoise privately. He had to stop bloody Rutter monopolising her all the time. He reassured himself that she would tire of the odious Tom Thumb and his oily charm. As Françoise hadn't formally rejected him, he felt that there was still hope. After all, she was usually polite and pleasant to him. Nevertheless, Françoise's eyes still sparkled at the mention of Rutter's name. This made One Ball want to puke. Consequently, he became more determined to expose the flaws of the arrogant rugby captain. Just because he was a sporting hero didn't mean that he was invulnerable. One Ball felt reassured as he lounged in his bubble bath like a Hollywood star. Yes, he would unmask the repulsive Lilliputian. After all, he didn't go through the rigmarole of getting his Johnnies hidden at the beginning of Exodus for nothing.

Hayes interrupted One Ball's reflections and returned to the Senior Lav End with his coat.

'Put it over there,' ordered an imperial One Ball, waving his hand dismissively.

Hayes moved towards some hooks by a radiator.

'Not there, squit, by the settle.'

'I thought you liked to keep your coat at a distance from your clothes,' reasoned Hayes.

'Well, you thought incorrectly.'

'Sorry.'

'Accepted'.

Just as Hayes was about to escape further interrogation, One Ball continued.

'Did you see the match this afternoon?'

'No.'

'We won.'

'Good.'

'Is that all you have to say, Hayes?'

'Well I didn't see the game so it's a bit difficult to comment.'

'Well we won 11-8.'

'Congratulations.'

Potts submerged deeper into his bubble bath, while observing his squit.

'What were you doing this afternoon, Hayes?'

'Practising with the colts.'

‘I see. Well you missed a tight game.’

‘Jayne Mansfield has one of those.’

One Ball immediately looked disconcerted.

‘What?’

‘A bubble bath.’

‘I’m not Jayne Mansfield, Hayes.’

‘I know that Potts.’

‘Are you suggesting that I’m effeminate?’

‘Not at all, Potts.’

‘Because I’m certainly not.’

‘I was just saying that..’

‘I have a bubble bath for relaxation.’

‘Of course.’

‘Not because, I want to be a woman’

‘I didn’t mean..’

‘And certainly not Miss Mansfield.’

‘Why not? She’s quite intelligent.’

‘That’s not the way she comes across.’

‘Surely we mustn’t just believe the papers, Potts?’

‘Hayes. This is not the time for a discussion about the press.’

‘Sorry, Potts.’

One Ball sank further into the bath, lapping water across his muscular torso.

‘I’m trying to relax after a triumphant win.’

‘Triumphant?’

‘Yes. I scored the winning try.’

‘Did you?’

‘I wouldn’t say so if I hadn’t, squit.’

‘Well congratulations, Potts.’

‘Thank you, Hayes.’

‘Well I’d better go and get ready for tea,’ said Hayes moving towards the door.

‘Just one thing, Hayes,’ cried One Ball, stopping Hayes in his tracks.

‘Yes’.

‘Have you seen Rutter recently?’

‘Why, Potts?’

‘Nothing. I just need to speak to him.’

‘No I haven’t seen him.’

‘Ok. I’ll find him.’

‘During tea. In the Dining Hall, perhaps?’

‘Maybe. And Hayes, how’s your mother?

Hayes paused as he didn’t want to go into details about his mother, particularly as Hannah had found the Christmas period difficult. It brought out her raw emotions. Certainly, Hayes enjoyed the usual seasonal trappings: the coal at the bottom of stockings, musical chairs, carols with his mother at the piano, the Queen’s Christmas message and of course presents. Despite such jovial rituals, Hayes felt a certain melancholy behind Hannah’s determined gaiety. He sensed that beneath her display of fortitude lay a deep feeling of hurt. Hayes now realised that it would take more time for her to erase the pain of her divorce. Therefore, he was quite relieved to meet up with his father and Bob for another match at Charlton. Bob, resplendent in his cheese cutter cap, enjoyed displaying a brown walking stick, which he’d received for Christmas from one of his girlfriends. According to Hayes’s calculation, during the afternoon he managed to say ‘old boy’ a record seventy times. However, he wasn’t going to relay such idiosyncratic personal thoughts to One Ball.

‘She’s fine. Teaching the piano,’ replied Hayes.

‘Good. Who’s her favourite composer?’ enquired One Ball.

‘Mozart, I think.’

‘Nice but too airy fairy for me.’

‘Really?’

‘I prefer something more earthy and dramatic.’

‘That’s why you like Wagner.’

‘Exactly.’

Hayes opened the lav end door and was about to depart, when he thought that he should reciprocate Potts’s enquiry.

‘How’s your mother?’

In fact, sometimes Potts had been finding it difficult to have a conversation with Martha. Over Christmas, she drank too much and occasionally got morose. When they went to the midnight service together, the vicar gave a rousing sermon about the relevance of the birth of Christ, to which the Farnham congregation paid polite but distant attention. On Boxing Day, the Kirwins came round with Len's younger sister Janet, her husband Stephen and their baby Rosie. Unfortunately, Rosie proceeded to be sick all over the drawing room carpet after eating the Potts' Christmas food. Despite this mishap, One Ball was grateful for the Kirwins' presence, as it diverted his mother's attention away from depressive brooding. A boisterous game of charades was particularly entertaining, with the Kirwins contorting their bodies into absurd shapes to get the Potts family to guess the right word. In fact, the fun of that occasion proved a catalyst for Martha as the following week she started looking for ways to get a better job. In the meantime, she continued to work part time.

'She's ok,' answered One Ball.

'Good,' acknowledged Hayes.

'She's helping out at a Red Cross charity shop,'

'Do send her my regards.'

'I will Hayes,' confirmed One Ball, before abruptly dismissing his squit by declaring, 'thank you, that's all.'

Hayes was about to leave when Potts suddenly called him back.

'And Hayes.'

'Yes?' queried Hayes.

'I hope my coat is spick and spam.'

'Of course. Nothing but the best from me.'

'I hope so, Hayes. All right, go.'

After the departure of his squit, One Ball washed his considerable frame with Palmolive soap and sank into his bubble bath.

It was late afternoon just before tea on a cold January afternoon. Brown and Bunter were listening to the radio playing 'Don't You Rock Me Daddy-O' by The Vipers Skiffle Group. They were standing on a bench, clapping and raucously singing the chorus, when Barrett entered the dayroom in a very excitable mood.

'Eden's resigning!' he screamed. Given such news, Brown and Bunter reluctantly agreed to turn down the exhilarating recording.

'Brown can you try to get the news? Barrett pleaded with unabated fervour. 'Maybe it's the end of the Tories,' he yelled euphorically as if revolution was in the air.

'I doubt it,' remarked a detached Brown.

'Why do you say that?' challenged Barrett with a contempt for non-believers.

'Because they have over a fifty seat majority,' elucidated Brown calmly.

'Yes but Suez has been a humiliating disaster,' claimed an angry Barrett.

'Governments can survive disasters when they have the numbers,' pronounced Brown, blunting Barrett's euphoria.

Bunter searched for the Home Service as Barrett came down to earth with a bump. Of course, Brown was right. They had the numbers. Their class and all those Old Etonians would close ranks when it came to retaining power. Like his father, Barrett was hopeful of something more lasting after the Labour government had laid the foundation of the welfare state. However, during the holidays in south London, Barrett was disappointed to discover that after years of austerity, too many people seemed to be more interested in getting a tv and a fridge on hire purchase than a creating a fairer society. Eventually, Bunter found a newsflash, read in a resonant voice by John Snagge, which announced that Eden was no longer Prime Minister. After the dramatic bulletin finished, Killer entered the dayroom, followed by an intrigued Hayes and Sully, so Brown turned off the radio and told them the news.

'Eden has resigned,' he announced, moving off his rocking position on the bench to terra firma.

'Really?' responded a bemused Killer, who had just returned from giving a chemistry lesson to some unresponsive juniors.

'I told you Brown. I heard from Mr Le Mesurier. A friend who works in Whitehall told him earlier on the phone. I met him in the Avenue,' clarified Barrett excitedly.

'On the grounds of health, apparently,' added Bunter.

'That's rubbish' insisted Barrett. 'He's resigning because he's been pushed out.'

'Because of Suez?' suggested Hayes.

'Yes. Barrett's probably right. Winston will be upset,' contemplated Killer.

'Why? I thought he'd resigned, sir?' queried Sully.

'Eden was Winston's chosen successor, Sully,' said Killer.

'After such a humiliating withdrawal, the PM was finished. The Yanks put pressure on Eden to leave,' stated Brown confidently.

By now, One Ball had joined the gathering, eager to assert his views.

'Eisenhower didn't want military action to take place just before the US election,' countered a forceful One Ball.

'That's very cynical, Potts,' observed Killer.

'I'm always cynical about politicians, sir,' declared One Ball.

'Eden will be spending more time in Jamaica now. He can go and visit Noël Coward and Ian Fleming,' propounded Killer.

'Do any of these rich exiles pay taxes in this country?' questioned Barrett.

'They're not there all the time, Barrett,' contended Killer.

'Well why is there criticism of just Coward then, sir?' posed Barrett.

'Maybe he owes more tax than the others,' commented Killer.

'You just want to undermine aspiration Barrett,' accused One Ball.

'I want a just system for a fairer society,' argued an insistent Barrett.

'Your piety has no limits,' exclaimed One Ball fervently.

'Ok Potts. Calm down,' interrupted Killer, pacifying his belligerent monitor.

'Sorry sir but I just don't think high taxes are the answer,' disputed One Ball diplomatically.

'To tax or not to tax, that is the question?' parodied Rice as he joined the ad hoc debating society.

'Well we know one thing. Sir Anthony won't be making those decisions anymore,' interjected Bunter.

'At least he can go and watch some good cricket,' thought Rice.

Brown then started a snatch of a celebrated song:

‘With those little pals of mine,’ he sang in calypso style while cueing in Bunter.

‘Ramadhin and Valentine,’ concluded the two rockers together.

Everybody laughed except One Ball, who wouldn’t smile even if he’d won the pools. Grim Jim was still feeling the embarrassment of Killer’s reprimand in front of the others, especially juniors. Even Killer relaxed and could see the funny side of Brown and Bunter’s double act, although he didn’t know the song’s origin.

‘Sorry but I must plead ignorance. Why is there a song about Ramadhin and Valentine?’

‘Cricketers sir,’ explained Rice.

‘I know that Rice but why the song?’ enquired Killer.

‘It’s a celebration sir, of the first West Indies Test Match victory in England,’ replied Rice.

‘When Sonny and Alf took a lot of English wickets,’ stressed Barrett.

‘Eden likes cricket,’ said Hayes.

‘Well, he’s got plenty of time to get to watch it now,’ joked Brown.

‘My neighbour’s going to be very upset,’ informed Hayes.

‘Eden’s secretary?’ queried Barrett.

‘Oh yes, I heard that you know her,’ corroborated Killer.

‘Yes. She’s been with him for years,’ affirmed Hayes casually.

‘Does she tell you anything?’ added a curious Barrett, itching to obtain some scandal on the former Prime Minister.

‘No, not me, but I get a bit from her son Andrew,’ confessed a conspiratorial Hayes.

‘What does he say? Go on, tell us,’ demanded Barrett.

‘That Eden hasn’t been well. And that he takes drugs,’ continued Hayes.

‘Good god!’ cried a surprised Killer.

‘What drug?’ asked Rice.

‘Are you sure, Hayes?’ stressed One Ball.

‘You mustn’t spread false rumours, Hayes,’ warned Killer, sceptical of such conjecture.

‘I only know what I’ve been told sir,’ maintained Hayes defensively.

‘Like what?’ pursued Barrett.

‘That he takes a drug to help his health difficulties,’ elaborated Hayes.

‘Cocaine?’ suggested Brown facetiously.

‘Hashish?’ proposed Bunter, echoing such levity.

‘Ok, boys, that’s enough,’ interrupted Killer.

‘It’s called Benzedrine, I think,’ said Hayes hesitantly.

‘The PM is a drug addict!’ exclaimed Rice.

‘Thank you, Rice,’ interrupted Killer, to stop further elucidation. ‘Still, that might explain some of his decisions,’ he resumed thoughtfully.

Killer then invited the boys to speculate on Eden’s successor. It was hard to call as the Conservative party don’t do anything as vulgar as actually elect a leader. He emerged from an inner cabal almost as of divine right. In any case, none of the boys could agree.

‘Rab’ speculated Barrett.

‘Butler? Too competent and boring,’ thought Rice.

‘Macmillan. A wily populist with all that Premium Bonds stuff,’ thought Brown.

‘Any other contenders?’ sought Killer.

The boys didn’t think so, although Brown did flippantly mutter under his breath the name of Tommy Steele, to which puerile proposal Killer gave a scornful scowl. They all agreed that whoever came into office was going to have to deal with re-establishing Britain’s relationship with America, dealing with the ever-growing desire for independence in the British colonies as well as a fragile economy. One Ball also mentioned the Cold War and the Soviet threat, while Barrett reminded everybody of the dangers of nuclear proliferation.

Killer enjoyed engaging with the boys about current affairs, so long as it didn’t get too heated and denigrate into a slanging match. It made a change from the usual conversations about sport and floggings. Even though he found some of their views naïve, he was proud of the way they were thinking about the world, despite Brown’s insolent desire to see a pop singer as Prime Minister. Although he believed in discipline, he was more concerned about citizenship. He didn't want to teach a lot of boring technocrats, who could just pass exams, but young people who were informed and open to new ideas and the wider world. Given the rapid changes since the end of the war, he was convinced that well-informed youth would give the country hope for the future. Such optimism was redemptive as the Suez debacle only confirmed to Killer that colonial Britain was on its last legs.

After the boys' attempts to reshape the nation, Pound, suddenly approached the group around the radio.

'Sorry to break up the cabinet meeting,' said Pound jovially.

'That's all right. We're only trying to save the world,' responded a grinning Brown.

'No. Just the British Empire,' insisted Bunter.

'Certainly not the Tory party,' stressed Barrett derisively.

'That's enough Barrett,' interjected Killer, firmly stopping any further political discussion.

It was now time for tea. Pound rang the bell. The boys ambled out of the dayroom. The Prime Minister was no more but the boys still eagerly awaited their cauliflower au gratin.

Hubert Aloysius Bayliss was delighted to be the director of the school play. He was particularly pleased as his choice was Henry V by England's greatest playwright. Bayliss saw Shakespeare's exploration of kingship and war as a 'patriotic entertainment'. In fact, he wanted this highlighted in the marketing of the production. Bayliss always had an eye for publicity and headlines. He would have made a good editor of a newspaper but lethargy stopped him entering the real world. He preferred to use his position in the well-paid closeted milieu of a public school to flirt with his ambitions. In fact, Bayliss had become so involved in his interpretation of the classic play that he'd forgotten to initially run his Shakespearean proposal by Basil Ponsonby-Smythe, the Head of the English Department. Basil was an effete eccentric, who always had a polka-dotted handkerchief in the top pocket of his various ostentatious jackets. His expansively imaginative classes were notorious. On one occasion, dramatising the shipwreck in The Tempest, he rearranged the whole classroom so that the boys stood on desks, swaying from side to side. It was so convincing that two pupils ended up in the infirmary with a sprained ankle and a pulled hamstring.

Basil liked Bayliss, so although he found his interpretative ideas very simplistic, he allowed his production to proceed. Anyway, he needed a break from directing school plays. After all, the previous year Basil had directed A Midsummer Night's Dream, which when on tour in Holland experienced considerable difficulties. The First Fairy got seasick on the Harwich ferry and the boy playing Hippolyta, replaced him. At the first performance in Amsterdam, the new Fairy managed not only to forget his words but also to invent new ones. The Dutch teacher, who was hosting the visit, wondered if it was a new version of the scene. Notwithstanding such artistic setbacks, the tour was a considerable success, even though Basil did have to spend a lot of the time making sure that the boys weren't over-friendly with the welcoming girls. Not least in Amsterdam, when young women dressed in traditional Dutch costume, including a lace bonnet and wooden clogs, presented various cheeses to the boys on stage. After such a long and exhausting project, Basil was willing to suppress his artistic doubts about the effervescent Bayliss and give him the opportunity to direct his 'patriotic entertainment'.

Bayliss was pleased to get the necessary support from Basil. He could rely on him as he wasn't an envious colleague. Although Bayliss was a history master, he certainly had an instinct for drama. For instance, during his class on the Crimean War, he would self-consciously allude to Florence Nightingale's purported lesbianism or when evaluating the Napoleonic Wars, refer to Napoleon's sexual dalliances with Josephine. Of course, this was grist to the mill to adolescent boys and Bayliss revelled in their curiosity. Tall, thin and debonair with a pale complexion, thinning fair hair and rosy cheeks, Bayliss liked a drink but managed to keep his imbibing under control. He was married to Mary, a warm, dumpy woman with dark curly hair. Mary used to work in the school's library but was currently looking after their five-month year old child, pretentiously named Augustus.

Bayliss was a lazy liberal cocooned in cynical detachment. Nevertheless, he still had faith in his country and its values. He saw his interpretation of Henry V as a glorious celebration of victory at war and honour in peace. Given that World War Two wasn't so long ago, Bayliss saw this as a perfect opportunity to celebrate the British values that had triumphed so resoundingly. Of course, Olivier started such thoughts with his film during the war but Bayliss believed that his interpretation was different. His production wouldn't be a rallying call to the troops but more a celebration of values. Bayliss seemed to underplay the wider humanity of the play-the doubts about leadership and war as well as the celebration of peace and reconciliation. The emphasis seemed to be on bombast and conquest. It wasn't that Bayliss wasn't insensitive to other themes. It was just that he felt that the subtleties of the play would be harder for the boys to negotiate, so he decided to direct a production which put greater emphasis on their strengths of energy and physicality.

Bayliss lounged in his study contemplating the casting of his epic. He wasn't a housemaster, so that gave him more time to concentrate on his production. He lived in one of the post-war detached houses off the Avenue in Copse Grove, next to Mr and Mrs Killer. The houses were functional rather than aesthetic but had modern amenities and were located at a suitable distance from neighbours. Consequently, Bayliss didn't hear Killer's rumoured rows with his wife. The house came with the job so he thought it a good acquisition, especially with a new baby in tow. Although he could have done with a bigger study to accommodate his books, overall he regarded his abode as satisfactory. As he sat back on his chaise longue and tried to focus on casting, much to his annoyance Augustus started bawling. As the baby continued to howl, Mary resorted to putting a dummy in his mouth to quieten him down. Eventually a sort of peace reigned and Bayliss resumed his role as casting director

Suddenly, Bayliss leapt up from his recliner, spilling some of his coffee over the brown carpet. He'd found his Henry. It had to be Andrew Macready of Tickle A. 'Macready has the stature and the voice; he also has the necessary hauteur and intelligence,' he assured himself. Bayliss circled his study, sipping his coffee with delight. He was confident that he'd found his lynchpin. Now, further ideas ensued:

'Madoc or 'Barrel' as the boys call him could be Fluellen, he's Welsh. Brown and Bunter could be Nym and Bardolph, they're sufficiently vulgar. The clever but dull Beckett could be the mundane Duke of Exeter.' Bayliss rushed to his desk, got hold of an exercise book and wrote his musings down, while intermittently gulping the remains of his coffee.

'But who could bloody well be the Chorus? Maybe that rather humourless boy, whose father died in the war, he'd do? What's his name? Ah yes, Potts. He certainly has the natural sense of patriotism that's needed. But the cast can't all come from James B. Ah, Rutter from Ironside A, he's a bit small but he could be the Dauphin. But what about the women? If only we could use the French women already employed here. 'Of course that's far too sensible to be allowed,' uttered Bayliss to himself, embracing some of the rebellious tendencies of his student days.

As he strolled theatrically around his study ruminating on the casting of his epic, Bayliss instantly confronted mundane reality. His wall clock showed that it was 1:50 pm. In ten minutes, he had to give a lesson on the build up to the First World War. He quickly grabbed his notes and put them in a black zip-up bag. In the hall, he got his navy coat and blue cashmere scarf out of the cupboard, took his fedora hat from a hook and made towards the door shouting, 'Mary darling, I'm off to class. I spilled some coffee on my study carpet. Would you mind cleaning it up? Must dash. See you in an hour.' There was no reply as the door slammed.

During tea, Potts noticed that Yvette was on duty not Françoise. One Ball saw this as an opportunity. He decided to take control of the situation himself and evaluate his chances of persuading Françoise that he was far more interesting than the dreadfully suburban Rutter. In fact, One Ball had never heard the elfin Rutter say anything of any import and thought that he had the intellect of a gnat. Rutter was studying A Level English and History but he wasn't going to get to Oxbridge. He'd be lucky to get into some second rate university up north. Yet, he was getting all this attention from Françoise. In comparison, One Ball didn't think that he himself was bad looking or lacking in conversational skill, but so far he hadn't had a chance to meet Françoise away from the Dining Hall and convince her of his allure. He was determined to rectify this. First, he would get an update at tea from Yvette on Rutter and Françoise's liaisons.

'How are you, Yvette?' remarked One Ball as he was about to receive his macaroni cheese.

'Well,' replied Yvette, politely detached from One Ball's effusive greeting.

'How's Françoise?'

'Off today.'

'Is she still seeing Rutter?'

'Would you like vegetables with the macaroni?'

'Yes, please. Where do they meet?'

'Spinach?'

'Yes. Thank you. On Open Way?'

'Why do you want to know? Potatoes?'

'Just a few. I'm just interested.'

'Or nosey? Anything else?

'Just curious. No nothing else thanks.'

'Au revoir then.'

'Au revoir.'

One Ball walked briskly back to his place near the top of the table, carrying his macaroni cheese and veg. He sat down and started eating voraciously. Pound and Boring Beckett noticed his petulant mood.

'Anything wrong, Jim? enquired Pound sympathetically.

'Not really,' responded One Ball defensively.

'Yvette didn't upset you, did she?' added a concerned Beckett.

'Not directly,' said One Ball evasively.

'Indirectly?' suggested Pound.

'What did she say?' pursued Beckett.

'I think it's best, I keep it to myself,' avowed One Ball decisively.

Pound and Beckett looked at each other, concerned that One Ball seemed to be unduly distressed.

Hayes continued going to lessons unenthusiastically. On this particular January morning, he was attending the English class of Mr R A Darbishire BA, a baby-faced teacher in his mid-twenties, who was a club rugby player. Hayes got to know Darbishire through his confident coaching of the colts squad. Unfortunately, when he came to teach English Literature, he was more insecure.

Darbishire's classroom was on the first floor in one of the blocks, next to Big Hall. Hayes, Binns and Sully attended this class among twenty other pupils. Darbishire entered the room diffidently wearing a light brown woollen jacket, matching trousers and shoes. In his hand, he had an attaché case. As he came in, the boys rose raggedly from their decaying brown desks.

'Please sit down,' insisted Darbishire, who placed his case on his desk and took out a copy of Oliver Twist and an exercise book with his notes. He then asked Binns to open a window as he found the classroom stuffy.

'But it's cold sir,' replied a defiant Binns.

'Then open it slightly, Binns,' suggested Darbishire.

Binns got up and moved sulkily past a peeling green wall with an old poster of British classical writers. He uneasily stretched to his full height in front of the window and just managed to let in a little air into the stuffy classroom. Darbishire then started to talk hesitantly about Oliver Twist, before the class proceeded to read sections of the novel aloud. The insecure master was making sure that there was less time for him to make judgements on the work. Nonetheless, Hayes enjoyed the reading as he was keen to hone his performance skills, in the hope that he'd be cast in Henry V. Neither Bayliss nor Basil had mentioned anything yet but he remained optimistic. Sully was also keen to be in the play because he thought that it would aid his operatic ambitions. However, he disliked reading Nancy as he didn't want to play a girl and he couldn't do a decent cockney accent. Binns was indifferent to public performance. He had no desire to be in the epic, not least because his habit of squeezing his hands together might present difficulties in performance. He certainly didn't want cries of 'mental' being shrieked in the middle of an important dramatic moment. Regardless of these reservations, he still enjoyed being the pompous and cruel Mr Bumble.

Unfortunately for Darbishire, the boys sometimes stopped the reading and asked questions, which weren't answered by the master's meandering analysis. Darbishire's responses tended to nervously kick most enquiries into the long grass. The beleaguered teacher repetitively said 'ok all right' in most of his replies.

Binns got fed up with such prevarication and pursued Darbishire for some clear answers.

'But surely you have some comments on Dickens's social views?

'Well. Yes, of course, Binns. Dickens was appalled by poverty, ok all right?'

'But who did he blame?'

'He certainly pointed a finger at institutions like the poorhouse, ok all right?'

'But what about the politicians, the rulers?'

'I don't think it's as simple as that, Binns, ok all right?'

'Was it that he saw good and evil in everybody?' interjected Hayes.

'Yes, exactly Hayes. Dickens creates good and bad characters in all classes, ok all right?'

'But what about the anti-Semitism in the book sir?

It's a larger than life creation, almost satirical. I'm not sure that it's anti-Semitic, ok all right?'

This part of the lesson seemed to get too demanding for Darbishire.

'I have a Jewish friend in Sutton Coldfield, who used to go to my primary school. He hates Oliver Twist because of the way Fagin is portrayed,' declared a passionate Sully.

'Well, maybe he's being a little unfair Sully?' thought a flustered Darbishire. As the conversation developed, Darbishire became increasingly uneasy. He gave answers without fully developing a dialogue with his pupils and after a short time he decided to close the conversation about racism, with his inevitable recurring response: 'I'll look it up for next time, ok all right?' He then evaded further scrutiny by instructing the boys to continue reading.

The class concluded with the section on Nancy's murder, during which Sully, despite his inaccurate accent, was inspired to levels of agitation not previously witnessed. While Sully's Nancy was in full flight, the bell sounded and Darbishire promptly concluded the lesson.

'See you all next time, ok, all right?'

Suddenly, Binns couldn't contain himself anymore and burst out laughing.

'What's so funny, Binns?' demanded an embarrassed Darbishire.

'Nothing , sir,'

'Oh yes, there is. Perhaps you'd like to share the joke with us.'

'No sir, I wouldn't.'

'Binns, I suggest you do so. Otherwise none of you will be free to leave.'

'You can't hold us hostage, sir.'

'No but I can delay you, if you're reluctant to cooperate.'

When Binns turned round for support, the whole class stared at him aggressively as they were eager to leave. This wave of indignation forced him to confess.

'I was laughing because you'd said 'ok all right' sixty times during the class, sir.'

The rest of the pupils struggled to contain their laughter.

'Stay behind Binns. The rest of you, go. Ok all right?'

The latter gathered their belongings and started to leave the room. As they did so, Hayes and Sully held their hands over their mouths to make sure their laughter didn't immediately explode. Others ran away like greyhounds chasing a hare. When they had all reached the corridor, an outpouring of hilarity was unleashed, like the release of sparkling champagne out of a bottle. The noise was so great that Darbishire abruptly opened the classroom door and robustly shouted 'Quiet!' The boys were shocked into silence by Darbishire's uncharacteristic venom and rapidly controlled their hysteria. As they started to saunter away, Darbishire returned to the classroom to talk to Binns.

'Binns.'

'Yes sir.'

‘I think you could use your time more profitably in class, by concentrating more on Oliver Twist than counting my mannerisms.’

‘I made a contribution, sir.’

‘Maybe, but you were also thinking about matters that were irrelevant and disturbed the class.’

‘I didn’t disturb the class, sir.’

‘Yes you did. They must have known you were counting.’

‘Some of them did. Not all.’

‘Don’t split hairs, Binns, ok all right?’

Binns bit his lip so that he wouldn’t laugh.

‘If you do that again Binns, you’ll be in detention, ok all right?’ continued Darbishire.

‘Yes sir,’ responded Binns, suppressing his giggles. His lip was now getting very sore.

‘Ok. So, next time settle down and concentrate on Dickens.’

‘All right sir.’

‘Ok. You can go, Binns.’

Binns duly gathered his belongings, made towards the door and turned towards Darbishire.

‘Sir.’

‘Yes Binns.’

‘Do you play for Harlequins sir?’

‘Yes, I do.’

‘Good luck on Saturday sir.’

‘Thank you, Binns.’

Binns then departed hurriedly as Darbishire sighed, put his exercise book and copy of Oliver Twist into his black attaché case and left the classroom.

As Hayes and Sully made their way across the Quadrangle for the morning break, they were still feeling the delirious after effects of Darbishire’s lesson and his sixty ‘ok all rights’.

‘He’s just got no idea he’s saying it all the time,’ said Hayes.

‘In future classes, Binns will be counting, ‘I’ll look it up for next time,’ remarked a cynical Sully.

‘No doubt.’

‘Darbishire’s a fool.’

‘In a way, I feel sorry for him, Sulls.’

'Really?'

'I think he's a decent person. Just out of his depth.'

'Maybe.'

'On the rugger field, he's a good coach.'

'I'm not interested in rugby, Hayes.'

'I know but it's just that he's a different character.'

'In what way?'

'Well for a start. He's more confident and helpful.'

'The conversation about Oliver Twist wasn't bad.'

'But his lessons always get side tracked by other stuff.'

'Ok, all right?'

'Exactly.'

'I hope Binns doesn't get a detention.'

'He'll be ok. Darbishire is quite liberal really.'

'Let's hope so, for Binnsy's sake.'

Hayes and Sully gathered pace as they got to the Avenue. PE was always a rush but one with which they were familiar. As the two boys moved purposefully towards James B, Sully broached his latest concern about One Ball.

'One Ball's obsessed with Rutter.'

'Why?' asked Hayes

'He wants to clear the field.'

'So he can meet up with Françoise?'

'Exactly.'

'I don't think he's got much chance there. If rumours are to be believed our rugby captain has been gallivanting over hill and over dale with his French maid,' elaborated Hayes, relishing tittle-tattle like a scandalous William Hickey journalist.

'That's why One Ball wants to do something about it before it's too late,' stressed Sully.

'What's he suggesting then?' questioned Hayes avidly.

'I'm not sure but he keeps enquiring about Rutter's movements,' divulged a hesitant Sully, struggling to fathom the inner recesses of One Ball's mind.

'Perhaps, he wants to blackmail him.' suggested Hayes excitedly.

‘You mean catch him with the French maid and then threaten to report him?’ suspected Sully, alarmed at the thought of contributing to such treachery.

‘Exactly,’ confirmed Hayes confidently.

‘But why does he think that I’d know Rutter’s whereabouts?’ probed Sully, worried about being drawn into some dubious, clandestine operation.

‘He wants power over his spy,’ proclaimed Hayes, understanding clearly the strategy of the perfidious One Ball.

‘I’m sure Rutter can deal with One Ball,’ believed Sully, looking to reassure himself and not get drawn into some dastardly conspiracy.

‘Not if he gets caught,’ replied Hayes, reminding Sully that Rutter’s love nest liaisons made him vulnerable to One Ball’s vengeful strategy.

As they made their way down the Avenue, eager to get changed for PE, Hayes also drew Sully’s attention to One Ball’s weaknesses.

‘Remember, One Ball has skeletons in his cupboard as well.’

‘Yes, like bullying. I still have those bloody miles to do,’ said Sully despondently.

‘Rank insubordination?’ enquired Hayes.

‘And outright duplicity,’ added Sully apprehensively.

‘I thought he’d water those down after my mother met Mrs Potts,’ responded a disappointed Hayes, appalled by One Ball’s intransigence.

‘No such luck. They’re still in the book,’ acknowledged Sully bitterly.

‘We must get comrade Barrett to tell Ryder about this.’ urged Hayes

‘Good idea. Last term at choir practice, Ryder told me ‘not to worry, it’ll be resolved,’ remembered Sully. ‘At the time, he was heavily involved in the chapel insurrection. So now Ryder’s less busy, Barrett can update him about my predicament. It’s better coming from him. He’s more political.’

‘In the meantime, let’s still keep a close watch on One Ball,’ emphasised Hayes.

‘By the way, Ryder is getting on better with Root this term,’ revealed Sully as a humorous grin spread across his freckled face. ‘I believe yoga has given the music master spiritual enlightenment.’

‘Blimey!’ exclaimed a perplexed Hayes.

The boys had now reached the house. They made their way through the porch to the dayroom, where they put their books in their locker. They then went quickly to the changing room to get prepared for the morning PE exertions.

Killer had been going through a difficult time in his marriage. Mrs Killer, more commonly known as Deirdre, didn’t really like the school and got easily bored. They had one small child, Barney. While initially the birth brought them closer together, they had now drifted emotionally apart. Although he was a busy junior housemaster and science teacher, Killer hadn’t shown much commitment to his domestic responsibilities. He enjoyed observing Barney get up to all sorts of antics but felt inadequate with babies. It was all too messy and unpredictable and he preferred to leave such matters to Deirdre. Deirdre resented Killer’s attitude, particularly as she was already feeling increasingly isolated.

They’d met in Newcastle when Killer started teaching at a local grammar school. Deirdre was working as one of the few female journalists on a local newspaper, investigating a report into indiscipline at schools. They had fun dating: going to see Die Rosenkavalier at the Theatre Royal, having a drink at the Quayside or taking a trip to Haydon Bridge. They married a year later. Soon afterwards, the school offered Killer a job. Deirdre didn’t want to move south, particularly as she’d worked hard to get employed by the paper. It was also difficult to leave her parents and community. However, she recognised that the salary and position were very attractive, and eventually she went along with Killer’s decision.

Left alone with Barney, Deirdre’s loneliness intensified. Killer was out for long periods and she didn’t know many people on the school estate. In any case, she disliked several of those she’d encountered. Mrs Percival from across the road was an exception and on occasions, they met for a chat over coffee.

Deirdre found these rendezvous reassuring as Beatrix Percival had two young boys and was sympathetic to her feelings. Deirdre confessed to Beatrix that she found her emotions going all over the place, often leading to rows with Killer. She'd experienced great joy in the birth of Barney, especially his eccentric murmurings like 'dobadee,' but also pangs of doubt. She didn't take easily to breastfeeding, wasn't sleeping well and had doubts as to whether she could cope with being a mother. Beatrix reassured her that this was not unusual, in fact she'd experienced similar feelings herself. When Deirdre mentioned Killer's lack of contribution, Beatrix let out a comic guffaw, believing that it was impossible to rely on men for such matters

Killer himself found it increasingly difficult to deal with Deirdre's moods. Having gone through the male bastions of school, university and the army, he wasn't best equipped to deal with the finer points of woman's feelings. He was courteous and respectful but insufficiently supportive. He certainly understood her frustration at not being able to continue her career and getting bored stuck in an insular community. He just resented the way she blamed him and had become emotionally distant. He also got exhausted with the rows. Recently, after she'd drunk far too much, she railed against corporal punishment and how she regarded him as its greatest instigator. When she started chanting 'Killer! Killer!' around the house like a demented hooligan, Barney woke up and started crying. Straight away, Killer took Barney in his arms and quietly sang a French song that his mother had sung to him: 'Frère Jacques, Frère Jacques, Dormez-vous? Dormez-vous?…' Killer's French was terrible and he wasn't much of a singer but he had fond memories of this particular song and his mother's soothing reassurance. Barney also seemed to like it as he gradually started to go to sleep. After Killer placed him firmly in his cot, he turned round to see Deirdre out for the count, sprawled across their bed, her skirt hoisted high above the knee, displaying her long legs. Killer placed a blanket over her inveterate body and then started undressing to go to bed.

During his house duties, Killer had noticed that the matron at James was taking a shine to him. In fact, as the term proceeded,

Marian's advances became increasingly unsubtle. Whenever, he was on duty, she was repeatedly asking him into her flat for a drink. So far, Killer had rejected such invitations but given Deirdre's recent extreme behaviour, he was finding the temptation less resistible. Marian was in her mid-thirties, single with a medical background She was always wearing a white coat like an orderly in a hospital and having her auburn hair tied in a neat bun. Marian was obsessed with playing draughts and frequently dragooned both boys and staff to play with her. She was a warm person but garrulous. She could also be very bossy. This could get on the boy's nerves and led to the sugar debacle with Boot. The elongated film fanatic discovered that Marian's abode, which was just below the junior dormitory, was unlocked and he took the opportunity to avenge the house matron for her withering criticism of his hygiene.

Marian wasn't resistant to sharing her bed with a suitable candidate if it was done discreetly. As she'd heard rumours about Killer's marriage and found his tall imposing stature attractive, she intended to test him. Since her husband died from polio, she felt that she'd lived too much like a nun. She missed Peter, particularly his Lancashire sense of humour, which helped him manage the travails of working in local government. Although, she found too many people down south snotty nosed and two-faced, she did like her job. Therefore, she knew that she needed to be careful regarding any romantic tryst.

On a late January evening, Killer was on duty in the junior dormitory. This time he'd accepted Marian's invitation for a drink after he'd finished with the boys and he felt recklessly excited. The boys noticed that Killer was in a more energetic, jovial mood. Usually, he had a pleasant but detached demeanour. This evening he was more verbose, describing anecdotes about a dubious businessman in Newcastle, who opened a nightclub in a residential area, without getting local authority permission. Killer revelled in dramatising the day that the police came to close the supposed den of iniquity. Scantily clad dancers, drugged musicians and a collection of drunken local villains, all tumbled chaotically onto the street. The owner, a barrel-chested Geordie, with a rose in the lapel of his blue suit, departed in handcuffs as the police bundled him into their patrol car.

'That was the end of Club Vegas, boys,' declared Killer.

'Were you actually at the club yourself, sir?' questioned Hayes.

'We went with friends after seeing a bad play. We needed further entertainment after experiencing a juvenile dramatic lecture,' regaled Killer.

'Didn't you know about the crook, sir?' enquired a sceptical Barrett.

'No, Barrett, we had no idea,' admitted Killer.

Killer continued in this talkative vein with a few army anecdotes and by the time the boys were in bed under the watchful eye of Pound, he left to meet Marian. Everything was calm in the dormitory, as Pound immersed himself in reading about fluvioglacial landscapes. Unlike when One Ball was on duty, there was a sense of sedate security in the dormitory. After Pound left, one of the boys switched on his illicit radio and tuned into Radio Luxembourg. A distinctive Australian voice was on the air. It belonged to a presenter called Barry Alldis, 'your DJ BA'. The personable Alldis was rattling through the likes of Cindy Oh Cindy, The Green Door and Just Walkin' In The Rain, much to the boys' satisfaction. Just as Alldis's show was finishing, Hayes started wondering if Killer was going to see matron. When Alldis duly signed off with his inimitable catchphrase-'whether at home or on the highway, thanks for tuning my way' and Radio Lux went to the adverts, Hayes aired his thoughts publicly about Killer and matron. While the other boys started giggling, Hayes decided to take the initiative. 'I'm going to do a recce,' he announced.

The radio was turned off as Hayes got out of bed and jogged across the dormitory to the window behind the monitor's table. He then peered down into matron's room. Killer and matron were sitting on a sofa. A draft board with black and white pieces lay on a nearby table. They had obviously just finished a game. Matron looked triumphant. 'Oh god' thought Hayes, 'she's won again.' Hayes remembered that such was her obsession with draughts that she kept a little book to record her wins. Each victory was accompanied by a scream of 'yes' in a guttural northern drawl. Thankfully, this evening she seemed to be in a mellow, romantic mood.

‘What’s happening?’ whispered Barrett from the other side of the dormitory, demanding a commentary.

‘Matron’s turned the main light off.’

‘What else?’

‘I think she’s going to seduce Killer.’

Suddenly the boys’ ears pricked up. Barrett and Sully walked barefoot to the window. Soon others followed. In no time, twenty boys amassed in a scrum, staring down into matron’s room, now lit only by a table lamp. Below, on a sofa, matron was passionately kissing Killer. In fact, she became so involved in her amorous activities that she’d forgotten to close the curtains, thus giving the boys a splendid ringside view. Killer was now responding to matron’s advances, by starting to take off her red roll neck sweater and reveal her white cupped bra.

‘Nice sight,’ cooed Boot, who was part of the inquisitive group.

‘I prefer white bras,’ insisted Binns sleepily.

‘Are you an expert, Binnsy?’ said Barrett cynically.

‘No. Just stating a preference,’ justified Binns defensively.

‘Good job Mrs Killer isn’t here!’ hooted Sully.

As the boys giggled vicariously, Killer was now on the floor with matron, struggling to get her stockings off from her suspenders.

’Maybe I ought to give him a hand,’ volunteered gangly Boot.

‘I prefer a woman with knickers,’ stipulated Binns.

‘There talks a man of experience,’ retorted Barrett derisively.

‘Oh shut up Barrett. You’re just as wanker!’ proclaimed Binns contemptuously.

‘Keep quiet for goodness sake.’ interrupted Hayes.

‘I don’t wank!’ stressed Barrett.

‘So what are those stains on your sheets?’ challenged Binns.

‘Have you been spying?’ accused an irate Barrett.

‘Didn’t you know, I’m the wanker inspector!’ exclaimed Binns, ridiculing Barrett’s supposed personal activities.

'Boys please. Look!' urged Hayes.

Killer had now finally finished taking off both matrons' nylon stockings. It had been a struggle but it did finally reveal her alluring, shapely legs. As the boys peered voyeuristically from their perched positions, they then saw Killer unclip Marian's bra and reveal her breasts.

'This is better than tv,' claimed Boot.

'This is our own James peepshow, boys,' decreed Hayes.

'I always wondered what was under that white coat,' reflected Barrett.

'I'll never think of matron in quite the same way,' said Sully gleefully.

'Nor Killer for that matter,' amplified a chortling Hayes.

In fact, matron was now unbuttoning Killer's shirt, with the odd kiss on his hairy chest as she did so. Having completed her initial task, she abruptly threw the shirt onto the sofa and started taking off his belt. Killer then gently interrupted matron and suggested that it might be easier if she took off his shoes and socks first. Matron did so and then resumed her main assignment of removing Killer's trousers. This she completed with military efficiency, leaving Killer just in his shabby boxer shorts.

'I think they're going to do it on the carpet,' claimed Boot.

'I couldn't get into an x certificate at the Granada Clapham Junction. Now I'm getting admission free,' divulged an excited Hayes.

'I don't think much of Killer's underpants. They look like leftovers from the war,' observed a critical Boot.

Marian was just wearing her suspender belt, Killer his archaic pants. Marian moved towards Killer and they started kissing. As they developed their carnal explorations, she could feel him getting increasingly excited. Just as she was going to take off his boxer shorts, she suddenly noticed that the curtains weren't drawn.

'Excuse me a moment, Killer.'

'What's the matter, Marian?'

'Just a minute.'

Marian moved swiftly to close the curtains. Just as she was about to confirm their privacy, she detected dim figures at the junior dormitory window. Much to her horror, these apparitions gradually became more discernible. They were a crowd of gloating boys, leaning over each other with grins on their faces, looking to get a grandstand view of their intimate cavorting. Quickly, Marian put on her sweater and abruptly closed the flower-patterned curtains.

Immediately, the boys scattered from the window and took refuge in their beds. With his head on his pillow, Hayes feared that Killer could become vindictive after being caught in flagrante delicto. Still, he thought it was worth it, seeing a bit of active foreplay. Anyway, he reassured himself that the junior housemaster could hardly punish anybody, when he was being unfaithful to his wife on the school premises. Hayes became confident that Killer would just let the inevitable rumours become part of unreliable school tittle-tattle. Meanwhile, Barrett, while settling down to sleep, was still annoyed with Binns. If he wanked, it would be on a Conservative-supporting paper of his choice, not his sheets. Nearby, Sully lay on his considerable back and wondered whether Mrs Killer would find out about her husband's infidelity. Opposite the celebrated window, Binns, as was his wont, squeezed his face and clasped his hands under his bedclothes. He enjoyed learning a few techniques of seduction and hoped to put them into practice sooner rather than later.

In matron's abode, Killer calmly reassured Marian that he would deal with the boys. She had nothing to worry about. This made her relax and she resumed removing Killer's pants.

After they'd made love, they remained naked and shared a bottle of Pinot noir.

'I should have poured this all over you and enjoyed further exploits,' said Marian, mischievously waving the wine bottle.

'Next time, Marian, next time. But don't tell me in advance. Just do it!'

'All right, Killer.'

'Oh no, not bloody Killer again.'

'Ok, Mr Roy.'

'Alex, please.'

'Alex.'

After they'd finished drinking Burgundy's finest, Killer got dressed, kissed matron goodbye and was about to leave, when she called him back.

'Killer. Oh sorry. Alex.'

'Yes, matron, sorry Marian.'

'See you again?'

'Certainly.'

'Mum's the word.'

'Yes. Mum's the word.'

Killer smiled and Marian returned the compliment. Killer then closed the door and quietly made his way back home.

A few weeks later, One Ball was sitting in his study desk, continuing his reading of General Lancelot England's grisly memoir. Some of the general's descriptions disturbed him and undermined his faith in British democracy and the rule of law. He felt particularly queasy about the killing of demonstrators, which let him wondering if similar violence had triggered his father's breakdown. Instantly, One Ball recoiled from thinking too deeply about such things. Anything that revisited his father's disintegration began to frighten him so sometimes he came to resent his mother for her honesty. He felt that she'd burdened him with her own disillusionment. Even though they'd got on with their lives, the ghosts of war still hovered in the background.

One Ball stopped reading about Boer War concentration camps, and focused on his responsibilities, in particular, his determination to inculcate the best of British values, in which he firmly believed. He took refuge from historical revelation by preparing for the arrival of Sully. When he checked the time on his watch, he discovered that it was 4:00 pm. Bloody Sully was late. 'That boy may have a father in the military but he's totally undisciplined,' concluded One Ball. In fact, Sully's waywardness reminded One Ball that the errant junior hadn't completed his punishments. Although, he couldn't afford to look weak and have his authority undermined, One Ball was now open to compromise. If Sully could give him information about Rutter and his liaisons with Françoise, he was prepared to be less punitive. After all, he had to eliminate Rutter at all costs if he was to have any chance with Françoise. As One Ball mulled over his devious strategy, the blubbery Sully abruptly interrupted his contemplation.

Sitting down in One Ball's armchair, while glancing at the imposing Wagner picture, Sully appeared perspiring and nervous.

'Why are you always late, Sully?' demanded One Ball, turning round on his chair to confront the junior.

'I had to wait for the shower after athletics practice,' explained an apologetic Sully.

'Athletics?'

'Yes,'

'Surely, not running?'

'No,'

'What then?'

'Shot putt.'

'I see. Well you've certainly got the weight for it!' affirmed One Ball sarcastically.

'Actually, I think I've got the balls for it,' asserted Sully.

It was only after he'd spoken that Sully realised the full implication of what he'd said. He wanted to laugh but One Ball's furious countenance stopped him in his tracks.

'I do hope you're not trying to be funny, Sully,' stated One Ball, with an intimidating stare.

'No Potts,' denied an apprehensive Sully.

'Are you aware of the language you've just used?' emphasised One Ball.

'Only after I spoke,' admitted a fearful Sully.

'Well bloody well think before you speak!' exploded One Ball.

One Ball then gathered himself, remembering the main purpose of the meeting, He refused to be deflected by irrelevant deviation. Too many meetings consisted of meandering opinions and no conclusions. He wanted a commitment from Sully to help him. Therefore, he would use the full extent of his power to get him to do so. One Ball rose from his seat and looked at the Wagner picture for inspiration. He then paced up and down in the confined space, whistling the opening bars of the Tannhäuser overture. Once the great composer's music enveloped him, One Ball was ready to deal with the impudent Sully.

'What's that you're whistling Potts?' asked Sully.

'Don't you know it, Sully?' replied One Ball, haughtily.

'I think its Wagner.'

'Of course, it's Wagner but what?

'I prefer Verdi.'

'You're in the choir. You want to be a singer. You should know it.'

'Sorry Potts. I can't remember the title.'

'Italians over elaborate. This gets directly to the soul.'

'But Wagner's operas are very long.'

'Because they're more ambitious and less simplistic.'

'Maybe.'

'There's no maybe about it, Sully. They just are. And for your enlightenment Sully, I was whistling the opening overture from Tannhäuser,' disclosed One Ball disdainfully. 'However, I don't want to discuss the various merits of Wagnerian and bel canto opera,' he continued irritably. 'I want you to know more about Rutter's relationship with Françoise.'

'Didn't you find him in the Dining Hall? enquired Sully.

'No I didn't. Anyway, it's difficult there,' justified a dismissive One Ball.

'I don't know Rutter, Potts.'

'You don't have to know him personally. I just want information about what he does with Françoise.'

'What kind of information, Potts?

'Where they meet. What do they do? Where they go?

'You mean you want me to be your spy.'

'No, I mean, well yes in a way.'

'I'm not spying on people.'

One Ball moved in front of the armchair and looked down mercilessly at Sully.

'Sully. You have two punishments to complete.'

'Yes. I thought you'd forgotten.'

'Well you thought incorrectly, Sully.'

'I was hoping that your mother might have persuaded you to be more lenient.'

'My mother isn't a monitor.'

'No Potts.'

'I make my own decisions. I'm not a mother's boy, Sully.'

'Of course not, Potts.'

'Your punishments stand Sully. They're in the book in my own indelible hand.'

'I know that, Potts.'

'Then you'll also know that you haven't yet completed a punishment in the allotted time.'

'Yes.'

'But if you give me sufficient information on Rutter and Françoise's activities, I'll sign them off.'

'How will the information be measured?'

'That will be left to my judgement, Sully. If it's just about their whereabouts, I'll strike off one punishment but if its more, shall we say, personal stuff, I'll let you off both.'

'I'll have to think about it.'

'No Sully. I don't want you to have a powwow with all your mates. They must have nothing to do with it. This is just between you and me. Yes or no.'

Sully was hesitant. He didn't want to spy, least of all for One Ball, yet the thought of the punishments going on forever was a millstone around his neck. Reluctantly, he decided to comply and look to avoid excessive betrayal later.

'All right, Potts. I'll do it,' agreed Sully.

'Good,' proclaimed One Ball with a beaming grin.

Sully got up and left uneasily. He felt like someone who had just joined the KGB.

Françoise was glad to be back at the school. During the Christmas break, she found her parents suffocating. They constantly probed into her time in England, which intruded upon her privacy. Further encroachment transpired, when she went for a stroll and bumped into her ex-lover, the English teacher, who tried to rekindle their previous relationship. Consequently, despite enjoying food like oysters and escargots and getting around the piano to sing carols such as Bel astre que j'adore, she was glad to return to Sussex. Although, she recognised that her parents wanted the best for her, she still found their attention oppressive. Nonetheless, she left on good terms after her father did a very good impression of Maurice Chevalier singing Louise.

During the early part of the term, she saw Rutter consistently. She enjoyed their furtive meetings, which always had an air of excitement. They both trusted each other and were confident that their liaisons remained secret. On this particular Saturday evening later in the term, they had been in the cricket pavilion for an hour. It was a bit cold but fortunately Rutter had miraculously found a two bar heater. Rutter and Françoise felt increasingly relaxed in each other's company. They enjoyed not only each other's bodies but also their intimate conversation.

Rutter expounded on the limitations of Purley as they drank some excellent Chardonnay. Even though he loved his family, he felt that their world restricted his horizons. He could talk to his father about sport but not much else. Mr Rutter ran a family printing business, which he took over after his own father died. During the war, he served in the 1st Battalion of The Royal Hampshire Regiment and had several army postings, including the D Day landing. Rutter believed that his father's violent war experiences had left permanent scars and had made him both sullen and volatile. Nevertheless, he still managed to be obsessed about his beloved Everton F.C. Rutter could never understand how a boy from south London could support a team from Lancashire, until he learnt later of the Liverpudlian club's success in the 30s.

Rutter's father met his mother before the war at the Locarno Streatham. They both loved ballroom dancing and later won a few local awards with their waltzes, sambas and tangos. They were inspired by Victor Silvester, whose BBC programmes became very popular. Rutter's parents were keen on education for their son, less so for their older daughter, who went to work in a bank until she got married. They managed to get representation to go to the school through a forces charity and were delighted when Rutter passed the entrance exam. Sadly, his father was no longer enjoying his work, his mother was finding it difficult to adapt after her two children were no longer at home and the dancing style they both loved was rapidly going out of fashion. As soon as they bought a television, an evening ritual seemed to emerge, whereby they stared at their newly acquired set as if it was some form of oracle. Rutter knew something was going awry in family life when he discovered both parents gaping at the screen, mesmerised by the interlude film of the Potter's Wheel.

Françoise enjoyed hearing about Rutter's domestic background as they worked their way through the French wine. In fact, she found his experience similar to her own. Although she was proud of Lyon being the centre of the Resistance during the war and the way it had been revitalised after bombings, she felt that she needed more space to develop herself. She thought that it was a good time to improve her English, especially as she found the post-war energy coming from the Britain and America exciting. She told Rutter about her affair with her teacher and how it seemed a good time to get out of Lyon, before going to study law at the Université de Toulouse. As they drank, Françoise revealed that her family were religious and that complicated matters. In fact, her younger sister was going to be a nun. On her return home, Françoise found going to church a penance, especially as the services were interminably long and in Latin. Although, like Rutter, she enjoyed the reassurance of the love of her family and its cosy domesticity, somehow it wasn't enough. Certainly, Paris was an attractive destination with its influx of American jazz musicians, the political debates between Camus and Sartre and the courageous feminism of De Beauvoir. Still, notwithstanding such cultural temptation, Françoise preferred a foreign adventure to consolidate her English.

After this long, intimate heart-to-heart, Françoise and Rutter finished the wine and started to sing a variety of songs. Françoise grabbed a flat white cap left for cricket umpires and started to launch into Juliette Greco's 'Je suis comme je suis'. She danced around the 1st X1 dressing room with tipsy abandon, to the accompaniment of Rutter's infectious laughter. On concluding the song, she flung the hat up in the air and collapsed on a bench; her dramatic slump causing a cricket bat to fall on the floor with a resounding thud.

After Françoise's attractive chanson, a merry Rutter gamely grabbed a nearby cricket cap and a broom, which he used as a mike, and burst forth into a rendition of Fats Domino's

Blueberry Hill. Rutter's attempt to lower his voice to Fats's raspy vocal was comic in itself. In fact, in his jaunty cap, he looked more like a schoolboy act than a blues singer from New Orleans. After Rutter reached the shattering climax of Fats's classic song, Françoise embraced him with a tiddly kiss. Recklessly, she then grabbed the exhausted Rutter by the hand and pulled him out of the pavilion towards the 1st X1 pitch. Amidst the developing gloom, she challenged him to show off his dancing skills.

'Come on. Show us your dancing!' cried an excitable Françoise, mercilessly pulling the besieged Rutter.

'Oh Françoise, please! We need to be careful.'

'Ah mon chéri est fatigué ,' mocked Françoise.

'Oui, tres fatigué.'

It was a cold January evening but thankfully Rutter had already put on his black coat, after their more intimate activities. A more carefree Françoise wore just a thick brown sweater, as she playfully pulled Rutter to the cricket square.

'Venez. You're from a dancing family. Dance. No one's about.'

'Françoise, this is a cricket pitch.'

'So what?'

'If Fred sees me here, he'll kill me.'

'You can blame me. Come on,' insisted Françoise, grabbing Rutter by the waist. 'What about a song?

'A song?'

'Oui. Of Course. While we dance.'

Finally, Rutter submitted to Françoise's seductive insistence.

'Ok,' he conceded. 'Ready'.

'Oui monsieur,' she replied with a broad smile.

As they started to move Rutter counted their waltz steps, before bursting into a rendition of I Could Have Danced All Night. Rutter glided with elegance, a chip off his Dad's block à la Victor Silvester-one, two, three, one, two, three, as he guided Françoise expertly around the hallowed cricket square. The two lovers danced in close harmony, inspired by the popular song. Their concentration was so intense that Rutter forgot that they were desecrating the sacred turf, which Fred nurtured like the most revered garden. After Rutter had completed the song, they kissed long and intensely. As they both got more aroused, a flashing light suddenly caught both of them in a compromising position. Immediately, they broke away from each other and gathered themselves together.

'Where the hell was that coming from?' asked a shocked Rutter.

'From over here,' said Françoise, pointing in the direction of the light.

'We'd better go there,' decided Rutter.

'Ok,' agreed Françoise.

They both moved quickly to the edge of the cricket boundary, opposite the colts' rugby pitch. After looking despondently at various nearby trees and foliage, they heard cries.

'Help! Help!' continued the desperate sound.

They discovered that the the cri de coeur came from the direction of a benign, bushy elm tree, just next to the main pathway.

'Who's there?' called Rutter.

'Me. Sully.'

'What are you doing up there?'

'I'm stuck.'

Sully wasn't very far up the tree. With his excessive weight, that wouldn't have been possible. However, with difficulty he had managed to clamber up to a position next to the first main branch. As he was now a spy, he wanted to get into a suitably camouflaged position. It not only gave him a better view but a greater sense of his dramatic importance. The only problem was that after the lovers had seen him, he panicked and couldn't get down. Unfortunately, Sully often suffered from such attacks during moments of extreme tension. He was particularly frustrated as he'd just got the evidence to give One Ball. Grim Jim had lent him his Kodak camera and he'd taken some revealing shots of the couple canoodling.

'How did you get up there?' enquired Rutter.

'Well I sort of found some footholds on the trunk, clambered up, made my way to the first big branch and wormed round into this cranny here,' described a ruffled Sully.

‘Well do the same, only in reverse,’ ordered Rutter.

‘But I panic. I start getting scared,’ admitted a fearful Sully.

‘But you’re only seven foot off the ground,’ argued Rutter.

‘I know, but to me it seems a lot higher,’ contended Sully.

‘Maybe now we’re here, you can try again,’ suggested Françoise reassuringly.

‘Oh yes, thank you. What’s your name?’ projected Sully, keen to make conversation with the female presence below.

‘Françoise,’ she responded benignly.

‘Sully let’s leave the introductions until you return to terra firma,’ interjected Rutter.

‘I was just being polite,’ maintained the offended Sully.

Rutter then gave Sully a series of practical instructions as to how he could overcome his psychological problems. This led to a tortuous sequence of events, by which a simple climb down became more complex than escaping from Colditz. To assuage Sully’s apprehension, Rutter told him to look at Françoise for reassurance if he had another panic attack. Sully gleefully appreciated that advice and gave her a cheeky smile, before resuming his efforts to descend from the tree. After a lack of initial progress, Rutter eventually managed to help him manoeuvre to near the trunk, but on his arrival the plump junior instantly froze. He just couldn’t trust himself to make further progress.

‘I don’t think I can do it,’ feared an agitated Sully.

‘Well, you’ve got a choice Sully,’ stated Rutter calmly.

‘What’s that?’ enquired an alarmed Sully.

‘You can either find footholds on the trunk or you can jump onto the grass?’ demanded Rutter, trying to stop Sully’s prevarication.

‘But I’ve my case and torch,’ pleaded Sully.

‘Ok. You can throw me the torch. And you can put the case’s straps firmly around your neck. Then you can jump,’ said Rutter, offering a practical solution.

‘Did you have help climbing up?’ mentioned Françoise.

‘A little. From a trustful groundsman,’ divulged Sully.

‘Ok then jump,’ reiterated Rutter, making the decision for him.

'Will you take me to the infirmary if I get injured?' requested Sully.

'You're a hypo,' accused Rutter.

'A what?' queried a confused Sully?

'A hypochondriac,' elaborated Rutter.

'I'm certainly not, Rutter. I just want you to promise as a precaution,' asserted Sully defiantly.

'Ok. We'll get you to the infirmary,' relented Rutter wearily.

Sully then took the torch out of his pocket and threw it to Rutter, which the agile sportsman caught with ease. As Sully anticipated leaping, he looked like a nervous young recruit taking his first parachute jump. Françoise gave him reassuring smiles as Rutter instructed him how to break his fall, a skill he'd learned from his father. Sully then manoeuvred to the lowest foothold he could manage, his small case dangling precariously around his neck and descended from the tree with a great thud, accompanied by a desperate primal scream. Rutter wasn't sure whether it was of delight or pain. On discovering a wide grin across Sully's face, it transpired to be the former.

'I fell well didn't I?' announced Sully proudly.

'Yes, you did,' assessed Françoise.

'Perhaps I should be in westerns,' declared Sully.

They both laughed. In fact, the idea of Sully appearing in such films was apt. His physical girth and tomfoolery certainly would lend itself to the ribald roistering in that cinematic genre.

'What's in your case?' continued the observant Françoise.

'Er, nothing,' replied Sully hesitantly, while wiping leaves off his coat after his dramatic fall.

'Show us then,' she challenged.

'It's private,' claimed Sully nervously.

'Open it up, Master Sully,' dictated Françoise.

Reluctantly, the beleaguered spy unzipped his case and displayed the Kodak flash camera.

'Bloody hell, Sully. You've been taking photographs of us,' an angry Rutter accused the junior.

'Yes,' confessed Sully.

'Why?' questioned Rutter, staring intensely into Sully's apprehensive eyes.

'Potts,' answered Sully disdainfully.'

‘Ah, bloody One Ball,’ acknowledged Rutter.

‘He wants to get to know Françoise, so he feels the need to discredit you,’ explained Sully.

‘Blackmail,’ confirmed an appalled Rutter.

‘Why do you call him One Ball?’ probed Françoise, with a gleam of devilry in her eye.

‘Because he only has one,’ said Rutter dismissively.

‘He lost the other in an accident,’ clarified Sully.

‘Oh dear,’ sympathised Françoise, grimacing nervously.

‘Give us the camera Sully,’ commanded Rutter.

‘I can’t,’ insisted Sully aggressively.

‘Why not?’ countered Rutter abruptly.

‘It’s One Ball’s. He’s bullying me. I have two punishments for running a mile. I can’t get them ticked off because I’m unable to run them to time. They’re like a noose around my neck. So when he told me that he’d start erasing them, if I could..’

‘Give us the camera,’ reiterated Rutter, firmly interrupting the junior’s tirade.

‘No!’ screamed Sully.

‘Sully. You don’t want to get us into trouble do you?’ warned Rutter.

‘Not really,’ attested Sully fearfully.

‘Well give it to me then,’ instructed Rutter.

‘Please Sully,’ entreated Françoise

‘What am I going to tell bloody One Ball?’ implored a distraught Sully.

‘We’ll deal with that,’ Françoise reassured him.

‘Will you?’ beseeched Sully incredulously.

‘Yes,’ corroborated Rutter.

‘But how?’ wailed Sully.

Rutter then told Sully how One Ball had been following him and giving him strange looks. Now that the senior monitor had sent Sully to spy on him, he’d no choice but to do something about it. Otherwise both himself and Françoise could be expelled. Sympathising with Sully’s predicament, he reassured him that he would challenge One Ball’s bullying. However, he’d only consider returning the camera when he’d examined the evidence.

After Rutter and Françoise calmed down the overwrought junior, the troubled spy started to relax and realise that he had strong allies. Suitably heartened, Sully gave Rutter the camera and took what looked like a coloured sweet from his pocket.

'What's that?' remarked Françoise.

'A gobstopper,' proclaimed Sully.

'A what?' replied an incredulous Françoise.

'A gobstopper,' answered Sully casually.

'What's this gob?' queried a bemused Françoise.

'Gob is slang for mouth,' disclosed Rutter.

'I like them because they change colours' explained Sully.

'Well, don't be sucking it when you see One Ball,' warned Rutter.

'No, I'll put it in my hanky,' revealed Sully.

'Spare us the details please Sully,' insisted Rutter.

'It's ok. I have a separate hanky for gobstoppers,' explained Sully reassuringly.

'It's late. We need to pick up our things and go,' Françoise prompted Rutter.

'You'll give the camera back?' implored an agitated Sully.

'After we've got the photos developed,' stressed an assertive Rutter.

'What in the hell am I going to say to One Ball in the meantime?' moaned Sully.

'Just tell him, you saw nothing. Right,' said Rutter, looking sternly into Sully's agitated eyes.

'Right,' agreed a reassured Sully. Somehow, instinctively he trusted Rutter much more than One Ball.

Sully was about to depart when he abruptly turned to the couple.

'I loved your singing and dancing. It was great,' Sully blurted out passionately.

'Merci,' responded Françoise warmly. She was pleased to have given enjoyment, even though she knew she couldn't sing like Julie Andrews or Juliette Gréco, for that matter.

'At least it made the spying entertaining. Bye,' replied Sully, who then started walking towards the Avenue singing Get Me to the Church on Time, his own personal favourite from the show.

Later on a Sunday afternoon, the Major drove Root towards town in his Land Rover, which was a bit of a rickety ride when going through narrow village roads. The Major had bought it off a war pal, who wanted to offload it before immigrating to Canada. The Major thought that it'd be good to go for tea at the Repton Hotel, a less known establishment on the periphery of the town. As the Major and Root entered the large tea room, it seemed as if everybody was over seventy. The place was full of grey-haired pensioners, several with hearing aids and walking sticks. A morose man with drooping eyelids was playing nostalgic tunes on a piano at the side of the room. His clownish face exuded a sense of detachment, as if his mind was concentrating on something more substantial than the light music he was playing. Despite his aloofness, he impressed Root with his subtle use of modulation.

The Major found a table for two at the far end of the red-carpeted room. It gave them the privacy that both he and Root wanted. Schools were small societies and you never knew if gossips were in the vicinity, even when outside the estate. Immediately, they ordered some egg and tomato sandwiches and a pot of tea from a young fair-haired boy in a smart black suit with enlarged velvet collars. The Major and Root then listened to the music medley and exchanged pleasantries until the waiter, with his neat matching bow tie and well-pressed white shirt, returned with their order.

'Thank you' acknowledged the Major courteously.

'A pleasure sir, anything else I can get you?' replied the waiter.

'Not at the moment thanks,' said the Major politely.

'Thank you sir,' answered the boy, nodding his head in acknowledgement.

After the boy departed, the Major poured the tea from a large china teapot, decorated with blue patterns of various trees.

'This is pleasant Bill,' observed Root.

'I thought you'd like it, Reg,' affirmed the Major.

They both enjoyed their Earl Grey tea as the pianist sauntered through another nostalgic medley, aimed at arousing the memories of his audience.

After the Major took a sip of tea and replaced his tree-patterned cup on its saucer, he turned to Root and resumed the conversation.

'So the yoga helps, Reg.'

'Yes, it has, Bill. I'm surprised. It's helped a lot.'

'Good.'

'I can now do Mountain Pose and Down Facing Dog.'

'Good God!'

'Yes strange names but they're just yoga positions.'

'Anyway, I'm glad it's been beneficial.'

'I can deal with Ryder now.'

'No more revolutions, then?'

'Not at the moment, anyway.'

'He's behaving?'

'Actually, we're working better together.'

'Good.'

'I've even agreed for the choir to sing 'Beautiful Dreamer'.

'You're becoming diplomatic, Reg.'

'Yes, Bill. I should work for the UN!' exclaimed Root, laughing nervously.

As the two men enjoyed their tea, Root accepted that he should have listened more to his pupils. Since last term's rebellion, he'd reflected on his methods, which had now led to him being more inclusive. Consequently, Root thought that the choir was singing even better, to which the Major concurred. Nonetheless, he still didn't trust Ryder. He thought that the choir leader would still use any situation to hone his political skills.

The Major and Root proceeded to drink their Earl Grey, while listening to the pianist coming to the end of Autumn Leaves. As they did so, Root revealed that it wasn't just the yoga that had helped him but sex. He'd found a boyfriend.

'Oh really?' queried the Major, hesitating to drink his tea.

'He's an actor. He was touring Birmingham at the Alex?' confided Root.

'The Alex?'

'The Alexandra Theatre. He was in a Rattigan play.'

'I see.'

‘I met him in the bar after the show. Then he introduced me to a club I didn’t know.’

‘What was it like?’

‘Exciting. Everybody knew it was a place to find a lover but outwardly everything was oh so respectable.’

The Major took a sip of his tea while observing the rejuvenated Root.

‘Where is your friend now?’ quizzed the Major, replacing his cup firmly on its saucer.

‘In Sheffield. Continuing the tour,’ elucidated an enthusiastic Root.

‘Will you be seeing him again?’ pursued the Major sceptically.

‘Oh yes,’ affirmed a buoyant Root.

The Major and Root tucked into their sandwiches and chatted, as the pianist continued playing from his extensive repertoire. Some minutes later, he was concluding We’ll Meet Again. Several elderly couples were passionately singing the lyrics; others just stared vacantly, alone with their memories. After the song finished, Root and the Major joined the appreciative clapping.

‘Wonderful tune that one,’ appreciated the Major.

‘Yes, effective but sentimental,’ judged Root.

‘Nothing wrong with sentiment, Reg.’

‘Trouble is it exploits emotion rather than portrays genuine feeling, Bill.’

‘Maybe, but it binds people together.’

‘I suppose so.’

‘It’s not Mozart Reg.’

‘Certainly not,’ corroborated Root emphatically.

The colleagues carried on with their afternoon tea as the inexpressive pianist progressed to a Carousel medley. The familiar tunes brought cheery smiles to the aged audience. At the end of the Rodgers and Hammerstein homage, Root hastily put his cup down.

‘Oh before I forget, I must tell you. I met Rattigan briefly. He was at the production that night.’

‘He writes damn good plays,’ enthused the Major.

‘Yes this one was about pilots during the Battle of Britain.’

‘He knows all about that.’

‘Exactly. It hadn’t been done for a few years. I think that’s why he came.’

‘So you had a good time?’

‘Yes. It was good fun. One of the older actors came with us to the club. He told us that he’d worked with an influential producer. Apparently, when this celebrated impresario came into his dressing room after a first night, this senior thespian refused to kiss him. He insisted that this was the moment that his career started to slide.’

‘But wasn’t he queer as well?’

‘No, I don’t think so. He just joined us for a drink. He’s married with two kids.’

‘Oh I see.’

The doleful pianist was now playing As Time Goes By, to which some of the audience were singing quietly to themselves. Root thought that the Major had made a good choice in coming to the Repton. Not only did it have a unique atmosphere but more importantly, no one from the school was likely to visit it. Consequently, Root wondered if the Major had brought Victoria to the hotel.

‘Well, yes. We have come once or twice,’ admitted the Major.

‘How is Victoria Wallace?’ mentioned Root.

‘Well. She’s joined my badminton club.

‘Did you see her over the holidays?’

‘Yes. The absence of the boys was helpful.’

‘I can imagine.’

‘We’ve also been going for walks. Sometimes, with Wallace’s terrifying dog.’

‘Is he an Alsatian?’

‘Yes. Victoria warned me that he doesn’t like strangers. Apparently, he bit Mrs Hackett at a garden party a few years ago.’

‘Some people would say that she deserved it.’

‘That’s a bit unfair, Reg. She means well.’

‘I’m not sure that she does. She’s constantly telling me how to do my job.’

‘There’s no harm in suggestions.’

‘Mrs Hackett doesn’t suggest, she orders.’

‘She’s an assertive woman, Reg.’

‘She’s an absolute pain. Goes on about Gilbert and Sullivan.’

‘Really?’

‘Accused me of playing too much music by foreigners.’

‘But her husband is in charge of the modern language department.’

‘I told her that the chapel services are full of English music.’

‘She does have some extreme views. She believes in hanging.’

‘Probably flogging as well. ’

‘They’re a strange couple because Jet is much more moderate.

‘She wants me to pitch for a Pirates of Penzance production.’

‘Sounds fun.’

‘Maybe. But I’m not a G and S fan.’

‘You’d like something meatier?’

‘Exactly. Anyway, that’s enough of horrible Hackett, what about Victoria?’

Before the Major could answer, the music stopped and the audience clapped, no doubt remembering Bogie and Ingrid in Casablanca. After the applause had died down, the melancholic pianist announced in an elocutionary voice that he was taking a short break. As he departed, the Major eventually responded to Root’s enquiry.

‘Victoria’s getting better at badminton.’

‘Does Wallace approve of your courting?’

‘Yes, I think, he does.’

‘That’s good; you’re over a major hurdle there.’

‘He’s always pleasant and encouraging.’

‘No sign of his vile temper?’

‘None thank God.’

‘What about Victoria?’

‘There are positive signs, Reg.’

‘Excellent Bill.’

As the Major and Root talked and relished their tea and sandwiches, the pensioners chatted away or meditated silently. Eventually, the bow-tied pianist in his formal grey suit reappeared and started playing a medley of Noël Coward songs. Several of the oldies swayed in recognition of the familiar tunes. Such was the pianist's demeanour that he looked more like an undertaker than a musician. However, as soon as he played, a metamorphosis took place and he transported his audience to the comforting world of memory. During his performance, the pianist neither smiled nor gave a full acknowledgement to any applause. A brief, wave of a hand, was the only rare gesture. He seemed impervious as to whether he was giving pleasure or not. Root wondered whether he disliked churning out song after song for so many hours. Maybe he aspired to play classical concertos, or perhaps he was a jazz musician who needed the money. Root wasn't easily enamoured by light music but in this particular case, he was enchanted by the mysterious pianist's delicate playing and his feel for melody. It was as if life's vicissitudes had worn him down but not diminished his talent.

'He's doing a good job, that chap at the piano,' observed the Major, finishing off the last of the egg and tomato sandwiches

'Yes he certainly is,' agreed Root, 'especially as he's playing without a score.'

'I hope he's getting well paid.'

'I doubt it, Bill. Probably a pittance.'

'Really?'

'Getting a musician isn't regarded as essential.'

'But I'm sure he's bringing people in.'

'That won't stop them paying as little as possible.'

'That's a shame. He deserves better,'

'The artist is too often a financial afterthought.'

'Maybe you're right, Reg.'

They then ordered a top-up to their tea. The young waiter with the large velvet collars duly obliged and the two friends continued their chat between sips of Earl Grey. The Major was delighted that Root was happier and more relaxed, even though he was sceptical about his new relationship. He had a suspicion that the actor in the Rattigan play was a ship that might well pass in the night. Consequently, he was afraid of Root becoming despondent if his expectations didn't materialise. Despite his newly acquired yoga routine and committed application of Down Facing Dog, the music master could still be a very emotional man with unpredictable mood swings. The Major didn't want his feelings to affect his work and incite another confrontation with Ryder and the choir as he didn't think Oliver would tolerate further conflict. In fact, he was certain that if one emerged, the harassed Oliver would sack Reginald Root. This could lead to the possibility of the music master descending into unparalleled depths of despair. The Major couldn't bear to think about such a prospect as he liked and respected Root. Reggie had a unique sense of commitment and a belief in high standards, which the Major found admirable. He had also helped him resurrect his own love of classical music. After his war experience, the Major found it redemptive reconnecting with the likes of Schumann and Beethoven. Somehow, he felt that their work embraced an eternal, universal humanity.

As he listened to the Major, Root thought that his friend was terrified of personal commitment. He obviously felt deeply about Victoria Wallace but was worried about the fifteen years age difference and of its social consequences. Root heard that the largely male environment of boys' schools and the army had dominated the Major's life. He was one of two brothers, who had both attended preparatory and public schools. He was cautious about women, probably too cautious. He had affairs, mainly at university and in the military. He was particularly keen on a secretary during the war but his posting abroad and his obsession with his job, led to a carelessness that denied real intimacy. Root was flattered that the Major had opened up to him so wholeheartedly. He reassured him that it wasn't age that mattered but compatibility and if he was in love he shouldn't have any shame. Root had only spoken to Victoria a few times but he thought that she was an intelligent woman, who shouldn't just be a secretary. Apparently, the Major wanted to propose but was scared stiff of doing so, in case she rejected him. Root encouraged him to be brave. He pointed out that he had suggested ways for him to deal with his feelings, now he should be positive about his own..

‘Thanks for that, Reg,’ said the Major as they awaited their bill, while the solemn pianist played numbers from Guys and Dolls.

‘It’s a pleasure, Bill,’ replied Root contentedly.

‘Will you see your actor soon?’

‘You mean Rupert.’

‘Oh sorry, Rupert.’

‘Yes. When he finishes the tour.’

‘Is he coming to the school?’

‘I hope so.’

‘Do be careful, Reg.’

‘I will, don’t worry.’

There was a pause while the Major drank his tea, gathered his thoughts and then declared:

‘It’s about time, they changed the law.’

‘The law?’

‘About homosexuality.’

‘Let’s hope they will. In the meantime, evading the police is quite exciting.’

‘I don’t think going to prison is exciting, Reg.’

‘No. I keep forgetting.’

‘I saw several chaps in the army get really distressed.’

‘What do you mean, Bill?’

‘They’d fallen for other soldiers.’

‘That must have been difficult.’

‘In fact, one fell for me.’

‘Really?’

‘Yes. Nice bloke. A colonel.’

‘What happened?

‘I told him I wasn’t interested?’

‘A bit difficult.’

‘Yes. But we just forgot it. Too busy trying to survive.’

‘That’s why I concentrate on work.’

‘Attractive chap. He’s now a bank manager. In Peckham.’

‘So you still see him, Bill?’

‘Only at reunions.’

The Major paused, finished his tea and remembered one of the bank manager’s unusual talents.

‘He was also a good ugly sister.’

'In panto?'

'Yes. The army's version of Cinderella.'

'He took to a skirt rather well.'

'He sounds rather adorable.'

Just as Root was beginning to fantasise about the various attributes of the Peckham bank manager, the waiter arrived with a broad grin on his face. As he placed the bill on the table, he gave Root a cheeky smile. Root responded with a hesitant acknowledgement. He realised that the waiter had heard the end of their conversation. The Major and Root each paid half of the bill plus a generous tip. The fresh-faced waiter looked down with pleasure at the notes and coins placed on the table. He gathered them carefully while checking the payment and placed the money on a salver, apart from the tip, which he unceremoniously stuffed in his pocket. He then took the teapot and cups from the table and put them and the salver on a large silver tray. Just as he was about to depart, he turned to Root and smiled enticingly.

'Thank you.'

'Thank you,' replied the Major, diverting his eyes from the waiter's gaze.

'I do hope you enjoyed your tea,' continued the grinning waiter.

'And the sandwiches. Thank you,' added the Major gratefully.

'I hope to see you again,' stressed the waiter, staring at Root.

'Yes indeed,' acknowledged Root nervously.

'Yes. Thank you,' concluded the Major decisively.

After the audacious waiter left, the Major and Root couldn't help laughing. When their mirth subsided, they just listened to the music. The room was now less populated but it didn't stop the pianist continuing with his extensive repertoire. He was now playing a haunting version of Lonely Town. The Major and Root stayed embedded in their seats as the wistful tune unfolded. It was as if they were both mesmerised by its feeling for the bereft. On the song's completion, they managed to drag themselves away, gather their coats and leave the Repton, as the pianist changed tempo with a breezy version of Oklahoma! The journey back in the Land Rover was bumpy yet exhilarating. As they approached the school and its resplendent English setting, Root broke out with unalloyed enthusiasm;

'Thanks Bill. A perfect Sunday afternoon'.

'Yes, it was good, Reg. '

'The Repton will be our little secret,' confided the Major.

'Far from the madding crowd,' uttered a jovial Root.

'Exactly,' confirmed the Major.

One Ball was in his study listening to Life with the Lyons. He didn't think that he'd like the Light Programme comedy series about an American family in London, but he was pleasantly surprised. The Lyons family had a great rapport, which wasn't surprising as they were a real family, not a manufactured one. One Ball enjoyed the absurd plots and the interruptions of the regularly featured characters like a Scottish housekeeper and various noisy neighbours. It was perfect listening for a rainy Sunday afternoon. Laughter calmed him down, especially before seeing Sully. As One Ball was listening to the end of the episode, there was a knock on his door. 'Bloody Sully,' he murmured to himself. 'Come in,' cried One Ball abruptly.

'Hello Potts I er,' stuttered Sully as he entered the study.

'Quiet! screamed One Ball, pointing to a seat and instructing Sully to sit down.

Sully obeyed One Ball's command and listened to the end of the show. Sully enjoyed the gentle humour but it wasn't his favourite. He preferred Ron and Eth Glum in Take It from Here. When the inevitable clapping signalled the end of the week's episode, One Ball let the music play as he gathered his thoughts. In any case, he rather liked signature tunes and this one had an attractive style. Nonetheless, as soon as the Light Programme announcer started the closing credits in hearty tones, One Ball got up and switched off the radio, which was on a small table near his bookshelf. After he returned to the chair next to his desk, he confronted the red-faced Sully, who had sunk into a small, decrepit armchair. One Ball could now easily look down on Sully, which he thought wholly appropriate.

'My Dad likes Bebe Lyons,' said Sully, trying to make small talk before admitting the failure of his spying mission.

'Bebe Daniels,' corrected One Ball.

'Yes. Bebe Daniels. My Dad thinks she's pretty. He told me she was a silent movie star.'

'I do know that, Sully.'

'Sorry Potts. Maybe you didn't know that she was harassed by a lunatic who wrote her hundreds of letters and threatened her several times.'

'Sully. We're not here to discuss Bebe Daniels.'

'I know but I thought I'd tell you what my father told me.'

'Fascinating Sully but we have other matters to discuss. As you well know.'

'I think that's why she left Hollywood.'

'Sully. Stop,' insisted One Ball.

'I just thought you'd be interested as you listen to her programme.'

'Sully, shut up!' shrieked a frustrated One Ball.

After a suitable pause, One Ball collected himself and asked:

'How did you get on?

'Get on?'

'Yes. With Rutter and Françoise.'

'Ah, yes. It was difficult. '

'Why?'

One Ball looked at Sully with violent intent, like a man possessed. Consequently, Sully hesitated before telling him of his conversation with Rutter on Open Way and the seizure of the camera. When he heard about it, One Ball exploded and spewed vile invective upon the assailed Sully. He was depending on this evidence to put pressure on the ghastly midget. Now he had no incriminating photos to undermine him. He couldn't understand why Sully had been so stupid. He'd made everything worse. The unravelling of the junior's idiotic strategy had given Rutter the opportunity to plot some awesome revenge. He dreaded that Sully's failure was going to make it even more difficult for him to extricate the rugby captain from Françoise. After all, he'd hoped that with the necessary proof and Rutter's fear of expulsion, he'd be able to stop him seeing her. He believed that this would give him an opportunity to know Françoise more intimately. Now, because of Sully's abject failure, his plans were in ruins. Then there were his rubbers. They couldn't stay nestled in Exodus forever. He bought them for a purpose, not as an object d'art. This dreadful news wrecked One Ball's Sunday. He knew that involving this fat fool was a risk but he didn't think that he'd fall at the first hurdle. The monitor's tolerance of Sully began to evaporate. It only reinforced his belief that his mother's pleas for moderation were feeble nonsense. He had to make it clear to Sully that he'd made things worse for himself.

'You've still got two punishments, Sully,' One Ball reminded the recalcitrant junior.

'I did my best,' claimed the agitated Sully.

'Well your best wasn't good enough.'

'It was difficult Potts.'

'They were in the pavilion weren't they?'

'I saw them on the 1st X1 cricket pitch.'

'What were they doing there?'

'Dancing.'

'Dancing?'`

'Yes. Dancing and singing.'

'Hells bloody bells.'

As Sully had warmed to the couple and appreciated their help, he just couldn't say that he saw them kissing. One Ball would have to discover that himself.

'I took a picture but they were a bit far away,' warned Sully.

'I gave you my Kodak Brownie Flash II especially,' One Ball reprimanded his squit.

'It wasn't easy Potts.'

'Why didn't you get closer, like the press do with celebrities?'

'I didn't want to be discovered.'

'You should have been more nimble and inventive, Sully. Then One Ball wouldn't have seen you.'

'I'm not one of the paparazzi, Potts.'

'You certainly aren't. And now Rutter has not only got control of the photos but also my bloody new camera.'

'Rutter said that he was going to meet you.'

'You've made everything worse, Sully!'

'You can see him during Henry V rehearsals?'

‘I rehearse my scenes on my own with Bayliss.’

‘I’m sure you can work something out.’

‘Work something out! You’ve got a bloody cheek.’

‘Well maybe you can still use the dancing on the cricket pitch bit.’

‘Not if I haven’t any evidence, idiot.’

‘I saw them.’

‘That’s not enough, Sully, if you haven’t the proof of a picture.’

There was an uneasy pause. One Ball rose from his seat and stared intensely at Sully.

Sully looked uneasily at the wooden floor. Then, after pondering his thoughts, he slowly raised his eyes to face the grim visage of One Ball.

‘Potts? enquired Sully.

‘Yes?’ replied One Ball, still irritated by Sully’s incompetence.

‘Why do you want to catch them?’

‘That’s my business.’

‘I see.’

‘Meanwhile Sully, you’ve still got those two punishments.’

‘What about changing the time limit?’ pleaded Sully.

‘Certainly not. You didn’t deliver anything. You’re no James Bond, Sully,’ answered One Ball derisively.

‘But I did try, Potts.’

‘Sully. You get nothing for trying, only achieving.’

One Ball had had enough of Sully’s bumbling foolishness. He glared at him like an unpleasant interrogator triumphing over a wilting victim.

‘Potts. Can I go?’ asked Sully, desperately wishing to escape the clutches of his oppressor.

‘Yes, you can. I’ll contact you shortly about doing your punishments at my convenience,’ declared an unrepentant, implacable One Ball.

Ok,’ mumbled a deflated Sully, as he got up from the armchair and opened the study door to the sound of ribald laughter in the dayroom

The debonair Hubert Aloysius Bayliss was finding directing Henry V very frustrating. He had limited time with his inexperienced cast, so he was under considerable pressure. Still, it was a challenge he relished, and certainly a necessary antidote to repeating his lessons on Napoleon's inexorable charge through Europe. Despite the limitations, Bayliss was pleased with the way rehearsals were developing. The boys weren't the greatest exponents of the iambic pentameter, but he'd seen worse. At his previous school, a grammar in Cardiff, he witnessed a production of Twelfth Night that was so unintelligible that it really needed subtitles. However, Bayliss believed that his current cast were a more talented group and that a combination of their intelligence and enthusiasm, would lead to an impressive production. He just wished that he didn't have to rehearse in the scout hut, which was freezing, even when the heat was on.

On this particular February afternoon, Bayliss was rehearsing the British camp scene. Sitting next to the director behind a large imposing table was Hayes, who was both the stage manager and playing the Boy. Bayliss felt frustrated that his rehearsal schedule had to accommodate so many other activities, not least incessant sport. Still, trying to change people's minds about an ethos embedded in the institution was impossible. It was almost like trying to overthrow the monarchy and he certainly wasn't for that, as his production was going to so aptly demonstrate.

Bayliss instructed Hayes to position various chairs to denote a tent and get a wastepaper basket for the campfire. He then pompously reminded everybody of the location of the exits and entrances, making an unnecessary joke about 'not bumping into the furniture'. They were just about to start the rehearsal, when Hayes pointed out that Macready was missing.

'Where is he?' insisted Bayliss.

'I saw him in the library, sir,' said Boring Beckett, who was playing Sir Thomas Erpingham.

'When?'

'This morning, sir.'

'Has anyone seen him this afternoon?'

Bayliss looked around at the assembled cast but answers there were none. He started to get angry. 'After all, he'd put faith in this boy, yet he can't be bothered to attend rehearsal on time,' he pondered broodingly to himself.

'All right, let's start without him. Hayes, you can read in Henry,' delegated Bayliss.

Sniggers greeted the decision. The idea of the callow Hayes being the King of England seemed palpably absurd to the rest of the cast.

'Shall I move it sir?' suggested Hayes.

'Why not? proclaimed Bayliss, looking to encourage initiative and company spirit.

Immediately, Hayes made a bold entrance and started the scene with Boring Beckett. Suddenly, Bayliss rose from his chair with restless despair.

'More colour, Beckett. Do it again.'

Boring Beckett looked confused and flustered. He nervously made his entrance again but he still struggled to bring light and shade to his few lines. Surreptitiously, Bayliss sighed heavily. Regardless of his efforts, he realised that Beckett's performance wouldn't change from the initial reading. He decided to give up on improving Boring Beckett's monotonous delivery. Unfortunately, he'd have to live with a very dull Erpingham. In contrast, Hayes's performance, much to everybody's surprise, had both variety and stature.

As the rehearsal proceeded, Binns, who had decided to take part after his acclaimed reading of Mr Bumble, made a lively, melodramatic entrance, revelling in Pistol's bad French. In response, Bayliss again got up from his chair and interjected.

'Have you never heard that less is more, Binns?'

'No sir.'

'Well remember it. Do it again.'

When they repeated the scene, Binns was more disciplined, concentrating on the character rather than trying to be funny all the time. What's more, he didn't constantly squeeze his hands together. Bayliss was pleased with his response. As the scene progressed, Hayes also surprised the director by the way he read the beginning of the scene, where the King disguises himself as an ordinary soldier. He did it simply and sincerely, without superficial flourishes. Then, just as an excitable Barrel as Fluellen and a greasy haired senior from Morton B as Gower were about to make their entrance, an out of breath, frenetic Macready burst into the room.

'Sorry sir,' apologised Macready before Bayliss could speak.

'Where the hell have you been? demanded Bayliss.

'I was learning my lines, sir.'

'But surely you knew we were rehearsing.'

'I lost track of time, sir.'

'Well keep track next time, please.'

'Yes sir.'

'You need to lead from the front, Macready.'

'Yes sir.'

'Just like Henry.'

'I will sir. '

'Good. Let's get on with it. We've got to Fluellen's entrance.'

Macready put down his script and went to where Hayes had been standing. He then tossed his head in the air with a sense of his own importance, while Hayes returned to his seat and his role as stage manager. His short reign as Henry V had come to a sudden end. Hayes was disappointed as he was enjoying himself and returning to stage management felt like a demotion. However, as he was keen to be involved in the whole enterprise, he wasn't going to sulk but continue to show commitment. He still wanted to be part of the school's theatrical community.

When the rehearsals continued and Fluellen and Gower had exited, Macready started playing the scene with lanky Boot, a burly senior from Goole A and a pimpled monitor from Jasper B, who were cast as the soldiers Williams, Bates and Alexander Court. Macready was off the book for the first time and was struggling to remember his lines. Suddenly he dried badly and screamed at Hayes:

'Yes!'

Hayes, still feeling the exhilaration of his own interpretation of King Henry, looked nonplussed and turned despondently to Bayliss.

'He wants a prompt,' explained Bayliss.

'Oh, right,' said Hayes, nervously looking at the script.

'Yes!' yelled Macready again.

'Where were you?' requested a tense Hayes.

'You should bloody know, Hayes. You're the prompter,' accused Macready, in a fit of prima donna pique.

'That's enough, Macready,' interrupted Bayliss. 'Let's take it from, 'Besides there is no king being his cause never so spotless.'

'Ok, sir. Sorry,' replied a seemingly contrite Macready.

Unfortunately, when he restarted Henry's speech, he dried again.

'Oh, fuck!' cried the frustrated Macready. 'Sorry sir, I knew it in the library,' claimed the leading thespian, apologising quickly to Bayliss before he was criticised. 'Yes!' reiterated the vexed actor, screaming at Hayes as if he was a servant from a bygone era.

Hayes, fearful of Macready's wayward temperament, hastily came in with the line 'What kind of god art thou….'

Bayliss was finding Macready's interpretation, mannered and hollow and before Boring Beckett re-entered, the director stopped the scene,

'You're singing too much,' commented Bayliss.

'Singing!' exclaimed the offended Macready.

Yes. Overplaying. You're talking to ordinary soldiers, not dukes and duchesses. Keep it simple and honest. From 'Upon the King. Do it again,' commanded Bayliss.

Macready looked aggrieved. 'Singing? What cheek!' he murmured to himself. He thought Bayliss should be pleased that he knew the lines so well, in spite of the fluffs. Reluctantly, Macready swallowed his considerable pride, took the note and made the speech more intimate. He had to admit that the others did seem to be listening more intently. Even Boring Beckett responded and helped Macready make Henry's soliloquy at the end of the scene, a stirring plea for victory.

'Better,' encouraged Bayliss, revelling in such inspiring patriotism.

The rehearsal then progressed well. Macready calmed down and brought more variety to his role. Hayes also started to feel much more positive about the production, notwithstanding the curtailment of his regal reign and Macready's temperamental outbursts. The cast left the rehearsal optimistic, purposefully avoiding their mercurial leading man, who stayed behind to apologise to Bayliss for his bad time keeping and foul language.

Sully departed from the scout hut with Barrett, after they'd both been measured for their costumes. He decided now was the time to tell him about his latest conflict with One Ball and his futile attempts to be 007.

'What an idiot!' exclaimed Barrett.

'I thought I could get rid of these bloody punishments,' justified a distressed Sully.

'Why didn't you tell me about this undercover escapade?'

'Because One Ball demanded secrecy.'

'And you trusted him?'

'Well what could I do?'

'Don't be so bloody gullible.'

There were times when Barrett despised Sully's stupidity. Nonetheless, undeterred by his manifest failings and absurd fantasies, he submitted to Sully's vulnerable charm. Obviously, he was no match for One Ball's ruthlessness and needed strong support.

'I think One Ball will see Rutter,' conjectured Sully, attempting to be strategic.

'To get his camera and photos,' maintained an intrigued Barrett.

'Yes.'

'That'll be interesting.'

The two boys chatted as they strolled amidst the asphalt spaces behind the houses, towards James B. Barrett concluded that it was best to wait and see how Rutter dealt with the brutal One Ball. Then, if necessary, he'd have to see the Major as Ryder had proposed. Sully agreed and while the two boys made their way past a long, frustrated queue at the tuck shop, Sully recalled what he'd observed on Open Way.

'They were dancing on the 1st X1 cricket pitch?' said Barrett incredulously.

'Yes, and singing.' added Sully admiringly.

'Lonnie Donegan?'
'No Barrett, sorry. I Could Have Danced All Night'
'Ok. But not as good as Digging My Potatoes'.
'They were kissing.'
'Blimey. They certainly take risks.'
'I don't think they care. They're in love.'
'Rutter could be in big trouble if he gets caught.'
'And Françoise?'
'She would be sacked.'
'They were really into each other'
'Having sex?'
'Not at that precise moment.'
'Careless rapture eh?'
'Yes. That's good. Careless rapture.'

Barrett then started to talk about his problems of achieving a Northern Irish accent for his part of Macmorris. Bayliss wanted it to be northern so that the production could represent the whole of the UK and fulfil his concept of a 'patriotic entertainment'. Although Barrett found reading the work of Herodotus difficult, mastering the rasping sounds of Northern Irish speech was becoming impossible. When Barrett practiced alone, contorting his mouth into different shapes in the mirror, he couldn't even understand himself. Just when he was in a state of artistic despair, he read an article in the News Chronicle about Danny Blanchflower, the captain of Tottenham Hotspur. As he was from Belfast, Barrett thought that he might copy his accent.

'How are you going to hear him though?' questioned Sully.

'Maybe he'll be on Sports Report?' suggested an unconvincing Barrett.

'You don't know if he'll definitely be on, do you?' answered a practical Sully.

Barrett realised that he'd got caught up in the emotion of his idea and that surprisingly Sully was the person being rational. He couldn't rely on listening to the radio, as those who had one illicitly wouldn't risk lending it to anyone, and in the house Brown and Bunter were always rockin' to AFN or Radio Lux. Then, as the two boys moved back into the dayroom, Barrett put forward an alternative.

'Wait. I've got another idea,' mentioned Barrett mischievously.

'What?' queried Sully.

'I'll get in touch with Carson.'

'Brilliant.'

Carson was a tall, wiry senior from Coleraine in Jasper A. He was nicknamed Chuck because of his obsession with the music of Chuck Berry. Apparently, he did a good version of Roll Over Beethoven.

'Yes, Chuck's your man.'

'He'll make an Irishman of you!'

On the two boys arrival, Brown and Bunter increased the volume of the radio and Bill Haley's Rip It Up boomed across the dayroom. Several of the boys were so enlivened that they started dancing. The joint was really rockin', when suddenly One Ball emerged from his study with a most forbidding countenance.

'Turn it down!' he yelled.

Brown and Bunter looked at him as if he was old fogey from another century. Warily, Brown reluctantly decreased the volume.

'I know it's nearly time to march to tea but some people are still working. Like me!' emphasised an incandescent One Ball, who departed slamming the door of his study.

'He wouldn't be so angry if it was classical music,' said Bunter.

'Like Wagner,' stressed Sully.

'I doubt if he's ever heard of Little Richard,' remarked Bunter.

'Nor Jerry Lee Lewis,' added Brown.

'Maybe I should try Lonnie Donegan on One Ball?' joked Barrett.

'It'd be hopeless. He'll never rock,' concluded Brown.

A few minutes later, the genial Pound entered the dayroom and rang the bell. He announced that it was time to get ready for parade and go to tea. Brown unwillingly turned the radio off and the boys made their way forlornly out of the dayroom.

Rutter was approaching the Quadrangle after an illuminating English lesson about sexuality in D.H. Lawrence, when he bumped into Smallman. Smallman or Pongo, as he was called for some eccentric reason, gave him a respectful acknowledgement. Thankfully, he didn't seem to suspect anything about his senior monitor's liaisons with Françoise or the defilement of the 1st X1 cricket pitch. Anyway, if he knew, he wasn't saying anything, probably to protect his cricket team and not expose any scandal in his house. In any case, Rutter had more immediate concerns on his mind, not least dealing with One Ball. As he contemplated his concerns, who should fortuitously emerge but none other than One Ball himself, walking briskly on the other side of the Quadrangle. It was a cold February morning and One Ball liked to keep warm, let alone give himself time to prepare for lunch. Rutter decided that he was going to confront his arrogant protagonist. This required considerable effort on his part, given that his short stature meant that he found it difficult to keep up with One Ball's lengthening stride.

As One Ball was about to enter the porch leading into James B, he suddenly heard his name being yelled all over the Avenue. He turned around in alarm to witness the sight of a breathless Rutter, smiling at him with a huge grin across his face. On discovering such leering, One Ball became tense and anxious. His first reaction was to ignore the beaming idiot and go into the house. He then thought that was cowardly and decided to challenge Rutter over his behaviour. If he was to have any chance with Françoise, he must defy his rival. Believing that was the chivalrous thing to do, One Ball walked defiantly towards the smirking pygmy.

'What do you want?' demanded One Ball with cold detachment.

'I've got your camera,' asserted Rutter gleefully.

'I think we'd better talk,' decided One Ball, who then indicated that they should move behind the house, towards the asphalt area in front of the running track. Inconveniently, this was full of juniors like Hayes, Barrett and Sully playing football, which One Ball found sacrilegious. 'After all,' he thundered to himself, 'we're a bloody rugby school.' As soon as

Sully saw One Ball and Rutter together, his face turned red. He feared that they might come to some agreement, which would make his situation worse.

'Hello Sully,' said Rutter reassuringly.

'Hello,' replied a tentative Sully.

'Go inside, you lot. It's nearly time for lunch,' ordered One Ball, while glaring at the highly inquisitive juniors.

Reluctantly Sully grabbed the football, while Hayes and Barrett picked up the various sweaters that represented the goal posts. One Ball watched them depart and decided that it would be better to talk to his diminutive rival in a more remote place. Consequently, he ushered Rutter to some bushes at the side of the athletics track. There, he found a hidden area next to a beech tree. At the base of the tree was a multitude of cigarette ends, the result of boys enjoying a subversive smoke. The various stubs were in extreme contrast to the bushy verdant foliage. It was hardly a setting for a noble resolution.

'Why were you spying on me?' asked Rutter, leaning casually against the tree.

'I wasn't spying Rutter,' refuted One Ball, offended by the rugby captain's supercilious posture.

'Who sent Sully then?'

'He was requested to observe your movements.'

'Stop the semantics, Potts. That's bloody spying.'

'Where's my camera?'

'I've got it.'

'Give it back to me.'

'Not at the moment Potts.'

'When?'

'When it suits me'

'You've obviously got incriminating evidence.'

'You think so?'

'Yes'

'So how do you know?'

'Sully saw you.'

'From a tree?'

'What?'

'Your MI5 man was stuck on a tree'

'Bloody idiot!'

‘Stop blaming Sully.’

‘He’d better have got some photos.’

‘Or what?’

‘I’ll deal with him’

‘And do what?’

‘That’s my prerogative.’

‘Stop the bullying, Potts.’

‘He’s a thicko, who needs discipline.’

‘And you’re a jealous fool.’

It was at that moment that One Ball wanted to hit Rutter. In fact, he only just managed to control himself. Yes, he had succumbed to jealousy but it was for a reason. He could never get a moment to talk properly to Françoise. Why should he be at such a disadvantage? It wasn’t as if the Lilliputian Rutter was an Adonis, far from it. He had a big nose and mean, thin lips. ‘How the hell did he inveigle himself into her company in the first place?’ he raged to himself. One Ball was too busy with his scientific studies and being a conscientious monitor to have time to plan seductive assignations. He was disturbed that he was playing by the rules and making no romantic headway, while the lascivious dwarf was running roughshod over protocol, dancing the night away with the woman he desired. Yet such was his delusion, he refused to contemplate the reality.

‘I’m not jealous of you, Rutter,’ claimed One Ball.

‘Yes you are. You want Françoise but you can’t have her,’ declared Rutter robustly.

‘We’ll see about that.’

‘What are you going to do?’

‘That’s my business.’

‘Get juniors to do your dirty work?’

‘Just give my bloody camera back.’

‘I will. When you show sufficient contrition.’

‘Contrition? What about you showing some repentance?

One Ball was appalled that Rutter wouldn’t return his property. He was just using the school as a plaything for his sexual antics. The revered rugby captain had no academic ambition. He was obviously content to end up in some depressing, rain-sodden northern town gaining a minor degree in BA Pleasure.

‘You’ll get the camera back later when the photos have been developed,’ stated Rutter deliberately. In fact, he’d already managed to drop it off with a local chemist, before a debate on hanging at the local grammar school.

‘It’d better be soon, otherwise I’ll report you as a thief’ warned One Ball.

‘And I’ll report you for bullying and spying.’

‘I mean it, Rutter’

‘It’s nearly time for lunch,’ said Rutter looking at his watch, ‘I need to get back to house’.

Rutter left the shrubbery quickly, without looking back at One Ball. In contrast, One Ball remained alone amidst the debris, depressed at his lack of romantic progress. He now wondered if he was ever going to use those bloody rubbers.

Reginald Root had just finished going through Henry Purcell’s ‘Hear My Prayer O Lord’, which was to be sung at Sunday’s Evensong service. Root was hopeful that the forthcoming performance of the choral anthem would prove to be an even more significant artistic development than his rendition of Prince Igor. After a rehearsal in the chapel, most of the boys had departed to do their homework, apart from Ryder. Meanwhile, Root was chatting with Sims, who seemed much more energised since he’d become officially engaged to nurse Beth. As Root was praising Sims for his organ accompaniment, Ryder moved determinedly towards them in the chapel aisle.

‘Can I have a word?’ enquired Ryder nonchalantly.

‘Of course. Do you mind, Tim?’ asked Root, referring to the rejuvenated Sims.

‘Not at all. I must get back anyway. See you tomorrow,’ replied Sims tactfully.

‘Thanks, Tim,’ responded Root apprehensively.

After Sims had made his way out through the vestry, Root turned to the choir’s leader. With his smartly swept-back hair and insolent swagger, Ryder emanated a contemptuous ease.

‘I was just thinking. Our services are full of English composers like Tallis, Byrd and Walmisley,’ proclaimed the choir leader, revelling in his knowledge of indigenous classical musicians.

'So what, Ryder. As you know, no one likes foreign composers more than me, but we are an English institution,' Root pompously reminded the choir leader.

'Exactly, so I was wondering if you might consider an exciting addition.'

'Not Stephen Foster again?'

'No sir, he's American.'

'I'm aware of that, Ryder.'

After Root's sharp response, there was a slight pause before Ryder revealed his hand.

'I was thinking of Hubert Parry,' divulged an exuberant Ryder.

'A minor composer, in my opinion.' commented Root disparagingly.

'The royal family like him.'

'What do they know about classical music?'

'Well, this piece does fit in with our British heritage.'

'I didn't know you were a traditionalist Ryder.'

'I'm not, but I do like this particular tune.'

'Which?'

'Jerusalem.'

'I knew there would be a political purpose behind this.'

'Not really.'

Root told Ryder to accompany him into the vestry. He didn't want to continue this conversation in the publicly cavernous spaces of the chapel. He ushered Ryder to a chair opposite a vestry table where various silver cups were placed, amidst a large jar of communion wafers and an imposing jug half-full of wine.

'The Reverend Elwyn got upset last week,' remarked Root critically, as he sat near the table.

'About what?' queried an inquisitive Ryder.

'Some boys came into the vestry and swigged half of the communion wine.'

'Oh yes, I heard about that.'

'You don't know who did it, do you?'

'No I'm afraid I don't.'

'And if you did, you wouldn't tell?'

'Well, there is that possibility.'

'I thought so.'

'You wouldn't want me to be a sneak, would you, sir?'

'I would like you to be honest though.'

'Such a moral conundrum doesn't exist, as I really don't know.'

Root didn't believe that such a diabolically devious operator as Ryder wasn't fully informed about such an outrageously profane act. Root thought that such deceit was evidence that he'd go far. This only made the music master even more determined to make sure that he wasn't exposed by Ryder's manipulative skills. Root didn't want to explore the 'holy wine' fracas any further. He wasn't particularly religious but he still found it shocking that some boys came especially to communion to have an alcoholic drink. In fact, Rev Elwyn told him of one boy, who when offered the sacrament, held onto the cup for so long that Elwyn uncharacteristically had to yank it violently out of his hands. Fortunately, Root was now able to deal with such a surreal event through his yoga meditation. He no longer rushed to anger. As he looked across at the, self-regarding Ryder, the music master appeared piously relaxed against a background of hanging surplices and vestments.

'So what do you think about the Parry?' challenged Ryder.

'Not at the moment, Ryder,' said an equivocating Root.

'It's a popular song.'

'I'm focused on more ambitious projects.'

'Like what?'

'Beethoven's Missa solemnis.'

Root spoke of the great composer's choral work with such exaggerated articulation, that Ryder found it hard to stop giggling at the music master's imitation of a pretentious Third Programme announcer. Eventually, after a salient pause, the choir's leader suggested a compromise.

'Can't we do both?' proposed Ryder diplomatically.

'Maybe. I'll think about it,' replied Root, pondering evasively.

Ryder rocked back elegantly on a vestry chair and then decided to use evidence to back his demand.

'I took a straw poll,' he announced abruptly.

'A what?' queried Root, taken aback by Ryder's initiative.

'I sent a questionnaire around the houses,' continued Ryder complacently.

'I see,' responded Root hesitantly.

'It came back with eighty per cent in favour of singing Jerusalem,' emphasised Ryder with a triumphant grin.

Root thought that Ryder was incorrigibly smug, as he sat on his chair with all the righteous certainty of a vain ideologue. He was obviously using Jerusalem as a rallying call for his socialist vision. In fact, Root had some sympathies with his aims but he disliked being pressurised by Ryder's agenda. He certainly had nothing against Jerusalem but he wasn't going to be bulldozed by the school's Lenin. After all, he was already struggling to get Missa solemnis off the ground, so naturally he didn't want to be distracted by controversial individual requests. Otherwise, where would it end? With straw polls demanding that Hound Dog is sung at Holy Communion? Root was now beginning to regret allowing Beautiful Dreamer to be accepted. He liked the song and thought that the choir gave a memorable rendition of Stephen Foster's evocative ballad. Unfortunately, it seemed to have opened the floodgates for the school to initiate their own version of Family Favourites and for none other than himself, Reginald Root, to be the school's disc jockey like Bill Crozier and Jean Metcalfe on the popular request programme.

However, as Root had been both transformed by meditation and received warm letters from Rupert, he felt able to handle comrade Ryder's machinations. Root knew that Oliver wouldn't want to hear about any further turmoil in the choir. The headmaster was a man for evolution not revolution and was already finding it difficult to cope with the increasing rise of popular culture and the power of youth. Ryder's disruption of Evensong had not gone down well and as that followed the drunken antics of Root's predecessor, the music master intended to proceed cautiously. After all, Oliver was a man of tradition and a creature of habit. Therefore, Root decided to kick Ryder's request firmly into the long grass.

'Ok, Ryder. I'll think about it and get back to you in due course.'

'How long will that take, sir?' pressed Ryder suspiciously.

‘Well you know these things do take time as I need to consult.’

‘Consult. With who?’

‘Who do you think, Ryder? The headmaster.’

‘Is that really necessary?’

‘Yes, it is Ryder. Especially, after your Evensong revolt.’

‘It wasn’t an attack on Evensong. It was an attack on you and your running of the choir.’

‘I don’t think we’ll reopen those wounds, Ryder.’

Ryder decided to avoid further confrontation with the newly becalmed Root. Nonetheless, lounging languidly on his chair, he was still determined to keep up the pressure for a performance of his socialist anthem.

‘I hope that the headmaster gives the proposal a fair hearing,’ Ryder declared ominously.

‘We all will, Ryder’, confirmed Root with nervous reassurance.

‘I do hope so as the boys want it.’

‘Your polling isn’t scientific, Ryder.’

‘No, but the response was so much in favour that it certainly wasn’t inaccurate.’

‘We can’t be running the school by referendums, Ryder. ‘

‘You can’t ignore popular choice either.’

‘We’ll see.’

‘We sing Rule Britannia, why can’t we sing Jerusalem?’

‘Rule Britannia isn’t a controversial choice, that’s why.’

‘It is to some, who aren’t enamoured of Britain’s imperialist legacy.’

‘In any case, Ryder, the school wouldn’t want to promote a socialist rallying call.’

‘But some regard Jerusalem as a patriotic song.’

‘That’s debatable, Ryder.’

‘Anyway, shouldn’t we encourage balance?’

‘Maybe, but many in Labour want to abolish public schools. So there may be a feeling that it wouldn’t be wise to promote your own death sentence.’

‘Surely, it’s up to the pupils themselves to make their own judgements, after hearing both sides.’

‘Possibly. Leave it with me and I’ll get back to you.’

‘Don’t leave it too long, sir. Please.’

Ryder rose in stately fashion from his chair, said goodbye to Root and departed from the chapel through the vestry door. He knew that the music master was playing for time. Prevarication was the oldest trick in the book. Nonetheless, he was still determined to pursue his advocacy of Jerusalem. To hear Blake’s words sung by eight hundred boys, would be an exhilarating experience. It would be celebrating an alternative narrative rather than a fustian empire. The likes of ‘Britain never, never, never will be slaves’ stuck in Ryder’s craw. Britain may have eventually abolished slavery but she’d profited off it for years. However, Ryder reassured himself that now at least change was happening in the colonies where independence was on the move. He believed that the school should reflect such developments, rather than bury itself in dubious narratives of the past. Ryder was going to pressurise Root to initiate suitable progress and Jerusalem would be a start. He strode into the dark night across the Quadrangle in imperious fashion, confident of victory.

After Ryder’s departure, Root tidied up the vestry in order to avoid an unholy outburst from the Rev Elwyn. He knew Ryder would pressurise him about Jerusalem but he wasn’t going to get embroiled in a cultural dispute. He would discuss it and make a decision. He needed to value his health. He didn’t want to become permanently cross again. He also wanted to protect his job and not upset people. Although the chapel protest was blamed on Ryder, it didn’t reflect well on him. Some believed that he should have managed the choir better, so that such an embarrassing disruption wouldn’t have happened. Therefore, he couldn’t afford to make changes to accepted practice without consultation. Root looked around the vestry to be sure that he’d cleared up sufficiently, not to upset the oversensitive Elwyn. He switched off the lights and headed into the stygian night. Root was going to cook some lasagne and listen to some chamber music on the Third Programme. That would be an appropriate palliative to Ryder’s inexorable demands.

Françoise had received a message in her pigeon hole in the kitchen. It was in a smart Basildon Bond envelope. When she opened it, she discovered it was from Rutter asking her to meet him after tea in the drying room, next to Ironside. Françoise had previously been in the tube, the long tunnel under the Dining Hall and all the houses, which was only accessed when the weather was severe, but she wasn't familiar with the delights of the drying room. Consequently, she was expecting another bizarre English experience.

At tea, Françoise served overcooked mince to pupils in Jasper A. Fortunately, she wasn't anywhere near James B and the dreaded One Ball. Since the revelation of Sully's spying, Rutter and Françoise had been more careful about their liaisons. They'd stopped meeting at the pavilion, fearful that rumours of their trysts there were becoming common knowledge. The thought of voyeurs observing their dalliances didn't fill Françoise with any further enthusiasm for that location. Unfortunately, Rutter had yet to find an alternative venue, so he resorted to the unromantic surroundings of the drying room as a temporary measure.

When tea finished and the boys started to depart, Françoise saw Smallman talking to the formidable Miss Pollard. Miss Pollard, aka Mrs Danvers, seemed to be laughing, which was a miracle in itself. This was in marked contrast to her two-piece black suit, which made her look as if she was going to a funeral rather than organising the Dining Hall. Françoise was glad that Madame Danvers was in a radiant mood, as she wanted to depart as soon as the boys had left the hall. In fact, she'd already arranged with Yvette to say that she wasn't feeling well. Normally, the icy kitchen supervisor was incredibly vigilant but today her flirting with Pongo gave Françoise hope that she was being unusually lax.

After all the boys had left, an eerie silence descended upon the Dining Hall. Only occasional voices, usually in a foreign language, echoed across vast space. When she'd cleared her serving table, Françoise teamed up with Yvette and they took their urns into the kitchen. On each arrival, swarthy Spanish and Italian cooks made inappropriate remarks and gave them licentious looks. The two women ignored this lustful cacophony and after depositing the last urn in the kitchen, they swiftly departed. Yvette then reassured Françoise that she'd deal with

Madame Danvers. In any case, that intimidating lady seemed to have mysteriously disappeared. As Pongo had also vanished, the two women believed that they'd both gone to have a tête-à-tête. So when Yvette whispered 'allez!' Françoise instinctively obeyed.

Immediately, she took the back stairs and descended into the subterranean world of the tube. When she reached the bottom, she could hardly see amidst the dim light. Gathering her bearings, she turned right in the direction of Ironside and made her way cautiously towards her destination. Françoise didn't think that Ironside was far away, as it was one of the first houses on that side of the Avenue. Then, just as she was trying to get her bearings, Françoise heard the sound of dragging feet moving towards her. Despite the dark, sinister setting, she decided to remain calm and keep walking at an even pace. Gradually the sound of footsteps got louder and she began to decipher a small, wiry man coming towards her. As he came more into focus, she recognised one of the housemasters looking drunk and tired. His dark brown hair appeared dishevelled and he wore a brown sports jacket, with patches on its arms. Françoise got alarmed when he started moving in different directions. As he got nearer, she watched this oscillating figure with intense scrutiny. Just as he was about to approach her, Françoise moved consciously out of his way. However, such an action became unnecessary, as he stopped a few yards away from her and politely acknowledged her presence.

'Good evening,' he said, slightly slurring his speech.

'Good evening,' responded Françoise courteously.

The man looked haunted and unhappy as he stared at her in the dark. His eyes were slightly bloodshot and anxious, like a frightened animal. Françoise waited for him to restart his walk and pass her. After staring at her giddily for a moment, he regained impetus and made his way down the dark, grimy passage with its murky electric wall lights. As Françoise continued her journey, she tried to remember the man's name but somehow it escaped her. She wasn't too far way now, as she was sure that she'd arrived near Rutter's house. She proceeded very slowly, looking carefully for a suitable door or opening that would signify the drying room. Just as she was beginning to despair, she heard a whispering voice calling her out of the darkness. Françoise moved slowly towards the sound and there bathed in shadowy light at the doorway emerged Rutter, garbed in just breeches and an open blue shirt.

'Where's your coat?' asked Françoise.

'It's bloody hot in here,' warned Rutter.

When Françoise moved into the musty drying room, she realised that Rutter was right. It was very warm. Rugby shirts, shorts, socks and boots wrapped around very thick, deteriorating grey pipes, enveloped the room. A wooden clotheshorse stood in the middle of the space, displaying various underpants and shirts. While removing her purple scarf, Françoise turned to the sweating rugby captain.

'A very romantic setting, mon chéri!'

'Sorry about that, but we've got to keep a low profile.'

'I've just met one of your housemasters.'

'Where?' enquired an alarmed Rutter.

As she proceeded to unbutton her coat, Françoise described her encounter in the tube.

'That's Bowen. He's Welsh,' revealed a relieved Rutter.

'I didn't hear an accent but he didn't say much,' Françoise reassured him.

'He teaches Maths. He's also our rugby coach.'

'He wasn't very fit for a coach. I think he was drunk.'

'He can be volatile. He once hit a boy over the head with The Times, when a pupil didn't get up as he entered the room.'

'Mon dieu!'

'Yes, strange man. I think he suffers from depression.'

'Surely he shouldn't be teaching?'

'Maybe, but he's a good coach.'

'This place seems more interested in sport than studying.'

'It's regarded as character building, Françoise.'

'Not for those who hate games, Artie?'

'Yes. I suppose there's limited accommodation for them.'

'Can't they do something else?

'Sort of. Like painting gates, repairs, that kind of thing.'

'It's ok for you because you're a sports king.

'I do other things.'

‘Like chase les femmes?’

‘Of course, when they’re as beautiful as you.’

‘Flattery will get you nowhere, monsieur.’

‘Remember, Françoise that in the school play, I’m the Dauphin, so watch your step!’

‘A Dauphin that can’t speak French.’

‘Sorry about that. I chose my subjects before I met you.’

‘You’re forgiven.’

‘Anyway, I’m learning French from you.’

‘Un petit peu.’

‘It’s better than nothing, Françoise.’

‘I can’t wait to see your performance.’

‘I think my Dauphin is beginning to sound a bit like Kenneth Williams.’

‘Who?’

‘An outrageously camp comedian. He’s on the radio quite a bit.’

‘Are you laughing at the heir to the French monarchy?’

‘I suppose we are. Blame the director. He sees the play in primary patriotic colours.’

‘Maybe, Yvette and I should protest.’

‘Don’t worry too much. Shakespeare’s humanity is bound to win through in the end.’

‘Thank God for that.’

‘Oh, I forgot. One Ball is a domineering Chorus.’

Françoise had now taken off her coat and put her scarf in one of its pockets. She preferred to hold it rather than risk dirtying it on the peeling pipes. The mention of One Ball reminded her that the battle with the conceited monitor wasn’t over. Consequently, she wanted to know if Rutter had received the printed photos.

‘Not yet, but in the meantime, I’m pressurising One Ball about his behaviour,’ said Rutter, outlining his strategy.

‘But he could still report us,’ maintained Françoise.

‘That’s a risk, I’m willing to take.’

‘I’ve heard he’s been bullying Sully.’

‘Yes, badly. So he needs to be challenged.’

‘What has he been doing?’

Rutter then told Françoise about the successive punishments for 'rank insubordination' and 'outright duplicity'. He also described the sadistic way One Ball insisted on Sully repeating his punishment mile, after being set times that he would never achieve.

'Let's put your coat on a hanger, Françoise,' volunteered Rutter, trying his best to create a more comfortable environment.

'Ok,' agreed Françoise cautiously.

'I'm sorry about this. Next time we'll meet at the Savoy.'

Rutter hung the elegant coat on the clotheshorse, next to the rugby jerseys. It looked a bit out of place, like crown jewels in a rubbish dump.

'That's better. I'm afraid we just can't go back to the pavilion at the moment but I'll find somewhere else. I just need a bit of time,' apologised Rutter, with as much charm as he could muster.

'I feel like I'm in Le Maquis, with all this hiding and moving about,' responded a frustrated Françoise.

'That's why you can help with this One Ball problem. We need to reel him in.'

'Reel? I don't know this word.'

'Like a fishing line catching a fish, and then winding it in.'

'Ah, I see. Reel. I must remember.'

Rutter realised that it was important that Françoise beguiled One Ball, so that he wouldn't report their affair. They both needed to survive the term at all costs. Accordingly, Rutter cautiously asked Françoise to be friendly with One Ball, to indeed 'reel him in'. He needed controlling so that the lovers avoided punishment. This would give Rutter time to assess the photos. In the meantime, he believed that One Ball could still use other means to get them both expelled. In particular, he was concerned that the aggrieved monitor would get Sully to talk. Rutter feared that the junior's trepidation of the monitor's relentless punishment regime could lead to unforeseen consequences. He was convinced that One Ball's irrational jealousy needed to be contained. Otherwise, it would rage unabated like a rampant bushfire. Rutter sensed that One Ball's animosity wasn't just about a spat about a girlfriend but insecurity about his sexual prowess.

'You mean he wants to exercise his one ball!' exclaimed Françoise.

'Exactly' confirmed Rutter.

'Well Artie, I'm not going to give it a test run!'

'Of course not, Françoise.'

'So what are you suggesting?'

'I'm just want you to be friendly, to calm him down, so it stops getting us both thrown out.'

'But we've done nothing wrong.'

'I know, but the powers that be don't look kindly on sexual relationships between pupils and staff.'

'We're old enough. It's not illegal and anyway I'm a kitchen maid, not an academic.'

'You're still part of the staff.'

'I find a lot of this very hypocritical.'

'I know.'

'What about the homosexual teachers lusting after boys?'

'But they're not sleeping with them.'

'Not as far as we know.'

'Unfortunately, that doesn't alter the fact that Sully is a potential witness.'

Françoise was disappointed by the sexual attitudes of the English, whom she thought too often behaved like deceitful Victorians. Thankfully, Rutter was an exception to the rule. Still, eventually she agreed to deal with the haughty One Ball, notwithstanding the absurd shenanigans. She knew that behind the bluster, he was insecure, vulnerable and damaged but that couldn't excuse his bullying. In any case, she didn't want to be sacked. Regardless of the difficulties, she was enjoying her work experience. She was getting the opportunity not only to increase her knowledge of the English language but also the delightful eccentricities of their way of life.

Françoise wasn't looking forward to flattering such a humourless bully. Still, it had to be done. She'd have to find a way to act as a femme fatale to handle le rendez-vous. Something in the seductive style of Barbara Stanwyck in Double Indemnity would be fun. She always liked her.

‘It’ll make up for you not playing Katharine,’ joked Rutter.

‘I’m not an actress,’ countered Françoise.

‘Nor are we actors, for that matter.’

‘Shakespeare is hard.’

‘But you’re French and Katharine is a French princess.’

‘But I’ve never been on stage.’

‘I’m going to tell Bayliss.’

‘It’s a play for the boys, not the kitchen staff.’

‘Ok, but you could at least advise on Katharine’s French.’

‘Maybe.’

‘No maybe, Françoise. We need French input.’

‘Who is playing Katharine?

‘Staines.’

‘I don’t know him.’

‘He’s in James B and a fitness fanatic. He’s a pleasant princess but his French needs work.’

‘Ok. See what Monsieur Bayliss says.’

‘But first One Ball.’

‘Yes. First, One Ball.’

After such agreement, they kissed in the middle of the cavernous drying room. Amidst a hanging naked bulb, they revelled in the dangerous excitement of their love. However, just as Rutter was beginning to get excited, he remembered that he had to get back to house. Pongo was on the prowl and his absence might confirm rumours that were already floating about, after Sully’s failed mission. He therefore gently and reluctantly disentangled himself from Françoise’s firm embrace.

‘Remember. I won’t return the camera until I see the photographs,’ said Rutter about to depart. ‘But first we deal with not getting expelled and One Ball’s bullying,’ he added, opening the drying room door.

‘Ok. You’d better go,’ accepted Françoise dismissively. Frustrated that they couldn’t continue expressing the intensity of their feelings, she gathered her coat from the hanger and aggressively dusted it down.

‘Bye’, responded Rutter, going over to give Françoise a reassuring kiss on the lips.

After Rutter departed, Françoise put on her coat and tied her scarf around her neck. She wondered if she’d got herself into a terrible tangle. Still, she was philosophical about her fate,'ce qui sera sera,' she concluded. In any case, she thought that it was definitely more exciting than staying in Lyon. She then cautiously moved towards the door and peered outside to both the left and right. Thank goodness the tube was clear. She didn't want to meet any more drunken housemasters. With confident strides, she moved in the direction of her lodgings.

Mrs Killer, aka Deirdre Roy, had become alarmed by the increasing rumours regarding her husband and Marian, the James matron. She felt demeaned by the scandal and was determined to confront Alexander Roy about such treacherous carnality. Killer wasn't on house duty this particular evening, so she intended to broach it during supper. As they were eating, Killer complimented Deirdre on her lasagne, which he felt went particularly well with the mixed salad and the bottle of wine. Initially, Deirdre didn't like cooking but given their family circumstances, isolated in a school, several miles away from the town, she expanded her culinary skills. In fact, it gave her solace and helped her relax, particularly with the pressures of a young child. As she observed Killer chewing the Italian dish and heartily swigging the Chianti, he looked handsome, with his alluring brown eyes and imposing stature. He also had a warm demeanour and a sense of humour. Nonetheless, Deirdre got frustrated that he seemed to live in his own secluded world. The school and the boys seemed to take over a housemaster's life. It was as if they were their real family, one in which women played a minor role. For instance, while Killer did play with Barney, he never considered bathing or dressing him. Deirdre needed some relief from constantly attending to their child, but no offer emerged from her husband. Hence, she was now determined to challenge Killer about his casual levity.

While eating their dessert, an apple pie Deirdre had picked up from a Premier supermarket in the town, they chatted about the boys, Barney and even the wiles of Harold Macmillan the new Prime Minister. Later, when they were drinking their coffee in their living room, Deirdre decided to pursue her personal concerns.

‘Are you seeing Marian the James matron?’ asked Deirdre directly.

‘What do you mean seeing?’ replied Killer suspiciously.

‘Having a relationship with her?’

‘When I’m on duty, I just go and talk to her.’

‘Really?’

‘Yes. I play draughts with her.’

‘In your underpants?’

Killer suddenly stopped drinking his coffee. After giving himself time to come up with a suitable answer, he decided to act as a bewildered innocent.

‘What do you mean?’

‘I think you know what I mean.’

‘I’m afraid I don’t.’

‘I was walking down the Avenue with Barney recently.’

‘So what?’

‘And some boys from James B were laughing.’

‘That’s not unusual.’

‘They were laughing at me.’

‘Were they juniors?’

‘Yes.’

‘Well, what do you expect?’

‘It was the way they laughed.’

‘What do you mean?’

‘Their gloating was humiliating.’

‘You should have taken no notice.’

‘I did but rumours circulate.’

‘What rumours?’

‘About you and the Witch of Wigan.’

‘Deirdre!’

Deirdre wanted Killer to feel awkward. Accordingly, she superciliously sipped her coffee before continuing.

‘Beatrix Perceval told me that she’d heard that the boys saw you in the witch’s room in your underpants.’

‘Do you believe gossip?’

‘You didn’t even close the curtains.’

‘This school thrives on fantasy, Deirdre.’

‘You were rolling around the floor with the witch.’

‘I was playing draughts.’

'More like strip poker!'

'Beatrix probably works for the News of the World.'

'She described your underpants. The sexless, military grey ones.'

'There's nothing wrong with my underpants.'

'So she was right. You were seducing the bloody witch!'

Killer placed his coffee hurriedly on their newly acquired walnut, table. As he lounged back irritably on the saffron coloured Danish sofa, he noticed that Deirdre appeared triumphant. There was a smug look on her face, which Killer found annoying. Bloody Beatrix. Why couldn't that woman keep her mouth shut for once? Moreover, why didn't Marian close those damned curtains? At the time, he was too involved in sexual pleasure, too often the architect of a person's fall from grace. Marian was good at getting him aroused and in the ensuing euphoria, reason rapidly vanished. She was certainly eager to make up for the lost time since her husband died. After their tryst, Killer tried to calm things down but Marian was very insistent and talked about 'wanting it regular'. Although, he'd enjoyed his fling, Killer didn't wish to lose Deirdre. He realised that he'd been negligent and that she'd been going through a difficult period after the birth of Barney. Killer just wished that she hadn't nagged so much, when he had so many lessons to prepare and duties to fulfil. Not only was he teaching and being a housemaster, but he was also an officer in the boys Combined Cadet Force, something that both he and the school took very seriously indeed. Still, he needed to placate Deirdre, otherwise she would vamoose up north to her parents with Barney.

'She deserved to have sugar in her bed,' affirmed Deirdre vindictively.

'Deirdre, please,' pleaded Killer.

'I'm tempted to congratulate young Boot on such splendid work,'

'You'll do no such thing.'

'Mind you, I'd have added some sticky egg custard.'

'Deirdre, calm down.'

'She slept with my bloody husband.'

'It won't happen again.'

'The woman has no conscience, no respect.'

'We got carried away.'
'And now you're a laughing stock in boxer shorts.'
'That'll die down.'
'Not when they're calling you Killer Pants-Off !'
'I'll deal with that.'
'How? By thrashing more boys?'
'By ignoring it.'
'It's you that needs the bloody thrashing.'
'Calm down, Deirdre.'
'For brazen infidelity!'

Deirdre sat triumphantly on a light green armchair. She was glad to have released her feelings about the Witch of Wigan. Still, she knew that more needed to be resolved with Alexander 'Killer' Roy than his exposure in boxer shorts. As they talked further, Deirdre admitted that she had been preoccupied with looking after Barney and lost interest in sex. She frequently felt worn out and irritable, especially as Barney was hyperactive. In response, Killer told her that he felt rejected and had become frustrated.

When Deirdre suggested that he might help with some domestic chores, Killer looked bewildered. 'Surely, bathing children and dealing with nappies was a woman's work?' he persuaded himself. He wasn't going to air his concerns publicly, as he realised that he had to compromise. So reluctantly, he agreed to do some nappy training and promise to carry out the task at least twice a week, once he became skilled in that delicate art. He also agreed to read Barney stories every night that he was at home and not on house duty. Eventually, he also accepted that he should do more washing up, an activity he hated. He just hoped that he'd be able to cope with such duties, which weren't the norm for most of the husbands he knew. The thought of cleaning Barney's crappy nappies didn't exactly fill him with inexorable enthusiasm. Still, he realised that if he wanted Deirdre to be more reasonable, he'd have to contribute more domestically. Consequently, he went along with it.

However, that still left Killer with how to deal with Marian, who wasn't going to be enamoured by rejection, especially as their affair had only just started. Killer thought it best not to personally engage with her but just be amenable over work matters. Killer didn't think it would be easy but he'd try. In contrast, Deirdre found the conversation with Killer very therapeutic. Her initial anger dissipated after she'd got him to face his responsibilities. Still, she was going to keep a wary eye on underpants Killer, as she certainly didn't intend to lose him to malicious Marian. Relaxed and confident, she came over to the sofa and sat next to him.

'No more dalliances with the Witch of Wigan?'

'Ok.'

'Let's make more time for each other.'

'Yes, let's.'

'What about the pupils giggling?'

'Don't worry. They'll stop. After all, I'm not called Killer for nothing.'

Deirdre laughed and moved her long, sensuous body closer to his. They kissed for some time. Eventually, Killer gently disentangled himself,

'A new start eh?' proposed Killer.

'Yes but get rid of that bloody woman,' warned Deirdre.

'You know Deirdre. She gets lonely sometimes. Like you.'

'Probably.'

'So don't make a melodrama out of it.'

'Ok.'

'Regard it as an aberration. '

'Yes, an aberration in boxer shorts!'

They laughed nervously and then kissed even more passionately until Deirdre suddenly drew away.

'I'd better check on Barney,' she said with concern.

'I'll come up with you,' volunteered Killer.

Deirdre moved quickly upstairs, while Killer looked around the drawing room, turned out the lights and followed her.

Hayes was glad to get out of the school and have a break from Sully, One Ball and Bayliss's patriotic Henry V. It was certainly good to see his mother and Poppy again and venture into the town. As they made their way to the local fun fair, Hannah gave him a warm, generous smile. He was pleased that she was happy. Hayes always knew that going through the divorce and restarting her life with two young children was never going to be easy. He felt guilty that he hadn't thought more about her. Somehow, during term time, the school took over everything and the family became more distant. They became people from whom you just received letters, especially as the boys weren't allowed to phone home. Hayes assumed this was part of the school's character building process to be independent and self-reliant. Unfortunately, this meant that he buried his family worries in the activities of the school: work, games, drama and of course the Sully-One Ball fracas. Consequently, their visits became a gateway to tenuous reconnection. Still, he was very happy to see them again.

As soon as they got off the local bus, Hayes and Poppy rushed to the dodgems. The funfair wasn't on a par with Battersea's. It was much smaller, being amidst rough spare ground, but it still had much to commend it, not least the dodgem cars that they both wanted to drive.

'Together or separate,' queried a young attendant with Brylcreem-saturated hair, tight jeans and a black leather jacket.

'Separate,' yelled Poppy, obviously relishing the thought of going bumper to bumper.

'Ok, love, that'll be 8 shillings for two,' demanded the attendant, holding out his hand in expectation.

'Mum!' implored Poppy, getting into a lather of excitement.

Hannah, who'd been quietly observing the proceedings, took out her purse from her handbag and handed a 10 shilling note to the young attendant.

'Thank you' said the young lad, putting the note firmly in a wallet and giving Hannah two tickets and her change. 'Over here,' he indicated, while walking at the side of the track.

'Here you are,' he proclaimed, hooking in a car with a long pole. 'Ladies first,' announced the young man, inviting Poppy into the car.

'How long have we got?' enquired Poppy, stepping into the vehicle.

'5 minutes love. You go when the siren starts,' instructed the attendant, leaving her in the car. He then told Hayes to follow him as he sauntered further down the circuit, while whistling an erratic version of Rock-A-Bye Your Baby.

'Right, now you mate. Here you are,' stated the attendant, hooking another car with his pole and dragging it closer.

'Thanks,' replied Hayes, excited at the prospect of some collateral damage.

'Like the gear, mate.'

'It's the school uniform.'

'Blimey I thought you came from a fancy dress party!'

'Oh, really.'

'Yeah, we get a lot of parties and stag dos.'

'Really?'.

'They go completely barmy. Total nutters.'

The attendant walked away chuckling as he moved towards a yellow booth and gave the thumbs up sign.

Meanwhile, Hayes made himself comfortable, equating himself with Stirling Moss at the starting line. Suddenly, the siren blared and although Hayes got off to a flying start, he soon discovered that a manic Poppy was just behind him.

'Got yer!' she screamed, as she bumped into the rear of her brother's car.

'Be careful!' exclaimed a despairing Hannah from the sidelines.

Ignoring such maternal advice, Poppy sped off to the other side of the track. Immediately, Hayes cut across the circuit and stopped her circling around, by hitting the side of her car.

'1-1!' shouted Hayes, while bumping her and triumphantly speeding away.

The two cars circled each other menacingly as Hannah sauntered around the edge of the track, fearful of how it might end. Poppy was now becoming a dodgem vigilante seeking vengeance, not only on her brother but also on all who got in her way. Mercilessly, she bumped into the back of a young father, who was in a car with his terrified young son. The Dad, smartly attired in a dark blue coat and a herringbone flat cap, smiled meekly at Poppy, while his young son, with a cub badge on his windcheater jacket, nearly choked on his stick of rock. Poppy then made a quick getaway as an increasingly confident Hayes pursued her. Just as her brother was about to pin her in a corner, she escaped, spun round and gave his car a hefty bump. '2-1,' she cried as she sped away, looking to pounce on another victim. This time it was a young mother in a blue woollen coat, who was with her bobble-hatted small child. As Poppy ruthlessly attacked the back of their car with a celebratory bump, the shaken young mum laughed nervously, while her daughter screamed and stared at Poppy as if she was deranged. In the meantime, Hayes was determined not to allow his sister to get away with her rampage and as she was leaving her latest victims, he bumped the front of her car.

'2-2,' yelled Hayes jubilantly, as he dashed away victoriously.

Poppy ignored her brother. She would choose her moment to retaliate. In the meantime, she cruised around the track looking for another victim. Eventually, she found some teds, who were just in front of her, and duly crashed into them. The teds turned round and confronted her. One was a young man with long sideburns and a large quiff, which dangled profusely over his forehead. He was sporting a velvet collared black jacket with a matching bootlace tie. He looked angrily at Poppy while his girlfriend, a young woman with a pile of curly blonde hair and wearing a long Edwardian coat, glowered threateningly.

'You made a mistake there love,' accused the ted.

'You certainly did,' echoed the lady ted.

'I don't like being surprised,' continued the ted.

'Nor do I. It upsets me' repeated the lady ted.

'Sorry,' said Poppy, 'but it is the dodgems.'

'I know it's the bloody dodgems. Do you think I'm thick?' challenged the ted.

'No, of course not,' refuted Poppy.

'I bet you do. You're posh and you think I'm thick as pig shit,' insisted the ted.

'I didn't say you were thick,' maintained Poppy defensively.

'Well I'm not. I was going to a grammar,' claimed the ted.

'That's right. He was second in the class at maths,' declared the lady ted admiringly.

'I had to go and work for me Dad on the stall,' disclosed the ted.

Observing this altercation in the middle of the track, the dodgem attendant was getting increasingly annoyed.

'Get moving!' the attendant screamed from the side. 'What you doing? You can't stop there.'

'Ok, mate, don't get shirty. We had a problem with Little Miss Muffet here,' the ted shouted back.

'I don't care if you had a problem with Muffin the Mule. Get moving. It's dangerous stopping,' projected the attendant loudly.

'All right. We 'eard you. Keep your hair on!' shouted the lady ted venomously, before confiding to her partner that 'he's worse than the cops.'

'You're a lucky lady, love. A very lucky lady,' uttered the ted, staring dramatically at Poppy, before racing off at such an alarming speed that the lady ted filled the air with orgasmic shrieks.

Just as Poppy was about to turn and start her patrol again, Hayes bumped into the back of her, to the accompaniment of Poppy's frantic scream.

'3-2,' he asserted triumphantly, darting away like Stirling from a pit stop.

Poppy was frustrated that the bloody teds had allowed her brother to bump her. As she stalked the track looking for revenge, Poppy saw Hannah looking on hopelessly from the side, like a despairing football manager on a touchline unable to control the actions of his players. When eventually she discovered Hayes chatting to two teenage girls that he'd just bumped, she drove into him from behind.

'3-3,' she yelled and departed swiftly into the traffic.

'Who's that?' said an aggrieved blonde.

'My sister,' admitted Hayes.

'She's a bit mental,' suggested the other girl, a wary brunette wearing a turquoise scarf.

'No she's fine, just rather competitive.' revealed Hayes. 'I'd better make sure she doesn't hit me. Bye,' and suddenly he spurted off to the other side of the track.

'What strange kids,' pondered the bewildered brunette.

'Don't worry about them. Let's get bumping!' exclaimed the blonde, driving towards the other cars with ferocious intent.

While Hayes scoured the track looking for his sister, his mother sat next to the circuit with her Manchester Guardian.

She was reading about how Dr Nkrumah was going to make Ghana a thriving independent state. She realised that it was the end of an era and that British colonial power was unravelling. She thought that the children faced an uncertain future, what with the decline of our empire, the cold war and the nuclear arms race. Hannah then hastily decided to move on to the arts page and find something more life affirming. Thankfully, she discovered that Laurence Olivier was due to appear shortly at the Royal Court Theatre. Apparently, he's going to play an old music hall comedian. 'Goodness,' she thought, 'that'll be a change after wearing all those tights over the years.'

Hayes tracked Poppy as she was circling a lively young couple. The driver was wearing a Panama hat and ostentatiously smoking a cigar, while steering with one hand. His female companion, who had a smartly parted fringe and long flowing curly hair, was laughing hysterically. Her bright, multi-coloured jacket with its array of Caribbean colours enlivened an overcast afternoon. Poppy decided to add to their hilarity by bumping them from behind, which only incited them to further delirium. Just as she turned her car away from this bedlam, her gleeful brother bumped her in the front and screeched '4-3!' However, before battle could continue, the siren wailed and all the cars ground to a halt. Poppy and Hayes reluctantly departed from their vehicles and moved towards Hannah, who was now engrossed in an article by Neville Cardus, who believed that The Magic Flute is the only opera that could have been composed by God.

After the exhilaration of the dodgem contest, Poppy made vociferous demands to go to the crazy house. Hannah then realised that her hopes for a leisurely return to the school had vanished. Instead, Poppy's relentless pursuit of visceral excitement, supported by Hayes's own enthusiasm for the bizarre attraction, won the day. Hannah relented with a benign, loving smile and they all made their way to experience some unconventional entertainment. Hayes and Poppy had been to the crazy house at Battersea Park and found it 'really scary', so they were eager to be terrified again. This one looked like something out of a grotesque fairy tale with its sloped white roof and slanted attics. Various bizarre hoardings advertised activities like ‘Fanny’s Fangs’ and ‘Bloody Mary’. A ghostly white lamppost and a green plinth, on which there was the head of a monkey with black sunglasses, surrounded the entrance. Hannah viewed such melodramatic absurdities with a satirical eye and had no fears about her children’s safety.

When Hannah went to get tickets, she encountered Madame, who was sitting in a slanted white cubicle. She soon discovered that in fact Madame was a man. Madame’s face was full of eye shadow, rouge and lipstick, a well coiffured brown wig, large golden earrings and various exotic bracelets. When she gave Hannah her change, she replied in a deep baritone voice. Hayes and Poppy were taken aback by the colourful person in their midst but it was no surprise to Hannah. She told the children that she’d seen such people during the war, when she went to nightclubs with friends.

As Hayes and Poppy climbed up the creaky wooden stairs, they confronted posters of James Dean and Marilyn Monroe. A frenetic electric guitar soundtrack, mixed with intermittent fearful shrieks, accompanied them on their journey. Suddenly, a white skeleton dropped down from the ceiling and Poppy yelled, throwing herself into Hayes’s arms. Although Hayes was also shocked, he reassured Poppy as best he could and they proceeded to ascend the winding staircase.

When they reached the first floor and opened a door, they confronted more cries and yells and a lady in a bath, supposedly dead. Lying across an enamel tub in a dark blue swimsuit, her silver hair, pallid face and grey lips conjured up some ancient waxen effigy. Hayes and Poppy were about to leave, when the lady abruptly arose, parading deadly fangs and laughing hysterically, as the volume of cacophonous music quickly increased. The two children then hastily left ‘Fanny’s Fangs’ and closed the door with a violent bang.

Hayes and Poppy looked at each other with nervous excitement. They held each other’s hands as they went upstairs, passing hysterical children who were moving down. When they arrived on the next floor, they discovered a young woman wearing deathly pale make up in a claustrophobic dark room. She wore a black bikini and a noose hanging from an overhead pole, was around her neck. Blood dripped from her lips and sinister shadows appeared ominously on the wall behind her. The atmosphere was compellingly macabre. Hayes and Poppy gazed at the vampire-like woman with anxious anticipation. Then, this strange creature swiftly burst free from the noose and started dancing. However, the accompanying music wasn't a soothing melody from Those were the Days but something more rhythmically harsh and anarchic. Arms akimbo, the lady in the bikini started moving haphazardly, rushing from one side of the room to the other in demonic fashion. She then raised her hands as if to summon greater spiritual power, banged the walls as if she was urgently demanding freedom and finally concluded with a terrifying cry as she did the splits. The power of 'Bloody Mary's' intense performance totally overwhelmed Hayes and Poppy.

Inspired by this outlandish act, they went upstairs to pursue further excitement. On their arrival, brother and sister moved eagerly to engage with the crazy mirrors, which grotesquely distorted the body. They entered a crowded room and started making faces at the surrounding glass, creating various malignant disfigurements. Meanwhile, disapproving parents ushered their progeny away from such threatening abnormality. Hayes and Poppy were in an irrepressible mood, sharing their inventions with mischievous devilry. Hayes was now creating his own version of Frankenstein, pulling ludicrously twisted faces at the mirror, while Poppy responded with helpless mirth. As he screwed up his face to become even more abominable, suddenly the contorted image of a fearsome One Ball confronted Hayes in the mirror. Immediately, the junior screamed as if he'd woken up from a nightmare.

'Hello Hayes,' proclaimed a severe One Ball.

'Are you ok, Tommy?' asked a concerned Poppy.

'I think so,' thought Hayes, tentatively, recovering from the shock of such a terrifying vision. 'This is my sister Potts,' he announced, looking to divert the conversation to more formal matters.

'I remember,' acknowledged One Ball.

'Hello,' said Poppy perfunctorily. 'We're leaving now,' she added hastily.

'So am I,' asserted One Ball with an alarming grin.

Hayes, Poppy and One Ball then started to descend the long and winding staircase. A commanding One Ball led the way without regard to the others. It was as if he was intent on showing leadership in front of his squit and Poppy. When they reached the first floor landing, they saw a blonde-haired woman in an exotic red and yellow dressing gown. The vivacious blonde was moving towards a door, which was engraved with the sign Private Staff Only. Hayes and Poppy recognised the woman as the lady in the bath. They now realised that when she was performing, she'd been wearing a wig.

'Maybe there's more than one lady in the bath?' queried Poppy, scrambling down the remaining steps.

'And probably another girl in the black bikini?' submitted Hayes.

'They must be doing it between acting or dancing jobs,' thought Poppy.

'Of course,' asserted One Ball abruptly, as if his two companions were on a significantly lower plane of intelligence. 'They have a rota. They couldn't be doing that kind of performance without a break.'

'I'm all for workers' rights,' declared Poppy.

'It's nothing to do with workers' rights. Just common sense,' replied One Ball disdainfully.

By this time, the group had reached the entrance, where they discovered Hannah and Martha sitting on a bench, having an animated conversation. Hayes proudly noted that his mother was wearing a fashionable green swing coat, in comparison to Martha's fustian grey one. The mothers greeted the children with warm smiles, while enquiring about their explorations. Poppy led the way by giving lurid descriptions of the fangs, hanging noose and monstrously deformed images. Hayes downplayed Poppy's hyperbolic fantasies, so that the mothers didn't become too alarmed. In contrast, One Ball was silent and brooding, but even grim James Potts admitted that the experience was worth the money, if a little ridiculous.

The mothers had decided that they would all travel back to the school together. One Ball dreaded the outcome of this decision. Extended social conversations with your squit were not to be encouraged. Being too friendly, introduced hierarchical complications. One Ball didn't think Hayes was a bad squit but neither was he a brilliant one. He still had things to learn, like polishing shoes so that one could see oneself in the tips. He also could be better at sewing as One Ball recently discovered when a button dropped from his coat while he bestrode the Quadrangle. One Ball was frustrated that his mother didn't understand how the school worked. It wasn't a community centre, it was a place of learning. There was a sense of companionship but there was also a pecking order and getting too friendly with juniors wasn't advisable. It undermined the natural order.

In any case, One Ball was suspicious of his squit's relationship with the hapless Sully. He had fears that Hayes was colluding with the blundering junior. He had recently observed them in earnest conversation in the lavatory, only to note that as soon as he entered to urinate, the discussion abruptly halted and the two boys resorted to incongruous small talk. Although he still intended to pressurise Rutter and use the photos as evidence to fully convince an indecisive Major, One Ball still needed Sully as a supporting witness. Consequently, he didn't want him distracted by a devious squit.

The train back to the school was late. A voice on a muffled loudspeaker informed passengers, in a scarcely audible estuary tone, that the delay was due to 'leaves on the track'. One Ball felt angry about such unacceptable inefficiency but the others were more relaxed. Martha, in particular, used the time to tell Hannah about her work at the Red Cross charity shop. While she didn't earn much money, she enjoyed meeting the customers. She was also now going to adult education classes to improve her chances of getting a decent job. Martha was studying sociology and was keen to get into social work. Hannah admired her tenacity and told her that she would be good at such a job. This flattering judgement was reached more by intuition than reason, as Hannah didn't have a detailed knowledge of such institutions. Poppy joined the chat and said that she didn't really know what she wanted to do, apart from go to university and study PPE. Nevertheless, she was sure that she wouldn't just get married and settle down. The mothers seemed to dismiss Poppy's radicalism with condescending smiles, as if it was just the consequence of the impractical dreams of idealistic youth.

Meanwhile, One Ball and Hayes meandered on the platform, eyeing each other warily. One Ball felt uncomfortable mixing his family life with his school one. He became increasingly irritated that his mother seemed insensitive to his position in James B and his responsibilities. He thought that the closer she got to Mrs Hayes, the more difficult it became for him to do his duties impartially. Hayes observed that One Ball looked isolated and tense. He neither seemed to relax with his mother nor with the Hayes family. Without the superficial authority given to him by the school, he seemed a diminished figure.

'How's the squit getting on?' enquired Hannah, eyeing One Ball's discomfort and looking to bring him into the conversation.

'He's doing all right,' replied One Ball tentatively.

Suddenly, the train arrived and the Hayes and Potts families got into the small and dusty empty carriage, with its jaded brown luggage rack and pictures of various British landmarks. The families sat opposite each other and settled down for the short journey. Hannah smiled at Martha, who then turned to One Ball and articulated her apprehension.

'I hope there's no bullying at the school, darling.'

'No none, is there Hayes?' replied One Ball, staring intensely across the carriage at his squit.

'Well no but..' stuttered Hayes.

'Can't you just call him by his name?' interrupted Martha, disliking such impersonal formalities.

'I just have mother,' insisted One Ball.

'I meant his Christian name,' clarified Martha.

'But to me he's Hayes,' claimed One Ball intransigently.

'Why?' persisted Martha.

'We don't call people by Christian names,' asserted One Ball.

'You know he's Tommy,' continued Martha incredulously.

'That's not how the school works,' emphasised One Ball.

'That's really odd,' thought Poppy.

'It's a form of objectivity,' stated One Ball.

'It sounds very militarised,' said Hannah critically.

'That's good. Everybody is treated equally,' countered One Ball.

'But you have privileges, don't you?' pursued Hannah.

'Only after I'm a senior and I've earned them,' explained One Ball.

'But you seem to be running the house not the masters,' remarked an agitated Martha.

'We're self-governing. That way, it's more efficient,' elaborated One Ball.

'From what I've heard, it seems that you have too much control,' interrupted Poppy.

'The masters can't be around all the time. So it makes sense for monitors to have authority on the ground,' argued One Ball irritably.

'Not if you abuse it,' asserted a perceptive Poppy.

'That's why there's concern about bullying, darling,' stressed Martha.

'Discipline and punishment isn't bullying mother,' disputed One Ball.

'I'm not keen on boys having so much authority,' responded Hannah.

'If we abuse it, we're punished,' deduced One Ball.

Until this moment, Hayes had been quiet. Now, he believed that this was a good time to put pressure on One Ball for his treatment of the bedevilled Sully.

'That's right, Potts but it could be hard to prove,' believed Hayes.

'What do you mean Hayes?' challenged One Ball rigorously.

'Well, the only people who can witness bullying are other boys and they can be silenced,' rationalised Hayes provocatively.

'There are other monitors and seniors around,' accentuated One Ball.

'Yes, but they could keep quiet so they're not accused of being a sneak,' maintained Hayes.

'That's highly unlikely Hayes,' insisted a supercilious One Ball. 'Boys are chosen to be monitors because they have impeccable credentials, like strong moral fibre.'

‘Strong moral fibre! My goodness darling that sounds a bit high and mighty,’ exclaimed a bemused Martha.

‘Maybe, but it’s true,’ avowed an offended One Ball.

The train was now not far away from the school station as the late afternoon turned to evening. From the window, figures in the rural landscape became less distinct.

‘I wanted you to go to the school to not only achieve academically but also to learn how to be a good citizen. I didn’t want you to be educated at a regimented military academy,’ affirmed Martha, energetically continuing the argument.

‘I agree with you wholeheartedly Martha,’ corroborated Hannah.

‘So do I,’ added Poppy, ardently completing feminine agreement.

As the train pulled into the station and both families gathered their belongings, Hayes was delighted that they’d rigorously questioned One Ball. Maybe he would now be more cautious in the way he treated Sully. Hayes certainly hoped so, as he clambered out of the carriage and made his way with the others towards the school.

Despite meeting One Ball and hearing his dubious opinions, Hayes enjoyed the afternoon. The visits of his mother and Poppy always made him feel buoyant. No doubt, he’ll be a little tearful later in the evening when he’ll feel their absence, but he thought that he’d get over it. As both parents and their children went out of the station, the irrepressible Poppy ran ahead and started playing hopscotch. A joyful Hannah and a smiling Martha both enjoyed the eccentricity of Poppy’s athleticism. Even One Ball stopped looking blankly ahead and grinned. An evocative evening sunset hovered over the playing fields and the school’s imposing buildings, as they all moved nearer James B.

Barrett had just finished seeing Chuck Carson for some help with his Irish accent. Although it was difficult to get the redoubtable rocker to stop talking about the turbulent background of his pop idol, he eventually gave him valuable advice on Ulster vowels. After leaving Jasper A and its Chuck Berry devotee, Barrett went and practised his Macmorris accent in the less conspicuous space of Open Way. While wandering down a path adjoining that vast area, a lumbering figure ran slowly towards him and he instantly stopped his theatrical endeavours. Barrett soon discovered that the struggling athlete in a black and white striped rugby shirt was an ungainly Sully.

'What are you doing Sully?' asked an incredulous Barrett, witnessing the bulky junior's desperate attempts to become Roger Bannister.

'Practising. I'm trying to improve my running,' justified a breathless Sully, stopping in front of his friend.

'Why Sully?'

'So I can show progress with my times?'

'Do you think One Ball will care?'

'He might show leniency.'

'I doubt it.'

'Don't say that Barrett. Ever since I got these punishments, they've been hanging over me like a dark cloud. It's beginning to drive me crazy. It's like being in a prison.'

'A prison?'

'Yes. A mental prison.'

Eventually, Barrett calmed down the fretful Sully and they sauntered together down the path.

'Has One Ball reported Rutter yet?' mentioned Barrett.

'No he hasn't,' corroborated Sully confidently.

'Interesting,' ruminated Barrett, contemplating One Ball's strategy.

They were coming to the end of the Open Way path before Copse Grove and returning to James B. As they were both free this Saturday morning, and wished to talk further, they decided to turn round and walk towards the pavilion.

'You know Hayes met One Ball and his mother in the town,' relayed Barrett as they approached the colts' pitch.

'Yes. He told me. At the funfair,' confirmed Sully, now jogging beside him in a feeble attempt to continue his fitness regime.

'Has One Ball summoned you for punishment runs since that visit?'

'No. He hasn't but he doesn't seem to have changed.'

'But the pressure is building?'

'What pressure?'

'Sulls. Mrs Potts and Mrs Hayes disapprove of the school's whole structure. They've threatened to talk to the Major.'

'But they haven't have they? And my punishments are still in the book. It's like being on death row.'

'Oh for goodness sake, Sulls. You sound as if you've been reading The People.'

'It's ok for you to laugh Barrett but you haven't been given the punishment.'

'I know it's hard, but you mustn't allow emotion to cloud your judgement. That's what bloody One Ball wants.'

'It's just that I'm getting really anxious about it.'

'Don't. There are others in an even worse situation.'

'Like who?'

'Rutter and Françoise. He could be expelled. She could be sacked.'

'I've heard that Rutter's still got One Ball's camera.'

'They must be planning something.'

'You really think so?'

'I'm pretty sure. So you need to stay calm. Do nothing. Just tell me if One Ball reminds you about the punishments. Then we'll respond accordingly.'

'Really? Ok. Thanks.'

'You need to think of something else, Sulls. Like Mistress Quickly.'

'Maybe.'

'Know your lines?'

'Sort of. But I hate being a woman.'

'I've been practising my accent. These gruff Irish sounds are bloody impossible.'

'Did you manage to listen to Danny Blanchflower?'

'I heard him once but it's really Chuck that's helping me.'

'Good. At least, that might stop him going on about his hero's illegal misdeeds.'

'I doubt it.'

The boys maintained their trundling progress, embracing a sunny spring day and the expansive green grass before them. After they reached the pavilion, Barrett turned round to his friend with a wide smile on his face.

'Oh by the way Sulls, you'll make a fabulous woman!'

Sully suddenly started to attack Barrett with mock punches, as they went past the pavilion towards the 1st XV rugby pitch. Barrett fended off the phantom attacks and the two boys continued around Open Way.

Later, after lunch on the following Sunday, Rutter met Françoise. They had made their own way to a discreet destination, a bench behind a small wood off the path to the pavilion. Rutter was in his school uniform and Françoise was wearing a brown leather jacket, tight blue jeans and black boots. Her hair was in a neat bun that highlighted her high cheekbones. Rutter looked around to make sure that no one was in the vicinity and then moved to embrace her. She willingly accepted the invitation and they kissed for several minutes, exploring each other with youthful verve and imagination. Before such cavorting reached the point of no return, Rutter remembered the main purpose of their meeting and reluctantly disentangled himself from Françoise's embrace.

'What's wrong?' said a disappointed Françoise.

'It's time for reeling,' demanded Rutter.

'I suppose so,' conceded Françoise, remembering that they needed to thwart One Ball.

'You should write a letter to One Ball,' proposed Rutter.

'A letter,' queried Françoise.

'It should be a letter with an invitation.'

'To do what?'

'To arrange an assignation with him?

'A what, monsieur?'

'A personal appointment, Françoise.'

'Ah, un rendez-vous.'

'Yes. Exactly.'

Françoise then paused and conjured up her role model for the so-called assignation.

'Ok. I'll summon up my inner Barbara.'

'Who?'

'Barbara Stanwyck.'

'Whatever reels him in, Françoise.'

'You and your bloody reeling!'

A railway track was next to the secluded area and trains chugged past, leaving a trail of smoke in their wake. Against this accompaniment, Rutter, placing his arm gently around Françoise's shoulder, reminded her that it was a case of playing a game that needed to be won, so that they both could remain at the school. Rutter was confident that Françoise could take advantage of One Ball's vulnerable desire to feel attractive. He was also convinced that she could control the situation, while being sufficiently encouraging. Rutter thought that the more One Ball had hope, the more he would be under Françoise's thumb. If One Ball felt that he could seduce Françoise, there was a good chance that he'd neither pursue them nor bully Sully.

When Rutter discovered that Françoise played tennis and had been coached to a reasonable standard, he had an idea. He suggested that she invited One Ball for a game on the court next to the athletics track. Rutter believed that now was the time for Françoise to indeed learn from Miss Stanwyck, and be a femme fatale who would ensnare a naive One Ball.

Although Françoise found the school a bewildering mixture of academic excellence, eccentric imagination and downright stupidity, she could no longer avoid meeting One Ball. Initially, the thought of seducing the conceited monitor filled her with revulsion. However, when inspired by Barbara, she felt more comfortable 'reeling in' the arrogant bully and then discarding him like rubbish. In fact, she was now looking forward to playing the role. As she embraced her alter ego, Françoise started imagining what she might wear to be a femme fatale extraordinaire. Rutter told her not to rush and warned her that it will take time to have One Ball under control. She should remember that One Ball wasn't unintelligent, even though he was emotionally immature. Rutter thought that initially Françoise should write him a letter, inviting him to play tennis.

'I'll need help with that,' admitted Françoise.

'May I be your teacher?' requested Rutter, miraculously producing a notebook and a ballpoint pen out of his coat pocket.

'You planned all this!'

'Let's say I had them available, if you agreed.'

'You're terrible.'

‘Ok, let Monsieur Le Terrible write the letter with you. You start,’ proposed Rutter, clicking his ballpoint.

‘Ok. Cher. Sorry. Dear One Ball.’

‘No, Françoise. Call him by his name. You’re Barbara, remember?’

‘I don’t know him by his name. Only as One Ball.’

‘Jim. Jim Potts is his name.’

‘Ok. Dear Jim.’

‘On second thoughts, it’d be best to address him as James. Conservative formality is more likely to impress him.’

‘Right. Dear James, I’m writing to see if you’d like to come and have a game of tennis.’

‘Ok, that’s the easy bit,’ said Rutter, scribbling away. ‘First, we’ve first got to flatter him, give him hope. Come on Barbara, you remember the letters you wrote to your lover, the insurance man, what’s his name?’

‘Fred MacMurray.’

‘Yes. That’s the man. You can bamboozle One Ball in the same way.

Rutter encouraged Françoise to fantasise. The letter needed to be personal and enticing with an offer that he was unlikely to refuse. Rutter encouraged Françoise to express delight that she’s now free to see One Ball. They enjoyed bouncing ideas off each other, as together they weaved a pattern that combined romance, sport and finally poetry. Françoise suggested a quote from Baudelaire but given One Ball’s implacable patriotism, Rutter thought it best to choose a romantic English poet like Rupert Brooke. Eventually, they both fell upon the bench laughing uproariously about their own creative concoction: the imaginary break-up of their relationship, the exaggeration of One Ball’s irresistible sexual allure and their deception by verse.

After they had recovered from their outburst of mirth, Françoise folded the draft letter and put it in the pocket of her jacket. She agreed to find a quote from the recommended Mr Brooke, send the letter on scented paper, place it in a colourful envelope and address it to Mr James Potts Esquire. Rutter thought that such formality gave the letter stature and class. One Ball would fall for that.

The two conspirators revelled in their strategic insolence and couldn't wait to see Potts appear on the tennis court. Rutter was confident that Françoise could control the emotionally fragile One Ball. In fact, the French maid was very much looking forward to being the Barbara Stanwyck of Sussex.

'Supposing he starts suspecting and becomes aggressive,' said Françoise, fearing the worst.

'Unlikely as he needs to be careful,' assured Rutter calmly.

'Why?'

'Being with a woman in a public place.'

'He could still turn nasty.'

'Don't worry, I'll be watching.'

'Where?'

'In the shrubbery. Next to the athletics track.'

'But that's too far away.'

'No it isn't. I'll have binoculars.'

'Anyway, I'll yell, if he goes crazy.'

'Don't worry. You'll twist him around your little finger. He talks big but emotionally he's a baby.'

'You're right. I'll concentrate on playing him like a piano.'

'You'll enjoy doing that. It could be fun.'

'You've never seen my musical skills.'

'I look forward to doing so.'

'So will One Ball!'

The two accomplices laughed, checked that no one was in the vicinity and kissed. They revelled in the excitement of their devilish ploy. They would have loved to go to the pavilion immediately and yet again defile the home dressing room. Frustratingly, it was still too risky to return to their preferred rendezvous. It just wasn't possible until they'd neutralised One Ball. Consequently, they looked around again to make sure there weren't any intruders and just as another train made its way to London, they kissed passionately. They were going to make the best use of the worn bench that they could.

By some quirk of fate, James B were to play Ironside A in the final of the House Rugby Cup Final. In other words, it was One Ball versus Rutter. In their semi-final, James B had narrowly beaten Morton B, who had suffered from mysterious injuries to their best players. In contrast, Ironside A won theirs easily against Wade A, their heavy scrum terrorising the opposition into submission. One Ball was determined that this wouldn't happen to James B under his captaincy, especially when the odious Rutter was the leader of their opponents. Therefore, for him this game was personal. In any case, James B had a reputation for sporting prowess and winning cups was second nature to its very ethos. The Major thought of it as a positive reflection on how he managed the house. Although he wasn't a sporting expert, he enjoyed basking in the limelight of the boys' success.

On the afternoon of the final, a substantial crowd congregated around the 1st XV pitch, which lay some four hundred yards beyond the pavilion. Hayes, Barrett and Sully, all wearing their uniform and the school's black scarf, were among their house's many supporters. Killer was also there in a gabardine grey raincoat and so was Marian aka the Witch of Wigan, wearing a boyish newsboy cap. Killer tried to avoid her but didn't succeed and Marian directly confronted him.

'Hello stranger!' cried Marian loudly.

'Hello Marian,' responded Killer apprehensively.

'I haven't seen you for some time,' she remarked with critical innuendo.

Killer suddenly moved away from the touchline, as he didn't want Marian to start making a scene in front of the boys. Some of them had already had enough amusement seeing him in his boxer shorts, let alone a revelatory sight of their matron. Thankfully, the consequences of that embarrassment had subsided and neither Killer nor Marian had reported any puerile, derogatory comments from the James B voyeurs. Such was Killer's menacing demeanour that the boys found it advisable to control their sniggers about his infamous sexual indiscretion. Nonetheless, the last thing Killer wanted was Marian to remind them of that calamity. Unfortunately for him, the resolute James matron, ignoring such sensitivities, insisted on holding Killer to account and pursued him relentlessly. Eventually she cornered him thirty yards from the pitch, next to a nearby willow tree.

'Why have you been ignoring me?' Marian challenged the junior housemaster.

'It's been difficult,' admitted Killer, looking for sympathy.

'I feel used,' said Marian accusingly.

'I have a wife and a baby,' explained Killer.

'That didn't worry you when your trousers were off,' observed Marian pointedly.

'Please Marian. We were going through a difficult time,' declared Killer adamantly.

'That doesn't mean you can discard me like toilet paper' retorted Marian angrily.

'Marian, the analogy is inappropriate,' claimed Killer. 'I like you.'

'To screw,' countered Marian venomously.

'Marian, it's difficult at the moment,' pleaded Killer.

'It is for me as well. Being rejected so casually,' insisted Marian forcefully.

'Look. Marian. I'll come and see you when I'm next on duty,' bargained Killer.

'When's that?' pressed Marian suspiciously.

'Next Wednesday?' confirmed Killer.

'You can't just treat me as a plaything,' stated Marian disdainfully.

'Ok, Marian. Now let's get back to watching the game. It's an important one for the house and they need our support,' emphasised Killer, nervously trying to change the subject by rallying community spirit.

'Maybe. But you can't just treat people so carelessly,' stressed Marian, tightening the belt of her dark brown coat.

'I'll see you on Wednesday,' repeated Killer.

'You'd better,' warned Marian.

As they began to walk back towards the touchline, Killer made an observation.

'I like the cap.'

'Thank you,' replied Marian cautiously.

'You can certainly deliver my paper anytime,' teased Killer, with a mischievous glimmer in his eye.

There seemed to be a hint of a smile on Marian's face, as they diverged and diplomatically moved to different areas of the increasingly large crowd. Hayes and his friends had noted Killer's tête a tête with matron. This had induced further hilarity, especially when Boot arrived and expressed his desire to add salad cream to the Wigan witch's bed. As Marian berated Boot incessantly, the junior thought that the house's matron made the weird sisters in Macbeth seem like girls next door. Binns then joined the group and noticed Françoise, in a tightly fitting red coat and a jauntily placed matching beret, coming towards them. On viewing this vision, Binns had a sudden desire to practise his French. Unfortunately, his thoughts didn't match his actions and as she passed the boys, he became speechless and just gave her a modest smile of recognition.

Meanwhile, Brown and Bunter approached the pitch, acknowledging the juniors while singing He's Got the Whole World in His Hands. Straight away, Hayes and co belted out the chorus as they clapped their hands to the gospel rhythm. Brown and Bunter then started changing the lyrics to accommodate the names of the James team. Accordingly, they all chanted, 'He's Got Captain Jim Potts in His Hands!' He's Got Captain Jim Potts in his Hands!' followed by 'He's got Randy Rice in His Hands! He's Got Randy Rice in His Hands!' reminding everybody of that boy's obsession with movie lovelies. The boys' version of the celebrated gospel song was getting so loud that it was attracting the attention of not only Killer but Smallman, who was now also on the touchline. The various masters gave stern looks towards the improvised choir, as if they were hooligans incarnate. After the singing subsided, Bunter talked about the gospel classic. He'd heard from his Dad, who was an engineer at EMI, that a teenager from Bethnal Green was going to record the song. His name was Laurie London but he reckoned that couldn't be his real name.

As kick off approached, Hayes saw the crowd swell considerably. As various groups emerged, Hayes discerned his bête noire Mrs Hackett, the frosty maths queen. Her laconic husband accompanied her while she held the lead of a shaggy dog. As Mrs H approached the coterie of boys, she greeted Sully like a long lost friend. To which he responded with cringe–making flattery. When Hayes thought that he'd diplomatically try to warm to his nemesis by complimenting her on her lovely collie, she rebuffed him coldly. Mrs Hackett announced in a lofty tone that he was a Polish lowland sheepdog. At that moment, Hayes realised that he was never going to be able to please Mrs Hackett, whatever efforts he made. He would just have to accept that she didn't like him.

Just as he was plunged into the depths of Hackett-induced despair, he and the other boys noticed the arrival of the Major with his shooting stick. The boys' housemaster was wearing a smart charcoal overcoat and thick black shoes. As he passed Hayes and co, he acknowledged them with a big grin and encouraged them to cheer loudly. He was followed by a somewhat disorientated Root, who didn't appear to be a natural rugby fan. The music master, attired in a navy raincoat, stood dutifully next to the Major and appeared unusually restrained. The Major then opened his stick and plumped himself on its seat as he liked to watch from a comfortable, strategic position near the halfway line. By now, Collins had also appeared, with an Ironside rugby shirt displayed over his several pullovers to enhance managerial credibility. He had agreed to be an assistant coach, only because he thought such an activity would help improve his health. Collins wasn't a rugby specialist but he felt that he knew enough about the game to help the team. In fact, 'Whistle' Boland, who accompanied him, was Ironside's chosen coach. A hefty former army man, who ran the gym rigorously, he also wore the house's rugby shirt in similarly conscientious fashion. The two coaches were chatting intensely with Smallman, who was puffing happily on his inevitable Senior Service cigarette. Observing this fraternity, Hayes wondered what plan Boland and Collins had conceived to win the game.

Further along the touchline, Oliver and the Rev Elwyn were having a lively conversation. Elwyn's hair was blowing in the wind, his dog collar was a little awry and his double-breasted camel coat too big for his frame. As usual, Oliver was puritanically sedate, his dull brown raincoat making him look like an inconspicuous clerk. Hayes surmised that it would be more than likely that they were discussing some contested theological point, rather than the forthcoming match.

With only five minutes to go, a plethora of staff invaded the touchlines like busy bees swarming around a hive. Bayliss and Basil looked like two aesthetes trying to adapt to an alien sporting world. Bayliss was wearing a deerstalker like a rural landowner going on a grouse shoot, while Basil's black fedora made that cultured man look like a nineteen thirties mobster. Long John then emerged in a grey mackintosh, hopping along with his walking stick next to Endersby, his burly junior housemaster and ridiculed biology teacher, who was clad in a thick gabardine overcoat and breathing heavily. They certainly made a bizarre double-act as they plodded towards the touchline.

When Sykes, approached, red-faced and impatient, Hayes alerted Binns, given his instinctive distaste for the conservative French teacher. With his tinted glasses, Cossack fur coat and black coat, Binns thought that his nefarious adversary looked like a sinister Soviet agent. Sykes approached Collins and exchanged pleasantries, while only cursorily acknowledging the non-academic Boland. In fact, both teams were receiving special coaching assistance for the final. The boys all agreed that James B were particularly fortunate to have Bowen and Darbishire in their ranks. Standing in their tracksuits at the half way line, they certainly looked the part. At least they'd both played the game at club level, while Collins and Boland had only been in their school teams during a bygone era.

Amidst more people arriving at the pitch, Barrett espied Macready, with his school scarf dramatically entwined around his neck. He was walking with a book in his hand while declaiming to fresh air.

'Look,' signalled an excitable Barrett, 'he's learning his lines'.

'Can he never stop acting?' beseeched Sully.

'He does have a lot to learn,' conceded Boot.

'Even so,' remarked Sully.

'Not exactly the best place,' agreed Binns.

As Macready approached the pitch, the assembled fraternity heard his booming voice projecting Henry V's clarion call:

'Once more unto the breach, dear friends, once more;
Or close the wall up with our English dead!
In peace there's nothing so becomes a man..'

'Macready,' called Boot, as the committed thespian approached.

'Yes, Boot,' replied the frustrated 'monarch', piqued at Boot's interruption and critical stare.

'The game's about to start,' Boot reminded the obsessive leading man.

'I know that Boot. Thank you,' retorted Macready contemptuously.

'Anyway, it sounded good,' flattered Boot, hoping to calm down the volatile artiste.

'Thank you Boot,' reiterated Macready, eagerly accepting his praise. 'I haven't come for the rugby,' asserted the school's 'royal' indignantly, 'I'm from Tickle A, so I have no particular interest in the outcome of this game. I just thought I'd look in as I shuffle around Open Way learning my lines.'

'Maybe you could give the half time team talk with one of your speeches,' suggested Barrett sarcastically.

'I'll be away by then Barrett,' insisted Macready, blithely unaware of the irony of the suggestion. 'At the French King's Palace, to be precise. In the meantime, boys make sure you know your own lines,' ordered Macready, glaring mercilessly at his theatrical colleagues. He then enunciated a self-consciously elongated 'goodbye', as he strode majestically down the touchline. When he stopped to talk to Bayliss and Basil, they listened to him with detached patience. Most of the boys believed that Macready took himself far too seriously. Bayliss and Basil seemed to agree, for as soon as the vain thespian had departed, they started laughing uncontrollably. No doubt, Bayliss was sharing some of Macready's more pretentious rehearsal moments, when his inflated ego flew into orbit.

As the final minutes ticked by towards kick-off, Le Mesurier and Wallace trundled towards the touchline while maintaining an animated conversation. They were a contrasting couple, given that Le Mesurier was small and wiry and Wallace big and bulky. Le Mesurier was wearing a cheese cutter cap and a blue raincoat, while Wallace's smart grey coat covered his inevitable plus fours. Le Mesurier approached the touchline cheerily but Wallace looked less comfortable, as if he was attending out of duty rather than enthusiasm. Wallace's tartan tie only belied a celtic unease amidst a very English occasion. Still his elegant flat golf cap or bunnet as his compatriots call it, gave Wallace an elegance and style, which belied his inner insecurity. After cursorily acknowledging the boys on the touchline, both masters gathered around the Major and the solemn, silent Root.

The appearance of Wallace made the boys wonder how the Major was getting on with Victoria, who was unable to attend due to tapping a typewriter for her estate agents. According to the more progressively inclined Barrett, cruel property capitalists selling houses at absurdly inflated prices, were slavishly exploiting her. Just as Boot was about to question Barrett's Marxist analysis, who should arrive but the school's Lenin himself, Francis Vladimir Ryder. With his immaculately combed hair and his belt placed provocatively low around his coat, the leader of the chapel uprising cut a swaggering figure. He told Hayes and co that he was making progress with Root about getting Jerusalem approved. This delighted Barrett but before the young radical could receive further advice about One Ball's bullying, Ryder had departed swiftly, like a royal dignitary avoiding the press. While passing Root, the choir's leader smiled perfunctorily, before placing himself at the far end of the touchline.

As the teams waited to enter the pitch, Yvette, wrapped in a light blue swing coat, trotted towards Françoise and kissed her lightly on both cheeks. A concerned Mrs Perceval in a drab cashmere garb followed her, running as quickly as she could. Perceval, who as referee, was waiting to go on the pitch with the players, looked at his wife with amusement, which Mrs Perceval acknowledged with a hesitant smile. Perceval was getting nervous as the kick off approached but witnessing Beatrix's endearing commitment calmed him down. He looked somewhat comic in a jaded green shirt, the only one he could find that didn't clash with the colours of the opposing teams. Nevertheless, he drew comfort that at least he'd stand out. When Perceval looked around, he was surprised at the size of the crowd. Everybody seemed to be there. Consequently, he was particularly aware that his performance would be scrutinised, not least by the experienced Bowen and Darbishire. Bowen in particular, could get fanatical if decisions went against him.

However, Perceval reasoned that as this match wasn't a 1st XV game he'd be less opinionated, but he wouldn't bet on it.

The two teams ran on to the pitch, led out respectively by One Ball for James B and Rutter for Ironside A. James B were wearing black and white hoop shirts, black shorts and socks, Ironside A red and blue shirts with blue shorts and socks. Perceval followed, struggling to keep up with the young players. Recovering his breath, Perceval summoned the two captains, asked Rutter to toss a coin and One Ball to call. When the James B captain responded with 'heads', Rutter looked at the coin, which had descended into a particularly muddy patch, and discovered that the opposition had won the toss. One Ball smirked at Rutter, who looked at his opponent with a facetious grin. This infuriated Potts, who impetuously declared that his team would kick off. An unconcerned Rutter responded by deciding to play initially against the prevailing wind, as he was confident that the Ironside pack would still dominate the game. When the two captains shook hands, Rutter felt that touching One Ball's palm was like coming into contact with a dead fish. For a moment, he wondered how this stern, obsessive boy would respond to Françoise's letter.

Having established the direction of play, both sides assembled like two opposing armies. James kicked off from the halfway line. The ensuing drop kick looped into the arms of a large Ironside forward, who thundered towards the opposition with all the speed and ferocity he could muster. The James forwards moved hesitantly towards the six foot three inch, fourteen stone monster approaching them. One Ball knew that you must make your presence felt early in a game and decided to show leadership. As the monster came towards him, he remembered Bowen's mantra about the necessary brutality of the first tackle. When the monster just charged forward relentlessly, One Ball realised that he was looking for a loose scrum rather than passing to the ineffective Ironside three quarters. Immediately, One Ball decided to bring him down and hope that his fellow forwards would be up with play to win a quick turnover. He duly crashed into the side of the monster with all his force. The monster collapsed and the ball went loose. Suddenly, another murderous looking Ironside forward arrived and fell on it. He was then followed rapidly by the rest of the Ironside pack, who heeled the ball back to Rutter at scrum half, who then kicked it a long way into touch near James's twenty-five.

At the lineout, One Ball rallied the troops. 'Come on lads. Concentrate. It's ours,' he cried. Such an exhortation inspired Boring Beckett to leap high with an impressive spring and win the ball. The James three quarters then made some progress until Ironside's gruesome forwards stopped them with powerful tackles. These mammoth youthful specimens were agile as well as powerful and managed to destroy any advantage that James gained. The game then proceeded in predictable fashion. James won their own lineouts but couldn't win enough set scrums, mainly because their hooker, 'Barrel' Madoc was struggling to make an impact. James were now clinging on, as Rutter worked the touchline with his kicking, keeping the ball close to his indomitable scrum.

One Ball was keeping an eye on the vociferous Rutter, who challenged his players with continual orders. As a wing forward, One Ball had an opportunity to tackle the loquacious scrum half. As he didn't want to get offside and give away a penalty, he bided his time. Eventually, an opportunity emerged. Ironside couldn't get a quick heel out of the scrum and One Ball pounced, thundering into the manikin's midriff and slinging him to the ground. As he did so, he shouted vengefully 'bloody well shut up!' but this didn't stop the inexorable attrition of Ironside's marauding forwards. Despite One Ball's efforts to inspire his team, the inevitable happened and Ironside's domineering pack pushed back One Ball and his scrum over the line for a try under the post. It was like an elephant squashing a fly. Rutter celebrated the breakthrough by manically jumping up in the air. Then, after the try was converted, he belligerently pumped his fists, looking in Françoise's direction as she and Yvette clapped enthusiastically.

Smallman, who was further down the touchline with his friend Collins, wasn't so enamoured. He disliked the modern sporting trend for histrionics and gamesmanship. He still believed in a gentleman's sense of fair play, not winning at all costs. He feared that he was becoming out of touch with an evolving amorality. Collins agreed with him and supported by a vigorous Boland, told Smallman that he had specifically told Rutter to calm down. Initially, the captain obeyed his request but later he reverted to type. In fact, it seemed that Rutter's aggression was a necessary catalyst to ignite his game. After taking the lead, Rutter started upping the ante. He shouted even louder to the scrum and kicked the ball further into touch. He was determined to use the power of his overbearing forwards to score again before half time. In fact, Rutter's aggression only made One Ball and the James team more resolute. They dug deeply into greater reserves of mental and physical strength. They found Rutter obnoxious and arrogant. His raucous behaviour only inspired them to punish the garrulous Ironside captain.

Eventually a moment emerged. During one of James's rare forays within their opponents twenty-five, Rice, James's fly half, dropped the ball twenty yards from the opposition's goal line. At the ensuing scrum, Rice whispered 'Mickey Mouse' as Rutter put in the ball for Ironside. Barrel as a devious hooker now made a significant contribution by managing to manoeuvre the ball quickly and surreptitiously towards Ironside's side of the scrum. Straightaway, the negligent Perceval impetuously blew his whistle for a penalty, thinking that Ironside had deliberately put the ball illegally into their own side. 'It worked,' mumbled One Ball, 'serves the bastards right when all they do is kick the ball.' Rice took the penalty kick and duly converted. It was now only 5-3 as Perceval imperiously blew the whistle for half time. As One Ball strolled past the deflated Rutter, he quoted the William Webb Ellis maxim which started the game, 'pick up the ball and run'.

'That's a myth, Potts,' retorted Rutter dismissively.

'You could at least try to play rugby not football,' responded One Ball disdainfully.

'You play to your strengths,' proclaimed Rutter proudly as if he was a professional coach.

'But you're not playing, Rutter.' insisted One Ball.

'Nor are you. You're cheating,' countered Rutter.

'What do you mean?' disputed One Ball aggressively.

'That penalty kick. I know how you cheated,' said Rutter emphatically.

'I don't understand,' claimed One Ball, feigning ignorance while wiping his muddy hands on his shirt.

'Mickey Mouse! exclaimed Rutter. That's got Bowen's fingerprints all over it. With the 1st XV, it was Dylan Thomas. We know his ruses.'

'See you in the second half, Rutter,' challenged One Ball.

'You certainly will,' affirmed the opposing captain vigorously.

The two touch line judges, selected from neutral houses not involved in the rigorously contested final, came onto the pitch and gave the teams their oranges. Both sides congregated around the centre circle but kept apart from each other. As they ate the sour pieces of Spanish citrus fruit and listened to their captains' rallying cries, the isolated Perceval prowled around the perimeter of the playing area, in preparation for the second half. He didn't want to mix with anybody at half-time otherwise he was going to get surrounded by various indignant voices. In fact, he'd already noticed both a querulous Collins and a swarthy Boland looking aggressively at him from the touchline. The classics master, with an obsession for martial combat and his colleague, the fanatical whistling gym master, obviously didn't think that it was a penalty. 'Well hard cheese,' thought a resolute Perceval, 'very hard cheese.' He got fed up with listening to the instant reactions of armchair experts, most of whom had never refereed in their life. Having nervously munched on an orange, Perceval then went to the touch judges and ordered them to collect the discarded peel from both teams. The touch judges obediently strode over to both groups with an air of indifference and collected the ragged remains of the fruit. Perceval gave them a few minutes to clear the pitch and for both teams to get into their positions, before blowing his whistle for the second half.

At 5-3, it was still anybody's game. This led to a furious start with both sets of scrums hurling into each other. Meanwhile, Rice as James's scrum half, was getting more vocal to counter Rutter's incessant wailing. One Ball's half-time oration, which traduced the opposition and called upon his team ‘to fight on behalf of the house, school and nation for a just cause’, was certainly having an effect. James became quicker in the loose and even Barrel seemed miraculously to gain a yard of pace. Their able three quarters came into the game, and ran confidently with the ball. As this transpired, Rutter became even more maniacal in hectoring his scrum, much to the increasing disapproval of the staff. He did not intend to be second best to someone like One Ball, with his reputation for despicable bullying and cheating. However, when the ball from the scrum came out very slowly to Rutter, One Ball took the opportunity to pounce, tackle him aggressively and yell:

‘Where’s my bloody camera, midget?’

‘In the Bahamas, One Ball!’ replied a mangled but defiant Rutter. In fact, the photos still weren’t ready. The chemist had sent him a card informing him that his assistant had flu, which meant that he was considerably behind with developing photos.

The crowd saw this confrontation but most of them didn’t hear it. Françoise looked on with increasing alarm at such tension, especially as she hadn’t yet completed her letter to One Ball. Rutter had given her further help but she still needed to fine-tune it into a sufficiently seductive missive. Given One Ball’s withering look at Rutter, Françoise feared that the James rugby captain might demand immediate retribution before she could pacify him. She now realised that she had to send the letter sooner rather than later. While Françoise frowned anxiously, Yvette found such personal antagonism during a rugby game bewildering.

In the meantime, Hayes and Co cheered One Ball while Ironside’s followers barracked him vociferously. Bowen and Darbishire thought Potts should just concentrate on the game. Getting involved in a punch up or ‘mixing it’ was going to give your opponent an advantage. Smallman was close to the incident and didn’t think that comments about the nature of a person’s testicles or their size for that matter, was appropriate in a game of rugby. Certainly, he’d have a word with the voluble Rutter about it. Collins understood his friend’s concerns but was more worried about how the spat would influence the game. At the same time, the Major, ensconced on his shooting stick, thought Potts should calm down and show leadership while

Root just revelled in the clash of young bodies. Even Bayliss and Basil got intrigued by the altercation but kept their thoughts to themselves.

As far as Ryder was concerned, the coercive Potts deserved everything that he got and he intended to liaise further with Barrett about a strategy to stop his unacceptable bullying. In contrast, Beatrix Perceval was bored by the whole macho spectacle and couldn't wait to leave. Concurrently, Le Mesurier and Wallace had so immersed themselves in a conversation about classical Greece, that they were oblivious to the details of the altercation. For his part, Oliver found it most distasteful and didn't want bad behaviour and disrespect to become the norm. The Rev Elwyn was concerned that it might undermine the school's religious and moral traditions. He then supported his argument with an obscure Latin quote, to which Oliver nodded approvingly. A few yards away, Sykes, ever suspicious and alert, wondered why Potts had mentioned a camera.

As the game progressed, James made considerable progress. Boring Beckett was now leaping higher than ever in the lineout and Rice was hassling Rutter with tigerish intensity. One Ball, with mud strewn across his face like a camouflaged soldier fighting guerrillas in the jungle, was not only pouncing on his abominable foe with vengeful ferocity but also inspiring his team with calm, vocal encouragement. Still, the score remained 5-3 as Rutter continued to hug the touchline, keeping the play close to his pack. The powerful and athletic Ironside scrum were like a superior army brutally chugging to inevitable victory. Yet, such was James B's intransigent resistance that Ironside just couldn't score another try to confirm victory.

After a scrum in the middle of the pitch, Ironside won the put-in against the head but the ball came out too slowly and One Ball tackled Rutter before he could throw the ball to his fly-half. As he disentangled himself from his nemesis, One Ball allowed his studs to engage brutally but discreetly with one of Rutter's legs. As usual, Perceval was on the wrong side of the play so he didn't notice the assault. Rutter yelled with pain and pleaded with Perceval that the James captain had committed a serious foul and should be sent off. One Ball smirked as Perceval gave both boys a dressing down and told them to get on with the game. His protestations ignored, Rutter now limped around like an injured war veteran.

James B got encouraged by Rutter's incapacitation and played with greater vigour. When they clashed on the field of play, One Ball repeatedly pressed Rutter about his camera and threatened to report him if he didn't give it back immediately. As Rutter put the ball in a scrum on James B's twenty-five yard line, he whispered 'you'll get it back, you bloody cheat.' This accusation didn't concern One Ball. The ignominious goblin deserved to be a victim of some innocuous gamesmanship. However, to get the ghastly gnome expelled, he needed possession of that photographic evidence. In addition to such personal issues, the Ironside captain had refused to give both One Ball and his team the respect they deserved. His supercilious attitude emanated from a belief that James were weak and that victory was inevitable. Consequently, One Ball believed that Rutter deserved to be 'given one' for his arrogance and sense of entitlement. He was delighted that Rutter was hopping on one leg like a wounded animal. Unfortunately, he forgot to remember the old sporting adage that wounded animals can be dangerous.

In fact, after the initial pain from One Ball's studs had diminished, Rutter looked to rally his team. The Ironside scrum half went into overdrive. His screeching became more hysterical, his kicking more accurate and his determination to win at all costs more resolute. Nonetheless, the score remained the same, as the teams entered the last quarter of the game. There was no doubt that despite their efforts, James were tiring. They started to get less and less possession and their legs began to wilt. One Ball responded by calling desperately for more energy and concentration. The crowd could now see that James were suffering and that like the unfolding of a Greek tragedy, the inevitable was going to happen. However, James, buoyed by their cheering supporters, refused to buckle. After a lineout fifteen yards from James's goal line, one of Ironside's big beasts brought the ball down, his scrum gathered around him and they all pushed towards the line. When the beast released the ball, Rutter made towards the line to score what was likely to be the winning try. Suddenly, One Ball flung himself heroically at the advancing scrum half before he could touch down. Thankfully, James survived the ensuing scrum and a kick from Rice released terminal pressure. Time was now running out and as the school timetable wouldn't accommodate extra time, the game would be replayed if it remained a draw.

The James team were exhausted. Barrel could barely run, Boring Beckett's spring in his jumps had diminished and One Ball's voice had become hoarse with his relentless rallying of his team. Still, while Ironside were unable to score again, they still had a chance. As the game advanced to its conclusion, the crowd became an extra man, urging on their respective side with thunderous support as Ironside continued to pummel the James goal line.

From a scrum ten yards out, Ironside went for a pushover try. As James felt the increasing pressure of the opposition's gargantuan scrum machine, One Ball desperately exhorted his teammates, as if James were fighting some malignant force of nature. Meanwhile, the Ironside beasts pushed and pushed. They were hungry for victory. They wanted to kill their prey and finish the contest. Meanwhile, the James scrum were like the passengers on the Titanic facing submission to an elemental power. Luckily, just as defeat stared them in the face, Perceval came to their rescue, blowing for another infringement. Salvation comes in many forms but rarely from a referee attired in leprechaun green.

Having survived at the death, James were relieved. Although they had managed the odd attack, for the spectator the overall spectacle was like watching a presentation of the Alamo, with James courageously withstanding wave after wave of attacks. As Ironside hadn't been able to score through the domination of their powerful scrum, towards the end of the game a desperate Rutter resorted to bringing his three quarters fully into play. When the ball reached a frail Ironside centre and he was rigorously tackled, the ball fell loose and was hacked away into Ironside's half. There followed a chase as if the James boys were pursuing an errant thief. Frustratingly for James, their centre lost control of the ball as he got near the goal line and it flew into touch. 'Thank God for that,' mumbled a relieved Rutter. For the James captain, the thought of losing to such a weak team was unthinkable. He just couldn't understand why his scrum couldn't deliver victory when they'd had so much of the ball. It now looked like he would have to accept that there was going to be a replay. He believed that this was not only very inconvenient but also wholly avoidable. It made him angry.

As the game was in its final minutes, there was a lineout for Ironside, just behind their twenty-five yard line. The Ironside throw was inaccurate and surprisingly none other than Boring Beckett miraculously found reserves of inner strength and leapt gloriously like a salmon dramatically jumping out of the sea. The revived Beckett caught the ball and threw it to scrum half Rice, who showed a sudden burst of pace and left Rutter floundering. Rice then sold a dummy to the opposing fly-half and made towards the posts. Just as several covering forwards were chasing him, he found the necessary swerve and acceleration to avoid them. In fact, he surprised himself with his ability to increase his speed when he was so exhausted. Yet, somehow the elation of the moment gave him the necessary impetus. As he dived over the line between the posts, avoiding the despairing lunges of the opposition, Rice felt a unique sense of exhilaration that he'd never felt before. It was even greater than the excitement engendered by Brigitte Bardot. In fact, he was feeling so euphoric that he nearly missed the conversion in front of the posts. His kick hit an upright of a goal post and only just bounced over the bar. After this fortunate outcome, Perceval blew his shrill whistle loudly to end the match. James B had miraculously beaten Ironside A 8-5.

Instantly, several of the James team collapsed on the pitch in a combination of relief, fatigue and exuberant jubilation. Others like One Ball leapt into the air in ecstasy. To him, this was what the school and country were all about-resolve, determination, discipline and irrepressible team spirit. He wasn't just proud of his teammates but also of himself. He'd driven them to victory against the odds. They couldn't match the ability of the Ironside scrum but by sheer will power they'd won. He was delighted to defeat the smug Rutter's intemperate barking and air of presumption.

One Ball looked at his rivals and saw the dejected faces of the defeated. As far as he was concerned, it served them right. To isolate their own three quarters for so long exemplified their arrogance. Consequently, when Ironside finally brought them into play, their confidence was fragile. It only needed a moment for Rice to easily breach their lines. In contrast to Rutter and a demoralised, fractious Ironside, One Ball felt that he had the confidence of the whole team. He had moulded them into a unit, in spite of their limitations. Only a few of them played for school teams but they had risen to the challenge through hard work, unity and endurance. Moreover, it was he, One Ball, who had given the team the inspiration to survive and win. He thought his father would have been proud of him. He wasn't so sure of his mother but then she didn't know much about rugby.

Rutter was shattered. He lay on the pitch massaging the leg that One Ball had assaulted. He was sure he would have stopped Rice's final run if he'd been fully fit. In any case, he would get revenge on the violent, cheating bastard at a moment of his own choosing. For a start, he'd ask Françoise to redo the letter. She would now be able to use One Ball's victory to express even greater flattery. Rutter thought that such bait would be irresistible to the conceited James captain. Françoise would ensnare him into her trap and they'd take control of their future. He looked across the pitch at the cocky captain, laughing and smiling with his teammates. Such a sight made Rutter sick. Despite One Ball's blatant cheating, to lose in the dying embers of the game against such a ramshackle outfit was humiliating. He felt like a boxer, who was knocked out in the last seconds of a fight. He was depressed and deflated. His house usually won, for god's sake. They had a scrum full of players in school teams while James had very few of that quality. As the school's rugby captain, he felt embarrassed. What's more, Ironside had controlled most of the game. James's victory defied logic. Conveniently, Rutter's ruminations had omitted that sport wasn't just always logical. In a one-off match, on the day, anything could happen.

The teams then made their way back to their respective houses. As they crossed Open Way, the James players kept jumping in the air, making celebratory sounds and giving their match winner bear hugs. Rice also cheerily acknowledged the James supporters on the adjoining path, who were repeatedly shouting ‘Super Ricey!’ The avid fan of Picturegoer with tonsured hair had become an unlikely rugby hero. Even One Ball, who wanted to highlight his own leadership, had to admit that without Rice’s ingenuity they wouldn’t have won. Still, as they approached the house, several of the team lifted captain One Ball shoulder high, while singing certain songs of dubious taste. They then carried him around the dayroom, much to the annoyance of the more studious boys, who were trying to study. The rugby mob continued regardless and after completing a victory circle, they went into the changing room and around the outside of the house, before finally depositing their captain in his study. Slumped on his chair, an exhausted One Ball felt triumphant. He’d remember this day as one in which belief in his values was fully justified.

Meanwhile, as they meandered morosely back to house, Rutter and Ironside received commiserations from a sympathetic Smallman and a detached Bowen and Darbishire. Smallman expected people to be honourable in defeat. He had an old-fashioned sense of chivalry. His friend, a red-cheeked Collins, was very disappointed and surprised. He thought his team had shown a lack of guile, particularly in the second half. He believed that Ironside’s tactics had become too predictable. Collins had told them to be more tactically flexible but they hadn’t taken his advice. Still, he accepted the defeat philosophically. After all, he was a classics master not a rugby coach and he was confident that Oliver would have noted his willingness to help. In contrast, Boland remained not only infuriated by Percival’s incompetent refereeing but also enraged by Rutter’s intransigence. He bitterly regretted that he’d too readily submitted to the obstinate captain’s strategy. Still, after taking a few deep breaths to calm down, he eventually managed to reflect more thoughtfully. Regardless of the loss, he didn’t think that he’d blotted his copybook. After all, he’d volunteered to manage the team and shown commitment. Accordingly, Boland believed that Oliver would evaluate his performance favourably, which would help his ascent up the school’s greasy pole. In the meantime, he'd return to running the gym, where no doubt he'd continue to blow his whistle incessantly.

In contrast, Bowen and Darbishire left the pitch elated. They didn't expect James B to win and feared that they would be on the losing side. Like arrogant, consummate professionals, they put the win down to their preparation and organisation. Nevertheless, Bowen was disappointed that the team didn't try any of his innovative attacking set pieces for the three quarters. Still, he was impressed with Rice. He couldn't believe he could show such skill. Of course, he put it all down to his coaching. He told Darbishire, that Rice had become the school's version of Cliff Morgan, Wales's celebrated fly-half.

Darbishire hoped that his contribution to the victory would earn him more respect. The derision that ensued from his constant repetition of 'ok, all right' had made him feel depressed. As hard as he tried to stop saying it, he just couldn't succeed. He was considering consulting a psychotherapist but he just didn't seem to have the time. He was also contemplating cutting down on his sporting activities, although giving up Harlequins and school rugby would be difficult. After all, one of the main reasons he got the job was because of his sporting ability. He was under no illusions that it was purely on academic expertise. In fact, it didn't take Darbishire long to discover that he struggled teaching bright boys. They asked too many awkward questions and when they got on your case, like the inexorable Binns, they were ruthless. Still, he liked to think that his was getting a greater grip on Oliver Twist. He was also trying to limit the 'ok all rights' by saying 'I must not say ok, all right' to himself as he walked towards the classroom. In fact, on one occasion, he must have repeated the mantra one hundred times. It did reduce his output of the phrase but he still said it many times and the boys didn't stop giggling. If it didn't improve further, Darbishire believed that he would have to seek professional help.

Like the staff, Françoise was also making her way home. She was disappointed that she couldn't talk to Rutter, particularly about his persistent yelling during the game. As the defeated captain limped across Open Way, he'd given her a despondent look. Under the darkening sky, he seemed a lonely and melancholic figure. Françoise was sorry that he'd lost but she was alarmed that he'd become a different person playing rugby. She didn't realise that he could be so aggressive. She consoled herself that boys needed to let off steam and that Artie hated the thought of losing to a notorious bully like One Ball. Even so, she found his constant clamour alarming. She just hoped that such invective wouldn't lead to any regrettable action.

As Françoise and Yvette got closer to their lodgings by the station, Françoise took a piece of paper from her coat and read her proposed letter to Yvette. Although Yvette enjoyed listening to it, she worried about Françoise. She thought that she took unnecessary risks. Nonetheless, in this particular case, Yvette was morally decisive and supported Françoise's ruse. She didn't want to see Françoise sacked so she realised that One Ball needed to be controlled. In any case, she found that the James' rugby captain embodied that English exceptionalism she disliked. The English seemed to have the insularity of an island people bound by a rigid class structure. Everything had to be on their terms. She was a great admirer of their culture but not so much of their way of life. She admired their inventiveness and creativity and she'd met some very likeable people. Yet she still found that some of them had traits that were too similar to untrustworthy, snobbish Parisians. Therefore, she felt compelled to see One Ball humiliated.

'He's so arrogant. He'll fall for your flattery,' remarked Yvette, commenting on the letter.

'It's not excessive?' queried Françoise.

'No. I don't think so.'

'Good. I'll have to change a bit though.'

'Why?'

'Now One Ball has won the rugby cup, I can flatter him even more.'

'I suppose so.'

'I'll consult with Monsieur Rutter.'

'One Ball may have done well at the rugby but I find him obnoxious, so does Barrel'.

'Obnoxious?'

'Very unpleasant.'

‘Thank you. I’ll remember that word. It might come in useful.’

‘Barrel, I mean Graham, taught it to me.’

‘It’s so easy to forget their real names isn’t it?’

‘Yes, they have a make believe world all of their own.’

‘Anyway, how is Barrel. Sorry Graham?’

‘Exhausted, I think.’

‘No. I mean how are you getting on with him?’

Yvette didn’t really like talking about intimacy. She believed in valuing privacy. However, she trusted Françoise. In any case, it seemed mean to be chatting about her escapades and never about herself. She admitted that she liked Barrel and his passion for literature, even though she found him rather obsessive and full of overwhelming energy. He talked a lot and most of it was interesting but she wanted him to be more of a listener. Still, he had a very good sense of humour but there were times when une période de calme would be appreciated.

‘What about emotionally?’ enquired Françoise, as they approached the white gates opposite the road to the gym.

‘I haven’t slept with him if that’s what you mean?’ revealed Yvette defensively.

‘Why not?’

‘Because I don’t love him.’

‘But you like him a lot.’

‘That’s not enough for me.’

‘Have you kissed?’

‘Yes.’

‘Well that’s something.’

‘Oh Françoise. I don’t have to sleep with every person I like.’

‘No but you don’t have to keep your body chaste either.’

‘I’ll awaken my body at the right time.’

‘Don’t leave it too long.’

‘I’ll know when I’m ready.’

‘Denial can become a habit.’

‘So can promiscuity?’

‘I’m not promiscuous. I have only one lover.’

‘Ok. Maybe you’re not. I’m just slower to find mine, that’s all.’

Françoise decided not to pursue the debate about Yvette's virginity so she diverted the conversation. They chatted about when they would hear about working on Henry V. They agreed that too many English people didn't seem very good at languages, so they were confident that they could help. Meanwhile, as they progressed down the small hill towards the cottages by the station, Françoise continued to worry about Rutter and hoped that he'd go to the infirmary and get his leg treated..

The spring afternoon was getting darker and a pervading murkiness gathered over the picturesque cottages. Françoise suggested that she'd use her Peugeot grinder for some real coffee. As they made their way down the paved entrance to the cottage, the women agreed that the thought of such a drink was a lot better than English tea with milk.

A week later, One Ball was returning from the ritual of the morning service. He casually collected letters from his pigeonhole and made towards his study. As he glanced through the correspondence, he noted the inevitable epistle from his mother, no doubt full of chastisement. Potts believed that Len Kirwin was influencing her, given that her recent letters were reading more and more like a Labour Party manifesto. For instance, she earnestly believed that we shouldn't be testing the H bomb, even though the Soviets were increasing their ballistic missile capability. One Ball was alarmed. The next thing she'll be wanting us to join the forthcoming Common Market. One Ball thought that his mother was starting to lose the sense of what makes us British. We're not socialists and we're certainly not continentals. He accepted the necessity of post-war reconstruction but now was the time to encourage enterprise not further state regulation. He feared that his mother was reading too much J. B. Priestley and George Orwell.

One Ball entered his study and put the letters down on his desk. Having recovered from the emotional impact of seeing his mother's writing, he observed the rest of the correspondence. One letter in particular, written in an elegant spidery hand on a pink envelope, caught his attention. He didn't recognise the writing so he opened it. Immediately, he looked at the end of the letter to see the signature. 'My God!' he cried, he couldn't believe it. It was signed 'Love Françoise'. For a moment, he stared blankly out of his narrow window, watching boys walking down the Avenue to their morning lessons. Then suddenly he roused himself from his stupor. He'd better go, otherwise he'd be late. He inhaled the fragrant scent of the delightfully feminine notepaper, put the letter carefully into the drawer in his desk, gathered his books and joined the lively multitude.

During the next lessons, he couldn't concentrate. He kept thinking about those two delightful words 'Love Françoise'. At the science lab, the nicotine-stained Moriarty, nicknamed 'phallic' for some sexually mysterious reason, was bewildered when One Ball failed to remember the principles of Faraday's electromagnetism. He became tongue-tied. During the break, he couldn't keep proper time doing the PE exercises. Things got worse in the next class with 'Pop' Bean, a scruffy man with one arm and an obsession with collecting toothpaste tubes. During a general discussion about Watson and Crick's recent DNA discoveries, 'Pop' was aghast that one of his star pupils was so inarticulate and uncertain with his answers. When he stared in shock at the stumbling senior, One Ball looked distracted. 'Pop' lost his arm in the war, during which his brother had also died. He had no children of his own, so he was particularly eager for the boys to do well. Therefore, to see his principal student, James Potts, unable to sufficiently remember a significant scientific development was disturbing. 'Pop' wondered if there had been bad news from home. He decided to have a word with the Major if the malaise continued.

As One Ball waited in his study for the bell to go for marching into lunch, he took a heavy breath and once more devoured the scent from Françoise's writing paper. He then looked intensely at the recently honed epistle before reading it carefully.

Dear James,

I want to congratulate you on winning the house rugby cup. It was a glorious achievement. Your Churchillian leadership was an inspiration not only to your teammates but also to me personally. I can only admire your vigorous athleticism and heroic defiance. You were calm, courageous and determined, showing us the best of Britain's bulldog spirit.

This was in complete contrast to Rutter your obnoxious opponent. His bawling tenor was like a crazy maîtresse losing her temper with a chambermaid. He ranted and raved like a juvenile delinquent while you showed maturity beyond your years. After the game, the verbose, egocentric adolescent was so rude to me that I have finished our relationship.

Happily, this leaves me free to see you at last. So, perhaps we could meet for a game of tennis. Why don't you book the court next to the athletics track for 2:30 pm on Sunday week?

I can't wait to see your superb physique in tennis clothes. I'm sure that you'll look magnificent.

In the meantime, I shall leave you with the words of one of your country's finest poets:

'Love is a breach in the walls, a broken gate.'

Love,
Françoise

As he read the letter, One Ball started to get excited. He felt flattered by such a wonderful patriotic compliment as 'Churchillian leadership'. To be equated with one of the country's greatest leaders was beyond his wildest dreams. To be admired for his 'vigorous athleticism' and 'heroic defiance', gave him recognition of not only his masculinity but also his resolute determination. One Ball basked in the glow of her compliments. He felt like a new man invigorated by a woman's flattery, especially as it was couched in recognition of his country's unique 'bulldog spirit'. One Ball was delighted that sport, which was embedded in values of the school, had alerted Françoise to his true character in contrast to the 'obnoxious' nature of the reviled Rutter. One Ball revelled in her description of the miniscule rugby captain as a 'crazy maîtresse' and a 'juvenile delinquent'. He knew that she'd see the light and reject the vile manikin.

Françoise's withering assessment of his diminished rival sent One Ball into a paroxysm of glee. He leapt up from his chair and repeated aloud: 'I have finished our relationship, I have finished our relationship, I have finished our relationship.' When he had exhausted himself from his euphoric outburst, he sat down and contemplated Françoise's tennis match proposal. Of course, he'd accept the invitation. After all, he was desperate to meet her alone. 'But I haven't got any damn tennis clothes,' One Ball groaned to himself. Nonetheless, he was ecstatic. Although the proposed date was in a fortnight, he decided to get a Fred Perry outfit straightaway. He would get permission from the Major to go into town. He'd persuade him that he needed to urgently buy some academic books.

One Ball rose and stared at himself in the mirror on the back of his study door. As he looked deeply into his own eyes, he repeated a phrase from Françoise's letter, 'superb physique'- 'yes, even if I say so myself, it isn't bad,' ruminated One Ball as he glared intensely at his reflected anatomy. In recognition of his physical attributes, he brought out a comb from the inside pocket of his coat and rigorously arranged his crinkly locks. After looking at himself for some time, and admiring the result, he reiterated the poetic quote, 'Love is a breach in the walls, a broken gate'. One Ball didn't know who wrote it but he didn't care, it was the romantic enticement that counted. Oh, how he wished to fill that breach! 'She fancies me, she fancies me, she fancies me..' he repeated to himself as he gazed mesmerically at the mirror. He reluctantly left his own reflection and hurriedly wrote down a reminder to reply to Françoise and book a tennis court. He would post the letter himself in the box at the Avenue. Having finalised his strategy, he couldn't resist looking back at himself in the mirror. 'I can see what she means,' he murmured complacently. He felt confident. He couldn't wait to meet Françoise in his new tennis outfit. He'll take it gradually, of course, but who knows maybe soon he might use those bloody rubbers.

Saturday couldn't come fast enough for One Ball, once he'd got permission from the Major to go into town. Initially, the Major received his request coolly, as he wanted to make sure that the 2nd XV were at full strength for their match in the afternoon. However, One Ball reassured his housemaster by promising that he'd be back by 12:45, quoting the train timetable to prove it. Such research impressed the Major, who surrendered to One Ball's commendable organisation. Having booked the court, One Ball wrote to Françoise, thanking her for the letter and confirming the date and time for their tennis game. In doing so, he controlled his more primitive emotions. He modulated his letter appropriately, showing sufficient enthusiasm without being ecstatic. One Ball thought that she was more likely to respect that.

On the forthcoming Saturday, One Ball set out after breakfast to go into town. As he passed the station cottages, he wondered if he'd see Françoise. He hoped not, as he didn't want to diminish the dramatic impact of presenting himself in his newly acquired tennis attire. After all, he was determined to look irresistible.

Françoise and Yvette were delighted when Bayliss accepted them as French advisors for his production. Not only did they get closer to the community but also Staines's pronunciation improved. This was a result of him adhering to their insistence that he must speak French every day. The play's princess followed this instruction with such diligence that 'she' walked around the Quadrangle greeting bewildered staff and pupils with an exaggerated 'bonjour!' When 'she' spoke Katharine's lines aloud, 'she' was so effective that a passing senior rudely shouted 'tart'. This upset Staines but when he informed Françoise and Yvette about such abuse, they told him to take no notice. In their opinion, it was a sign that he was convincing. Françoise said it should make him realise that the insults women receive from some men is quite common. Staines seemed surprised but revealed that as Katharine he was having similar difficulty with Macready. Apparently, the school's leading man had an insatiable sexual appetite and made lewd insinuations to the blonde gymnast. At one rehearsal, while Bayliss was boring the cast to death about the diplomatic implications of Burgundy's seminal speech in Act V, Macready put his arm around Staines, calling him 'my darling Katharine', to which Staines responded by violently elbowing 'the great actor' in the chest. As he struggled to regain his breath, Macready pleaded that 'he was only trying to be friendly' and was ‘exploring the part’. Staines also confided to the two women that when he came to rehearse the courting scene, Macready always appeared to have a lecherous look on his face. He was also constantly suggesting that he should rehearse with Katharine privately. Interestingly, not only Staines but also Bayliss rejected this proposal. Perhaps, the play’s director was only too aware of Macready’s sexual proclivities. Still, despite Macready’s inappropriate behaviour, Françoise and Yvette had to admit that Staines was convincingly feminine when he wore the blonde wig, especially hired from Nathans. His lithe figure and boyish look combined with an alluring period dress, made him appear splendidly royal. As for the licentious Macready, the two French women advised Staines to humiliate him through ridicule if he continued his reckless pursuit. If that failed, he should definitely complain to Bayliss.

Françoise enjoyed preparing to play her own part of a femme fatale. At the cottage, she’d washed and ironed her tennis clothes rigorously, much to Yvette’s amusement. Françoise was going to wear a short dress that would show her slender legs to advantage. It had light abstract patterns on its top but otherwise it was pure white with an enticing but contained bare neckline. Yvette thought that the dress was appropriately feminine and sexy. Françoise had also bought something called Meltonian to whiten her tennis shoes. Yvette helped her apply the liquid and after the shoes had dried, Françoise gathered her white socks together and announced that everything was ready. Notwithstanding such preparations, Yvette insisted that Françoise went upstairs and changed into the whole costume, so that she could give her a final inspection. Françoise duly agreed and disappeared into her bedroom.

In the interim, Yvette turned on the radio and heard a programme called Have a Go presented by a person from Yorkshire called Wilfred Pickles. During the broadcast local people told their personal stories and the audience joined in singing some traditional songs. Although their accents made it difficult for Yvette to fully understand the conversations, she still realised that they evoked a wonderful sense of community. A different side of England, she didn’t know. As Wilfred told a joke and the programme finished, Françoise reappeared. She descended the stairs of the cottage in her shimmering outfit and submitted herself to her friend's critical eye.

'Magnifique!' cried Yvette, combating the laughter coming from the radio.

'English, Yvette!' Françoise chided her friend.

'Oh, sorry. Magnificent,' articulated Yvette, correcting herself, while doing an imitation of an upper class English male dignitary with a plum in his mouth, deigning to engage with a mere minion.

As she sank herself into the nearby sofa, Françoise laughed at Yvette ridiculing English society.

'After the wonderful fashion display, can I ask you a question?' said Yvette with a radiant smile.

'Certainly,' replied Françoise playfully.

'Have you actually got a racquet?' pursued Yvette mischievously.

'Yes. It's a 'Little Mo' Vintage Wilson,' confirmed Françoise defiantly.

'Who's Little Mo'?' enquired a mystified Yvette.

'Maureen Connolly. American champion,' elaborated Françoise.

'Ah, of course,' acknowledged Yvette, remembering the Grand Slam winner. 'But what about the balls?' she added urgently.

'Oh mon dieu!' bellowed a distressed Françoise.

'English, Françoise!' demanded a stern Yvette, acting the schoolmistress.

'Ah, pardon. Oh my god!' enunciated Françoise, imitating the formidable Miss Pollard. The two women sat back on the sofa, cackling with laughter at Françoise's imitation of Madame Danvers of the kitchen. When eventually the delirium subsided, Françoise confronted the reality.

'I'll get some balls from Monsieur Artie Rutter,' she asserted with an erotic twinkle in her eyes.

'Good!' exclaimed Yvette, trying to suppress her giggles.

'Probably wise, when you're playing a player with just one,' professed Françoise, chortling uproariously.

Yvette's conservative sexual beliefs eroded as the two women hooted with laughter, while the Light Programme played in the background. An aged vicar on the People's Service was giving a sermon about the meaning of responsibility.

When the following Sunday proved to be a sunny spring day, Françoise was delighted. It gave her excuse to wear her white-framed sunglasses, like Barbara Stanwyck in Double Indemnity. Barbara might have come to a bad end in the film but she was still a strong, inspiring woman. She certainly knew how to control a man. Like Barbara, Françoise was going to remain detached and ruthless.

As she made her way towards the tennis court that morning, she reminded herself to regard the whole exercise as a performance. Attired in a light green raincoat, clutching her covered racquet and a box of balls, she moved gracefully past the rugby pitches. In the far distance, she could see a boy practising his serve. He seemed a desolate figure in the sporting landscape. As she got closer, she could determine that it was One Ball. He appeared energetic and obsessive as if he was preparing for Wimbledon, not just a friendly game. Françoise decided to walk diligently to thc court via the athletics track behind the houses. Nobody seemed to be using the facilities, apart from one tall blonde boy, who was practising the high jump in the middle of the track. Unfortunately, his attempts were consistently ending in failure. Various shrill cries accompanied his frustration and as Françoise passed, he gave her a rueful smile. Françoise responded with a sympathetic grin but her sunglasses lessened its impact. Dejected, the lanky boy took refuge in making another effort to clear the bar.

As Françoise continued on her journey, she looked at her watch. It was 2:35, not too early, not too late. She believed that was just right. As she got closer, she thought that the court's wire mesh surround seemed more suitable for a military compound. She found the setting strange. She had assumed that English courts were all made of grass, like Wimbledon. On reaching the perimeter of the asphalt court, she hailed One Ball with a gushing greeting. Suddenly, he stopped his serving action in mid-air. Françoise was speaking from behind the wire so One Ball politely steered her through the entrance to a seat, where she could leave her belongings.

'Sorry, it's rather primitive,' apologised One Ball nervously.

'Don't worry, that's fine. Lovely to see you,' replied Françoise seductively as she took off her raincoat and left it neatly on the bench. 'I've got some balls here, if we need more,' she mentioned, while unzipping her racquet.

'Thanks. I think I've got enough but let's see how we go,' suggested One Ball.

'You look very smart in your shorts and shirt,' observed Françoise, flattering James B's latest sporting icon.

'Thank you. They're from Fred Perry,' disclosed One Ball earnestly.

'Who?' queried Françoise, who'd never heard of the British tennis star.

'Fred Perry. He's the only British man to win Wimbledon. He has a sports clothing business,' explained One Ball, like a benevolent teacher.

'Oh. Yes, now I remember. Well they look very good,' mentioned Françoise flirtatiously.

'Thanks,' beamed One Ball.

'I don't think any French player has won Wimbledon recently,' remarked Françoise.

'I'm sure it'll happen again one day,' declared One Ball despite having no specialist knowledge of the game.

'I do hope so,' stated Françoise with patriotic optimism.

'Well, let's start,' proclaimed One Ball as he began to move confidently onto the court.

'Shouldn't we toss up first?' proposed Françoise.

'Oh yes, of course,' said a perplexed One Ball.

'Rough or smooth?' requested Françoise.

'Rough,' chose One Ball nervously.

Françoise then spun her racquet, which landed on the tarmac.

'Smooth,' revealed the serene French maid. 'I'll serve first. Which end would you prefer?' she asked her opponent.

'The one towards the school,' replied One Ball instinctively.

One Ball had never previously tossed for a game of tennis so he was taken aback by the ritual. He knew nothing at all about rough and smooth. Still, he was delighted that his Fred Perry purchases had made an instant impact. He was now confident that nothing was going to prevent him from showing off his tennis prowess to his admirer. As they knocked up, Françoise managed to return most of One Ball's shots but she worried about her backhand as it still wasn't very secure, despite her coaching lessons. She also wondered if One Ball would unleash unprecedented power in his shots or play more diplomatically.

In fact, he had decided to do the former as he couldn't resist wanting to assert himself. Consequently, he returned Françoise's service with all the force he could muster. At first, Françoise was scampering around the court to no avail. However, as the set progressed, One Ball started getting tense. He couldn't find his range. He lost points double faulting and firing too many ambitious shots out of play. Françoise got encouragement. Her serve may have been powder puff compared to One Ball's thundering brutality but she was more strategic. In fact, One Ball got so frustrated with Françoise's variation of pace that at the end of one game he yelled 'damn' with ferocious venom. Immediately, he apologised to his opponent, who took the mild expletive in her stride.

Françoise was delighted to undermine One Ball and expose his weaknesses by mixing up her game. She felt a particular satisfaction in putting the skills that she'd learned into competitive action. Françoise didn't like One Ball's assumption that he could impose his game upon her just through power. She was determined to destroy such chauvinism. As the set progressed, One Ball started losing many games. This was mainly due to a reluctance to be cautious with his second serve. Instead, of placing the ball conservatively in the box, he couldn't resist going for an ace to impress her. As a result, he found himself at 4-4 with Françoise serving to take the lead. One Ball felt his body sweating. He'd only recently become a sporting hero in his house. Just a few weeks ago, in his celebration speech, the Major referred to his, 'dynamic and inspirational leadership, his courage and will to win'. He just couldn't lose a tennis match to a woman. He'd be the laughing stock of the school. Although he concentrated ferociously to counter Françoise's beguiling top spin, he just couldn't deal with it. He seemed to be getting his feet in the wrong position and he didn't know how to correct it. His mother had paid for some coaching in the local park but that was years ago. As tennis wasn't his main sport, he'd neglected to develop his skills and now he was paying for it. This led to Françoise leading 5-4 with One Ball serving to save the set.

One Ball composed himself. He was good in a crisis. He needed to stay calm. He was going to pressurise Françoise's vulnerable backhand. He would pummel the ball ruthlessly in that direction and inevitably she would capitulate. In fact, One Ball became so obsessed with his aggressive strategy that he became tense and started with a double fault. In fact, his second serve was so inaccurately violent that it flew like a missile and narrowly missed Françoise's head. One Ball apologised, which Françoise accepted with an apprehensive smile. Exasperated by his performance, One Ball was now finding Françoise's sunglasses a distraction. 'It isn't that bloody sunny,' he murmured to himself. Françoise asked if there was anything wrong as she threw the battered ball back in his direction. 'No fine,' he lied. In fact, One Ball thought that playing tennis in sunglasses was showing unacceptable levity. He'd never before played anyone wearing them. Certainly, nobody as attractive as Françoise. 'It's like playing against a bloody model. It's putting me off,' he muttered.

The Barbara Stanwyck effect was bamboozling One Ball. However, as he gathered the ball to serve, he still believed that the 'beautiful model' could be his. After all, she wanted to meet him. She flattered him with evocative descriptions of his stature and appearance. She was the one who wanted to play tennis. Nonetheless, despite his earnest intentions, One Ball was getting outfoxed by Françoise's tactics. First, he couldn't reach her drop shot, then she passed him cross court with a powerful forehand and after he had relentlessly attacked her backhand, he netted an overhead slam. Enraged by his poor play, One Ball elicited a primitive cry that made Oedipus's loss of eyes a prick on a finger. One Ball was now shaking with nerves. The more he muttered agitatedly to himself 'calm down, calm down', the more anger and humiliation raged throughout his body. It was now set point and One Ball was facing ignominy. When his first serve was an ace, he felt hopeful. 'This is where she'll crack. She won't be used to the pressure of seeing out the match,' he reassured himself. Sadly for One Ball, far from submitting, Françoise felt more confident and relaxed. She didn't take the game too seriously and just enjoyed playing her shots. She could see that across the net there was a flustered opponent, so she relished imposing her game on the agitated bully. As it became more difficult for One Ball to hold his serve, he began to lose control. He became wildly aggressive when he needed to be tactical. This meant that he missed simple opportunities. During one exchange, with the court completely open, his loose forehand sent the ball careering into the wire mesh. To complete his humiliation, he served a double fault to lose the set.

Françoise swinging her racket casually wandered up to the net to meet a thwarted One Ball.

'Shall we sit down?' suggested Françoise, raising her sunglasses enticingly above her head.

'All right,' agreed a bruised One Ball.

Françoise moved her belongings and they sat next to each other on the fading grey bench at the side of the court.

'That was fun,' asserted a cheery Françoise, consciously crossing her legs.

'Yes. You're pretty good at tennis,' complimented One Ball, wondering how she produced that 'bloody top spin'.

'Not really I just learnt a bit with a professional,' clarified Françoise.

'In France?' continued a polite One Ball, masking his vexation.

'Yes, in Lyon. There's a club near our family home,' specified Françoise.

'Well, you got some good tips,' said One Ball admiringly, continuing to hide his disappointment.

'Yes, enough to have a proper game but I'm not that good,' thought a modest Françoise.

One Ball suddenly realised that if she didn't think that she's any good, 'what does she think of my game?' He felt demeaned.

He needed to play another set with her so that he could win and redeem himself. Losing to a woman was embarrassing.

Tactfully, Françoise quickly moved the subject to his rugby triumph. She developed the theme of the letter that she and Rutter had so carefully crafted. Françoise talked about how it was such an amazing finish to the game and how he had led the team so splendidly. She knew that such flattery would make One Ball forget his tennis defeat. Françoise then diverted the chat to the forthcoming school play. She listened to One Ball's concerns about the length of Chorus's speeches as he effortlessly turned the conversation to himself. He told her that when he started to bring some energy and attack to his speeches, he ran out of breath. Bayliss helped him break them down but he still found sustaining them difficult. One Ball thought that it would be easier if he was actually talking to another character but Chorus only has soliloquies, which he condescendingly explained is when a character speaks thoughts aloud by himself. He felt isolated, especially as he only rehearsed with Bayliss until there were run-throughs. Then he got tense when he rehearsed in the same place as Rutter.

Surprisingly, Françoise found One Ball's acting problems interesting. She could understand his sense of alienation and his fear of making a fool of himself, especially in the presence of her lover. He was more humane when he was relaxed and prepared to expose his vulnerability. However, having expressed his fears, One Ball then reverted to protecting his status. Without any consideration for Françoise, he ploughed on about his hopes for the future. He told her that he was determined to get into Cambridge. With blithe assumption, he was confident of getting the necessary grades. In defending his academic aptitude, he became rigidly obstinate. It was as if he was scared of his real self.

One Ball enjoyed chatting with Françoise. Somehow, because she was an outsider it was easier. He hadn't much experience of women and was nervous about how to establish a relationship. His father died too young to guide him and his mother, scarred by bereavement, opted out of such intimate concerns. Consequently, only Doctor Mates could illuminate him on such matters. The good doctor's sex lectures were one of Oliver's more progressive initiatives. Although Mates was instructive about the mechanics of lovemaking, his observations about the needs of the female sex were somewhat simplistic. His pronouncements steered conservatively towards marriage. In fact, at the end of his final lecture, Dr Mates drew a rather bad picture of a house and an approaching path. He then turned to the boys and declaimed 'this is what she wants,' while rigorously tapping the chalked home on the blackboard. One Ball didn't think that such an instruction was very helpful as far as Françoise was concerned.

Just as Françoise was beginning to feel sorry for One Ball, she wondered what Barbara Stanwyck would do in such circumstances. In Double Indemnity, Barbara never lost sight of her main goal: getting the insurance money through the death of her husband. Similarly, Françoise was determined to concentrate and learn from Barbara. She must keep to her objective of stopping One Ball from getting herself and Artie sacked before the term ended in a few weeks' time. She needed to make sure that she could permanently placate him.

'Tennis clothes really suit you,' said Françoise, raising her sunglasses and staring bewitchingly into his eyes.

'Really?' queried a disconcerted One Ball, looking away nervously from her intense smile.

'Definitely. They fit you very well,' amplified Françoise, continuing to stare intently at him.

'Thank you.' responded One Ball, who began to feel like a cat purring after incessant stroking.

In spite of such flattery, One Ball still had doubts about Françoise's commitment. He found it hard to believe that she had completely rejected Rutter. After all, they had been hand in glove for some time. Therefore, he wanted to make sure that the school's Tom Thumb wasn't using him. One Ball regarded Rutter as a Machiavellian character who couldn't be trusted. As far as One Ball was concerned, Rutter had inveigled himself into a position above his station. In fact, Rutter had a way with women that One Ball envied and he didn't think that the school's rugby captain would accept rejection easily. After Françoise's rhapsodic compliments, One Ball decided to air his fears.

‘Are you really not seeing Rutter?’ probed One Ball suspiciously.

‘Oh no, we had a terrible row. And that’s it,’ acknowledged Françoise, acting the wronged woman.

‘When?’ insisted a suspicious One Ball.

‘After a rehearsal. When Rutter escorted me home. We were discussing his role as the Dauphin. Well, for some reason, this led to him going on about the French during the war. He said that many of our citizens were collaborators and that’s why our government were looking to restore national pride by making it difficult for the UK to join the Common Market. When Rutter arrived near the back of the Dining Hall, he started shouting that the French were all cowards and supported the Nazis. It was terrible. I had relations Le Maquis. It was insulting. Not everybody supported the Vichy government. I didn’t want to see him ever again. I was very upset,’ confessed an emotional Françoise, engaging her best Barbara to deliver her hyperbolic, melodramatic untruths.

‘Goodness. That must have been terrible. I know how I’d feel if my country was insulted like that,’ sympathised One Ball.

Françoise thought that he’d fall for her story, given his lack of emotional insight. No academic course could teach him that.

‘Yes, it was so hurtful,’ stressed Françoise, ‘one of my uncles was killed by the Germans. He was a member of Le Maquis. He refused to give them intelligence information. Rutter showed no respect. He just went on regardless. It was a surprise. I knew he could become vicious on the rugby pitch but I never knew that he had such horrible views.’

In fact, One Ball regarded those views sympathetically. He thought that the French had been either cowardly or collaborators and that the British came to their rescue. Still, he certainly wasn’t going to express such sentiments to Françoise. He couldn’t understand how a practised ladies’ man like the manikin could be so bloody insensitive. Surely, there must be something more to their break up?

‘We also had a blazing row about the qualities of English food,’ maintained Françoise, purposefully contradicting her previously light-hearted cuisine conversations with Rutter. ‘It was ridiculous because everybody knows that English food is terrible. Rutter started defending British bread. I told him that French baguettes were not only more tasty but considerably more stylish. He then went crazy and started shouting that the French are too concerned with style and not enough with substance. Too much Christian Dior and not enough Bertrand Russell. I replied that the British had too little Jean Paul Sartre and too much Tommy Steele. Then he started calling my friend Yvette 'The Virgin Queen' because she didn't want to have sex with his friend Barrel. It all got rather ugly.'

'I can't stand Tommy Steele,' admitted One Ball. 'Too much like a pale imitation of the Americans.'

'Exactement. I only heard heard him a few times and there was no soul,' agreed Françoise.

'I agree with you,' concurred One Ball. He was happy to agree about the ability of a pop singer but not English food. In his opinion, it wasn't that bad. He loved good old English fish and chips and shepherd's pie. He believed Stafford Cripps and his relentless rationing was to blame for the diminution of the national diet. All that tinned fruit and evaporated milk,

'There's a young singer called Jacques Brel. He's very soulful,' mentioned Françoise.

'I'm afraid that I've never heard of him' confessed One Ball.

'He's new on the scene. He's from Belgium but sings in French,' said Françoise.

'Tell me a title and I'll look out for him,' requested One Ball.

'Quand on n'a que l'amour' whispered Françoise seductively, looking deeply into One Ball's grey eyes.

'A translation please,' pleaded One Ball, embarrassed by Françoise's intense stare.

'When we have only love,' continued Françoise, penetrating One Ball more deeply with her gaze.

Immediately, Françoise realised that she'd managed to completely captivate One Ball. It was a seminal Barbara moment. Ms Stanwyck, incomparable in sunglasses at the supermarket, would have been proud of her. This specimen of English manhood was crumbling before her very eyes. Amidst all the bluster and posturing, One Ball was even more vulnerable than she initially thought. She would now ruthlessly encourage him to believe that their relationship had a future. Of course, it did as long as One Ball obeyed her. She was going to train him like a dog. He was going to be her poodle. This was cruel but necessary. One Ball was a bully and was vengeful because he was insecure. Consequently, he hated her lover with extreme virulence. One Ball needed attention. He was a narcissist who basked in the glory of his own image, so she would flatter him appropriately.

As One Ball sat on the bench, he relished the French words pouring into his ears. He'd better quickly find out about this Jacques Brel. As Françoise looked into his eyes with such unwavering power, he felt important. He started to get aroused and his one ball became deeply activated. However, One Ball knew that he needed to control himself. In the middle of the afternoon at a tennis court was neither the time nor the place to make a pass. In any case, he knew that if he tried to kiss Françoise, he'd be rebuffed. Nonetheless, it was difficult to resist as she transfixed her brown eyes upon him and stretched her naked legs. Thankfully, his sense of discipline just about managed to stop him doing anything inappropriate. His one ball started to relax and he managed to challenge Françoise's tempting demeanour with a pertinent question.

'When will I get my camera and photos back?

Françoise was prepared to deal with the challenge of One Ball's enquiry. She reassured him that she'd get the camera from Rutter and bring it to one of the final rehearsals of Henry V. More importantly, she said that she looked forward to seeing him again. Perhaps next time, they could go for a long walk. One Ball seemed satisfied by her replies. Although he still had a burning desire to avenge his shameful loss, he didn't want to undermine the revealing intimacy that she had initiated, so he agreed to the long walk. As Françoise wanted to plan such a venture strategically, she suggested that they arrange a date later at rehearsal, after she'd checked her schedule. One Ball accepted her proposal. Above all, he wanted to develop their relationship.

Eventually Françoise and One Ball decided to leave the court. Françoise zipped up her racquet, and put on her chic raincoat. After she took her box of unused balls from the bench, they departed. One Ball left without any tracksuit. He thought that such exposure made him appear more masculine. He opened the tennis court gate for Françoise and respectfully let her go out first. As Françoise exited, she thought that she saw Rutter by a nearby copse, pointing binoculars in her direction and then hurriedly disappearing into the bushes. Rapidly, she drew One Ball's focus away from such vigilance to the athletics track, where a boy in a Jasper B shirt and all caked in sand, was practising his long jump. After discussing the boy's impressive progress, Françoise and One Ball made their way to the back of James B. When they arrived near the house, One Ball thanked Françoise for the game.

'I didn't know you were so good,' admitted One Ball.

'Not really. Still, merci,' replied a bashful Françoise.

'Well,' hesitated One Ball, 'see you at rehearsals.'

'Yes, I look forward to that,' responded Françoise, as she reasserted Barbara by self-consciously lowering her sunglasses. She was about to depart, when she turned back to One Ball and took off her shades. With a captivating smile, she reminded him of the romantic Belgian chanteur.

'Don't forget Jacques Brel.'

'No, I won't,' acknowledged a smiling One Ball, as he departed through the porch into the house.

Hubert Aloysius Bayliss was finding the technical rehearsal of his production very stressful. As a result, he was soon swigging whisky from a black flask, which hung precariously around his neck. Everything seemed to be happening at a snail's pace and the director was becoming increasingly frustrated. Members of the school orchestra, who were providing the incidental music, were being consistently late with their cues. The lighting designer, a bespectacled burly senior from Tickle B called Zuckerberg, was also creating problems. This ambitious artistic practitioner was so concerned with chiaroscuro and German expressionism that the cast called him 'the prince of darkness'. Matters came to a head when Bayliss, aided by his intake of the hard stuff, told the Teutonic upstart 'to light the bloody actors'.

Meanwhile, Anne Becker, the designer, was trying to infiltrate some of her Brechtian views into the set, which was becoming more and more austere. Originally, she wanted captions but Bayliss disliked dry, intellectual theatre and certainly wasn't going to allow a German communist to influence his production. Bayliss hated modish direction. He had recently witnessed a Marxist Hamlet, which was set in some kind of Kremlin where everybody was dressed in Bolshevik costumes. The critics described it as radical but Bayliss hated it, regarding it as utterly phony. So when he told Anne that her set looked like the foyer of Barclays Bank, she got very upset and flounced out of Big Hall. Bayliss promptly followed her into the pouring rain. When eventually he caught up with her under the cloisters, he apologised and implored her to return to the rehearsal. After some hyperbolic flattery from a drenched Bayliss, a soaked Anne, whose progressive theatrical views were manifestly at odds with the director's patriotic interpretation, eventually agreed to come back. As they both returned to the rehearsal, Anne, furiously wiping her half-moon spectacles, contended that the colour 'would be in the costumes', which she was also designing. Bayliss certainly hoped so as he thought that the set was grimness personified. Although Bayliss accepted that Anne was both inventive and idiosyncratic, he found her a dreadful slave to ghastly, fashionable thinking.

On arriving at Big School, Bayliss discovered Macready walking around the stage, rehearsing some of his speeches. Bayliss took a swig from his flask and told his leading man to depart speedily. When he informed him that the technicians and stage management needed a clear stage to make adjustments, Macready took offence. The school's leading thespian insisted that he needed to try out the acoustics. While drying his hair with a provided towel, Bayliss abruptly dismissed his demand with a perfunctory, 'not now, not now, Macready'. Upset by such a rejection, Macready stormed off the set.

As the technical rehearsal continued, the problems mounted. For instance, One Ball, as Chorus kept entering from the wrong place. Bayliss wanted him to appear at different parts of both the stage and auditorium. This was supposed to give him a good link with every section of the audience. One Ball, costumed in a magnificent cloak and tights, told Bayliss that several doors were locked and he couldn't access the relevant areas. Bayliss then summoned the caretaker, a Mr Seamus O'Reilly. O'Reilly was a querulous Dubliner, who hardly had a good word to say about anybody. He was also was a great admirer of W B Yeats and at the annual staff party, he had given a rousing rendition of Easter 1916. Ever since his stirring performance, the staff became wary of the passionate Irishman. They were uncertain whether his choice of poem was an act of cultural subversion or a homage to a great poet. Certainly, O'Reilly gave the impression of being the school's resident Guy Fawkes, substantiated by rumours that his family had IRA connections. Despite his seditious status, Bayliss knew that O'Reilly actually liked plays. He'd told Bayliss that he'd been to the original Abbey Theatre before it was burned down and that he had met Sean O' Casey. Thankfully, this was a hopeful sign and the cantankerous Dubliner eventually opened the doors for the rehearsal.

Unfortunately, dealing with the entrances of the Chorus was only one of Bayliss's increasing problems. The Archbishops played by Boot and Rice couldn't hold on to their props. The various parchments, which underpinned Henry's legal claim to France, kept fluttering all over the stage. Of course the two boys, fitted in solemn religious regalia, found this hilarious and couldn't stop laughing. Bayliss hastily intervened and crudely told them to 'deal with it'. Later, a fractious French court confronted the director, arguing about the furniture and their positions. Inevitably, Ryder was at the centre of this discussion. So insistent was his argumentative rhetoric that Bayliss was convinced that his King of France would argue that two plus two didn't actually make four. No wonder he wanted to be a politician. Bayliss decided that the only way to stop such bickering was to take control calmly. With his flask dangling in the air, the director leapt up on the stage and made sure that the chairs were in the right place. He then asked Hayes as stage manager to come out and mark the new positions. Gradually, the tension subsided as Hayes brought out some black gaffer tape and started crouching on the stage. When Bayliss saw the tape's colour, he ordered the stage manager to change it to white as it wouldn't be seen in the black outs. When Hayes said that he didn't have any white tape to hand, Bayliss irritably told him to 'keep it black and change it later.'

Bayliss then went back to his position in the middle of Big Hall, where he was sitting at a table with an Anglepoise light. 'Thank God, I don't do this for a living,' he muttered to himself. He had wanted to be reassured that working with professionals would be easier. In fact, he'd heard from university contemporaries who worked in the theatre that this wasn't necessarily the case. Just after Bayliss had sat down, Rutter, his irritation accentuated by One Ball's gleeful gloating, complained that he couldn't sit comfortably in the Dauphin's chair because of the thickness of his costume. At once, Bayliss shouted for Anne. When she didn't appear, he persisted in yelling her name to the heavens. Eventually, the sceptical designer cautiously emerged from the upstage centre entrance, carrying a needle with a dangling thread. Hearing Rutter's complaint, she looked at him disdainfully before observing both the bulky medieval costume and the chair. Anne didn't want further tension with the conservative director, so she reassured him that she'd find a solution.

'Good. Good. Thanks Anne,' appreciated Bayliss, desperately trying to keep up morale.

Just as the rehearsal seemed to be developing smoothly, Barrett, incandescent in tights and chainmail, came racing up to Bayliss requesting a credit in the programme for Chuck Carson.

'He deserves recognition, sir,' urged an earnest Barrett.

'Not in the middle of the tech, Barrett,' entreated Bayliss tetchily.

'He's from Belfast, sir,' mentioned the excitable Barrett.

'I don't care if he's from Outer Mongolia, Barrett,' vowed Bayliss haughtily.

'He's not in the play sir,' clarified a determined Barrett.

'I know he's not in the play, Barrett,' responded Bayliss irritably.

'He's been very helpful with my Irish accent,' stressed Barrett.

‘Ok, Barrett, leave the details here and I’ll see what can be done at this late stage,’ conceded Bayliss, peering over his tortoiseshell-framed glasses with a weary smile.

The exhausted director then hastily called for the rehearsal to continue as Barrett departed, satisfied with the conclusion of his negotiation. After there was progress with the lighting and sound cues, it transpired that the Governor of Harfleur, a very tall slender boy from Jelly B, was in difficulty. He was to enter on highly raised rostra but just as he was about to speak, he complained of suffering from vertigo and looked like a pale ghost. Apparently, he could only make his entrance via a precarious ladder, which made him very nervous. Bayliss instantly summoned the reliable Higginbottom, who came onto the stage in brown overalls, raised a hand above his forehead to counter the stage lights and peered to the back of Big Hall. The bulky manual teacher then reassured the fraught director that he’d find a solution to securing the gates of Harfleur.

Eventually, Harfleur was stabilised and the technical rehearsal moved on apace. The musicians came in on cue, Zuckerberg toned down his expressionistic excesses and the stage management did the scene changes without sounding like a herd of elephants. Nonetheless, Binns as Pistol became maniacal with his swordplay and needed to exercise restraint. Immediately, Bayliss told the moustachioed Mr Rivers, the school’s fencing master, to work with the dangerously erratic Binns in a nearby room. The urbane Rivers, splendidly attired in an immaculate white tracksuit, graciously accepted the invitation. He didn’t want to be responsible for an accident and would reiterate the importance of cueing discipline.

Later, Bayliss confronted an even bigger problem. He’d hired a smoke device at considerable cost to give the camp scene greater atmosphere. Alas, the smoke got so totally out of control that the actors were no longer in the middle of the Agincourt camp but in some bizarre, hazy, twilight zone. Gradually, coughing became infectious and barely decipherable human figures struggled to leave the stage. The hapless Bayliss looked on in horror. His pièce de résistance had turned into a nightmare. He demanded an explanation. Eventually, the bedraggled, bleary-eyed figure of Hayes emerged from the smoke and between sporadic coughs, he told Bayliss that the effect was difficult to control. An incredulous director then went backstage to examine the apparatus for himself. While bending down and observing the inadequate equipment, Bayliss discovered that Hayes was right. He was furious that his only opportunity to realise a directorial coup de théâtre had been lost. Consequently, he was adamant that the manufacturers should pay for such negligence. How could smoke for a fire circulate like Victorian fog?

As a deflated Bayliss made his way back to his seat amidst the swirling smoke, he took a big swig from his flask, followed by several deep breaths. 'Cut the smoke,' he bellowed to Hayes 'and break for fifteen minutes'. In fact, it was another half an hour before the fumes dissipated satisfactorily. Hayes then disconnected the link with the fire and removed the disgraced smoke appliance. Much to Bayliss's annoyance, Zuckerberg took an eternity relighting the scene. It was if he was determined to emphasise the importance of his artistic prowess to the whole company. Eventually, after a laborious hiatus, 'the prince of darkness' finally rejigged the design to his satisfaction. By this time, Bayliss had made considerable inroads on the contents of his flask. As he leaned back nervously on his chair, he relished the full effect of Scotland's finest whisky. He then barked out bellicose demands to Hayes to get the full company on stage. On their arrival, Bayliss stood up unsteadily and gave a short oration. He told everybody that the tech must be finished by the end of the session, so 'let's do it.' While the boys departed, Bayliss shouted at the stage management to set up and get ready to restart. Everything progressed satisfactorily until it came to the battle of Agincourt and various maroons didn't function. When Macready mentioned that Henry was fighting with bows and arrows, and that there were no bombs at Agincourt, the director took offence.

'I'm well aware of that Macready. I inserted the maroons as a form of bellicose, musical accompaniment.'

'But they're not going off, sir,' replied a querulous Macready.

‘They will do. They will give extra thunder to my patriotic interpretation,’ postulated Bayliss.

‘Won’t we lose authenticity?’ queried Macready.

‘The authenticity will be in the music. The maroons will be mixed in with it,’ stipulated Bayliss. ‘It’ll be wonderful.’

‘Yes, sir,’ said Macready dubiously.

‘It’ll have echoes of the Battle of Britain,’ trumpeted Bayliss.

Bayliss dismissed shilly-shallying Macready and continued the rehearsal. This wasn’t the time for doubting Thomases only full believers. He’d deal with his vacillating leading man later. That’s if the vain artiste wasn’t too busy fine-tuning his medieval hairstyle. Thankfully, the rehearsal progressed without further alarms until Staines had problems with Katharine’s wig, which comically slipped to one side of his face. Bayliss once again summoned Anne, who appeared holding a dress in the middle of the French palace. She looked aghast at the incongruous sight and assured Bayliss that she’d correct it. The harassed director responded by diplomatically thanking the Brechtian fanatic, before continuing with the rehearsal.

Eventually, they got to the end of the play. However, Bayliss’s problems weren’t over as Macready started to control the curtain call. In response to these narcissistic antics, Bayliss rose from his chair and overrode Macready’s manoeuvring. He then corralled the cast to enter in various groups from different sides of the stage. Consequently, Macready got upset that he wasn’t given a solo bow and started to mope. Bayliss responded by articulating his reasoning to his sullen King Henry.

‘It’s a school production. A group effort. Not a star vehicle,’ Bayliss reminded his leading man.

‘But I’m playing the title role,’ claimed Macready.

‘Macready, you’re giving a good performance but you’re a schoolboy not Laurence Olivier,’ countered a determined Bayliss.

‘Maybe but I’m playing the same role as Olivier,’ reasoned Macready.

‘Yes, but as part of a school production,’ emphasised Bayliss.

‘It’s still the same play, sir,’ insisted Macready.

'But in a completely different context, Macready,' concluded Bayliss emphatically.

After this exchange, Macready went into a predictable sulk, while Bayliss proceeded to thank the whole company. The rehearsal had finished much later than expected and as the cast and crew departed, Bayliss sat on his chair alone and isolated, irritated by Macready's juvenile egotism. He noted that everybody left the building very quickly. Instinctively, he took these abrupt departures as a rejection of his direction but after another swig from his flask, he reflected more rationally. It was late, he'd overrun and the boys needed to return to their houses for bedtime and the staff to their families.

Bayliss gathered his things together and put them in his black leather bag. He then decided to go on stage and check the set. As he did so, he noted that the furniture was too untarnished like something newly imported from Scandinavia. He also thought that the walls were similarly impeccable. Regrettably, he doubted if there was time for them to be broken down. As he was about to continue his obsessive wanderings, he heard a yell at the back of Big Hall. It was the effervescent O'Reilly.

'Have you finished? shouted O'Reilly, wearing a brown working coat and holding a ring of variously sized keys.

'Yes. Thank you, O'Reilly. Just give me a minute,' requested Bayliss, who clambered off the stage and collected his bag.

'How did it go?' enquired an intrigued O'Reilly.

'Let's say, we got there in the end,' responded Bayliss wearily.

'It's hard work these plays. I know that from the brother,' divulged O'Reilly.

'Is he an actor?' asked Bayliss.

'Well sort of. He's a carpenter but he won the All Ireland,' proclaimed O'Reilly proudly.

'What's that O'Reilly,' queried a bewildered Bayliss.

'The biggest amateur drama competition in the country. He won the Best Actor award,' stressed the effusive O'Reilly.

'For what?' questioned Bayliss.

'Joxer Daly in Juno and the Paycock,' asserted O'Reilly. 'He thought of going professional but he was too busy.'

‘Busy?’ probed Bayliss.

‘With his carpentry, of course,’ added O’Reilly brusquely. ‘He couldn’t be footling around doing plays all the time.’

‘I see,’ pondered Bayliss, taken aback by O’Reilly’s artistic assertions.

‘Anyway, all those Abbey people are messers. Look what they did to O’Casey,’ declared O’Reilly. ‘A friend of the brother rang him in Devon for advice about Juno and somebody with a thick Dublin accent answered and said ‘I’ll see if he’s here’. After a pause, the same person came back and insisted adamantly ‘no, he’s not here!’ and then slammed down the phone.’

‘Who was he, then? enquired a confused Bayliss.

‘O’Casey of course,’ stated O’Reilly. ‘Ireland made him very bitter, you know,’ he remarked.

‘That’s a pity O’Reilly as bitterness can be very corrosive,’ contemplated a philosophical Bayliss.

‘Don’t I know it? I had an uncle who was an actor. He was very bitter about the British. He took to the streets in 1916 and killed a policeman. He was regarded as a hero.’

‘I see..’ hesitated an alarmed Bayliss.

‘He was a good catholic though, always went to mass. He didn’t really like O’Casey’s work. He had small parts in his plays at the Abbey but felt uncomfortable. He was very conservative. O’Casey was too much of a communist for his liking.’

‘O’Reilly. I hate to interrupt this fascinating conversation but perhaps we can talk another time,’ suggested Bayliss. I’m a bit tired and need to get some sleep.’

‘Oh sorry, Mr Bayliss. I just thought you’d be interested,’ assumed an offended O’Reilly.

‘I certainly am. I don’t know enough about Ireland and would like to learn more. It’s just that I’m exhausted after the rehearsal.’

‘I understand Mr Bayliss. Ireland is only regarded as an afterthought to the British.’

‘You’re probably right O’Reilly but let’s discuss Anglo-Irish relations after the play has finished.’

‘There are still problems over there and it could blow up in the Brits’ faces, if you get my meaning.’

‘Thank you, O’Reilly. Please, let’s leave now.’

Eventually the garrulous O’Reilly stopped his insistent rhetoric and the two men moved towards the exit. O’Reilly made sure all the practical lights were off and closed the huge exit door with a dramatic bang. Following these decibels, he ceremoniously held the keys up to a nearby quadrangle light, made his choice and locked the door. Bayliss, who had patiently been observing this ritual, then said ‘goodnight’ to which O’Reilly gruffly replied. After that uneasy moment, the two men departed their separate ways and made their way back to their respective homes.

During the final rehearsals, Bayliss’s teaching became increasingly erratic. His grasp of European history started faltering. So much so, that he got the events of the 1848 revolutions mixed up and hastily had to consult the oeuvre of A.J.P. Taylor. Directing Henry V had made Bayliss exhausted, nervous and bad tempered. Unsurprisingly, his wife Mary had become tired of the whole enterprise. She thought that she’d married a witty, urbane schoolmaster but instead she was living with a tense, alcoholic play director. While she was sympathetic to his creative endeavours, things would have to change. After the play finished, she was going to sit down and have a good talk with Hubert Aloysius Bayliss.

In the meantime, Augustus, their baby boy, was becoming more of a handful and was peeing in his pants at regular intervals. Bayliss kept reassuring Mary that it would all be over shortly and that they’d have a good break in Bath, during the holidays. Despite imploring her to be patient, Bayliss realised that Mary couldn’t wait much longer. She was finding his lack of support a severe strain. Nonetheless, the languid Bayliss realised that he had to be obsessive and ruthless if he was going to get his epic into acceptable shape. He now understood those film clips of Cecil B DeMille bellowing through a megaphone. With a huge cast of amateurs, he needed to constantly drive them so they didn’t become an undisciplined rabble.

Everybody connected with the production attended the dress rehearsal, including Françoise and Yvette. Françoise, wearing a brown coat to protect herself from the freezing hall, came early to see Rutter backstage in an empty classroom. Rutter was delighted to hear more details about Françoise's tennis victory, given that he couldn't fully appreciate the game's fluctuations, while camouflaged in the distant shrubbery and being attacked by undiplomatic gnats. After all, he'd only recently recovered from One Ball's vicious studs' assault.

Rutter told Françoise, that he'd finally managed to collect the photos and camera from the chemist. He'd got permission from Pongo to go into town on the pretext of buying a specialist book on wicket-keeping. He discovered that the photos were indistinct and blurred. They looked more like the abstract experimental work of an art student on drugs than reliable forensic evidence. As a result of this desecration, Rutter gave Françoise the camera and photos to return to One Ball. When they conferred surreptitiously before the dress rehearsal, they felt frustrated that their strategy had undermined their access to intimacy. Their love affair was now reduced to occasional, clandestine snogging. Nonetheless, they reluctantly accepted that they must keep to their plan and let One Ball down gently.

When Françoise returned his photographic property before the dress rehearsal, One Ball regarded it as confirmation of her commitment. The way Rutter continuously looked angrily at him, only emphasised his seductive triumph. In fact, during the final rehearsals, One Ball hadn't talked to the ludicrous Dauphin. Instead, he'd just given him disapproving glances, which were reciprocated with contempt. He would challenge this disdain after he'd looked at the photos. In the meantime, One Ball intended to revel in his newfound love and enjoy performing a play by England's greatest playwright.

Françoise was surprised that One Ball wasn't in period costume but in modern dress: a t shirt with 'Henry V' inscribed on its front, light blue jeans and plimsolls. Such a costume seemed more appropriate for a musical than a Shakespearean production. One Ball explained that Bayliss wanted a contemporary connection with the audience and for the Chorus to be visually outside the action. Apparently, Anne had persuaded the director to make this significant change at the last moment. One Ball believed that it was the designer's way of infiltrating some form of Brechtian alienation into the production. Initially, Bayliss reluctantly agreed to the change to keep Anne quiet. However, contrary to his previous protestations, he secretly enjoyed putting his personal signature on the production, especially given the abandonment of his smoke effect. As much as he hated being fashionable, he couldn't resist making a self-conscious directorial statement, even though he didn't really believe in it. Françoise understood the thought behind the change but wasn't totally convinced that it would work. Consequently, she resorted to blandly telling the struggling thespian that it sounded 'interesting'. One Ball felt indifferent to his new attire but was delighted when the kitchen maid was keen to set up their next assignation. Françoise, reverting to Barbara Stanwyck mode but without the sunglasses, temptingly arranged for them to meet at the back of James B next Sunday after lunch, to go for that long walk. She was determined to keep him close, right to the end of term.

Meanwhile Hubert Aloysius Bayliss got himself ready for the dress rehearsal in the only way he knew how, by imbibing more whisky. He hadn't drunk so much for years and was worried that it might become a habit. Certainly, Mary had concerns, not least when he was driving. Bayliss dismissively brushed these aside, denying that he was an alcoholic and telling her that he'd drunk very little. Luckily, the black, neutral flask around his neck nullified accurate measurement. Publically he combatted such concerns with talk of a 'wee top-up'. By using a Scottish phrase, Bayliss tried to trivialise his alcoholic intake and make it more acceptable. Privately, he knew he had a problem. In fact, he'd noticed the boys giggling derisively when he took a swig. He just hoped that after the ordeal of the school play, he could revert to less conspicuous consumption. Unfortunately, the progress of the dress rehearsal didn't help his path to abstinence.

One Ball gave a new definition to the word monotonous. He was so nervous that he just blasted his lines like an unhinged general shouting at his troops before battle. Rice and Boot as the Archbishops were slow and indistinct. Macready, loving the sound of his own voice, seemed to be acting in a play of his own. Sully as Mistress Quickly couldn't be heard. The Governor of Harfleur's vertigo hadn't disappeared. Katharine had 'no tits' and her wig still slid comically to the side of her head. The lights for the fire in the camp scene didn't come on, plunging all the characters into semi darkness. The sound for Agincourt was neither at the right volume nor from the correct direction. The French court lurched alarmingly into caricature, Macready was inappropriately crude in his courting of Katharine and the curtain call was still a mess. Apart from that, everything was fine!

At the end of the dress rehearsal, there was a smattering of applause from the auditorium.

Bayliss then ordered the whole company to assemble on stage. He had about thirty minutes to give notes. He tried to be encouraging and make his points simply and clearly. First, he diplomatically invited Françoise and Yvette to comment on Staines's accent, to which they responded with a mixture of encouragement and constructive criticism. Bayliss then complimented the cast on their energy but appealed to them to be more focused and not gabble their lines like a strained recitation. He stressed the need for the audience to believe that they were actually speaking for the first time. Bayliss then pointed out some extremely late lighting cues to a surly Zuckenberg, asked Anne to make Katharine's perpetually moving wig tauter and requested Higginbottom to secure the rostra even more tightly for the vertiginous Governor of Harfleur. He then recommended that Staines got hold of the Sunday Pictorial and put some of its pages into his bra to bolster his 'breasts'. He also urged the ever-vain Macready not to play the scene with Katharine as if he's about to assault her. He reminded him that it's a gentle, courtly scene and to woo her gradually. To avoid obliterating his fragile ego, Bayliss praised his leading man for his terrific 'Once more unto the breach' and its precise and thrilling rendition. A bit of an exaggeration, but nothing like a bit of flattery to build up confidence. Bayliss ended by congratulating everybody on their committed work and assured them that the performance would be a great success. The boys immediately burst into applause, embracing their own enthusiasm. They then hastily departed from the huge, freezing building as Bayliss shouted after them to be in good time for the performance. Several discordant 'yes sirs' were yelled back as the cast returned to their houses with morale high.

The next day, an hour before the performance, the cast assembled in the classroom block next to Big Hall. The male characters changed in Burke's classroom. Burke was a young, fair-haired maths teacher from Crewe. He was nicknamed 'Johnnie' after the American crying crooner Johnnie Ray, who was renowned for controversial performances, which incited teenagers into a lather of hysteria. Like the singer, Burke had a hearing problem and wore a deaf aid, so the boys made the association with the frenzied singer. In fact, Sully, while in the shower did a good imitation of Johnnie Ray, singing Build Your Love (On a Strong Foundation). As water poured water over his well-upholstered, youthful body, he worked himself into comic blues mania, which had his surrounding audience laughing uproariously.

Maths master 'Johnnie' was known for throwing chalk at boys who weren't concentrating. On one occasion during a summer term, Burke missed the object of his attack and his missile flew through an open window and hit the irascible O'Reilly, who was doing some maintenance. Their relationship never recovered and O'Reilly took it as a deliberate attack on his republican views. He even threatened to inform Oliver of the 'savage assault'. However, after some reflection, he realised that he wouldn't be able to win against the bastions of the British establishment. He preferred to do his job well, take the money and be the resident dissident.

Brown's new Sony transistor blared across Johnnie's classroom as the boys changed into their medieval costumes. The ardent rocker had successfully managed to get permission to use his parents' birthday present for the run of the play. Although Radio Luxembourg was a bit faint, the sound of Don't Knock the Rock and Cumberland Gap helped to give the boys not only entertainment but energy. Hayes as stage manager but attired in the costume of the Boy, kept coming into the classroom at various intervals, telling the unruly mob how much time was left before the performance. Meanwhile, One Ball disdainfully observed Ryder, who despite his socialist views had deigned to play the King of France. Occasionally, the radical choir leader exchanged tense looks with a smug Potts, transmitting his contempt for the infamous bully. In response, One Ball just blithely ignored him. Having seen off the nefarious Rutter, he wasn't going to succumb to the school's dastardly Lenin.

Those with leading roles were more subdued while those with smaller ones rock 'n' rolled to Radio Lux. For instance, Macready, after looking at himself in his mirror and assiduously applying his makeup, left the classroom and strode slowly up and down the nearby corridor. He believed in makeup and the necessity of artifice, even if others didn't. It was part of the whole process of illusion. He didn't care for the new naturalistic trends coming from America through the method and Brando. He thought that British style and technique were superior. Alas, for 'the great actor', a lot of the cast didn't agree with him and had been seduced by On the Waterfront and mumbling Marlon. Macready was particularly disappointed that Bayliss had only insisted on the female characters being made-up. In fact, Anne was helping them in the adjoining classroom, away from the noisy rockers.

The school's King Henry now thought that a lot of the cast looked dramatically anaemic. He feared that they would appear like insipid apparitions under the lights. As he bestrode the corridor, he went through his main speeches sotto voce, or at least less projected by his ostentatious standards. He then went to the lavatory to make sure that he wouldn't have an accident on stage. He stayed there for some time, continuing to rehearse his lines, concentrating on his first scene. He believed in getting those opening exchanges really fixed. To him, they were like the first steps of a child walking. If you succeeded in confidently asserting your initial presence, you were on your way. In fact, he became so engrossed with the part that he'd forgotten the time. Suddenly, he heard the desperate cries of Hayes in the corridor like an old music hall song-'Macready, Macready. Has anyone seen Macready?' Having registered

Hayes's calls, he yelled from his seat on the loo with considerable projection, 'I'm here!' Hayes then moved swiftly to where the sound emanated and entered the nearby classroom bog.

'Thank goodness you've got such a theatrical voice,' acknowledged a relieved Hayes, speaking in the lavatory.

'What is it Hayes?' enquired Henry V dismissively while pulling a chain.

'Ten minutes, Macready,' warned Hayes, focusing on Macready's cubicle.

'Thank you, Hayes,' said Macready as if the stage manager was a professional callboy.

'Please remain in the classroom,' pleaded Hayes.

'I'll be walking up and down the corridor,' pronounced Macready grandly.

'All right, Macready. I'll look for you there,' conceded Hayes, exiting hurriedly.

The audience were now gathering in Big Hall. Oliver was dressed in a smart blue suit, while his wife had taken the precaution of wearing a light green swing coat. Even in spring with the heat on, the large building could still be cold. Pongo Smallman's only concession to his trademark grey trousers and jacket was a blue handkerchief in his top pocket. He moved towards a designated staff area in the middle of the auditorium with his friend Collins, who'd come dressed in a blazer, more suitable for a sporting occasion. They were joined by Basil Ponsonby-Smythe, who was looking swaggeringly erudite in his herringbone suit and red tie. At a distance behind them, Bayliss was sitting next to his wife Mary in the back row. A strategic position from which to beat a hasty retreat if the production proved to be a disaster.

The play's director had reluctantly dispensed with his flask and his black casual attire and had changed into a grey suit. 'Back to being a bloody schoolmaster,' he lamented to himself, 'probably the end of my days as a bohemian director.' Mary had managed to get a baby sitter, the daughter of one of the science teachers. She was a bit concerned that she was only thirteen but Bayliss reassured her that she was a sensible girl and mature for her years. However, Bayliss's nerves weren't helped by not being able to indulge in the contents of his flask. Mary, wrapped in a beige coat, noted his apprehension and held out her hand to the fearful director. Bayliss clasped it nervously and thanked her for her support.

Gradually all the boys entered noisily into the towering hall. They were full of loquacious gaiety because the term was about to end. They moved merrily towards the front half of the auditorium, found the area allocated for their house and started to read their programmes. They either brooded over its contents or laughed boisterously at the absurd transformations that were going to take place, particularly those involving a change of sex. Oblivious to such puerility, the staff continued to make their way to their allotted seats, ignoring the boys' antics. A spruce Killer and a doleful Mrs Killer, the stern Mrs Hackett, and Jet, her bored husband, who again looked as if he'd prefer to be on another planet, had all come to support the artistic enterprise.

When Marian entered the building, she did so tactically. She moved deliberately and self-consciously to her seat in her tightly belted brown raincoat with its black-bowed matching hat. She passed Killer and gave him a menacing smile as she hadn't heard a dickybird from him since the house rugby final. He nervously adjusted his purple tie and buried himself in his programme. His wife observed her husband's insecurity and whispered intensely through gritted teeth, 'bloody well give us back our 53 pounds'. Killer, knowing Deirdre could explode venomously, implored her to be quiet, especially as he was still trying to persuade Illingworth and Son that he was fraudulently exploited. She responded wearily with a cynical 'yes sir, no sir, three bags full sir'. In fact, Deirdre was only attending out of perverse loyalty. She hated Shakespeare, mainly because a horrendous teacher at her school whacked pupils with a ruler when they forgot the bard's speeches. Thus, she looked forward to the whole ritual being over as soon as possible

As the time for the performance approached, more and more staff and pupils poured into the imposing edifice. Among them were a wary Sykes with his bloodshot, gimlet eyes, Le Mesurier in an outmoded double-breasted forties suit, cheerily greeting all and sundry and the Rev Elwyn wearing his formal dog collar, his eyes intermittently blinking while occasionally looking heavenwards as if in search of elusive spiritual inspiration. Some boys, fearing that they were late, charged into the building like demented buffaloes, breathless and unkempt, relieved that the performance hadn't started. In contrast, the Major, together with Victoria Wallace and Root, made their way to their seats in a relaxed and elegant fashion. Various boys stopped their babble and noted how attractive Victoria looked in her fur collared red coat. In fact, the Major and Victoria were appearing for the first time in public as a couple. The boys saw this as quite a statement. The way the Major displayed courteous behaviour by standing in the aisle and making way for Victoria to find her seat, only substantiated their views. In addition, the Major was wearing a new single breasted check suit. Such was the transformation that the boys concluded that Victoria had inspired the senior housemaster to do a Cary Grant.

In contrast, the bedraggled Mr and Mr Bowen followed, walking hurriedly with the solitary Darbishire not far behind. Boys and staff greeted Mrs Bowen, a warm, ashen-faced woman, in an unbecoming blue coat. In contrast, her husband, the small wiry Welshman, wrapped in a gloomy dark suit, looked sombre. His eyes only seemed to light up when talking about rugby. However, the genial Darbishire had obviously made an effort and was wearing a dashing burgundy sports jacket. He talked to everybody in his usual polite way, making sure that he didn't say 'ok, all right'. Regrettably, this didn't stop a group of cheeky boys, muttering the oft-repeated catchphrase.

With everybody assembled, O'Reilly approached Bayliss and told him that he'd locked the main door and that latecomers could enter discreetly via the side entrance. O'Reilly reassured him that he'd quietly usher the stragglers into some vacant seats at the back. After wishing the tense director good luck, the caretaker departed.

Within a few minutes, the play started and One Ball as Chorus set the scene. Thankfully, Bayliss thought that his textual substitution of 'red brick box' for Shakespeare's 'wooden O' made total sense, given Big Hall's proscenium stage. Although he was obviously nervous, One Ball was still authoritative and clear. Bayliss was pleased that he seemed more accessible in the new costume. He was delighted with his own inventiveness, conveniently forgetting that the idea was Anne's. In any case, the apprehensive director was relieved that there was a good start. Thankfully, Boot and Rice then managed to get a few laughs as the Archbishops, although Bayliss regretted not cutting their interminable opening scene more radically. Boot forgot his words but Rice covered his error quickly and Bayliss didn't think anybody noticed. Overall, the director adored the British swagger of the production. Macready embodied this style with an imposing Henry, who appeared more disciplined than in his previous histrionic efforts. Everything was going swimmingly until the tennis balls scene. Initially it started well and Beckett as Exeter was less boring than usual. Unfortunately, he became so immersed in his efforts to be dynamic that when it came to the line 'what treasure uncle?' Beckett couldn't open the chest to give a reply. Bayliss closed his eyes and prayed, as Mary put her hands around his shoulder. 'I know,' whispered Bayliss, 'this production's going to be about a bloody chest.' Just when Bayliss thought that the play would grind to a halt and that he might even have to make an announcement, Beckett yanked at the lock so violently that the chest suddenly sprang open like a maniacal jack-in-the-box. Immediately, Beckett forcefully exclaimed, 'tennis balls, my liege!' So aggressive was his intonation that he gave the impression that he wasn't only criticising the impertinence of the French court but also the disobedient chest. In contrast, Bayliss just sighed with relief that his production could continue.

In the next scene, the audience certainly enjoyed the performances of Brown and Bunter as Nym and Bardolph. Bayliss thought that this was because they came across more like modern rockers than medieval soldiers. Nonetheless, he persuaded himself that at least they communicated strongly. Later, Binns got a wholly inappropriate laugh for 'Pistol's cock is up', much to Oliver's displeasure. Then Hayes was late for his first cue as the Boy and out of breath for his initial dialogue. He had been looking urgently for the French court, who had left the classroom and were nervously sharing a Woodbine in the toilet. After his initial annoyance, Bayliss convinced himself that Hayes's mistake made the Boy more vulnerable.

In fact, Bayliss was delighted with the production's visceral sweep. He particularly liked Macready rushing forward with his soldiers and delivering 'Once more unto the breach' with such inspirational passion. In fact, Macready got so excited that his crown dropped onto the stage. Bayliss didn't think it mattered as the emotional impact of the scene was so exhilarating. Anyway, Macready astutely used the situation to his advantage, with remarkable aplomb. Having taken the crown from one of the soldiers, he raised it in the air before declaiming 'Cry 'God for Harry!' He then placed the crown triumphantly on his head at the end of the speech and exited, amidst a hullabaloo that made a football crowd roar a faint, nebulous murmur. Bayliss was thrilled as this truly exemplified the emotional heart of his interpretation. A celebration of British values against an oppressive enemy. After all, wasn't that what World War Two was about?

The quality of Barrett's accent as Macmorris, also surprised the director. It seemed convincing, at least to his ear anyway. Bayliss had to admit that the Carson boy had indeed made a significant contribution. Later, he was relieved to see that the Governor of Harfleur didn't collapse in a dizzy faint. The ever reliable Higginbottom had managed to build a surreptitious handrail to one side of the rostra, which Anne regarded as visually incoherent, but at least it gave the distraught Governor the confidence to surrender the town without the fear of making a fatal descent. Bayliss was also thankful that the regal music covered most of the noisy scene change to the French Palace, which sounded like the work of cantankerous removal men. During Katharine's initial scene, Mary whispered to her husband that Staines looked gorgeous. Bayliss didn't want to get into the minefield of the boys' sexuality. He was just pleased that his wig had stabilised and that Staines's French had improved since Françoise and Yvette's input. Yet, there were some still some O level errors, which frustrated the director. Why, for instance did he still sound an r in 'doigts'? Maybe he was getting mixed up with 'droit'. Didn't our princess realise that there's a difference between 'fingers' and 'right'?

Overall, Bayliss was glad that the cast got to the interval without major mishaps. He just wished that he could now get hold of his beloved black flask and continue his relationship with Scotland's finest export. Infuriatingly, this was impossible, especially with Oliver on the prowl. Still he'd make up for it later. In the meantime, he told Mary that he'd like to go backstage, to which she diplomatically agreed.

Bayliss was just going to give a few practical notes and some encouragement. First, he looked for Hayes. When he found the conscientious stage manager in 'Johnnie' Burke's classroom having an argument about props with the petulant Macready, he calmed both of them down. He then went through the positioning of the fire and the logs in the camp scene. After which, he assured them that they were doing well and the play was going splendidly. Bayliss then went out to the corridor to assemble the whole cast. In doing so, a frenetic Binns, dressed in chainmail and a feathered hat, almost decapitated the director, while practising his swordplay with the benign Rivers and a similarly clad French soldier. When Bayliss finally got everybody together, he told them to keep up the energy and concentrate right to the end. He then wished them good luck and departed.

By going backstage, Bayliss was able to avoid bumping into opinionated members of staff. However, on his return to Big Hall, he encountered a tactful Basil, who thought that he'd 'got a lot out of the boys', whatever that really meant. He then made his way back next to the steadfast Mary, who was gorging herself on a bar of Nestles milk chocolate. Bayliss accepted her offer of a piece and ate it voraciously. It wasn't exactly a substitute for the Scottish liquid but at least it offered some comfort. He also whispered in her ear that he appreciated her patience with all 'this theatrical madness' and that he promised to contribute more domestically after the play had finished.

Suddenly, the shrill sound of trumpets heralded the second half and out came One Ball as Chorus, setting the scene with 'Now entertain conjecture of a time…' Bayliss thought that One Ball was a little over the top but at least he woke up the audience and rapidly got them back into the play. Binns as Pistol was also melodramatic and still waved his sword dangerously but fortunately Macready narrowly escaped unscathed. 'Still,' thought Bayliss 'at least we have energy and pace'. This helped to accommodate the camp scene, giving Macready time to revel in the contrasting intimacy. He did this surprisingly well and Bayliss felt that his 'Upon the King!' was the best he'd ever done. It was both heartfelt and moving and what's more, even the fire lighting worked. In contrast, the boys in the French court still played their scenes too broadly, as if they were performing sketches in a student's revue. 'At least the audience laughed, which was something I suppose,' Bayliss reassured himself.

As the play progressed towards its denouement, it was clear that the egotistical and infuriating Macready was holding the production together. Bayliss thought that the boy was a terrible pain in the posterior but he had to concede that he had talent. While his St Crispin's Day speech was a little mannered, you could certainly sense the audience listening carefully to the power of Shakespeare's words. In contrast, the music and effects for the battle of Agincourt dramatised the unabated violence of war that Bayliss envisaged. Even though a couple of maroons didn't go off and some of Zuckerberg's lighting states were still more suitable for a Wagnerian opera, Bayliss relished the raw theatricality and youthful energy that the cast brought to the action. Bayliss felt that it vindicated his vision of a 'patriotic entertainment' and of standing up resolutely for what was morally right.

It also transpired that Barrel Madoc was so relishing the part of Fluellen that the leek, which was attached to his hat, became dislodged and dangled precariously like a puppet on a string. In his final comic altercation with Binns's volatile Pistol, the vegetable became such an encumbrance that Barrel decided to rip it off and stuff it under his belt. This didn't seem to matter. In fact, it brought extra amusement to the scene, not least from Yvette, who laughed uncontrollably. She was experiencing another part of Barrel's character, not least hearing him speak with such a pronounced Welsh accent. Unfortunately, neither she nor Françoise could fully decipher what he was saying.

When the play moved to the final scenes of reconciliation and the King's Palace at Troyes, Bayliss feared that Macready might launch into crude histrionics. He did start with a declamatory swagger but as he proceeded to woo Katharine, he managed a greater sensitivity than usual. Consequently, Staines, the blonde fitness fanatic, responded to Macready's charming tone and they bonded well. So much so, that they even managed some delicate humour within their dynastic negotiations. Bayliss was delighted that the personal blended seamlessly with the political, Henry showing the same resolution in wooing as he did with his territorial claims on the battlefield.

However, Bayliss thought that he should have trimmed Burgundy's speech at the end. He found some of the pastoral imagery overwrought, although the stilted delivery of a gargantuan member of Ironside A's rugby scrum didn't help its execution. Finally, One Ball came forward centre stage to conclude the play with the final speech, with its glimpse into the future and a final homage to the audience: 'In your fair minds, let this acceptance take.'

As soon as the lights started to dim, the applause rang out, interspersed with hearty cheers. The curtain call remained a mess but by that time, no one seemed to care. Macready bowed so low that Bayliss thought that he'd end up kissing his own feet. Wolf whistles hailed Staines as Katharine, about which Oliver looked decidedly uneasy and glared intensely at the offenders to little effect. When various boys stood up while continuing their anarchic noisy clamour, the staff also sheepishly rose. Meanwhile, Oliver was becoming deeply disconcerted. He didn't believe that such appreciation should invite unruly behaviour. The boys' response was more like an American hoedown that he'd seen in some vulgar Hollywood musicals.

However, Bayliss was delighted. He couldn't believe that he was getting a standing ovation. All right, it wasn't The Old Vic or Stratford-Upon-Avon but it was still a standing ov. He looked around to see his colleagues, a lively Pongo Smallman, an appreciative Collins and a delighted Major and Victoria, all applauding incessantly. Even Root was smiling, leaning forward and telling the Major, 'I just wish Rupert could have seen this'. Françoise and Yvette were repeatedly shouting 'Bravo! Bravo!' Mrs Hackett rose, clapping insistently as she hauled her sleepy husband to his feet. There even seemed to be a hint of a smile beginning to emerge across her taut face. The cheery Le Mesurier and the eerie Sykes also stood up while they nattered away. Marian's Lancashire accent bellowed 'well done lads'. Killer, standing straight-backed to his full height, applauded the boys as if he was observing an admirable military parade. Mrs Killer, was less formal, waving her hands in the air as if she was welcoming sailors back to port. She'd obviously come to the conclusion that Shakespeare wasn't that bad after all. In contrast, a harassed Rev Elwyn and an awkward Oliver were clapping more demurely. It seemed that they found extremity of emotion embarrassing. Bowen and Darbishire were less inhibited. They certainly saw it as a win in sporting terms and were putting their hands together as if they were celebrating a rugby victory. Next to them, the small, frail figure of Mrs Bowen, was on tiptoe, clapping above her head. Meanwhile, the effete Basil Ponsonby-Smythe was beaming happily. After all, such success would only add to the prestige of the English department.

Everybody revelled in sharing a positive experience. It was a unique occasion where staff and their families came together with the boys. It wasn't a success because the cast were all budding Oliviers, although Macready would certainly dispute that. It was because the company brought spirit and enthusiasm to the work of England's greatest playwright and shared it with their community.

Afterwards in the classroom dressing rooms, there was a release of nervous energy, which led to loud euphoric outbursts, accompanied by Little Richard's Long Tall Sally blasting out of Brown's transistor. The cast were both relieved and exhilarated as they laughed and hugged each other. An elated Bayliss came round, congratulated everybody, thanking them for their magnificent efforts and then disappeared, excusing himself by saying that he had to get up early. On his departure, the boys started to dance to the ecstatic rock 'n' roller in celebration of their endeavours.

On leaving the classrooms, the cast ignored the vigilant Anne's earnest pleas and left their costumes in a bedraggled state, sprawled across the rooms like the remnants of a disaster.

When the boys evacuated the building, Macready started going wild, chasing the heavily made-up Staines across the Quadrangle. As he ferociously pursued the PE expert, followed by some delirious cast members, Macready kept shouting: 'Katharine! Katharine! My queen! My queen!' Fortunately, by now the masters had all returned to their homes and anyway the dim lights surrounding the area couldn't easily discern the chasing figures scurrying across the dark landscape. Zuckerberg, the resident purveyor of lighting gloom, was one of the attendant group, and relished every moment of this murky expressionistic drama. As the prince of darkness followed the anarchic Macready pursuing his prey, the pervading atmosphere only confirmed to him that he could have produced something much more visually imaginative, if Bayliss had been more radical.

When Macready eventually got closer to his object of desire, he urged Katharine to kiss him, calling him 'my beautiful queen,' 'my gorgeous, French lovely' and various other hyperbolic epithets. Staines angrily confronted the despairing 'King of England' and told him to 'piss off'. Undaunted, Macready made a despairing lunge at Staines, which the nimble gymnast sidestepped; leaving Macready spread-eagled on the Quadrangle grass like a rugby player failing to stop an opponent from scoring a try. The other cast members, who were following their leading man's hounding of the cherry-lipped blonde, were prompted into further hysteria. Meanwhile, the agile Staines ran back to his house to avoid the baying mob and any further lascivious attention. As he disappeared into the distance, Macready lay on the turf forlornly shouting, 'Katharine! Forgive me! My beautiful queen!' Eventually, Brown and Bunter picked up 'the great actor' and gave him a swig of Dom Pérignon, which the cast shared surreptitiously. As the boys partook of the appealing beverage, nobody seemed to care where the rockers had acquired the wine. Their alcoholic intake just inspired them to sing a lively version of There's No Business Like Show Business as they went back to their respective houses.

After the closure of the Henry V production, the school was to break up the following week so there was little time to reflect on theatrical success. Although One Ball disapproved of the undisciplined shenanigans of some of the cast and detested being in the proximity of the abominable Rutter, he'd still enjoyed taking part in the drama. After all, it concluded a good term. He had triumphed in rugby, done well in the school play and most importantly won the affections of Françoise, with whom he'd had an enchanting walk near the strategically remote Byron Wood. The only downside was that although he'd got his camera back, the accompanying photos didn't reveal anything apart from Sully's abject failure as a photographer. The pictures were so obscure and taken at such absurd angles that they would never have the slightest chance of being used as evidence. The matchstick men in a Lowry painting were more decipherable.

One Ball still regarded Sully as a problem, given the abject failure of his mission. However, while he was smitten with Françoise, he chose to marginalise the difficulty. The French kitchen maid had definitely finished with Rutter and having witnessed his dreadful, effeminate Dauphin, he was confident that she wouldn't have regretted her decision. In fact, One Ball looked forward to seeing her more regularly next term. Still, he knew that he had to be cautious if he wanted to make more progress with his work. While his cogently argued essays always got good marks, he had to embark on serious revision if he was going to confirm his university place. He told himself that he mustn't get too excited about a woman, who would be leaving the country at the end of next term, even though he still wanted to use those damn rubbers. He decided not to think about such matters until he returned to the school. In the meantime, he needed to make sure that he was prepared to deal with his mother during the holidays.

At the same time, Hayes, Barrett and Sully were checking that they had sufficient belongings for the break. Although, they were glad that the term was over, they all felt a sense of achievement being in the school play. Hayes was particularly pleased about the praise that he received for both his portrayal of the Boy and his stage management. In fact, he found his part more interesting than he'd originally thought. Contrary to the more bellicose intentions of Bayliss's production, it made him think about the terrible consequences of war. However, he did find it difficult to lie dead convincingly for so long. Thankfully, the audience were at a sufficient distance not to witness his heavy breathing.

Similarly, Barrett was happy with his Irish accent and grateful for Carson's help. He thanked the Chuck Berry obsessive, who was delighted with his inserted credit in the programme. Nonetheless, despite the elation surrounding the theatrical adventure, he would still observe One Ball carefully. He'd noticed that he'd softened recently but Ryder had advised him to be vigilant and get in touch promptly if the monitor returned to his authoritarian, bullying ways.

As for Sully, he enjoyed being in the play, although he found that wearing Mistress Quickly's wig was like having a brick on your head. He certainly relished scrunching up the News of the World to form his 'tits' as he hated the scandal sheet anyway. He was also delighted to receive so many compliments, particularly from an adoring Mrs Hackett, who shook his hand so intensely that he thought that it might fall off. The exhilaration of being in the play made Sully forget the punishments hanging over him. Although One Ball hadn't mentioned them for many weeks, Sully feared that this could be a temporary aberration. Still, at least he was getting support from Barrett and Ryder to combat any despotic resurgence from the intimidating monitor. He couldn't forget the injustice of 'rank insubordination' and 'outright duplicity' but he was still determined to enjoy the vacation. He was particularly looking forward to seeing some opera for the first time. His father had booked seats for Covent Garden, so who knows, maybe he'd see Maria Callas?

Although the cast enjoyed their theatrical experience only Andrew Macready, the production's self-proclaimed star, wanted to join the profession. He had already decided to apply to drama schools, not just universities. For him, Henry V was only the start of his insatiable ambition but as the term drew to a close, Macready, like the other boys, looked forward enthusiastically to the holidays.

Summer Term

One Ball returned to school rejuvenated. After his rugby and theatrical triumphs, he felt confident that he could eventually seduce Françoise. In fact, One Ball had done some revision during the holidays to give himself more space to see the French maid, despite being interrupted by his mother's desire to socialise. Among such excursions he had to endure was a visit to see an appalling local pantomime and meet the leering, bald-headed director. Then there were the incessant visits from the Kirwins, who were constantly harping on about the inadequacies of Macmillan and his Etonian cabinet, while conveniently forgetting the limitations of the de Valera's priest-ridden regime in their beloved Ireland. Although One Ball was pleased that his mother was so active, he had suspicions that she might be having an affair with Peregrine, the ghastly director of Babes in the Wood, whom One Ball thought was a 'pretentious wanker' and he felt that was being polite.

One Saturday in the second week of term, One Ball suddenly decided that he needed to go for a run. In the changing room, he took off his school uniform, which in summer was a white shirt, dark blue blazer, grey socks and trousers or shorts if you were a junior. Having discarded his summer attire, One Ball started to put on James B's rugby shirt, shorts and plimsolls. He felt he needed a bit of exercise after the indulgence of the holidays and withstanding his mother's burgeoning social life. He also wanted to calm down his desire for Françoise. He certainly found her very attractive and yes, he certainly wanted to use those bloody rubbers. However, he also knew that he needed to control himself, take his time and proceed with his studies. In the circumstances, he concluded that a run was just the tonic.

One Ball ran around the perimeter of Open Way's huge stretch of green, just as he had commanded Sully to do. Only he was doing it better and with more purpose than the feeble junior. After all, he was an able athlete, who once came tenth in the school's gruelling, long distance steeplechase run. One Ball's outstretched bare legs pounded the path around Open

Way with an insistent and constant rhythm. For a change of scenery, he decided to divert his journey and go towards a path close to the railway line. As he ran past various shrubberies, he saw two figures on a bench, staring lovingly into each other's eyes. As he got closer, a horrible vision came into focus. It was Françoise in a light green coat and Rutter with black-rimmed spectacles.

One Ball decided that he had to lance this boil and confront the traitorous Françoise and her diminutive accomplice. He slowed his run and gathered his thoughts while trying to contain his rage. As he got closer, the image became more torrid when he saw them laughing and smiling as only intimates can. He stepped onto the grass and ran towards the bench. Immediately, Rutter alerted Françoise to his arrival. She turned round anxiously and discovered One Ball glaring menacingly at her, like an intelligence officer trapping a guilty suspect. He hated betrayal and disloyalty, so he challenged Françoise directly.

'You told me that you'd finished with him,' accused One Ball rigorously.

'Yes I did,' confessed Françoise.

'Well have you?' continued One Ball resentfully.

'No I haven't,' replied Françoise defiantly.

'Why did you lie to me?' demanded One Ball angrily.

'Because I..' blurted out Françoise.

'We didn't want you blabbing about our relationship,' interrupted Rutter.

'I see. So, Françoise, what you wrote to me were lies,' insisted One Ball.

'Not entirely. I thought you did well at the rugby and I do enjoy playing tennis,' justified Françoise evasively.

'But you have no romantic inclinations?' asked a despairing One Ball.

'No,' acknowledged Françoise firmly. 'But I would like to be friends,' she added as a diplomatic afterthought.

'I see,' replied a distraught One Ball. 'I'd better go.'

One Ball ran speedily off the grass. Once he got back on the path, he slowed down and exercised more sedately. He was burning with inflamed anger. Françoise was treacherous and deceitful. She had used him in an unacceptable way. She was only interested in keeping him quiet. She had no real feelings for him. She was a cold manipulator. As One Ball jogged his way past the surrounding thickets, he thought about how he could crush Françoise and her miniscule lover. The more he considered his options, the more frustrated he became. There was insufficient evidence, thanks to Sully's ludicrous, technical incompetence. The photos were useless. 'Going up a tree? Why didn't he take a photo through the pavilion window and run away like the press do with Marilyn Monroe?' he deliberated disdainfully. He increased his speed and then started thinking of the bespectacled Rutter, swanning around as if he's about to meet Jean-Paul Sartre on the left bank. 'Why is he wearing those glasses? To reinvent himself as an intellectual? That boy is a phony and a fool. I hate the bastard,' One Ball concluded angrily.

As One Ball accelerated his run, his anger didn't diminish. He believed that someone needed to pay for this. No wonder Rutter didn't challenge him during the play. He'd been used and humiliated. But how should he respond? How could he get revenge? Telling the Major about Rutter's sexual exploits without sufficient evidence, would just be regarded as a puerile vendetta against a rival senior. Then as he ran around Open Way, an idea suddenly came to him. He needed to get Sully to go to the Major and say that he saw Françoise and Rutter having sex in the pavilion and give a graphic account of their lovemaking. Yes. That's the only way. Then the Major would have to act. He would have to protect an innocent junior and report Rutter and Françoise's behaviour to Oliver.

At last he had a clear plan. Having made a decision, One Ball increased his pace as he bounded past the science lab. 'There are a lot of lunatics who teach me there,' thought One Ball, 'why is this school made up of so many oddballs, misfits and eccentrics?' Unable to unravel this mystery, he advanced briskly. When he got closer to James B. he slowed down and turned right, jogging past Killer's house. He crossed the Avenue and went through the porch into the dayroom. He proceeded to walk quickly past Barrett, Brown and Bunter, who were arguing about forthcoming British nuclear testing. He closed his study door abruptly and collapsed into his armchair. 'Yes,' he concluded, 'Sully's got to testify.'

Marian knew that she was called the Witch of Wigan. In fact, far from railing against the boys' rudeness, she felt rather flattered by their description. It meant that she'd made an impact. It was that terrible boy Boot, who'd invented her nickname. Marian regarded him as not only rude but horribly unhygienic. She often discovered mouldy food and smelly pyjamas in his settle. Her efforts to change his revolting habits led to him putting Demerara sugar in her bed. The result of this sabotage was that Marian experienced the most unpleasant discomfort in the inner crevices of her posterior for several days. However, as the constant application of Vaseline had erased most of the resulting sores of the embarrassing ailment, she became more committed to practising her retributive skills against negligent Killer than a vindictive boy. He still hadn't come to see her as promised and Marian was certain that his wife was behind this absence.

Even though both of them came from the north, Marian disliked Deirdre Roy. She was one of nature's moaners. Everything was always wrong: if it wasn't her husband, it was little Barney, if not Barney it was bloody southerners, if it wasn't southerners, it was posh Tories and on it went. She could certainly understand Killer tiring of the patron saint of moaning. Marian thought that the only thing that Deirdre seemed to like was the money and home that came with the job. She was quite happy to acquire all that, yet she criticised the school at every available occasion, while eulogising state education.

Marian didn't agree with her polemic. She realised that the school wasn't perfect and reflected some of the anomalies of the British class system. Nonetheless, it did provide a pathway for boys from less well-off backgrounds to access higher education. Anyway, Marian thought that Deirdre should keep her own political views to herself and not bite the hand that fed her. She also got tired of hearing how much she missed her job. If that was the case, surely at least she could do some freelance work from home. In fact, the Witch of Wigan found the feckless Deirdre Roy part of a spoilt middle class that she despised.

Marian had come up the hard way. Her father was a milkman, who had next to nothing during the thirties' depression. She'd made the best use of her opportunities by working hard and showing initiative. She hated listening to Mrs Killer's constant bleating, so she didn't feel at all guilty about sleeping with her husband.

Marian also wasn't going to accept Killer's neglectful thoughtlessness. Her mother, who had slaved with self-denial to make a home and bring up three children, accepted things too readily. She was determined not to do the same. Accordingly, Marian decided to concoct a plan to embarrass Killer and his smug Geordie wife.

She'd already rung a masonry company from Wakefield, pretending to be a school secretary, and asked them to send a headstone to the Killers. Engraved on white marble would be 'Alexander 'Killer' Roy 1921-1957, Philanderer and Corporal Punishment Executor, May He Rot in Hell'. The firm did question the wording but Marian assured them that the headstone was for a school play. When the amiable Yorkshireman at the end of the phone asked for the title of the drama, Marian hastily replied The Great Fornicator. She explained that it was a new drama, written by one of the older boys. When the firm requested Mr Roy's telephone number, Marian gave them the private number of Mr Fairfax, the Britannia publican. The Yorkshireman concluded by saying that they'd ring at 3:00 pm this afternoon to arrange delivery details with Mr Roy himself.

In fact, Marian had already arranged for Mr Fairfax, who was a former actor, to play the role of Killer. She'd got the compliance of Mr Fairfax through the good offices of Mrs Butcher, the manager of the tuck shop. Mrs Butcher, who frequented Mr Fairfax's pub repeatedly, was only too willing to help. Not only was she very friendly with Marian but she also had a natural propensity for drama, so she took the afternoon off to participate in the ruse.

Marian and Mrs Butcher decided to meet up at the Britannia and have a drink at lunchtime before the enactment took place. This gave them plenty of time to imbibe before Mr Fairfax received a call from the Wakefield firm after the pub closed.

Mrs Butcher was in a playful mood, exemplified by her Rupert Bear sweater. Mrs Butcher told Marian that her children had similar jumpers as the adventures of the comic strip character captivated them in their infancy. Marian, who was enjoying a pint of lager, recognised the iconic animal and complimented Mrs Butcher on her choice. Unhesitatingly, Mrs Butcher responded by clinking her glass with Marian's and indulging in a very loud 'cheers'.

Such was their obsession with gossip that the two women were still drinking after closing time. Eventually, Mr Fairfax told them to finish quickly so as to avoid any confrontation with the local constabulary. While the publican collected the glasses and emptied the ashtrays, he assured Marian that he'd trained Mrs Fairfax to answer any future calls as his personal secretary. He told her that his wife could always contact him on the intercom, if the masonry company called while he was in the pub.

As he cleared up, Mr Fairfax got so excited about his forthcoming performance as Killer Roy that Marian had to remind him to be very polite and formal and not to use the schoolmaster's murderous nickname inadvertently. She stressed that it was important to reassure the firm, especially as she'd already inveigled them to accept a cheque on delivery. She also told him that if they enquired as to why the school weren't making a stage headstone, he was to tell them that the director wanted greater authenticity and for it to be in real marble.

'How about saying that the director had been reading about the work of Lee Strasberg and was a great believer in the method?' suggested an enthusiastic Mr Fairfax.

Neither Marian nor Mrs Butcher knew anything about Mr Strasberg and his acting philosophy but it seemed impressive, so they went along with Mr Fairfax's suggestion.

'Ok, Mr Fairfax, that sounds good,' agreed Marian encouragingly.

'I'm not a method man myself but it's very fashionable these days,' conceded Mr Fairfax.

'That'll make it really convincing,' thought Mrs Butcher, duly drowning more of her lager.

After Mr Fairfax had finished his cleaning, he invited the two women to accompany him upstairs to the flat.

Marian and Mrs Butcher brought up several bottles of drink and sandwiches before parking themselves on a rust coloured sofa. Suddenly, Mr Fairfax wanted to be excused and mysteriously disappeared, while the two women continued consuming their beer. After ten minutes, Mr Fairfax returned, dressed in a smart maroon suit.

'I do like to dress for the part. I find it helps,' he pronounced vainly.

'Oh I see,' said a surprised Marian.

'I'm old school. I used to do weekly rep at Folkestone. A new play, every week. You got used to playing many different parts. When you could remember them,' divulged an ebullient Mr Fairfax, laughing nervously.

'I like your handkerchief,' observed an admiring Mrs Butcher, referring to the pink linen protruding elegantly from the top pocket of his jacket.

'Oh, thank you,' indulged Mr Fairfax, revelling in such flattery. 'It just helps to remind me that I have to do it in style.'

'Now, remember my description of Mr Roy,' underlined a forceful Marian, insisting that the publican concentrated on his part.

'Yes, formal, polite, a bit old school military. Pleasant but tough if needs be. Good Queen's English,' remembered an obedient Mr Fairfax.

'Excellent. Where's Mrs Fairfax?' demanded Marian.

'Gone to see her mother,' clarified Mr Fairfax.

'Good,' commented a relieved Marian.

'She said that if she stayed, she wouldn't be able to stop laughing,' continued Mr Fairfax affectionately.

'Then it's probably better she's not here,' declared Marian.

'I think so. When she starts laughing, she can get delirious quite easily,' admitted Mr Fairfax.

'Really?' pursued Mrs Butcher, who wasn't without hysterical tendencies herself, particularly when she'd drunk excessively.

'Yes. She can get over excited sometimes,' revealed Mr Fairfax.

‘At least she’s got a sense of humour,’ interjected a sympathetic Mrs Butcher.

‘I suppose so,’ replied Mr Fairfax wearily, as if his wife’s excessive jollity had often worn him out.

Mr Fairfax then moved to a gilt mirror and stared at himself, much to the surprise of the two women. He turned at various angles to inspect his profile with absurd vanity. He then took a bottle of Imperial Leather brilliantine, strategically placed on the top of a nearby chest of drawers, and plastered it all over his rapidly thinning hair. Returning to the mirror, he produced a comb out of the inside pocket of his jacket and started carefully covering his emerging bald patches. After several minutes of this ritual, Mr Fairfax turned round to the women and invited their appreciation.

‘How do I look?’ preened Mr Fairfax, inviting flattery.

‘You look splendid but not like Mr Roy, more like a waiter at the Burlington,’ observed Marian.

‘The Burlington!’ exclaimed a dumbfounded Fairfax.

‘A hotel of dubious repute in Manchester,’ elaborated a cynical Marian.

‘Oh never mind. They’re not going to see me. It just gets me in the mood. I’ve loved dressing up since I was a boy,’ confessed Mr Fairfax.

‘Mr Fairfax. Please let’s concentrate on the job in hand,’ asserted an irritated Marian.

‘Yes, of course,’ agreed Mr Fairfax meekly, intimidated by Marian’s bellicose insistence.

‘Have you got the address?’ commandeered Marian.

‘Oh my God, now where is it? fretted an anxious Mr Fairfax, searching his pockets nervously.

‘Do you want me to write it down?’ questioned Marian like a teacher reprimanding an errant pupil.

‘No, I’ve got it somewhere. Let me think,’ struggled a hesitant Mr Fairfax, pacing up and down like a distraught performer in the wings.

‘Please hurry up Mr Fairfax, they’ll be ringing shortly,’ entreated a despairing Marian in her broadest Lancashire accent.

‘Yes. We’ve only got five minutes, Mr Fairfax,’ shouted a loud Mrs Butcher, who thought that Mr Fairfax’s farcical preparation was much more entertaining than going to the pictures.

‘Ah, I’ve got it!’ cried an excitable Mr Fairfax, stopping in the middle of his worn out green carpet.

‘So where is it?’ asked a fervent Marian.

‘In the toilet. I was excusing myself,’ remembered Mr Fairfax.

The agitated publican then departed to the cream coloured lavatory, in which there was a poster above the seat showing a picture of a long-legged young woman in a bikini, next to an inscription stating that ‘Sprinkles are for cupcakes. Not toilet seats!’ On the linoleum floor was a scrunched piece of paper, which Mr Fairfax hurriedly unfolded. ‘Thank God,’ he murmured to himself as he retrieved his notes and scampered back to the living room. On returning, he settled by his phone, which was parked on a solid wooden chess table. Mr Fairfax liked chess. The game both challenged his mind and calmed him down, especially after dealing with virulently rude customers. It was also something that he shared with Mrs Fairfax, who was a skilful player and often battered her husband into submissive defeat. Apparently, she celebrated her victories with such expansive jubilation that you’d thought that she’d just won a bet on the Derby. Marian also noted the table and wondered how much it cost. She had no interest in chess. It was too intellectual. She preferred her beloved draughts or something with more of a direct emotional impact. For instance, when opting to play cards, she favoured the hysteria of snap to the intricate guile of poker.

Mr Fairfax, took out the crumpled paper that had decorated the lavatory floor and observed it intently. As he did so, Marian exerted further authority by reminding the former repertory actor of the intention behind his role. First, he should remind the firm of the white marble headstone with its quote engraved in black, which had already had been ordered by the senior school secretary, a role Marian herself had already successfully enacted. He then should give them the address, arrange a delivery time in the early afternoon when moaning Deirdre was likely to be at home and get them to send the bill to Mr Alexander Roy. Mrs Butcher laughed at the thought of seeing Killer accept the delivery. As she paraded her mirth, she eagerly grabbed another lager bottle, which she'd placed conveniently near the sofa. Marian was worried that Mrs Butcher's alcoholic consumption was going to undermine her plan. Consequently, she gave her a disdainful look as the tuck shop supremo poured another Carlings.

Just as everybody had settled down ready for the phone call, singing emanated from the stairs. Mr Fairfax looked alarmed as he realised that it was Mrs Fairfax warbling Singing the Blues. He rose abruptly from his chair and moved rapidly to the door. In doing so, he nearly bumped into his wife, who was in the midst of climaxing her vocal refrain. After finishing the popular song, Mrs Fairfax reminded everybody that until recently she'd been a singer, who'd toured all over the country. She then started talking about her good friend Ruby Murray, the Belfast vocalist, who'd had five hits in the top twenty in one week. Just as she was about to continue her gossip about the Irish singer, the phone rang. Before he answered it, Mr Fairfax screamed at his wife to go into the kitchen. Immediately, Marian unceremoniously ordered the inveterate Mrs Butcher to accompany her. The tuck shop manager duly obeyed, hurriedly taking her glass of lager with her like a supportive friend. Mrs Fairfax didn't object to departing so long as she still had an audience, so she started to regale Mrs Butcher about Ruby's current suitor.

As soon as his wife and Mrs Butcher were out of the room, Mr Fairfax picked up the phone. Marian looked on intently, hoping and praying that Fairfax wouldn't overact. At first, he seemed to enunciate like somebody in a bad production of a West End play. However, after some hectic semaphore from Marian, he gradually sounded more like a human being. Marian was pleased that he talked authoritatively, with that sense of pomposity that she thought came naturally to certain middle class southerners. Marian knew that although such arrogance was likely to offend northerners, at least it sounded authentic. Nevertheless, there was a slight pause when Mr Fairfax had to confirm the inscription and Marian hastily grabbed a nearby

Daily Mail and biro, before writing down the devastating quotation above a lurid headline. After Mr Fairfax steered his way through a challenging exchange about the ribald wording and the director's insistence on Strasberg-like authenticity, he arranged for the delivery to take place in two weeks' time on a Thursday afternoon. However, when there was a request for a backup contact, Mr Fairfax, keeping his hand over the receiver, whispered desperately to Marian, like an actor looking for a prompt. Thankfully, Marian responded swiftly and turned the paper to the sports page. She then scribbled the name and address of Mrs Perceval, that notorious purveyor of scandal, as a neighbourly contact. Therefore if required, the wife of the controversial rugby referee and history master, had unknowingly volunteered to deal with a surprising visitor. When Mr Fairfax finally put the phone down, Marian congratulated him on his excellent performance.

'Thank you, Marian. You know I couldn't have done it without dressing up a bit. It reminds me that I'm not myself,' divulged Mr Fairfax, wiping his brow with his pink handkerchief.

'You were very good Bert but if they ring again, you do know how to guide them to the address?' enquired Marian insistently.

'Yes, don't worry, I know the way but I'll have a map handy just in case,' replied a reassuring Mr Fairfax.

'If it's about anything else, say you've got to consult the wife, meaning me. Then phone and we can decide what to do. Understand,' demanded a forthright Marian.

At that moment, Mrs Fairfax and Mrs Butcher entered from the kitchen, somewhat the worse for wear, having furthered their relationship with Carlings lager. As everything had gone so well. Mrs Fairfax felt it called for a celebration and moved purposefully towards the Pye Black Box record player in a corner of the room. While she did so, Mr Fairfax asked his wife why she had returned so early from visiting her mother. He discovered that his mother-in-law had forgotten the appointment and told her neighbour, a very nosy woman called Mrs Cooper, nicknamed 'The Informer', that she'd gone to the dentist. 'I'll ring her later!' screamed the ex-night club singer as she put Guy Mitchell's Singing the Blues onto the turntable.

As the pub didn't reopen until five, Mrs Fairfax insisted that her husband brought up more drink, which he did reluctantly. Once the booze arrived, all the ladies relished more beer, while the abstemious Mr Fairfax contented himself with a Robinsons Lemon Barley Water and a corned beef sandwich. Mrs Fairfax then led the singsong and they all raucously sang Singing the Blues. Feeling inspired, Mrs F then launched into a version of Pat Boone's I'll Be Home, which she certainly sang with more passion than the bland all American boy. A few drinks later, Marian decided to improvise her own song entitled The Death of Killer. Such were its rude contents, not least about his boxer shorts and him being the sadistic, flogging Führer of the school, that it eclipsed even Mrs Fairfax's heartfelt efforts. By this time, Mrs Butcher was in such fits of laughter that she split half of her lager on the well-worn carpet. As the tuck shop manager sank hysterically into the sofa, Marian relished the applause from her audience, which she acknowledged with a mock-curtsy. She was delighted that she was going to embarrass Killer and whinging Deirdre. As far as she was concerned, the junior housemaster's cruel negligence deserved punishment. With the aid of Mr and Mrs Fairfax and the support of the formidable Mrs Butcher, it was a case of mission launched.

One Ball lay back in his armchair and listened intensely to the Tristan and Isolde Prelude pulsating away on his record player. The embattled monitor revelled in the magnificent power of such ethereal, romantic music. He found listening to Wagner redemptive, especially in his current state of mind. It helped him to relax and focus. Then, just as he was luxuriating in musical ecstasy, there was a knock on the study door.

'Come in,' commanded One Ball.

Sully entered cautiously into the study and apprehensively waited as One Ball rose, went over to the record player and stopped the euphoric Wagnerian recording.

'Sit down there, Sully,' instructed One Ball peremptorily.

The overweight boy settled in a wooden chair that One Ball had strategically placed in the middle of the small room. He then faced Sully and told him that he was going to give him another chance to erase his punishments. If he didn't want to keep running miles to the end of time, he must cooperate. He accused him of failing to get the photos through blatant ineptitude and monstrous incompetence. Hence, he had to make amends. He must be a witness and confirm that Françoise and Rutter were having sex in the pavilion. Sully should tell the Major that he was shocked and traumatised by what he saw and that the lascivious scenes have continued to haunt him and severely affect his well-being.

'But I didn't see them having sex,' insisted Sully.

'You must have,' stressed One Ball, prowling menacingly towards Sully.

'I only saw the couple dancing on the 1st X1 cricket pitch.

'And?'

'They were laughing. They were happy.'

'And what else?'

'I couldn't see them clearly.'

'What happened?'

'I tried to take another photo but they saw me.'

'But they were previously in the pavilion?'

'I didn't see them there.'

One Ball thought that Sully was telling the truth but that wasn't of any use to him. He didn't think the truth would bring justice, so he would have to use other means. There had to be a way to make the facts bend towards his objective. Isn't that what good lawyers do? After all, just because you can't prove something, doesn't mean that it isn't true.

'Sully. I want you to tell the Major that you saw them having sex in the pavilion,' said One Ball, circling forbiddingly around Sully's chair.

'But I didn't!' yelled an insistent Sully.

'That doesn't matter.'

'You want me to lie.'

'Depends what you mean?'

'It means not telling the truth, Potts.'

'What's the truth, Sully ?' You don't know that they didn't have sex in the pavilion. You didn't look there so it's still quite probable. If they were on the cricket pitch, it's likely that they were in there earlier doing it. After all, Rutter is captain of the rugby team. He has easy access.'

'I can only admit to what I know.'

'Then you will continue to do the punishments. If you tell the Major of Rutter's sexual transgressions, I'll tick them off.'

'I'm not going to be bribed by your lies, Potts.'

'Lies? How do you know they're lies? '

'Because there's no evidence.'

'Exactly and that's how so many criminals escape justice.'

'Rutter isn't a criminal. He's a boy in love.'

One Ball stopped his threatening movement and looked at Sully incredulously.

'In love. How in the hell do you know he's in love?'

'I've seen it in his eyes and Françoise's?'

'Françoise's?'

'Yes, I could see that when they talked to me.'

'Sully, you're not a bloody psychiatrist.'

'No, but I could see it by the way they looked at each other. Their movements.'

'Movements. What do you mean?'

'The way they related to each other. Physically.'

The thought of such intimacy only further incensed One Ball's angry sense of betrayal.

'Sully. I don't want to hear anymore. If you don't want to do the punishments, you need to tell the Major that they were having sex in the pavilion. And that's the end of it.'

'No, I'm not going to say that. I'm not going to destroy two people in love.'

'Stop being sentimental. Love is often temporary.'

'Not always. Anyway, how can I judge without evidence?'

'Evidence! Truth is relative Sully. Sometimes you don't need evidence. You just know. You can smell it. You feel it. It's an instinct that is greater than facts. And I know that they've been screwing in the pavilion. I just know it.'

'You tell the Major then.'

'It should come from a junior, Sully. Then it has a greater sense of corrupted innocence. It's a more compelling narrative. Anyway, you're frequently on Open Way. Doing your punishments.'

‘Or spying for you, Potts.’

‘There’s no need to mention that, Sully.’

‘You want me to do your dirty work for you.’

‘It’s not as if you’re not getting something out of it.’

‘I’m not going to do it, Potts. Not even to escape your punishments. Anyway, I don’t even know what ‘rank insubordination’ and ‘outright duplicity’ actually mean.’

‘All right Sully. Report to me next Thursday at 3:40. Then you can try to run one of your miles within the given time,’ said One Ball, retiring exasperatedly to his armchair

Sully stared blankly at his nemesis. He then stood up defiantly and resolutely confronted a frustrated One Ball.

‘You know who you remind me of?’

‘What are you on about now?’ queried a bewildered One Ball.

‘That McCarthy man. Another bully telling lies as he goes about his witch-hunt of communists.’

‘Get out, Sully.’

‘Don’t worry. I’m going Potts.

The more One Ball’s bullying got ferocious, the more Sully became emboldened. He gained articulacy through a hunger for justice. He was proud that he’d defied One Ball’s tirade. Strangely, for the first time he didn’t care about the consequences. The support from the likes of Ryder and Barrett had given him a new confidence. Sully would do his best with his so-called punishments but he wasn’t going to be incessantly servile. If One Ball maintained his reign of terror, Sully now decided to look for further support.

‘Don’t just stare at me Sully, I told you, get out!’ shrieked a manic One Ball.

‘Yes Potts,’ said Sully, quietly but firmly.

Sully stood still like a condemned man going to the scaffold, who felt liberated as death approached. Everything became a lot clearer to him. In contrast, One Ball was a victim of his own frustrations. Now that he had been betrayed, he felt righteousness was on his side and he’d use any morally devious method to get revenge. He would destroy this supposed love of the treacherous Françoise and the hideous Rutter by laying bare their antics to everybody. Once he had discovered Françoise’s duplicity, any remnant of liberal instinct disappeared from him forever like a condemned friend. One Ball was going to fight Sully's intransigence and get Françoise and Rutter punished. Meanwhile, Sully had concluded that although One Ball's use of the school rules was callous and cruel, it had been allowed to become an inevitable part of the status quo. This realisation only increased his resolve to challenge that injustice.

'I told you, Sully. Get out. Now!' reiterated an incensed One Ball, suddenly rising from his armchair.

Sully departed with an assured look on his face that One Ball found offensive. One Ball didn't like Sully's new-found. conviction. He'd obviously been in touch with those bloody Marxists like Ryder. He was all for justice but not histrionic gestures. One Ball thought that Ryder was both self-serving and devious. He admitted that he'd cleverly conceived a campaign against Root. Nonetheless, he believed that its purpose was more to increase the choir leader's power rather than any genuine altruism.

As One Ball moved towards his record player, he regretted missing out verses 2, 4, 6, and 8 of hymn number 250. He realised that Ryder had manipulated him by his forceful personality. He hated himself for his weakness and recognised that it wasn't only the Germans that were prey to powerful leaders. After putting on Tristan and Isolde and listening again to the melodiously intense Prelude, he wondered how Wagner would have navigated Nazi Germany, given his anti-semitic views. One Ball found it hard to believe that a second rate Austrian artist would have fooled a man of Wagner's stature, but 'who knows?' he speculated. Eventually, One Ball, decided to forget such hypothetical conjecture. After his frustrating exchange with Sully, he preferred to sink into his armchair and just let the music wash over him like a liberating shower.

Pongo Smallman relished the summer months, especially if the weather was good. He was in his element managing the cricket team and getting away from the ritual of his more predictable duties. This term he felt that his 1st X1 would be very competitive. The batting was solid, they had a couple of challenging quick bowlers and some decent spin, so he was optimistic about getting good results. This would not only enhance the school but also be a personal feather in his cap. He would then feel a sense of achievement before departing to the Norfolk Broads with Collins.

Fred Ord, the cricket coach, was with Pongo at the nets. Fred didn't know why Smallman was called Pongo. One of the boys told him that it was because he walked like a penguin. Fred still didn't really see the connection, although intuitively he thought it suited the cricket team manager. Pongo or no Pongo, Fred thought that Smallman wasn't the worst of the masters and was genuinely amenable. He was also a decent batsman. On the rare occasions that he played, he wore an elaborately coloured cap. At least it wasn't as multi-coloured as that dandy Basil Ponsonby-Smythe, even though it was still too flash for Fred's taste. Despite his propensity for ostentation, Pongo tended to take Fred's advice most of the time, apart from when he showed a weakness for favourites.

Fred was in charge of the nets, which were erected in an area behind the boundary of the 1st X1 cricket pitch. Pongo tended to stand back at a distance and observe while Fred did the coaching. As this particular session progressed, you could hear Fred call out 'well played, 'well bowled' in his distinctive midlands accent. He would instruct batsmen about their feet and head movement so that they played straight. He would also tell them to feel where the stumps were from their guard and how to judge the line and length of the ball. He would then turn his attention to his bowlers and put marks down, where he wanted them to pitch the ball. He wanted accuracy 'like Brian Statham, the Lancashire bowler, then batsmen get frustrated. I know I was one of them,' he'd tell the boys. He also encouraged his quicker bowlers to pitch the outswinger on the middle and off stumps, not on the leg side. 'That's four runs,' he'd cry if the bowler strayed. What's more, he guided the boys to make sure that the inswinger attacked the stumps. 'More chance of an lbw then,' advised Fred.

Later, Fred started working with Rutter as wicket keeper. 'Don't snatch at it, let it come to you,' he told him. Fred thought that Rutter was a good keeper but he needed to concentrate and cut out his loud, frenetic appealing, which Pongo didn't like. He wasn't personally upset by the histrionics but he advised Rutter not to be too hysterical as 'we don't want to upset Mr Smallman now, do we?' When Rutter's wicket- keeping session finished, Fred thought that he'd enquire about his extra-curricular activities as he secretly admired his devilry. In fact, he knew that he was 'doing something' with a girl in the pavilion but it wasn't his business, so long as the place was kept clean. He'd heard from one of the groundsmen that it was a maid from the kitchen but he wasn't going to gossip. As far as he was concerned, there was already too much tittle-tattle at the school.

When Fred enquired about the welfare of his girlfriend, Rutter, reassured by Fred's saucy grin, replied that she was fine.

'It's just that I heard that she was playing tennis with someone else,' said Fred, throwing a cricket ball up in the air and catching it expertly in one hand.

'That's nothing, Fred. Just a friend,' elucidated Rutter, starting to take off his wicket-keeping gloves.

'Ok. Just thought I'd mention it,' remarked the cricket pro, splendidly attired in whites and his Worcester CCC blazer. Fred then told Rutter to get ready to bat, as he wanted him to face some fast bowling. He'd recently seen potential in the tall, wiry Irishman Chuck Carson, who had helped Barrett with his accent for Henry V. Chuck was originally more of a batsman but Fred discovered that he could bowl quickly and at a rangy six foot three inches, he believed that he could dig the ball in uncomfortably. Rutter didn't know anything about Chuck as a bowler so he was confident about facing the rock 'n' roll fanatic. However, the first ball Chuck hurled down whizzed past Rutter's leg stump like an errant missile. It was fast, much quicker than any bowling that he'd previously faced. Immediately, Rutter became slightly apprehensive and decided to concentrate more intensely.

'Just bowl fast Carson, don't worry about anything else,' exhorted Fred, watching eagerly at the top of the nets like a master of ceremonies.

Rutter did manage to get his bat on a couple of Chuck's missiles, even if he only saw them at the last moment. Chuck wasn't consistently accurate but he was very quick. As Rutter didn't know where the next ball might go, it made the rock fan's bowling unpredictably dangerous. In fact, when Chuck hurled a bumper at Rutter, he only just ducked in time. Thankfully, Rutter's lack of height was an advantage in getting safely underneath the projectile.

'Well bowled,' said Fred encouragingly. Chuck's considerable pace so impressed the coach, that he became blissfully unaware of the physical danger to the beleaguered batsman.

Rutter managed to cope with most of Chuck's bowling, until he tried to hook a short ball, which kept unexpectedly low and clattered violently against the flimsy box that covered his testicles. When Rutter fell in a heap, dropping his bat in the process, Fred came down to him, followed by Pongo, who had been observing Chuck's ferocious pace with a mixture of delight and alarm. Initially, Chuck, the terminator, kept at a distance, quietly observing the effects of his assault, but when he realised that Rutter was badly hurt, he apologised. Fred responded resolutely by exonerating Chuck.

'Don't say sorry, Carson,' he insisted, 'it wasn't your fault. It's part of the game.'

Fred and Pongo lifted up Rutter and got him to put his arms around their shoulders. When they got to the pavilion, Pongo demanded that Rutter went to the infirmary for a check-up. Pongo had parked his Morris Minor at the back of the pavilion and with the aid of Fred, he took Rutter to the car and carefully placed him on the back seat. After Fred wished him a swift recovery, Pongo drove away. He reached the infirmary in five minutes, where a ginger-haired Nurse Archer took charge of proceedings. Realising that Rutter was in considerable agony, the talkative but attentive nurse wanted him to stay overnight. She informed Pongo in an official manner that Dr Meissner could see him in the morning. In the meantime, she would give him some cream for his private parts, as she delicately described them. On that note, Pongo thought it was diplomatic to leave. As he departed, the suffering Rutter thanked him for his support. Pongo accepted his appreciation and left, hoping to see him return shortly. After all, he needed his wicket-keeper.

Rutter was taken to a ward where there were six other patients. It had a good view of the infirmary gardens and was homely and comfortable. There was a table with papers and periodicals plus chairs and a sofa, in addition to an accessible bathroom. Rutter realised that he mustn't stay too long. Although it was an appealing retreat, he needed to do some work, what with exams approaching.

After he'd settled in a bed, Miss Archer returned with an appropriate cream.

'Here you are, Rutter. Go into the bathroom and put some of it on the relevant part. It's soothing.'

'Can't you put it on him nurse?' piped up a cheeky voice from the other side of the ward.

'No I certainly won't,' replied the blushing nurse as she started to depart. 'And if you want anything else, just ring the bell. Tea is at six o'clock.'

'Thanks nurse,' acknowledged a fragile Rutter.

Rutter went into the bathroom and prepared a warm bath. As he sank into the water, he wondered what Françoise was doing. He couldn't wait to see her. He was glad the game was up with One Ball, as now it was too late for either of them to be removed from the school. By the time any investigation concluded, it would be near the end of term when they were both leaving, making any punishment redundant. In any case, One Ball had no concrete evidence to use. Rutter had received confirmation of this from Ryder, who'd been reliably informed by Barrett, who was fast becoming the school's baby Lenin. Rutter was also glad to also hear that Sully had found a moral backbone. He just hoped that it would remain to be the case. In the meantime, he'd step up his studies if he has to convalesce for a few weeks. Although he wasn't a natural academic, he wanted to go to university, not least for the sport and social life. Then there was Françoise's departure to France. That was going to be heartrending.

Rutter felt much better after the impact of the cream and at tea, he enjoyed his sausage, egg and chips. While chatting with the other patients, he discovered that Miss Archer was a Scrabble addict. Such was her expertise at the game, that she was nicknamed Nurse Scrabble. Her devotion was so total that she always locked up the tiles and board in a special cupboard, so nothing was ever missing. It was rumoured that she hadn't lost a game for two years. Rutter wasn't the best at word competitions, so there wasn't much of a chance that he'd ever beat the Scrabble queen.

The next morning the all-conquering Nurse Scrabble told Rutter to attend Dr Meissner's surgery.

Meissner was a portly grey-haired man, who was always wearing a white coat and had a rather officious air. Rutter thought that he looked like a Victorian superintendent controlling patients in a lunatic asylum, so he ventured into his surgery with trepidation.

'Ok. Drop your pants,' ordered Meissner, who in fact was a refugee from Berlin.

Rutter was reluctant to let the good doctor inspect his testicles but he had no choice.

'Hurry up, Rutter. I've got a lot of boys to see.'

Rutter eventually lowered his trousers and pulled down his pants. Dr Meissner then bent down so he had a clear view. Somewhat eccentrically, he tapped the testicles gently with a light stick, continually enquiring 'does this hurt?' 'What do you feel?' 'Is this painful?' Although there were occasional 'ows!' Rutter managed to survive the German doctor's mild flagellation and put on his clothes.

'Just bruising. I'll officially prescribe your cream,' concluded the doctor. 'You can take it away with you. Administer twice a day for two weeks and then come back to see me at morning surgery.'

'Thanks Doctor. '

'How did it happen?'

'Cricket. Got hit in the balls. Sorry Doctor, testicles.'

'Cricket. Crazy game. I just can't understand it,' admitted the perplexed German.

A week after his clash with One Ball, Sully prepared to do the first of his punishments. Having changed into his James B rugby kit, he presented himself to a disinterested One Ball. The sight of the inordinately corpulent Sully in the middle of the afternoon wasn't a vision that would inspire the monitor's studies. One Ball was working on some revision and didn't want to be interrupted by the cumbersome junior, whose current obstinate attitude he regarded as thoroughly impertinent. In fact, Sully's audacity surprised One Ball as he always thought of him as a bit of a thicko. He certainly didn't expect him to be referencing the infamous Joseph R. McCarthy. One Ball hadn't forgotten that abuse and found it extremely offensive. He certainly wasn't a bullying Commie-bater like the alcoholic American senator. However, eventually One Ball reluctantly looked up from his book on Newton's experiments and stared at the revitalised Sully.

'Sully, I'm going to make a concession.'

'What's that Potts?'

'You must complete your punishment not in 7 minutes but 7 minutes 30 seconds'.

'Thank you for the thirty seconds.'

'It's a pleasure Sully.'

One Ball detected a cynicism in Sully's replies, which he regarded as disrespectful. He wondered why Sully had become more audacious. Having observed his father on one of his rare visits, he found the RAF Group Captain genial and intelligent. His beloved son certainly hadn't inherited the required mentality of a military man. Therefore, One Ball wondered if Captain Sully had managed to inculcate a strong sense of justice in the blundering junior. Maybe that was why Sully was becoming less acquiescent. Whatever the reason for this rebellious development, One Ball felt the need to reassert his authority. He stopped his work on Frederick Newton and took his stopwatch from the mantelpiece. He then opened the study door.

'Ok Sully. 7 minutes 30 seconds. Ready.'

'Yes Potts,' replied an alert Sully.

'Go,' screamed One Ball, firmly pressing down the silver button on the watch.

Sully sauntered through the dayroom, where at the far end, Brown, Bunter, Hayes and Barrett were discussing the possibility of the Russians getting a Sputnik into orbit.

'He's never going to make it,' thought Hayes, apprehensively observing Sully's initial exertions.

'It's One Ball's form of torture,' observed Barrett.

‘What makes Sully run eh?’ contemplated Brown.

‘Bullying. That’s what makes him run,’ responded Barrett bitterly.

‘You’re right. It’s not fair,’ agreed Bunter.

As Sully arrived at Open Way, he bumped into Rutter, clad in his cricketing whites, having now recovered sufficiently from Carson’s bowling bombardment. In fact, he was on his way to risk another battering from Chuck in the nets. Sully told him that he couldn’t stop, so they both jogged on the surrounding path. As they did so, he notified him on how One Ball was reasserting his authoritative rule.

‘That’s because he found out that Françoise wasn’t interested in him,’ divulged Rutter, running beside the punished junior.

‘Françoise?’ repeated a confused Sully.

‘Yes. Last term, she flirted with him to stop him causing trouble,’ explained Rutter.

‘No wonder, he went berserk when I said you were in love with Françoise,’ clarified Sully.

‘You said that?’ queried Rutter, taken aback by such an intimate revelation.

‘Yes. But it’s true isn’t it?’ insisted Sully, surprised by Rutter questioning his commitment.

‘Yes, it is. Here I leave you, Sully. Remember One Ball’s a bully. Good luck,’ cried Rutter, running off the path towards the pavilion.

‘Agreed,’ concurred Sully, while trying to accelerate his run. ‘Yes, One Ball is indeed a bully,’ he repeated to himself.

As Sully continued to waddle around Open Way, admiring the expansive verdant surroundings, with its numerous cricket and rugby pitches as well as the occasional elm tree, he realised that he was going to be the eternal long distance runner. He had to stop this sadistic ritual and erase One Ball’s callous culture. By the time he’d made his way across the Avenue back to James B, he came to a decision. He wasn’t going to run another bloody mile.

‘You’re late!’ declared One Ball, gleefully celebrating his captive’s failure. ‘9 minutes 40, Sully. In fact, you’re 2 minutes,

10 seconds out. I'm afraid,' stressed One Ball, leaning back smugly on his chair.

'So what happens now?' challenged a fatigued Sully, standing steadfastly by the study door.

'You'll do it again, of course.'

'No.'

'What do you mean 'no'?'

'I'm not going to do another mile.'

'You've got to.'

'I haven't got to do anything Potts.'

'They're your punishments.'

'Dubious punishments.'

'There's nothing wrong with them.'

'Rank insubordination means disagreement. Outright duplicity means avoiding cruelty.'

'That's your interpretation, Sully.'

'It's the truth and you know it.'

'Don't tell me what I know, Sully.'

'You use the system for power not justice and certainly not enlightenment.'

'What you don't understand Sully' said One Ball leaning forward and looking the junior searchingly in the eye, 'is that there have to be rules. The rules are there to maintain order and prevent chaos so that every boy feels free and safe.'

'But they're not there for bullying.'

'I'm not a bully Sully. I just want you to accept the rules and do your punishment accordingly.'

'That's nonsense Potts. You bend the rules to inflict pain.'

'No. To set challenges. To have a sense of achievement from punishment.'

'But I'm not John Landy. You know that I won't complete such times.'

'That's where you're wrong Sully, I'm not requiring you to do an under four minute mile. I set fair targets to encourage aspiration and achieve high fitness levels. After all, you need to lose weight.'

'Your aspiration is for control over people like me, whom you despise.'

'I only exert control to encourage improvement.'

'Bullying would be more accurate.'

'Sully. Stop it now!' bawled One Ball, standing up and staring intensely at the insolent junior.

'No I won't stop it. I'm not going to do any more of your punishments,' emphasised a defiant Sully. I'm going to see Mr Aizlewood, Potts. You've given me no alternative.'

'Do what you want, Sully. The Major has total confidence in his monitors.'

'We'll see.'

'We certainly shall.'

'You're a cruel bully Potts.'

'Get out! Get out!' screamed Potts, moving furiously towards the defiant junior.

Sully abruptly left One Ball's study. He passed Brown, Bunter, Barrett and Hayes, who still hadn't come to a consensus about Russia's space aspirations. As Sully ignored them and looked nervous and upset, they realised that there had been some serious reckoning with One Ball.

Deirdre Roy aka Mrs Killer was just recovering from giving lunch to a bawling Barney, when there was a knock on her door. When she opened it, two cheery men in blue dungarees appeared. They informed her that they'd come from Wakefield to deliver the headstone that Mr Roy had ordered for a play. Mrs Killer looked bemused, as she knew nothing about it. She told the two men that the school play finished last term.

'Well this is what we've been told to deliver,' vowed the more substantial of the two men, in a blunt Yorkshire accent. His toothbrush moustache only added to him looking like the comic film star, Oliver Hardy.

'We got the order from a Mr Roy. That's your husband isn't it?' asked his colleague, a small, impish looking man. His humorous face reminded Deirdre of Stan Laurel, one of the north east's finest comedians.

During this conversation, Barney was continually crying for attention. As the child reached a wailing climax, Deirdre told the two men to excuse her for a moment. She then made her way into the kitchen and extricated the bawling child from his cot. As soon as Deirdre released Barney, he calmed down and relished his mother's embrace. She then carried the pacified child while returning to the door to continue the conversation.

'Sorry about that' said Deirdre apologetically.

'That's all right love,' replied the burly Hardy sympathetically.

'He seems quite a handful' observed the diminutive Laurel.

'What's his name? enquired Hardy.

'Barney,' stated Deirdre proudly.

'That's a good name,' thought Hardy.

'A bit different, I'd say,' inferred a curious Laurel.

'Well it's not John or Michael,' retorted Deirdre.

'If you don't mind me asking, how did you choose it?' mentioned an intrigued Laurel.

'We got the name from a guitar player we liked,' proclaimed Deirdre.

'He's got something to live up to. Haven't you, young lad? said Laurel, smiling amusingly at the baby. 'Maybe he'll be the next Bert Weedon?' he continued, mischievously, peering at the young innocent with his twinkling eyes.

Laurel and Hardy then burst out laughing, until Deirdre interrupted their mutual mirth and demanded to see the headstone. Immediately, the two workers guided Deirdre and Barney to their vehicle, which they'd parked on the adjoining road. Hardy released the back of the truck and clambered up towards an object covered by a roped, grey tarpaulin. This entity looked mysteriously eerie as the sun filtered through the nearby trees and bounced off its camouflaged protection. Hardy dutifully untied the rope and revealed the headstone in all its glory. Deirdre was appalled when she saw the inscription.

'Who asked for this?' insisted Deirdre, holding on to her bewildered son.

'Mr Roy,' confirmed Hardy.

'It can't have been. It must have been someone else,' asserted Deirdre.

'That's the name we've been given,' said Hardy casually.

'We were told that it was for a play,' clarified Laurel.

'That they wanted a real headstone,' continued Hardy earnestly.

‘We presumed Mr Roy was ordering it for theatrical realism. Sounded interesting,’ pondered a curious Laurel.

‘Anyway, it’s not our place to question artistic motives,’ claimed Hardy.

‘Oh my God!’ cried a despairing Deirdre.

‘We just did our job,’ justified Hardy defensively.

At that moment, who should drive up the road but none other than Killer in his recently acquired Ford Anglia. After he’d parked, he gazed suspiciously at the visiting Yorkshiremen and asked Deirdre what was happening. When he viewed the headstone, he looked like he’d been struck by lightning. Straight away, he decided to corral everybody into the house.

Killer then composed himself and made initial efforts to be amenable. While everybody was having coffee in the kitchen, he told them that he’d come home early because several boys in his class were experiencing debilitating flu symptoms, which were spreading around the school. Exercising caution, he dismissed the class and drove the sick boys to the infirmary as Dr Meissner had instructed. After he’d digressed further with a few pleasantries about the invigorating Yorkshire landscape, Killer then put his cards on the table:

‘I didn’t order the headstone and there’s no play, so it’s clear that I’ve been the victim of an unpleasant practical joke.’

‘Well, our boss Mr Trueman assured us that the booking was made by a Mr Roy at this address and that we’re to leave an invoice and collect a cheque as agreed,’ Hardy announced earnestly, producing an envelope from his dungarees’ pocket and placing it ceremoniously on the kitchen table.

‘What’s this? insisted a suspicious Killer.

‘The invoice,’ said Hardy brusquely.

As Deirdre looked on, perching a mollified Barney on her knee, Killer opened the envelope and stared at the piece of paper as if he was confronting his own mortality. He couldn’t believe it. It was for 53 pounds. At that moment, he felt so angry towards Marian, that he wanted to go and shake the living daylights out of her. Thankfully, the presence of Laurel and Hardy from Wakefield made him control his baser instincts and try to look at the matter more calmly.

‘It’s for 53 pounds,’ confirmed Deirdre, reading the invoice.

‘53 pounds including carriage,’ amplified Hardy firmly.

‘A lot of skilled work goes into headstones, Laurel elaborated.

‘I’m sure it does,’ accepted an exasperated Killer.

‘Mr Carter. He’s from Hull. He’s an excellent engraver,’ assured a perky Laurel.

‘I’ve got to talk to your Mr Trueman. I want to know about his contact for the job as it wasn’t me,’ pronounced a forthright Killer.

‘Who was it then? Do you know?’ asked a fascinated Laurel.

‘No. But I’ve a good idea,’ added Killer ominously.

‘It’s very intriguing. Can you tell us?’ pursued an enthralled Laurel.

‘No, I can’t now but I’ll inform Mr Trueman later,’ disclosed an irritably resolute Killer.

When Laurel and Hardy had finished their coffee, they asked where they should leave the headstone. Killer wanted it to be returned to Illingworths but they said that wasn’t possible, as Mr Trueman had told them that they must deliver the order and receive a cheque. They needed to do that, otherwise they’ll get an awful earful from the boss, especially after coming so far.

Killer didn’t want to get the two workers into trouble, so he negotiated a compromise. He allowed them to leave the headstone in his garden, so long as it was covered by the roped tarpaulin and put in an inconspicuous place. Hardy was somewhat reluctant not to take the covering, because he’d already had trouble with local truants trying to steal it. However, after a protracted discussion, the men agreed when Killer guaranteed the tarpaulin’s return. The enraged housemaster would discuss the matter of the money with Mr Trueman. He didn’t request the order and wasn’t going to pay. When the two men observed Killer’s intransigence, they realised that they couldn’t pursue the situation any further. They just hoped that Mr Trueman would tolerate what they’d agreed.

The Yorkshiremen duly dumped the covered headstone, near a cluster of daisies at the back of the garden and then made their way to the truck. Killer accompanied them to the vehicle.

‘Well it’s a bit of a mystery this one,’ confided a perplexed Laurel.

‘I’ll get to the bottom of it,’ declared a determined Killer.

‘Let’s hope so,’ remarked a sceptical Hardy.

‘Somebody has been impersonating me,’ claimed Killer.

‘You think so?’ probed an excited Laurel.

‘I know so,’ affirmed Killer.

When they got to the truck, the two men lifted themselves into the cab. Laurel then wound down his window and leaned over to the beleaguered Killer.

‘Well good luck Monsieur Poirot.’

After Killer responded with a rueful smile, the two workers waved goodbye as Laurel drove into the Avenue, on the way back north. After their departure, Killer marched back to Deirdre and Barney. He was furious. He would deal with the bloody Witch of Wigan.

The Major sat in his study awaiting the arrival of Sully, who had requested to see him. Above a fireplace, a painting of Field Marshal Montgomery in military uniform dominated the room, highlighting the importance of the senior housemaster’s war service. In fact, the Major had thought of installing a picture of Archibald Wavell, but reluctantly decided on Monty as it sent out a more positive statement, given his boss’s sacking after the failure of Operation Battleaxe. Below the portrait, on top of a mantelpiece, there were family pictures and a brown ornamental elephant with ivory tusks.

The Major lounged in his leather wing armchair near the fireplace. After some reflection, he turned to a nearby side table and started taking his St Bruno tobacco from a yellow pouch. He then neatly installed it into his brown, black-stemmed pipe. After striking a Swan Vestas match, he started puffing relentlessly until he was satisfied that the pipe was alight. Placing the used match in a copper ashtray, he lay back in his armchair and wondered what was on Sully’s mind. During his conversations with his monitors, he’d heard about that boy’s difficulties with certain disciplines but nothing too extreme. Still, he’d do his best to resolve any tensions. After another satisfying puff on his pipe, the Major glanced at his watch. It was approaching 6:35. The boys should be coming back from tea shortly.

After a few minutes, there was a knock on the door and the Major called Sully into his study. He then told him to sit on a chestnut tub chair opposite the housemaster and explain his concerns. Sully then proceeded to tell the Major of how he was receiving ill-defined punishments from Potts, with running time limits that he had no chance of completing. He added that the monitor had also told him to spy on other boys. The Major listened to the complaints while continuing to puff on his pipe and relish the ensuing the aroma. He then brought Sully's attention to his 'outright duplicity' offence and the accusation of cheating.

'I only cheated, sir, because I was set such impossible times,' remonstrated Sully.

'Why were they impossible?' challenged the Major.

'Potts knew that I could never achieve them, that's why he set them in the first place.'

'Are you implying that Potts is sadistic?'

'Yes sir.'

'But you were impertinent to him. So although 'rank insubordination' and 'outright duplicity' may be hyperbolic, they're essentially true, aren't they Sully?'

'Hyperbolic, sir?'

'Exaggerated, Sully.'

'Thank you, sir. I only cheated because the punishment was unfair.'

'But Sully, times are there to be beaten. That's how progress is made.'

'I'm not an athlete but Potts treats me as if I'm a good runner.'

'You should be flattered, Sully.'

'There's too much emphasis put on sport, sir'

'Sport is important, Sully. It helps boys develop teamwork, courage, endurance and responsibility. It also gives a sense of pride, particularly to the less academic.'

'Maybe sir, but there are other ways of honing those skills.'

‘Yes, Sully. And we accommodate them. Look at all those who object to the Combined Cadet Force. They do various public works. Thank God there’s not too many of them.’

‘Why sir?’

‘Because I don’t believe in pacifism, Sully. Nor does that man there,’ stressed the Major, rigorously pointing to the painting of Monty.

Sully turned his head round to face the Field Marshal’s supercilious scowl.

‘He doesn’t look very happy sir.’

‘Nobody’s cheerful fighting a war, Sully.’

‘I should hope not.’

‘But it can be exhilarating.’

‘How sir?’

‘War is horrible Sully. But once you accept it, there’s the excitement of combat, the thrill of a winning strategy.’

‘What about losing, sir?’

‘There’s humiliation. The stakes are high.’

‘That’s how I feel. Humiliated.’

‘By Potts?’

‘Yes sir.’

The Major paused and puffed dramatically on his pipe. After he’d once more inhaled the comforting fragrance, he decided to get Sully’s point of view in more detail.

‘Sully. Why did Potts punish you for ‘rank insubordination’ in the first place?

‘Potts was taking coat inspection. The first time I showed my coat to him, he got hold of a penknife and started aggressively pointing out tea and food stains. I accepted his criticism and rectified the situation. This still didn’t satisfy Potts, who didn’t think the coat was ‘sufficiently immaculate’ and pointed out some butter stains that I’d missed. I corrected this and returned for another inspection. Potts then discovered what he described as ‘disgusting snot’ nestled in the top corner of my coat. I disputed this description and told him that it was the remnants of a fizzy drink. Once more, I went back to the changing room and spent a long time making sure that there were no further blemishes. On my return, he dug a knife into a minute area of the coat, screamed ‘dirt!’ and repeated that my coat should always be 'immaculate'. By this time, Potts's continual instructions made me feel exhausted. I thought that he'd never be satisfied with my efforts. I informed him that he was being 'unnecessarily fussy'. To which, he yelled that I would be punished for 'rank insubordination', when I'd only made the mildest of comments.'

The Major listened carefully to Sully's description as he puffed on his pipe. He admired Sully's candour and independence. He was standing up for himself. Although it did seem that Potts had been a bit over zealous, he found it hard to be too judgemental. Masters couldn't be around a house all the time so they had to depend on monitors. If monitors were seriously undermined then the whole system would break down. For a monitor to be disciplined, there needed to be very clear evidence. So far, he wasn't sufficiently convinced that Sully's case was strong enough to reprimand Potts. Still, he was concerned about the spying accusation, which sounded rather fanciful.

'It seems Potts wanted your coat to be really pristine, Sully.'

'Pristine?' queried a confused Sully.

'Spotless Sully,' illuminated the Major.

'Thank you, sir,' acknowledged Sully.

'Now, Sully what about the spying?' insisted the Major.

Before seeing the Major, on Barrett's recommendation, Sully had consulted with Ryder after a chapel service. The school's Lenin had warned him that the Major would take some persuading to cancel the punishments and admonish One Ball. Although it was a necessary step to take, the Major seemed to be confirming Ryder's doubts by not wanting to upset the status quo. Nonetheless, Sully still told him about One Ball's unsuccessful attempts to bribe him and catch Françoise and Rutter in flagrante delicto. As he relayed the whole absurd plot, the Major had a wry smile on his face.

'It sounds like a boys' version of something from those St Trinian's cartoons,' said an amused Major.

'I only did it sir, so that I could avoid the punishments,' divulged Sully.

'But you failed.'

'Yes. They're friendly but I didn't see them having sex.'

'Thank God for that.'

'They were just enjoying being together.'

'What a relief. There's a time for getting to know the opposite sex but not on school grounds.'

'Yes sir.'

'Sexual scandal would be disastrous for the school. Or any public scandal for that matter. It would batter our reputation.

'I understand that sir but what about Potts bribing me?'

'You could say he was being vigilant on the school's behalf.'

'He didn't have high motives sir.'

'How do you know?'

'He was jealous of Rutter because he fancied Françoise?'

'Who is Françoise for goodness sake?'

'A French woman. She works in the kitchen.'

'Have you any evidence of Potts's feelings towards her.'

'They played tennis together.'

'Sully, playing tennis or any other game for that matter isn't evidence of either strong feelings towards the opposite sex or an intimate relationship. I can't reprimand Potts for playing a game with a member of the staff, even though she works in the kitchen.'

The Major's response to his woes disappointed Sully. The senior housemaster just wanted to avoid conflict and any possibility of controversy. Consequently, Sully decided to make a final plea like a desperate supplicant to an implacable judge.

'Sir. I can't run a mile in 7 minutes 30 seconds. I'm fat. My weight is coming down but not enough to get anywhere near that time. I'm not a natural athlete. Potts wants to control me by making sure that I never make the time that he chooses. Then I'm constantly under his thumb. It's not fair. He's bullying me.'

'Sully you've made your case. I'll talk to Potts and ask him to reflect on the times he's setting you. Still, you must realise that I can't easily usurp a monitor's authority.'

'What's 'usurp', sir?'

'Take over, Sully.'

'Thank you, sir.'

'I mustn't undermine monitors unnecessarily.'

'I see.'

'Still, let's see if we can work out a good old British compromise.'

On that sceptical note, Sully left the pipe-smoking housemaster. With Field Marshal Montgomery in his military regalia overseeing him, the Major appeared as part of an establishment pageant.

On a sunny Saturday morning, Hayes was waiting in the dayroom for his father to take him out. He hadn't seen him for some time so he looked forward to his visit. Phil had been touring around the country with a small jazz group and Hayes had received his various postcards, which he duly stuck on his locker door. However, to a Londoner, the likes of Weston-Super-Mare and Scarborough were as remote as a town in another country. Phil had also made sure that International Stores sent him a parcel every month. Hayes really welcomed that, especially the pineapple chunks and tomatoes as they were his particular favourites. His father wrote briefly about how the tour was going while updating Hayes on the progress of Grantham FC. Hayes found his support of the Lincolnshire club bizarre considering he came from East Ham. Later, when he discovered that his father was based there during the war, his support appeared more rational. Although he appreciated the cards and food, Hayes felt it was like receiving correspondence and presents from a distant uncle rather than a father.

When Hayes saw Phil in his banged-out, cream coloured Triumph parked in the Avenue, he left the dayroom and immediately went to meet him. As he came out of the porch, Phil was walking towards him and they hugged each other affectionately. Hayes relished the embrace as he felt like a warm blanket had been wrapped around him. While they strolled to the banger, Phil suggested that they go for lunch at a café near the local park. Hayes agreed and away they went.

As Phil drove, he started talking about the tour. Apparently, it was hard with a new gig in a different venue each night. There were difficulties as the drummer was an alcoholic and the bass player took drugs. 'But we got through it,' exclaimed a relieved Phil. He then started to extol the virtues of Blackpool- 'not a jazz town but lively and distinctive. More a town for variety performers.' In fact, Thora, his loquacious landlady, couldn't stop telling him about all the stars who'd stayed at her digs like Elsie and Doris Waters, Vic Oliver as well as Irish singer Joseph Locke, who was always evading the taxman.

When Phil arrived outside the town, he ventured into smaller roads and started to 'mock-accelerate', which gave Hayes an enjoyable fright, as his father drove fast and then suddenly slowed down. This anarchic motor drama sent both father and son into gales of shared laughter. It only emphasised Hayes's delight at getting out of the school. Wearing shorts and sporting a blue cravat at the top of his open white shirt, also made him feel comfortable and relaxed. Phil was dressed in a sand linen jacket and jeans. He didn't seem like a typical Dad. Hayes took pride that his father appeared more modern than the others he'd met.

Phil parked the old banger just outside the park. They then went to a café where they encountered waitresses shouting like sergeant majors. Hayes and Phil sat down and a middle aged, ample woman in an austere black dress, accepted their orders indifferently, before continuing with her yelling. Later, while they were eating macaroni cheese, there was a massive scream from a child at a nearby table. Apparently, a mouse had been discovered, which neither did anything for Phil and Hayes's digestive systems nor their faith in the café's health standards. Consequently, father and son proceeded with their meal cautiously, although the rodent crisis didn't stop them ordering desserts: fruit salad for Phil and pumpkin chiffon pie for Hayes.

While they ate their food, the surrounding drama didn't abate. Suddenly, a woman shouted that she hadn't been given the correct change. The cashier, a tall blonde lady with dark-rimmed glasses dangling from a long protruding chain, looked upset as she locked her till and called for the manager. Eventually, a bald middle-aged man in a dark blue suit appeared. His drooping, bushy brown moustache and sullen face made him look like a sad walrus. After, several minutes of negotiation, the irate customer, a petulant elderly lady in a large red hat, was satisfied with the resolution. It was obviously a diplomatic triumph for the walrus.

When Hayes and his father had finished their desserts, they left the café and went for a stroll around the park. Children were paddling in a pool, splashing each other indiscriminately. Families were tucking into their picnics on a nearby lawn. Ducks and swans glided elegantly as if human behaviour was of little consequence. A mother was trying to protect her child from an overzealous Labrador. On the surrounding path, eager cyclists in singlets and shorts, intermittently weaved their way around the swelling crowd.

As father and son continued their journey, they discovered that by a lake small rowing boats were for hire. Instantly, Hayes asked his father if they could go for a session. When Phil discovered that Hayes couldn't row, he offered to teach him. They joined the queue and within a few minutes, Phil was getting tickets from a middle-aged man with a grey goatee beard and a strong West Indian accent, who was standing next to a wooden hut. Phil discovered that he came from Barbados, so he took the opportunity to chat about the merits of Sonny Rollins' recent jazz calypso, St Thomas. After exhausting their shared appreciation of Sonny's musical invention, Phil took his change and went with Hayes to the departure bay. On their arrival, a brawny young man in a blue t-shirt and jeans, tore the tickets. This muscular lad, with a hairstyle like James Dean, trimmed at the sides, tapered at the back with a swept back wavy quiff, then attached a pole to a boat and Hayes and his father scrambled into the craft. Phil held the oars, as the boat drifted out into the lake. Just as he was starting to row, the young man's cockney voice resounded into a megaphone. 'Remember, you've got 30 minutes. You're number 80.'

Phil steered the boat into the middle of the lake. Once there, he carefully changed places with his son and the lesson started. Phil didn't regard himself as an expert but he tried to give his son some guidelines. He went through the basic stroke movements and encouraged him to hold his head steady, concentrate on the rhythm and timing of the oar and not just use force. Under his father's tuition, Hayes gradually started rowing well. Once Hayes had established control of a straight-ahead journey, Phil taught him how to navigate the boat in different directions, sometimes using each oar separately. Hayes enjoyed his father's lesson as the more they talked about each task, the closer they became. Hayes realised that through the divorce of his parents, he hadn't got to know his father. He had become a distant figure, whom he saw sporadically. This was a rare occasion where they maintained some intimacy.

Just as Hayes was developing his rowing expertise, a group of girls in another boat interrupted his flow. All three teenagers were giggling hysterically. Two, in jeans and check shirts, were sitting together while drinking from bottles of beer. The other, a tall girl with long legs and wearing short pants, was supposedly rowing but seemed more inebriated than the others. Suddenly, they all started singing Michael Row the Boat Ashore. As they became engrossed in the traditional American spiritual, they sang louder and became more anarchic. The tall girl, forgetting about her rowing, stood up in the boat and imitated a gospel singer. She then screeched intensely, supported by cries of 'Hallelujah!' from her friends. As she worked herself into a lather of drunken passion, the boat started careering precariously . On reaching the final chorus, the park's Mahalia Jackson lost her footing and fell into the lake. For a moment, there was a pause while the self-styled gospel singer didn't emerge from the water. Then suddenly, much to everyone's relief, she popped up looking less like a musical icon and more like a drowned rat. Eventually, the delirious rat clambered aboard to safety.

Meanwhile, Phil had extricated their boat from this drama by parking next to a small island, which was full of various trees, shrubbery and wild life. Initially, Phil had contemplated going to rescue the singing diva but thankfully, it wasn't necessary. The girls calmed down and one of the less intoxicated members of the group started rowing back to the landing bay. After the gospel choir departed, Phil and Hayes enjoyed listening to the various sounds and sights emanating from the island. They played a game trying to outdo each other naming various birds, like herons and kingfishers. When they progressed to trees, Hayes became more confident in differentiating a weeping willow from an oak. He wasn't very good at nature and Mr Endersby's teaching hadn't rectified his ignorance. Now, with his father's guidance, he also learnt more about animals and plants. He began to discern otters and dragonflies as well as water lilies and marigolds. Hayes really enjoyed this exploration. Going to football certainly cemented a sense of fellowship but a discussion about nature felt more profound.

Eventually, a barking voice from a megaphone announcing 'number 80-your time is up!', abruptly interrupted Hayes and Phil's nature idyll. In response to this stentorian directive, Phil challenged Hayes to row back to the bay. Hayes accepted the challenge and carefully gathered the oars. He then navigated his way away from the island and rowed towards the shore. As his strokes grew more confident, Phil became proud of his son. He felt that he could really achieve things. He didn't know what exactly but that didn't matter. He was becoming capable. As they approached the bay, the boy in the blue t-shirt was smoking and laughing with his West Indian colleague. When Hayes and Phil drifted into port, the young man ostentatiously threw the remnants of his cigarette into the water. On their arrival, he attached the hooked pole to the boat and helped father and son embark safely. When his two customers had landed, the vigorous, quiff-laden blonde turned to them grinning.

'You're late but Isaac over there didn't want to charge you extra,' he said, referring to his colleague, who'd gone back to the hut to attend to the disruptive gospel choir.

Phil and Hayes could see Isaac overseeing the drowned rat, who was furiously drying her hair with a multi-coloured towel, while being supported by her backing group.

'Sorry. We were having a discussion about nature,' revealed Phil.

'Nature?' queried the bewildered young man.

'Yes. Identifying the names of different trees and animals on that little island,' continued Phil.

'Oh, right. You're not really meant to go there,' responded the young man disinterestedly, 'but Isaac over there didn't want to punish a jazz man.'

'I'll thank him.'

'Jazz doesn't do it for me. It's my Dad's music.'

'It's worth giving it a go, you know.'

'I prefer Elvis. Rip It Up, now that's rockin'.'

‘Have you heard of Lester Young?’ quizzed Phil, attempting to impart his musical faith.

‘Who?’

‘Lester Young. A jazz saxophonist. He plays very soulfully.’

‘Ok, I’ll check him out when I’m relaxing with my bird.’

‘Good.’

‘We go dancing at the Alligator on Saturday nights.’

‘Sounds fun’

‘Yeah, it can get lively there.’

‘Anyway, thanks.’

‘That’s ok, mate.’ The young man looked thoughtful and then added, ‘right. Lester Young. I’ll remember him.’

This conversation evoked sad memories for Hayes, as Phil had played a record of Lester’s when he visited him at Woolwich. It was after a Charlton game and it was the first time that he’d met Amy. He was upset meeting his father’s girlfriend, so Lester’s plaintive, bluesy tone suited his mood.

While Hayes and his father moved away from the landing bay, Isaac was still dealing with the three girls, telling them that in future they should obey the rules and row more responsibly. The gospel singer, followed by her backing group, then moved inside Isaac’s hut to dry herself more thoroughly, joking that it was a pity that he didn’t have a dress available. When father and son passed the hut, Phil greeted Isaac cordially.

‘Thanks for letting us off the extra charge and allowing us to go on the island.’

‘You’re welcome man,’ declared the affable Isaac.

‘Really appreciate it.’

‘Anything for a real jazz man.’

‘I was exploring nature with my son.’

‘That’s good. We can all learn a lot from that.’

‘I hope to see you again.’

‘Yeah, that’d be great. I’d better go back and try and find some clothing for the wet lady.’

‘Good luck.’

As Isaac was about to disappear inside the hut, he turned back to Phil with a cheerful smile.

‘Saint Thomas is something else. That’s calypso jazz, man.’

Hayes and his father left Isaac oscillating between helping the soaked gospel singer and dealing with some newly arrived customers. Phil then initiated a stroll through the park. It was turning out to be a bright, enervating summer's day. Families were having picnics on the grass and boys were playing cricket with a drinks crate as a wicket. One young, intransigent bespectacled batsman was refusing to accept that he was out.

When they reached the other side of the lake, a father and son were fishing but didn't seem to be having any luck. Not far from them were two boys playing conkers, one of them, a small tubby infant, was violently attacking his opponent's chestnut. As Phil and Hayes passed the contest, the two boys were having an argument about whether tubby had completed a legitimate three strikes. Father and son observed the argument with shared amusement, before ambling up a nearby hill. Here, several children were playing hide and seek, disappearing behind bushes and shrubbery as well as inside their parents' clothes. When they eventually reached the hill's high summit, Phil found a bench from where they could survey the whole park. As they both relaxed, they viewed the mass of humanity below. Looking down from a distance, Hayes thought that everybody seemed remote, like abstract figures from another world.

The young schoolboy decided that this was a suitable time to talk more intimately about his parents' divorce. He hoped it would clear the air.

'Why did you leave Mum?' Hayes asked intensely.

'We grew apart,' Phil replied nervously.

'How? I remember you being very much in love.'

'The war intensified things.'

'What do you mean?'

'Well. People fell in love quickly. Nobody knew what tomorrow would bring.'

'You lived for the moment?'

'Yes. Sort of. There was a lot of fear about.'

'I see.'

'But that made it exciting. Your mother and I had a lot of fun.'

'Fun? In what way?'

'Music. Concerts. Dances.'

Hayes thought that his mother had to make too many sacrifices and that Phil's charm glossed over his responsibilities. He felt that now was the time to challenge his father about his neglect.

'But Mum had to give up her career as a pianist.'

'To look after you and Poppy.'

'Surely she didn't have to stop her recitals altogether?'

'That's what society expects.'

'That the mother must just look after the children?'

Phil paused. He was beginning to find the conversation awkward. After looking at the children below noisily celebrating finding their hidden friend, he turned to his son.

'Yes, I suppose so,' he responded hesitantly.

'But you're doing what you want,' stressed Hayes.

'I'm just trying to make a living in a difficult profession,' said Phil quietly.

Hayes loved his father but suspected his motives. He obviously put his own career first. Hayes felt the need to remind him of the suffering he'd caused.

'Mum got very upset after the divorce.'

'I'm sorry about that.'

'She was living off very little money. She doesn't get much from you. She had to ask granny for help.'

'I'm giving what I can afford.'

Hayes didn't really believe him. When he had money, his father seemed to spend it on expensive holidays in places like the South of France. However, he decided not to pursue this area but instead reverted to the other consequences of his parents' break-up.

'There's quite a stigma about divorce. Other boys mention it. It's like you've failed society.'

'It's easy to simplify things.'

'I think Mum's religious in a quiet way. She believes in marriage.'

'Yes she does.'

'So failing is like breaking a vow.'

'I suppose so. It's just your mother never understood the music business. Or my side of it anyway.'

'What do you mean?

‘When I married your mother, I was more of a flight-lieutenant. When we came back into Civvy Street, I was a jazz musician and we had to start all over again. It just didn’t work out.’

‘But you left her with two very young children.’

Below, Phil saw a young girl in a bright red dress desperately looking for an innovative hiding place. While she explored possibilities, the other boys and girls had their eyes closed and were dramatically counting down the last seconds before they hunted her down. After she had hidden behind some remote undergrowth and her friends began to mount their search, Phil eventually replied:

‘Yes. I feel bad about that. I just did my best.’

‘You took the easy way out, Dad.’

‘No. It was never easy. I loved your mother.’

‘Then why did you break up our family?’

Phil looked at his son. He saw the upset and hurt, the depth of the scars. He realised that he underestimated how his children would react to the divorce. Hayes certainly seemed to be suffering a lot as his eyes were beginning to turn moist.

While Phil and Hayes made their way down the hill, they observed the girl in the red dress being discovered behind a bramble bush, much to the delight of her ardent pursuers. When they ambled through the park to the car, Phil tried to talk about the present. He wanted his son to accept Amy so he spoke about her forthcoming album. However, Hayes wasn’t interested as he felt that she’d contributed to the break-up of his parent’s marriage. On the way back, they stopped off at restaurant for a meal where they both enjoyed a large steak. Hayes began to feel better and he and Phil chatted about Surrey’s chances of winning the cricket county championship again. Their shared interest in sport dissipated the previous tension. After Hayes had demolished an ice cream and apple pie, his father drove him back to the school. Once they’d both got out of the car, Phil embraced his son.

‘Good luck, Tommy. See you soon.’

‘Thanks for a good time, Dad.’

Phil smiled and departed to his battered Triumph. Hayes walked into the house. He enjoyed seeing his father but it didn't dispel the pain of him leaving the family.

Ryder wasn't surprised when before choir practice, Sully told him about the Major's refusal to reproach One Ball. 'Liberal conservatism always avoids taking the necessary radical action. It's like a patient swallowing an aspirin, when they need an operation,' he brooded to himself during the rehearsal. Ryder now believed that this matter was becoming even more serious than Root's avoidance of adding Jerusalem to the choral repertoire.

The choir were preparing Anton Bruckner's Te Deum, which the music master described as an 'Evensong Special'. In fact, while singing the Austrian composer's uplifting religious music, Ryder's mind wandered to less spiritual matters. He decided that now was the time to initiate specific action against One Ball's bullying. The Major's idea of compromise was just a way of preserving the unacceptable status quo. He hadn't responded seriously to the charges and without his support, it was hopeless trying to persuade Oliver, who was vacillation incarnate and would do his best to bury any bad news. Therefore, Ryder concluded that the boys must take the matter into their own hands.

While Root meandered on about the devout Bruckner's intentions, Ryder started thinking of a plan. He decided that he must gather an insurrectionary cell together and initiate a strategic attack. After the rehearsal finished, Root gave Ryder a stern look. He was aware that the choir leader was preoccupied and he knew that meant trouble. As Root didn't want to be ambushed again by any further protests, he reassured the insolent choir leader that Jerusalem was still being seriously considered. Ryder superciliously thanked him for the update. Then, once out of the chapel, the school's Lenin relayed his new plan to Sully and told him to liaise with Barrett about gathering together sufficient rebels. Meanwhile, he'd book a room for a meeting at the Music School on Saturday morning at 9:30. While returning to his house, he'd also drop in at Ironside A and talk to Rutter.

When it was time for the meeting, the conspirators gathered in room five of the Music School. The room, which was at the back of the building, oversaw Open Way and was very small. Consequently, some of the plotters were standing, which gave the gathering a natural anarchic and spontaneous ambience. After the stragglers like Sully, Hayes and Barrett finally arrived, Ryder, standing imperiously by the piano, did a quick count. Once he'd decided that sufficient members of the insurgent cell were present, he started to speak.

'It's good to see you all,' he announced flatteringly, 'but do remember, this is a meeting for a singing practice. In fact, I've borrowed some hymn books from the chapel for the occasion. There's one for everybody,' claimed Ryder, passing them around. 'Have the book in your hand at all times, in case someone uninvited enters. I shall sit at the piano and play the role of accompanist. From time to time, we must sing. So make sure you do so loudly and heartily until I tell you to stop. We need to give the impression of an extra-curricular rehearsal. So let's start by singing hymn number 487, Eternal Father Strong to Save. You all know it as it's one of Elwyn's favourites. Come in after my short introduction. I'll cue you like this,' illustrated Ryder, raising his hand and then dramatically lowering it.

The boys looked at each other in disappointment before reluctantly finding the hymn. They wanted to be part of an uprising not choristers. Nonetheless, they accepted the school Lenin's diversionary tactic and after the self-appointed maestro's hand came down, the rebels bellowed bellicosely, 'Eternal Father, strong to save….'

All the conspirators immediately became choristers. Rock 'n' rollers Brown and Bunter sang lustily, even though to them an ancient British hymn wasn't the same as Whole Lotta Shakin' Goin' On. Boot performed with a vengeful, angry fervour while Binns was suitably manic, inevitably squeezing his hands together as he roared away. Rice just about held the tune. Barrel was belligerently passionate, Sully impressively mellifluous, Hayes stridently cacophonous and Barrett just loud.

After completing all four verses, Ryder thanked the conspirators fulsomely. Just as he was about to propose a strategy, Rutter, splendidly luminous in whites and a blue blazer, entered the room carrying a cricket bag.

'Sorry, I'm late, Ryder. Pongo wanted me to sort out some juniors. Then I had to get ready for the game against Old Owls. It starts at 11:30.'

'The Owls. Terrible cheats,' affirmed Rice with the passion of somebody who'd suffered from a bad personal experience.

'Thanks Rice. I think we need to proceed,' insisted the leader. 'Oh, Sully give Rutter a hymn book. You're attending a singing practice Rutter,' stressed Ryder, smiling conspiratorially at the newly arrived cricketer.

Rutter appeared confused. He felt as if a merciless cult had abruptly abducted the uninitiated. However, such fears didn't stop the leader continuing his oratory.

'We know without doubt' proclaimed Ryder 'that James Potts, known more colloquially as One Ball, is a bully. You all know of the way he's enslaved Sully through dubious punishments, blackmail, and oppressive enforcement. On my advice, Sully appealed to Mr Aizlewood but the Major equivocated. Why did he equivocate? Because that's the cowardly way of siding with a serial bully. Why didn't he stop the bullying? Because he didn't want to undermine a monitor's authority. Why didn't he confront a cruel monitor? Because the monitors run the houses not the housemasters. That's the system. And it's unjust. No boy should have to succumb to what Sully has gone through. Such power shouldn't be in the hands of an unelected elite.'

'So what are we going to do about it?' shouted Boot.

Suddenly there was a sound of vigorous movement in the corridor. At once, the leader swung round to the piano and miraculously transformed into a music master.

'First verse again everybody,' yelled Ryder.

With an appropriately fraternal gesture, Rice shared his hymn book with Rutter and guided him to nautical hymn 487. The swelling sounds of Eternal Father, Strong to Save, then resounded again throughout room five. In fact, Ryder's opening speech had inspired the conspirators to increase the intensity of their vocal efforts. After the verse ended, the leader gave an abrupt signal to stop, worthy of Root at his most robustly Teutonic.

'As I was going to say before I was rudely interrupted,' continued the leader amidst mild titters, 'to answer your question, Boot. Sully's tried to reason with the monitor. No response. He's tried to appeal to the senior housemaster. The Major sides with the monitor. We know that Oliver never interferes in such matters as he's afraid of undermining the housemaster. In any case, he's weak and ineffectual. Therefore, my friends, I conclude that we must take action,' declared Ryder emphatically.

'Violent action?' asked Binns excitedly.

'Let's not get ahead of ourselves, Binns,' warned a cautious leader.

'What then? demanded an insistent Boot.

'I believe One Ball needs to be reminded about injustice,' stated Ryder.

'But how? In what way?' pursued Boot.

'You're like an evasive politician, Ryder,' maintained Rice.

'He needs to be lured into the changing room,' suggested Bunter.

'Then what?' questioned a concerned Rutter.

'Give him the once over?' proposed Barrel.

'That's too crude,' responded Barrett. 'We need to be more subtle.'

'We could surround and intimidate him,' added Brown.

'After that, what are we going to do?' challenged Rutter.

'Well, we could take off his clothes and string him up,' elaborated Brown.

'That's a bit melodramatic, Brown,' said Sully derisively.

'I'm only trying to help, Sully,' claimed the offended rocker.

'Yes. It could work. Expose his ball,' exclaimed Binns, rubbing his hands with glee.

'What about facial recognition? asked a perceptive Brown

'I've got an idea,' announced a fervent Barrel. 'I could get masks. My Dad's got a friend in Merthyr Tydfil who makes them. He does satirical ones. Of politicians and royalty.'

'That sounds fun,' enthused the leader.

'Yes, we could surround him with masks,' eulogised Binns.

‘What about voice recognition?’ mentioned Barrett, ever the precocious junior.

‘We could just imitate the posh voices of various politicians and royals. It doesn’t matter if we’re useless at it. It’ll be fun,’ urged Bunter.

‘That sounds good. So, as this will have to be a James B project,’ evaluated the leader, ‘who’s going to be in charge?’

‘I’ll deal with it,’ asserted Barrett enthusiastically, although of course, I’ll need to remain in contact with you, Ryder,’ he acknowledged nervously.

‘Of course,’ confirmed Ryder, delighted that he could be a mastermind above the fray.

‘So when are you going to apprehend Potts?’ probed Rutter, establishing a semi-detached status.

‘Not yet. It’ll need more planning. In a few weeks’ time,’ thought Barrett, strategically prevaricating.

‘Meanwhile, we can practice being old Etonians like most of the cabinet,’ mocked Brown.

‘Jolly boating weather and a hay harvest breeze!’ sang Bunter in satirical refrain.

‘Do please keep in touch with me as well,’ pleaded an insistent Rutter, not wanting to appear unsupportive.

‘Don’t worry I will,’ replied Barrett, embracing his new leadership role.

‘And what happens after this action?’ queried a forceful Ryder. A deafening silence followed. It was clear that no one had really evaluated the consequences of their brutal plan.

‘They could expel us and cover it up,’ submitted Barrett.

‘These are the risks you take when fighting injustice Barrett,’ emphasised Ryder, launching into a tirade. ‘But it’s my belief that they’re worth taking. It’s not just about Sully, although that’s bad enough. It’s about an unfair system that needs changing. A system that’s been going on for years. A system that enables the powerful and exploits the powerless. This has to be stopped. We have tried to negotiate reasonably but the system has failed us. So, we have no alternative but to engage in rigorous action to support Sully and stop continual abuse and injustice. In short, we’ve got to storm the barricades! Good luck my friends!’ cried the euphoric Ryder.

Ryder's speech had the intended effect and incited resounding cheers. When the radical exhilaration had died down, the school's Lenin thought that the conspirators should end the meeting with a suitable song to inspire their revolutionary action. He proposed that they all should sing The Red Flag.

'Even those who aren't committed socialists can't deny that it's a passionate call for justice. I took the liberty of typing out the words. Take one and pass them on, Barrett.' instructed Ryder, exultantly taking paper sheets from the top of the piano and handing them to his prodigy, the school's baby Lenin.

After distribution was completed, Ryder returned to the piano and once more addressed his fellow conspirators.

'If somebody comes in and objects to our socialist elation, we'll say we're exploring the influences on Bertolt Brecht. Ok? Now everybody, who knows the tune?'

Only Barrett and Barrel put their hands up.

'Ok. I'll play it through once unaccompanied, then you two come in strongly and the rest can follow as best they can.'

This Ryder duly did with stylish élan, declaiming 'here we come One Ball! One, two, three! before pointing at Barrett and Barrel, who led the others into the socialist anthem: 'The people's flag is deepest red....'

Despite most of the boys not knowing the song, its visceral spirit gradually transported them. Such soaring defiance and commitment transformed the conspirators into a united army of rebellion.

Killer pounded the dormitory floor as the boys washed in the lav end. Later he was going to confront Marian about the bloody headstone, which was still stuck in his garden like an eternal ghost. He certainly wasn't going to settle the outstanding bill for 53 pounds. No, Marian must do that and pay for her puerile joke. Killer didn't realise how bitter she'd become. She knew he was married with a child. Why did she wish to humiliate him so brutally? And why hadn't she kept her bloody curtains closed?

Killer was on duty in the dormitory with One Ball, who had brought up several books to accelerate his work schedule. Killer could talk easily to One Ball because of their shared scientific interests. On this particular evening, One Ball was waxing lyrical about Einstein's Quantum Theory, when the gangly Boot interrupted his flow.

'Excuse me, Potts.'

'Yes. What is it Boot?'

'It's Saturday.'

'That's right Boot.'

'So is there going to be a reading tonight?'

'Yes'.

'Who's doing it, Potts?'

'Binns.'

'He didn't say. Do you know what he's reading?'

'Yes.'

'What?'

'The Devil Rides Out.'

'Good. Scary stuff!' enthused Boot, as he departed gleefully to his bed.

After Boot's interruption, One Ball continued his Quantum Theory thesis but Killer didn't feel like discussing atoms and subatomic particles. As he was still contemplating how he'd deal with Marian, he wasn't receptive to One Ball's theorising. In any case, Killer thought that One Ball was grandstanding. He was the eager student, wanting to show off his knowledge to a specialist audience. After acknowledging his expertise, Killer diverted the conversation. He wanted to get away from work and the headstone fracas so he enquired about One Ball's family. When the monitor responded hesitantly, it was clear to Killer that his father's death still loomed over him. This wasn't uncommon. Killer had several friends whose families suffered because of the war. They were struggling both emotionally and financially. Although Killer was glad that the school was able to educate the children of such people, it was a drop in the ocean compared to the legacy of the psychological scars. When Killer attended reunions with his old regiment, he could hardly recognise some of the veterans. Many had aged quickly, their faces wizened by stress, others had become alcoholics and quite a few were divorced. Killer realised that in addition to his unfortunate accident, Potts was suffering from the aftermath of a missing father. The junior housemaster saw through Potts's protective mask of authority and concluded that although he needed guidance, this wasn't the time to offer it. Maybe he could give it before the end of term. He hoped so, as he found the school deficient in providing support for a boy's personal difficulties.

Eventually all the boys left the lav end and took to their beds. This didn't stop an animated conversation between Boot and Hayes about whether Frank Sinatra performed a concert in Blackpool. Hayes didn't think so, nor did Barrett or Sully. Looking for an answer, Boot appealed to Killer.

'Sir, which of us is right? asked Boot, hoping for a definitive judgement.

'I've no idea, Boot. I know Sinatra came over here a few years ago but I thought he appeared only in London. Do you know Potts?' enquired Killer, looking to deflect his ignorance of popular music.

'I'm not a Sinatra fan,' said One Ball indifferently.

'I'll just have to ask Rice. He's a Frankie obsessive,' decided a determined Boot.

'Well you can't now because he's in the other dormitory,' insisted Killer resolutely.

'He's always going on about Frank's great backing,' added a weary Boot.

'Ok, Boot. That's enough on crooners,' demanded Killer.

'Sorry, sir,' apologised Boot, not wanting to inflame Killer's wrath.

Killer called for the reading to start. Sully and Hayes in their striped pyjamas, then wheeled Binns in his bed to the centre of the dormitory. One Ball then got hold of a large pole by the door and pulled the central light down, a few feet above the assembled reader. Once everybody settled down, he turned out the rest of the lights, returned the pole and went back to his desk, surrounded by an ostentatious pile of books. With everything organised, Killer decided to leave and confront Marian.

'All right, I'm off,' announced Killer, approaching One Ball's lit desk.

'Ok, sir,' accepted an acquiescent One Ball.

‘Goodnight boys,’ projected Killer, before exiting in the dark towards matron’s abode.

Dissonant cries of ‘goodnight sir’ followed Killer on his way. Once the door was closed, Boot couldn’t resist making a comment.

‘ I think he’s gone to visit the witch’.

‘Shut up, Boot,’ reprimanded One Ball.

‘Maybe he’s wearing his boxer shorts,’ imagined a mocking Barrett.

‘That’s enough, Barrett,’ warned One Ball, keen to immerse himself in his revision.

‘I wonder whether he’ll close the curtains,’ contemplated a chuckling Sully.

‘Sully!’ snapped an irate One Ball.

‘The James Witch Project!’ trumpeted Hayes, as if trailing a horror film.

‘Right. Stop it! Stop it right now!’ commanded One Ball, shouting while he moved towards Hayes’s bed. He then turned and addressed the whole dormitory. ‘Otherwise, there’ll be no reading. Silence!’ he thundered demonically.

Such was the force of One Ball’s outburst that he cowered the boys into submission. You could hear a pin drop.

‘Ok. Go ahead, Binns,’ instructed One Ball.

The single light over Binns’s head gave him a dramatic, menacing, shadowy profile, which suited the macabre narrative. As he leaned confidently against his white pillow, he started reading Dennis Wheatley’s disturbing story of black magic and the occult.

When Killer entered Marian’s room, she was sitting on her turquoise sofa reading an article in the Daily Mirror about developments in Cyprus. Suddenly, she forgot about Britain’s colonial struggles and gave Killer a seductive smile.

‘Ah, would the infamous Killer like a game of draughts?’

‘No he wouldn’t,’ replied Killer tersely.

‘What a pity I need some relaxation after reading about the danger confronting the world.’

‘Stop the play acting Marian.’

‘British forces’ operating abroad is a serious matter.’

‘That headstone isn’t funny.’

‘What are you talking about?’

‘You know bloody well what I’m talking about.’

‘You seem to be very agitated, my darling Killer. I think you’d better sit down and have a drink.’

‘I don’t want a drink.’

‘Well, just sit down and relax. In the meantime, I’m going to get one for myself,’ declared Marian breezily while departing to her kitchen.

Killer reluctantly plonked himself down on Marian’s sofa. He realised that he needed to calm down and gather himself. As he did so, he stared at Marian’s bookcase, which amidst various grisly thrillers included Patricia Highsmith’s To Love and Be Wise. ‘Easier said than done,’ thought Killer. Eventually, Marian reappeared from the kitchen with two tumblers and a bowl of ice cubes, which she placed on a nearby coffee table.

‘I’ve brought you a glass in case you change your mind,’ said Marian enticingly, as she went over to collect bottles of gin and tonic water from a glass cabinet. Reluctantly, Killer accepted Marian’s offer of a drink, in the hope that such consent would make her more amenable. As she prepared the drinks, Killer contemplated his next move, while continuing to observe Marian’s alarming selection of crime books. Eventually, Marian handed him his cocktail.

‘G and t. A good pick-me-up. Cheers,’ exclaimed Marian, returning to the sofa..

‘Cheers,’ acknowledged an anxious Killer.

They both drank in silence before Killer mentioned Marian’s literary taste.

‘I see you’ve been reading Strangers on a Train,’ broached a curious Killer, trying to avoid any further tension by turning to literature.

‘Yes, it’s very disturbing. I loved it. Did you see the film?’ enquired Marian gleefully.

‘Yes I did,’ responded a suspicious Killer, who couldn’t help wondering if the psychopathic protagonist of the classic thriller could have inspired Marian’s recent behaviour.

‘Peter loved that film. We went to the local Gaumont to see it,’ remembered a playful Marian.

‘Marian, you’ve got to pay for the headstone,’ blurted out Killer, no longer able to contain himself.

‘That and United. He loved the Busby Babes,’ continued Marian blithely.

‘It can’t stay in my garden,’ confirmed Killer, ignoring her tactical digressions.

‘He really wanted to be a doctor, you know,’ revealed a prevaricating Marian.

Killer realised that Marian was going to continue taunting him unless he was more assertive. He’d had enough of her reminiscences about her beloved husband. He took a quick swig of gin and delivered an ultimatum.

‘Marian. Your prank wasn’t funny. I’ve got a bill for 53 pounds because of your facile joke. I’m not going to pay it. I’m going to contact Illingworths. I’m going to tell them to redirect the invoice to you. Not only have you upset me but also my family. Your escapade was callous and demeaning. I didn’t know that you could be so vindictive.’

Marian sat back on the sofa and observed Killer’s fretting with considerable pleasure. He was inconsiderate and selfish so he only had himself to blame. She deliberately put her glass down on the table, arched her back and looked him sternly in the eye like a brutal barrister about to humiliate a witness

‘The invoice is addressed to you, so Illingworths won’t help. You ordered it so you must pay for it. I didn’t risk our liaison lightly. Ok, I was a bit randy but so were you. I knew you were unhappy and as I was attracted to you, I wanted to know you better. You seemed to feel likewise but after one night of intimacy, you start panicking, running back to your grumbling Geordie and ignoring me as if I didn’t exist. That’s not showing respect. So you deserve humiliation. That’s justice. You made your bed, as the saying goes, so now you must lie in it.’ Having concluded her invective, Marian picked up her glass and calmly resumed drinking.

Marian’s venom made Killer angry. He still didn’t think it was fair that he should be forced to pay for something that he didn’t order. It would leave a hole in his finances and invite Deirdre’s wrath. He grudgingly accepted Marian’s invitation for more gin as he contemplated what to do. Killer realised that he had underestimated Marian's need for commitment. He thought that she'd like being his mistress and would be satisfied with intermittent frolicking. He was wrong. Behind her northern bluster, he detected a vulnerable hunger for love and allegiance. She'd become wounded by loss and thought that he could fill that emotional hole. She obviously felt that life had treated her unfairly. This left her with little regard for his family and responsibilities. Killer concluded that she was frightened of loneliness. Something you'd never suspect when you observed her efficient organisation of the dormitories and the boys' laundry.

Following her splenetic outburst, Marian proceeded to pick up her Daily Mirror, only Killer didn't believe that she was really reading it. As she lounged superciliously in her tight fitting jeans, showing her slim figure to advantage, Killer found her alluringly attractive. However, this time he resisted temptation and once more tried to settle their dispute.

'I have a family Marian,' Killer reminded her.

'And a wife you don't like,' countered Marian.

'We were just going through a hard time,' clarified Killer.

'That's not what you told me,' maintained Marian.

'I've got to think about Barney,' emphasised Killer.

'You should have thought of him earlier,' prompted Marian.

'I'm sorry, yes, I should have,' admitted Killer contritely.

'It's too late now,' Marian affirmed scornfully.

The gin drinking resumed but neither of them spoke. Eventually, Killer broke the wordless impasse and made a proposal.

'Marian, what about us splitting the bill, that's only fair,' bargained Killer.

'No!' 'You ordered it. You pay for it!' reiterated Marian.

'But you know I didn't order it!' exclaimed Killer forcefully.

'That's not what Illingworths say,' stressed Marian.

In the ensuing silence, Killer realised that he wasn't going to make any further progress. The injustice of it made his blood boil. If there was no resolution, news of their altercation was bound to circulate. 'Leaks were as prevalent as fresh air in this school for scandal,' he thought to himself, so he needed to get closure quickly. Unfortunately, Marian's stubbornness meant that he'd now have to give her time to feel at least minimally repentant. If she didn't compromise, he'd have to urgently reconsider his strategy. Whatever the conclusion, hopefully it'll secure his marriage.

He tersely thanked Marian for the drink and made towards the door. After opening it, he turned round and demanded to know who was impersonating him.

'Well, it wasn't me,' vowed an innocent Marian.

'I know it couldn't be you Marian,' verified Killer sarcastically.

Marian nonchalantly glanced at her paper before Killer resumed his interrogation.

'Well then, who was it? insisted Killer.

'I've no idea. You'll just have to put it down to magic,' replied Marian, refusing to expose the artful character acting skills of the indispensable Mr Herbert Fairfax. 'Goodnight,' she concluded indifferently.

'Goodnight,' mumbled Killer resentfully and shut the door. He trudged home no wiser about Marian's vengeful strategy. Still, that wouldn't stop him trying to expose the damned impersonator.

After the school cricket team lost badly to Brighton College, Rutter avoided Pongo and Fred, said his goodbyes to his forlorn teammates and trundled back to house. At least, now he had more time for meeting Françoise. The pressures of the final term had made it difficult for him to see her. He had a lot of revision to do as his exams were rapidly approaching. Playing cricket had become so time consuming, that he'd even resorted to working on the coach when the school travelled away. Still, it was now Saturday evening and he needed a break. To celebrate seeing Françoise, he'd sneaked a bottle of wine into a satchel. The desired liquid was a clandestine purchase from his parents' last visit, when he'd wandered to an off licence under the guise of going to the toilet. He wanted to surprise Françoise, whom he'd arranged to meet at the back of the fives courts.

It was a cool summer's evening and Rutter felt smart and confident in his school blazer and blue cravat. Yet at the appointed time, there was no sign of Françoise. After ten minutes, he started to get anxious. Did she get my message? Had something suddenly cropped up?. He went and looked vainly towards the main pathway, which bisected the rugger pitches, but she still didn't appear. He was about to resign himself to a lonely fate, when an excitable figure wearing a red beret and a light brown jacket, emerged from a narrow footpath at the side of the nearby running track. Initially, Françoise looked flustered but when she eventually saw Rutter, she was relieved.

'Where is this fives?' she pleaded as she approached.

'Sorry, I should have explained, it's a court near the athletics field,' revealed a repentant Rutter.

'Court? Why are you so obsessed with royalty in this country?'

'No court, like a tennis court'

'Oh, ok. Another court?'

'Yes'

'There are a lot of courts in England.'

Rutter laughed and looked intensely at Françoise.

'Anyway, great to see you,' he whispered.

'And you Artie,' said Françoise quietly. As they couldn't be more intimate in such a public place, she then resumed her enquiries.

'So, what is this bloody fives? she insisted.

'It's a game.'

'I know that.'

'Well it's bit like squash, only you hit a hard ball with your hand not a racquet.'

'Sounds masochistic.'

'You wear special gloves so it's not too painful.'

'You do play some strange sports here and people like you go crazy playing them.'

Rutter didn't want to get into a further discussion, either about the idiosyncrasies of rugby fives or his competitive instincts, so he suggested that they found a quiet place to talk. As they made their way towards the tuck shop, Rutter didn't really know where he was going. He just hoped that something reclusive would emerge. While strolling aimlessly, they arrived at an asphalt area in front of the manual school. There, several juniors were so obsessed with a game of marbles that they completely ignored the advancing couple. Rutter and Françoise took advantage of this rejection to move surreptitiously around the edge of the school building. Stepping quietly onto a gravel path, they advanced aimlessly around bits of discarded wood and metal, until Rutter discovered a small hut.

Inside, amidst some neatly stacked furniture, he blew dust off two chairs and a table, using a nearby rag to give them a wipe. Rutter then invited Françoise to sit down. When she'd settled, Rutter dramatically revealed the 'poison' from his satchel, to his own trumpeting accompaniment. This revelation delighted Françoise, who accepted a glass of wine in one of the assembled paper cups that Rutter had taken from the Dining Hall. They then both started to enjoy the Sauvignon blanc like two rebellious children playing truant. Eventually, after a few drinks, Françoise disclosed that One Ball was writing short, angry letters to her, calling her a traitor and worse.

'I wouldn't worry about One Ball,' Rutter reassured her.

'But he's continuing to harass me,' replied an agitated Françoise.

'One Ball is going to be dealt with.'

'By who?'

'James B boys.'

'In what way?'

'They're going to physically confront him.'

'Do you mean hit him?'

'I don't think so.'

'Violence won't help.'

'He's a bully Françoise. His housemaster won't deal with him, nor will other monitors.'

'What if he gets badly hurt?'

'I think it's more to give him a scare.'

'I certainly hope so.'

Françoise took a swig of wine. She was concerned that such an encounter could get out of hand. It made her feel responsible. She'd only deceived One Ball to keep him under control. If the current plan was to accost him deliberately, she feared that a mob of volatile boys could be savagely cruel and violent. After all, didn't even the school's rugby captain get very angry just playing a game. In response, Rutter articulated that sport was different because it involved controlled aggression monitored by others, not a free for all. It exorcised any violent feelings and aided good behaviour off the field. Although Françoise could accept how his theory applied to himself, she thought that others, particularly juniors, could respond differently in a group or gang. Consequently, Rutter didn't elaborate on the conspirators' plans. Instead, he looked to alleviate Françoise's concerns, by reassuring her that seniors would control the showdown and that frightening One Ball would make him change his tune. Rutter was certain that the conspirators wouldn't throw punches but he believed that the boys were forced to act because of the school's negligence. Eventually, when his passionate rhetoric had finally convinced Françoise of the strategy, she decided to forget about the forthcoming encounter and just enjoy the wine.

'Anyway, what about us?' asked Rutter looking tenderly into her dark brown eyes.

'We're both going to university,' replied Françoise tentatively.

'I hope.'

'You will.'

'If I get more work done.'

'You'll go if you want to.'

They both sipped their wine and looked away from each other.

'I'll miss you,' avowed Rutter, putting his cup on the battered table.

'I'll miss you as well Artie,' confided Françoise.

'Do you think that we'll see each other again?'

'I don't know. I hope so'

'We should.'

'That would be good.'

'We must remember to exchange addresses Françoise.'

'Of course.'

'There's still plenty of time.'

'Yes, There is.'

Rutter and Françoise then consciously stopped discussing their future. They reverted to indulging in school gossip about the carnal progression of Yvette and Barrel's friendship, Bayliss striding the Avenue like a theatrical knight and Mrs Butcher being suspected of being part of a cabal that sent a defamatory headstone to Killer. When Françoise heard about the inscription, she became delirious and the two lovers revelled in their amorous intimacy.

Hayes had seen the masks and thought that the designs were impressive. Apparently Barrel's contact, an illustrator for a left wing periodical, was willing to loan them to him. After keeping the camouflages hidden in 'a mysterious location', Barrel invited everybody into the changing room on a Saturday evening, the day before the attack, so that the conspirators could try on their disguises as Ryder had insisted. Hayes was to be Princess Margaret who looked carefree and tipsy. A rather ample, complacent Queen Mother was given to Sully. The Queen, looking regally chaotic with an askew crown, was handed to Brown. An imperiously bloated Duke of Edinburgh with 'Phil The Greek' inscribed at the bottom of his face, Barrel allocated to himself. Harold Macmillan, the Prime Minister, portrayed as a distracted, out-dated Edwardian relic of empire, was the role ascribed to Barrett. Bunter was a mean, Scrooge-like, Peter Thorneycroft, the Chancellor of the Exchequer and Binns, an eccentric, batty-looking Lord Hailsham, the Minister of Education, whose hair seemed to fly to the heavens. Boot became Lord Home, Secretary of State for Commonwealth Relations, who looked dim and distracted, and Rice took on the role of Duncan Sandys, the Minister of Defence, who was vividly characterised as a British Führer. Barrel's spare mask depicted Selwyn Lloyd, the Foreign Secretary, as an obsequious flying Sputnik.

After the conspirators felt comfortable in their various transformations, Hayes as One Ball's squit, informed his fellow rebels that tomorrow afternoon, the abusive senior was to play a game of fives with Ransome, a monitor in neighbouring Morton A. Apparently, Potts had booked the court for 2:30, so Hayes assessed that he'd be coming back into the changing room any time after 3:15. Following a prolonged discussion, they all agreed that they should be ready at 3:00.

The meeting then moved on to strategy. The group decided that one person should give the orders. After a discussion about suitable contenders and a show of hands, the majority thought that Barrett should delegate his authority to 'The Queen' alias Brown, the most senior conspirator. Having been only recently appointed as Ryder's coordinator, Barrett felt undermined by this coup. As the school's baby Lenin, he was keen to implement revolutionary action himself, especially as he'd already carried out Ryder's orders efficiently. However, like a good socialist, he submitted to the majority's view and reluctantly gave way to Brown's greater years, physical strength and East End street experience. Having quickly accepted the leadership, Brown outlined how the conspirators should operate as an organised unit. In doing so, he instructed them to take up tactical positions to prevent One Ball from escaping. He then elaborated on how the attack would evolve.

Just before the meeting concluded, Barrel reminded everybody to revel in their posh voices and create confusion. He then held out his hand and the conspirators all laid theirs, one upon another, on top of the Welsh boy's palm. Sully, the victim of One Ball's bullying, called for a rallying cry to inspire them in their just cause, When nobody could conjure up a memorable phrase, an anxious and red-faced Sully, instinctively blurted out 'stop the bloody bullying'. The group immediately responded by repeating the words in passionate unison. As soon as the conspirators withdrew their hands, Barrel collected the masks and moved them speedily to his 'mysterious location'. Eventually, the conspirators all drifted away to enjoy the rest of the evening. Although they were apprehensive, they were also excited. The day of reckoning was nigh.

The following afternoon, One Ball was in a good mood. He was making excellent progress with his revision. He felt that he had a grasp of his subjects and every chance of taking up his university place. He'd got over Françoise. Anyway, he was now too busy with his studies to think about her. He realised that he'd stupidly fallen into a trap. He certainly wouldn't make such a mistake again. Nevertheless, anger about her deceitful letter still lingered. Unfortunately, the rude comments he'd already made hadn't fully exorcised his demons, so if a moment occurred when he could confront her he'd exploit it. Still, he wasn't going to consciously seek vengeance as he didn't want to be diverted from his efforts to get to Cambridge.

Nonetheless, One Ball didn't intend to renege on Sully's punishments. In fact, he'd become even more determined to exact retribution, now that Sully had showed pugnacious defiance. To One Ball, Sully was a coward, who couldn't face his punishments honestly. Instead, he tried to cheat and cut corners. That was deceitful and dishonest. What's more, when he had the opportunity to erase them by getting evidence of Rutter's lascivious roguery, he failed ignominiously. Such behaviour meant that One Ball had no pang of conscience about the calamitous Sully.

In contrast, he was feeling more positive about his mother. He recently received a letter from her describing her enjoyment of her classes and her desire to be a social worker. Apparently, she was seeing a lot more of the Kirwins. One Ball wasn't fully convinced that this was a good thing. He found them too left wing for his taste, although he admitted that they could be amusing. Anyway, the most important thing was that she was enjoying her studies. One Ball respected that. It took a considerable determination for her to change her lifestyle. His mother had listened to him and looked to the future, instead of wallowing in the past and living through him. He was now confident that she'd get a job. In her letter, she also gave hints about a new admirer. One Ball wondered who that might be. It certainly would be a relief if she found a new husband. Hopefully he'd like her suitor, so long as he wasn't a radical friend of the Kirwins or Peregrine, the ghastly amateur theatre director.

As One Ball relaxed in his study, digesting his roast beef and Yorkshire pudding, such thoughts raced through his mind. In half an hour, he'd start to get ready for his game. As he wasn't a very good cricketer, during the summer he concentrated on fives. He regularly met up with suitable opponents to both improve his ability and keep fit. Sunday afternoon was a particularly good time for a game as it was quiet and more boys were available. Ransome, One Ball's adversary, was a modern linguist who was in the school's 2nd Fives Team, so he knew that he had to play well to win. When he'd finished his break, One Ball, changed, gathered his gloves and made his way to the courts at the back of the house. By the time he arrived, Ransome was practising. One Ball greeted him amiably and joined his knock-up.

Brown, who had been monitoring One Ball's movements while posing as an innocent bystander, alerted the conspirators with a subtle nod of the head. At this signal, the various agitators stopped their dayroom activities. Hayes no longer wrote to his mother. Barrett stopped reading Colin Wilson's The Outsider. Boot and Binns quit their chess game. Sully ceased pretending to do his homework. Barrel finished reading Albert Camus's play about an assassination attempt on a member of the Romanov dynasty. Bunter and Rice concluded listening to the Light Programme's A Life of Bliss. Gradually, the conspirators filed into the changing room, not as a group but either singly or in pairs. On reaching their fateful destination, Barrel issued them with their masks.

After a close game, One Ball left the court a triumphant winner, two sets to one. As he made his way back to house, he chatted amiably with his defeated opponent. Apparently, Ransome's family cat called Eugene had recently caught eczema and he was concerned that the disease wasn't contagious. One Ball professed ignorance on feline matters but was glad to hear that Ransome's mother had contacted a vet. They then both wished each other well in their forthcoming exams and departed to their respective houses. One Ball was ecstatic about his victory as it was the first time that he had beaten a member of one of the school's teams. He had a real spring in his step going to his study to deposit his gloves. Fit and confident, he started whistling Getting to Know You from The King and I. He wasn't a fan of musicals but that particular tune suited his mood. Elated by his triumph, he looked forward to having a refreshing shower before getting down to some serious study. First, he'd bathe his hands to remedy the considerable battering they received during the game. In fact, when he took off his gloves he could see bluish bruises. Whistling cheerfully, much to the surprise of nearby seniors, who knew him only as dour, grim Jim, he left his study. One Ball indulging in the levity of popular taste when he had constantly championed the artistic supremacy of classical music, made those in the dayroom wonder how such a cultural revolution had taken place.

As One Ball made his way to the changing room, he was surprised that no one was by the radio, which was now transmitting Sidney Torch's Melody Hour. He deduced that such soporific light music would hardly interest obsessive rockers like Brown and Bunter, the resident radio gatekeepers. One Ball maintained his whistling refrain as he passed through the dayroom swing door and made his way to the changing room. While he filled a basin with cold water, he wondered if Deborah Kerr had actually sung the song herself or whether she was dubbed. After all, he'd read that many film stars couldn't sing a note. As he considered Miss Kerr's singing ability, One Ball allowed both of his hands to sink deeply into the basin. Although he felt the pain of his bruises, he withstood the cold water and prided himself on his stoical endurance.

Just as he was about to withdraw his hands, One Ball was confronted by some boys wearing masks. Before he could escape, 'Lord Home' and 'Peter Thorneycroft' surrounded him. One Ball thought this was just an amusing prank, which even made him smile. Initially, he wondered if one of the boys had designed the masks with help from the eccentric Anne Becker, but concluded that they probably came from a shop. After his jovial response to the surrounding clowns, One Ball started to walk past the 'Tory cabinet members'. As he did so, a sudden, strange, enunciated regal cry, proclaimed, 'arrest him!'

'Lord Home' and 'Peter Thorneycroft' quickly grabbed One Ball's arms and aggressively forced them behind his back. This didn't stop the assailed monitor from using his body to stop the assault. As he swayed powerfully from side to side, the momentum sent all three boys careering towards the shower. This propulsion led to the release of the on button and cold water rained down on the trio as they struggled in the communal trough. Instantly, a cohort of 'the monarchy' and the rest of the 'cabinet' came to the rescue. 'The Duke of Edinburgh', 'The Queen Mother', 'Princess Margaret', 'Harold

Macmillan' and 'Lord Hailsham' all attacked the hapless One Ball with the venom of vindictive teddy boys. They'd made preparation for each of them to grab a particular part of his anatomy and they executed the plan with ruthless efficiency. When 'Lord Home' turned off the shower, 'the British establishment' dragged a sodden One Ball into the inner recesses of the changing room, where the removal of some hanging clothes had left an ominous space.

'Debag him!' cried 'The Queen' with an imperial screech. At once, nine obedient conspirators surrounded their victim while the soaked 'Secretary of State for Commonwealth Relations' and the drenched 'Chancellor of the Exchequer' continued to hold the desperate One Ball's arms behind his back. Then the rest of the establishment, like wet vultures devouring a corpse, followed their leader's orders. They forcefully ripped off One Ball's shirt, shorts pants, socks and plimsolls, throwing them all away like disposable hankies. One Ball was left naked to the world.

'You're all going to pay for this. You cruel bastards!' yelled One Ball.

'Shut your mouth!' ordained 'The Queen', in an incongruously grand, falsetto voice.

'Otherwise, we'll get some tape,' warned 'Peter Thorneycroft', growling pompously.

'You never listened. You just bullied,' bellowed 'The Queen Mother', with imposing matriarchal authority.

'You were the cruel one. Using your power to exploit the vulnerable,' accused 'The Queen', pointing a hand at the indicted like a belligerent prosecutor.

'You bastards are finished. You'll be expelled,' shrieked One Ball.

'String him up!' decreed 'The Queen' as if demanding an execution

'No!' implored One Ball.

'Yes!' shrieked the merciless 'Queen'.

In the prepared space, 'Lord Hailsham' and 'The Duke of Edinburgh' started rigorously attaching belts to the clothes pegs on both sides of the changing room. While they did their work, the other conspirators held One Ball tightly as he wrestled and pleaded for mercy.

'Too late,' replied a vengeful 'Queen', glowering at the despairing bully.

Fully fastened, the two conspirators then tied the struggling One Ball's hands and legs to the belts. After an oscillating struggle, they eventually attached him securely to the pegs. One Ball was now swinging in the middle of the changing room, his one ball exposed to all and sundry.

'Get the blacking,' dictated 'The Queen' in her posh falsetto.

At once, 'The Duke of Edinburgh' brought forward a big metal tin, which he'd obtained from the boot room.

'Now the brushes,' instructed the sonorous 'Macmillan'.

'Princess Margaret' eagerly brought forward the several shoe brushes 'she'd' collected.

'Black the bully's ball,' ordered 'The Queen'.

'May you rot in hell, you bloody bastards. I'll get even with the lot of you!' yelled One Ball.

'Start the blackening,' demanded 'The Queen' vehemently.

It was appropriate that Sully as 'The Queen Mother' led the attack. He got hold of a brush, dipped it into the huge tin of black polish and made sure that he had a suitable large dollop. He then looked down on the victim, swaying in his imprisoned hammock. After observing his naked area carefully, he brushed a huge dollop around his penis, ball and pubic hair, taking no notice of the ensuing cries from his prey. He then stared at his abuser and mercilessly yelled 'bully!' This was followed by further ritualistic blackening by 'The Duke of Edinburgh', 'Princess Margaret', 'Prime Minister Macmillan', 'Duncan Sandys', 'Lord Home', 'Lord Hailsham', 'Peter Thorneycroft' and finally 'The Queen', who did so with brutal ceremonial dignity. The same vocal outburst of 'bully!' accompanied each dollop deposited on One Ball's private parts. By the time the rite had reached its conclusion, a mire of thick, black shoe polish covered One Ball's remaining testicle. The polish had seeped into his pubic hair and trickled down his bare leg. His eyes darted from one assailant to the other like a frightened rabbit.

The conspirators then proceeded to revel in further humiliation of the bully. They were in a state of vengeful euphoria and while continuing to use their posh voices, they worked themselves up into belligerent hysteria. They moved tauntingly in front of him while taking turns to shout various abusive epithets, as if they were taking part in some macabre rite. One Ball was terrified that he would be left defenceless to even more extreme physical attacks. Witnessing her 'fellow royals' and 'cabinet' behaving like thugs, 'The Queen' fearing an outbreak of violence, suddenly shouted in a shrill, anguished voice, 'stop!' Despite her powerful command, 'The Queen Mother' 'Princess Margaret' and 'Prime Minister Macmillan' persisted with their ritual, thrusting their masks aggressively into the face of the distraught, hanging boy. Their anarchic behaviour gave 'The Queen' no option but to get the physical assistance of 'The Duke of Edinburgh', 'Lord Home' 'Duncan Sandys' and 'Lord Hailsham'. They duly obliged and grabbed hold of the lunatic fringe before they got totally out of control. While they hauled the over-exuberant provocateurs away from the abused One Ball, 'The Queen' reprimanded the hooligans with despotic monarchical authority, by giving an imperious order. 'Stop it! No more! Scatter!'

As the conspirators left the changing room, the blackened, sodden One Ball was left hanging despondently. Gaffer tape, which 'The Queen' had formally sealed across his mouth, silenced his desperate appeals for help. As his muted cries persisted, the boys made their way to the toilet where Barrel collected the masks, which he hastily put in a box. Brown then told everybody to depart quickly but to relax and 'act naturally, like they did every Sunday.' When Sully, Hayes and Barrett briefly apologised for their unruly behaviour, Brown waved them away. Before leaving, those conspirators involved in the shower fracas like Boot and Bunter, hurriedly dried themselves and changed some of their clothes. Brown told them all to hurry up and not only leave separately but also stagger their return to the house to avoid suspicion. As One Ball's muffled cries increased, the conspirators started to leave by the back entrance to avoid seeing their suffering victim. Eventually, Barrel departed with the masks to his 'mysterious location', Sully,

Hayes and Barrett ambled off for an innocent Sunday afternoon walk while Boot and Binns went to have a quick Philip Morris fag behind the nearby bushes. Brown, then made his way through the front porch to the dayroom radio, followed at prearranged intervals by Bunter and Rice. The radio gatekeeper then moved the dial from the bland Melody Hour to AFN. By the time the others arrived, Sinatra's You Make Me Feel So Young was blaring away

'What about that backing?' enthused Rice.

'Not bad but I prefer Nat King Cole if you like that kind of singer,' replied Brown derisively.

'Nat's good but Frank's better,' vowed Rice.

'I prefer Jerry Lee Lewis' chipped in Bunter

'Nat's got a show on American tv,' imparted Brown.

'I haven't seen it,' admitted Rice.

'The first network show hosted by a black American,' stated Brown authoritatively.

'That won't last,' said Bunter.

'Listen to that arrangement. Nelson Riddle, he's brilliant,' urged Rice, lost in the music.

'All those bigoted southern states,' remarked Bunter.

'Thank God, we've got the BBC,' lauded Brown patriotically.

Brown was glad that they had a musical subject to talk about after the One Ball massacre. It helped to create the illusion that nothing had happened and that it was just a normal Sunday. Brown didn't regret orchestrating the assault. One Ball needed to be seriously confronted and only a collaborative revolt could do that. However, there was no guarantee that there wouldn't be repercussions, even though Ryder had recently assured Barrett that he would get the whole school to go on strike if there was extreme retribution. Brown now realised that the school's Lenin regarded the Root insurrection as a rehearsal for wider mobilisation. Although he respected Ryder's political acumen, Brown hoped that the sharp shock inflicted on One Ball would be sufficient to bring about radical change.

In the meantime, the debate about Frank and Nat continued. Rice was reluctant to concede that Nat sang a ballad better than Frank and he was certain that Frank swung more than Nat.

Regardless of these ardent opinions, Brown and Bunter didn't really want to talk about either of them. They belonged to the past. They were history like the bloody bobby soxers. When Sinatra's ditty finished, Ray Charles's I Got a Woman followed and the radio gatekeepers relished the musical change. Brown and Bunter inevitably responded by shaking and wiggling their anatomies in time to the music. While the rockers rocked, Rice tried to retain the sound of 'The Chairman of the Board's voice and Nelson's backing. Such efforts of retention were exerting the mind of the Sinatra obsessive, when Boring Beckett appeared and laughed at the rockers' antics. The former Duke of Exeter briefly enquired about the singer before proceeding to the changing room. As Boring Beckett exited, the rockers stopped dancing. The three conspirators wondered how the senior monitor would react to the sight of the abused One Ball.

Beckett was hardly a rocker but as he made his way to the toilet, he tried to whistle Ray's tune. Just as he started to enjoy his endeavour, he heard some strange sounds. He walked halfway down the corridor of the changing room and there on his right was the gagged, naked One Ball. The sight he beheld, shocked Beckett profoundly. You couldn't see either his private parts or pubic hair for thick black polish. Potts looked like a victim of a terrorist atrocity.

Beckett instinctively ripped the gaffer tape from his mouth and asked, 'what happened?'

A stunned One Ball was unable to reply. He was lost for words.

Oliver knew that he had a crisis on his hands. If the news of the assault on Potts became public, the school's future would be seriously compromised. Therefore, Oliver realised that he must make sure that there were no leaks to the press about the attack. The thought of impropriety at the school appearing in the News of the World brought shivers to his spine. He could see the headlines: 'Ball Turned Black at Public School', 'Mob Rule Blackens School' or 'Public School Yobs on Rampage'. The Labour Party would respond by advocating abolition even more forcefully. All his good work would be ruined. Oliver realised that he needed to put this fire out immediately. Nobody must speak about this incident publicly. Everything must be kept within the school. However, first he had to talk to Aizlewood before he appeared at the Disciplinary Committee. That's why he'd summoned him to his house.

As he lay back on his red sofa, waiting for the James B housemaster, Oliver had doubts about Aizlewood's management. Surely, he should have intervened to stop Potts's relationship with Sully descending into such vile incrimination. Still, he liked the Major. He was a decent man, if not the greatest teacher of geography. Nonetheless, he admired his splendid work for the Combined Cadet Force. Such an achievement was essential, given the school's military had royal patrons. In fact, Aizlewood's company always had very high marks for shooting, ordnance survey and parade discipline. They also did very well in the military exercises that took place regularly in Keats Wood. In the mock battles, they always 'killed' more boys than anyone else. Aizlewood had also created a much happier house than most over the years. However, Oliver wondered if his courting of Victoria Wallace had made him grow negligent. He was well aware of Victoria's irresistible charms but he felt that Aizlewood's feelings for her should inspire greater commitment not laxity. After all, that's what his love for his dear wife had done.

Oliver looked at his watch. It was 7:25 pm and Aizlewood would be arriving in a few minutes. Notwithstanding his concerns, the headmaster was thankful that after the abhorrent assault, the school still seemed to be functioning normally. Even so, he was relieved that the end of term wasn't far away. Oliver was particularly mindful of the Asian flu pandemic, which was now spreading across Europe. As it had already reached the school, he feared that any acceleration could cause chaos in the infirmary. This was a problem that he didn't feel qualified to manage. He'd have to depend on the advice of the dogmatic Dr Meissner. Meissner dealt with an earlier mild outbreak satisfactorily but he was concerned that this particular epidemic might be more intractably dangerous and widespread. He just hoped that if such contagion occurred, Dr Meissner wouldn't erode his authority. Otherwise, he feared that he might not be able to regain it.

Oliver tried to stop such negative thoughts. Usually, he was an optimist but he had a cautious nature and was immune to undue risk. While he diverted his mind by looking carefully at the notes that he'd prepared for the meeting, the doorbell rang. In response, Oliver gathered himself and Mrs O formally ushered Aizlewood into the room. The Major looked apprehensive and politely rejected an offer of tea. After Mrs O smiled graciously and departed, the Major sat down in a leather armchair. After apologising for what happened, he reassured the headmaster that Potts had begun to recover and that he'd identified the various conspirators.

'How do you intend to deal with them?' challenged Oliver.

'Well, I don't think we should give them running punishments,' replied the Major.

'What then do you propose?' continued Oliver, looking searchingly into the Major's apprehensive grey eyes.

'I think some form of public service work, like that for conscientious objectors,' suggested the Major.

'Oh no, Aizlewood. No. I have far too many pacifists already. If it goes on like this, they'll outnumber the CCF,' retorted a disturbed Oliver.

'I think any more severe punishment could present difficulty,' reasoned the Major, putting a hand nervously through his hair.

'Aizlewood. You're an army man. You know the value of military discipline. That's part of the ethos of the school. We march to meals, for god's sake. Yet, I get an increasing number of parents writing to me, insisting that their children don't take part in 'war games', imparted a frustrated Oliver, rising from the sofa and pacing up and down on his elegantly patterned Persian carpet.

'That's a reaction to the cold war and nuclear armament, headmaster. Actually, I think it's understandable,' thought the Major, leaning back in his armchair while straightening his navy blue blazer.

'But surely they deserve greater punishment?' stressed Oliver, stopping his patrol and staring intensely at the Major.

'I think further punishment presents greater problems,' countered the Major.

‘Why, Aizlewood? Surely, it’s suitable atonement,’ claimed Oliver with quasi-religious potency.

‘Headmaster. I think anything more extreme could lead to some kind of uprising,’ warned the Major, looking calmly at a perplexed Oliver.

‘Uprising! Aizlewood, we’re not Russians!’ insisted an adamant headmaster.

‘I’ve heard that Ryder would look to mobilise the whole school into some form of strike,’ revealed a concerned Major.

‘The sooner that boy leaves this school the better. He continually uses situations to impose his own political views on the rest of the boys. He’s a red menace!’ yelled an infuriated Oliver.

‘Maybe, but he’s rather good at it, headmaster. He’s also popular. Mr Root’s difficulties could be a minor skirmish before a full out war,’ advised the Major, while casually observing Oliver’s anaemic rural paintings.

‘War, Aizlewood. What pills are you on?’ bellowed an unusually splenetic Oliver.

‘None, headmaster. I was speaking metaphorically,’ clarified a seemingly repentant Major.

‘Thank God. Just the thought of Ryder organising some form of widespread revolt, I find appalling,’ confessed Oliver, returning to sit on his sofa in an attempt to calm down. He was finding it difficult to manage the crisis and present his usual temperate demeanour.

‘That’s why, it’s better to settle for a punishment that is more conducive to the public good. It fits in more with Ryder’s apparent socialist principles,’ counselled the Major,

‘How do you know all this Aizlewood?’ pressed a stern Oliver.

‘I’ve talked extensively to all concerned. Ryder was the mastermind behind the attack. Sully and his friends lost complete faith in the system. They looked to him for help,’ elucidated the Major.

‘Why didn’t you deal with this before the assault, Aizlewood? That’s what senior housemasters are for,’ emphasised Oliver.

'I tried. I talked to Sully and Potts but both of them refused to compromise,' maintained the Major.

'I hope your courting of Miss Wallace isn't distracting you from your duties, Aizlewood,' hinted Oliver slyly.

'Miss Wallace has nothing to do with this matter,' replied the Major with controlled exasperation.

'I'm glad to hear it Aizlewood, but it's up to you to look after the boys in your house, and that includes monitors,' highlighted a flustered Oliver.

'But the system works through delegation, headmaster. We trust the monitors to carry out their agreed duties. They only report to housemasters if they want advice over particular difficulties,' argued the Major authoritatively.

'You've forgotten oversight, Aizlewood,' insisted Oliver, reminding the Major of his duty. 'You have the ultimate responsibility to oversee all the members of your house.'

'I do, but a sense of trust is built into the system. I can't be a spy,' disputed the Major.

'Maybe you should have some form of network,' proposed Oliver.

'You mean of informers, headmaster?' queried the Major incredulously.

'Call them what you like, Aizlewood. You need to exert overall control. We can't have monitors bullying juniors,' asserted Oliver, looking accusingly at his housemaster.

'Of course not, headmaster,' responded a reluctantly compliant Major.

The Major realised that he couldn't continue the conversation. Oliver was terrified of the thought of any scandal. He obviously feared being eventually hauled before the Board of Trustees and losing his job, so he needed someone else to blame. While Oliver deliberated over his notes, the Major's thoughts were diverted by the headmaster's Bechstein piano. 'Maybe when Oliver calms down, I could ask to play on it,' thought the housemaster. After all, he'd recently progressed from Jingle Bells and was studying Chopin's compositions with Root. Perhaps, he could tinkle the ivories at some future soirée. Then, just as his thoughts lingered on one of the Polish composer's beguiling mazurkas, Oliver resumed his interrogation.

'Is Potts really recovering?'

'Well, he's working hard for his exams but he seems scarred by the experience. Hardly surprising,' thought the Major.

'In what way?' sought Oliver.

'He's less robust and assertive, which is good but he's gone too much into his shell,' disclosed the Major.

'I suppose not having a father doesn't help,' thought Oliver.

'Especially as he was a controversial figure,' added the Major.

'Yes. That's not an easy legacy to process,' concluded Oliver.

'Let's hope his work is a sufficient palliative,' affirmed the Major with diplomatic optimism.

'Indeed. But is he bitter?' enquired Oliver.

'A bit but I think he'll get over it,' divulged the Major, trying to reassure the beleaguered headmaster.

'He's not going to start getting the law involved?' pursued an anxious Oliver.

'Oh no, headmaster. He's just concentrating on getting to Cambridge,' reported the Major calmly.

'Thank goodness for that. Have you phoned his mother?' enquired the inquisitorial Oliver.

'Yes. I told her that some of the boys got up to an unacceptable prank and that her son was a victim. I said that they thought that he was a bully. When she heard the details, she was very upset,' imparted the Major deliberately.

'We've got to keep Mrs Potts onside. If she starts gossiping about the incident, God knows what could happen,' exclaimed Oliver while fiddling with his papers.

'I don't think she'll go to the News of the World or the Daily Mail,' contended the Major.

'How do you know, Aizlewood?' doubted Oliver.

'I think that she's more of a Manchester Guardian reader,' answered the Major, attempting reassurance.

'But that's worse,' spluttered Oliver, who was a Daily Telegraph man and detested The Manchester Guardian's consistently negative view of the country.

'Anyway, the Potts are a proud family. They wouldn't want to wash their dirty linen in public,' believed the Major, looking to mollify Oliver's accumulating fears of the press destabilising the school.

'You've got to keep tabs on her, Aizlewood. Parents Day is approaching, so we need to launch a charm offensive, not only with Mrs Potts but also with all the parents of the infamous nine offenders. I think its best that we deal with a group like this face to face, rather than separately on the phone. Then we can go through the grisly detail when they're all here. Nothing like the personal touch,' thought Oliver, presenting his forthcoming strategy. 'Of course, I'll expect your support, Aizlewood,' demanded Oliver, glaring at his colleague.

'Of course, headmaster,' acknowledged the Major with detached obedience.

'In the meantime, Potts should be checked out,' instructed a concerned Oliver.

'How?' probed the Major.

'By a doctor, Aizlewood,' replied Oliver bluntly.

'I suggested that possibility to Potts but he was very reluctant,' explained a wary Major.

'Try again,' ordered Oliver. 'I'll inform Meissner.'

'If you insist headmaster,' said the Major wearily.

'Yes I do insist. He may need psychiatric help for all I know,' judged Oliver.

'I doubt it,' countered the Major.

'But we need to be sure, Aizlewood,' accentuated Oliver.

'Ok, I'll tell him to contact Dr Meissner,' ceded the Major diplomatically.

'Good. I'm meeting the Disciplinary Committee shortly, so I'll consider your comments,' confirmed Oliver, looking to avoid any possible criticism. 'In the meantime,' he continued 'we need to cover all our bases, Aizlewood. I don't want news of this debacle spreading like the current flu,' proclaimed Oliver, fearing an apocalyptic scenario.

'Yes, it's beginning to spread across the country,' admitted the Major.

'If the infirmary becomes overrun, we may have to evacuate the dormitories in some houses. They could be needed as temporary wards,' revealed Oliver, calling upon his inner Churchill.

'That's a bit drastic isn't it?' questioned the Major.

'I've told Meissner that we need a plan for next term, just in case,' replied Oliver dismissively. 'I'm also writing to all staff, reminding them of their responsibilities to the school. They mustn't talk to anybody about the assault,' declared Oliver.

'We're putting a gag on freedom of speech?' queried the Major incredulously.

'Exactly,' affirmed Oliver purposefully.

'Sounds a bit like Soviet censorship headmaster,' claimed the Major cynically.

'I don't care Aizlewood. I'm going to recommend it to the committee. The reputation of the school comes first. We can't risk this great institution being ruined after a glorious four hundred years,' emphasised Oliver.

'I see,' responded the Major sceptically.

'We've got to use Parents Day to reassure the boys' fathers and mothers of what we offer their children. That's education at the highest level exemplifying the best of British. We can't afford a whiff of any scandal. So please use your inimitable charm on Mrs Potts and the families of the odious assailants,' requested a buoyant, revived Oliver.

'I'll do my best,' agreed the Major languidly.

'Good. Well that's all. Thanks for coming Aizlewood,' replied Oliver, rising from the sofa.

'Thank you, headmaster,' echoed the Major, lifting himself from his armchair.

The Major was about to leave the room when Oliver decided to confront him directly about his leadership.

'Aizlewood. Why didn't you contact me earlier about all this?'

'I thought that the matter could be dealt within the house,' confided the Major, who wasn't confident of Oliver's ability to manage such a crisis.

'I see,' pondered Oliver, implying criticism of the Major's role in the calamity. He wondered if Aizlewood's slow response could help him get exonerated when the trustees interrogated him.

Oliver ushered the Major into the hall. As they both made their way towards the front door, Oliver suddenly mentioned a matter that was troubling him.

'Aizlewood. Why is Potts called One Ball?'

'Because he's only got one,' corroborated the Major candidly.

'Oh, I see. I thought it had something to do with sport,' said an embarrassed Oliver.

'No, headmaster,' clarified a bemused Major.

'Do you mind reminding me how that happened?' asked Oliver, rigorously pursuing his curiosity.

'He tried to hurry through some barbed wire that ripped through his testicle,' elaborated the Major gingerly.

'Oh my God, poor chap. That might well create psychological damage. Yes, he definitely needs to see Dr Meissner,' reiterated a shocked Oliver.

'All right, I'll tell him to get in contact,' agreed the Major.

'Just give me twenty-four hours first so I can put Meissner in the picture,' requested Oliver as he escorted the Major into the hall.

Oliver opened the front door and the Major went outside, lingering on the doorstep.

'Ok, headmaster. We'll look forward to a positive end to the term,' exhorted the Major, wanting to end on a more optimistic note.

'Scandal free,' whispered Oliver.

'Yes, scandal free,' repeated the Major, not wishing to inflict further worry upon the besieged headmaster.

They looked like two tawdry politicians engaging in a cover-up.

Hayes usually found Parents Day a chore but on this particular occasion, there was a special attraction. This was the presence of the celebrated conductor Sir Malcolm Sargent or 'Flash Harry' as he was widely known, due to his sartorial panache. Sir Malcolm was visiting his friend Anne, the art teacher and erstwhile designer of Henry V. Consequently, the annual art school exhibition had stardust sprinkled upon it. When Hayes arrived at the event with an excitable Poppy and a more philosophical Hannah, Sir Malcolm was holding forth in front of various admirers. Among the inevitable sycophants were the school's leading narcissist, Andrew Macready and its in-house Peter Brook, Hubert Aloysius Bayliss, who was now less reliant on the hard stuff since the closure of his production. Sir Malcolm was impeccably dressed as usual in an immaculate dark suit with a silver tie and his trademark white carnation in his buttonhole. The sycophants formed a circle around the English conductor and attentively listened to his every word, as if he was a charismatic preacher imparting a faith.

Hayes and his family decided to ignore the school's celebrity visitor and view the exhibition. As they wandered around the gallery admiring the creative talent on display, Hayes reflected on how One Ball had changed since the assault. Unsurprisingly, the authoritarian monitor had become remarkably subdued. He no longer barked orders like a parade ground sergeant and he rarely used the word 'squit'. In fact, Hayes now felt like a nurse helping a patient. One Ball had become more reclusive, often staying in his study for hours at a time. Hayes no longer heard the powerful sound of Richard Wagner resounding from his study but instead the soothing intimacy of Bach's Preludes. One Ball only intermittently engaged with other monitors and seniors. He didn't look anybody in the eye and had become increasingly distrustful.

Initially, Hayes was fearful that One Ball would castigate him for being 'Princess Margaret' but it seemed that he hadn't fully discerned his attackers. In any case, he still needed his services and preferred to blame 'that bloody Marxist Ryder' for being the brains behind 'the cruel strategy'. Despite flashes of bitterness about what he regarded as the school's unjust handling of the attack, One Ball was careful to be more temperate publicly. Apparently, the Major had advised him to resist the temptation to be belligerent, while promising that his abusers would be punished. That seemed to be the bargain.

Meanwhile, the troubled Oliver caved in to the Disciplinary Committee's recommendations, which supported the Major's analysis, although it did agree with the headmaster's purdah policy. As the committee were fearful of a school strike, Ryder, who was leaving anyway, was mildly rebuked for holding 'a seditious meeting' and lost his privileges as a monitor. The perpetrators, the conspiratorial nine, ended up doing various public works like painting school gates and fences. During this tedious activity, they broke the monotony by singing songs such as Harry Belafonte's Day-O. They enjoyed fantasising that they were workers loading bananas at a dock in Jamaica, rather than schoolboys doing a punishment for assault in Sussex. Unsurprisingly, this outcome didn't satisfy One Ball's desire for justice.

As Hayes contemplated the likely repercussions of the committee's decision, he and his family finished looking at the boys' bizarrely imaginative paintings. Immediately, Anne invited them all to come over and meet 'Flash Harry'. They accepted her request and joined the sycophants. On their arrival, Sir Malcolm tactfully stopped talking about choral music to acknowledge their presence. After shaking their hands, he asked Hayes:

'So what do you want to do?'

'Go to university,' said Hayes shyly.

'Excellent. Where?' enquired Sir Malcolm with a dazzling smile.

'I'm not sure yet sir,' admitted Hayes.

'I can recommend Durham,' trumpeted Sir Malcolm.

'Why particularly?' pursued Hayes inquisitively.

'Because I got a degree there!' exclaimed Sir Malcolm, laughing self-consciously at his own sense of humour. He then turned to Poppy, 'and you, young lady, what about you?'

'I want to read PPE-philosophy, politics and economics,' stressed Poppy earnestly.

'Good God! That's ambitious,' claimed Sir Malcolm, taken aback by her venturing into such demanding subjects.

'There's nothing wrong with ambition,' insisted an assertive Poppy.

'Certainly not, I have a bit myself,' divulged Sir Malcolm, laughing nervously and turning to the sycophants, who duly did likewise.

'She's got to get a few O Levels first,' maintained Hannah, trying to mitigate any possible conflict.

‘Of course. Just as long as she doesn’t start looking to conduct the Proms!’ warned Sir Malcolm, turning once more to Anne, Macready and Bayliss for humorous, theatrical effect.

‘I’m more interested in rock ‘n’ roll so you’re probably safe,’ Poppy reassured the maestro with a humorous smile.

‘Thank God for that!’ roared Sir Malcolm, in mock relief, much to the amusement of his obsequious admirers.

Hannah took this moment to leave, thanking Anne for the exhibition and the opportunity to meet Sir Malcolm. As they departed, Sir Malcolm turned to his clan and resumed talking about his formative experiences with the Huddersfield Choral Society.

On leaving the art school, Hayes led his family across the Quadrangle to show them the classrooms. Eventually, they all ventured into ‘ok, all right’ Darbishire’s academic abode. After whispering conspiratorially with Hayes, Poppy got up onto the teacher’s dais, sat in a chair behind a large desk and started to imitate Eamonn Andrews compering What’s My Line?

‘Will the next challenger sign in please?’ announced Poppy, attempting an Irish accent.

Hayes duly obliged and scrawled his name Albert E Bloggs on the blackboard.

‘Will you give us your mime Mr Bloggs?’ instructed Poppy as Eamonn.

Hayes then did his best to mime being a lavatory cleaner. He seemed to get himself into such physical contortions that a simple job became absurdly complicated.

Poppy then impersonated panellists David Nixon, Lady Isabel Barnett, Barbara Kelly and the gruff Gilbert Harding, who thought that the mime was ‘very unhelpful’. As Eamonn, she also kept the score, while Hayes continued to play the part of Bloggs the lavatory cleaner, answering Poppy’s insistent enquiries such as ‘do you work outside?‘ ‘Is your job domestic?’ ‘Do you provide an essential service?’ Poppy also illustrated the countdown to ten, by pretending that she was flipping numbers. After nine nos and just before she ran out of questions, Poppy, reverting to being the irascible Harding, decided to throw caution to the wind and guessed correctly.

Hayes congratulated her and they both fell into gleeful hysterics. After a pause for recuperation, an amused Hannah and her offspring left 'ok all right's' classroom. The name Albert E Bloggs remained on the blackboard.

After a visit to the manual school, where Poppy sat on a newly made chair as if it was a throne and impersonated the Queen, the Hayes family made their way to the Dining Hall. As they did so, Hayes was constantly throwing and catching a tennis ball that he'd concealed in his pocket while Poppy brought out a yo-yo and started practising her tricks. It was now time for tea and for the parents to meet the masters. Hayes suddenly feared that the Potts family might discover that he was the 'Princess Margaret' conspirator. He stopped his catching ritual and became contemplative. He was concerned that his mother would become seriously alarmed about his role in the attack, without fully understanding the context of One Ball's bullying. As they progressed to the Dining Hall, Hayes quickly diverted his worries by looking to bowl his tennis ball to Poppy. He was progressing with his cricketing skills and hoped to get in the colts' team soon.

'Here's my Jim Laker,' yelled Hayes doing an imitation of the Surrey off spinner, who'd bowled out the Aussies.

'Oh no, you're just using me for practice,' cried Poppy, reluctantly, putting away her yo-yo and picking up the ball.

'I'm only bowling Poppy, I haven't a bat,' pleaded Hayes.

'In the holidays, you had me bowling in the corridor of the flat,' Poppy reminded him.

'That's how you improve Poppy. Constant practice,' contended Hayes.

'Then you wanted me to name the whole Surrey team. Surridge, May, Lock, Laker, Bedser A, Constable..' Poppy was going through the county championship winning team by rote when Hannah, observing her children's dilly-dallying, called loudly from afar.

'Tommy, Poppy, come on!'

Later, when the family entered the Dining Hall, it was full of parents and their children as well as masters and their guests. Françoise and Yvette were serving tea and coffee at the far end of the building, opposite the headmaster's dais, where various sandwiches and cakes were also available. Assembled tables and chairs were spread around the hall, while still allowing plenty of space for everybody to circulate. It was noticeable that the masters and their spouses were all very smartly dressed. In fact, it wasn't long before the Major, in an immaculate white linen suit, came towards Hannah and enquired about her well-being. After a brief exchange of pleasantries, he departed to welcome other parents, continuing his efforts to reassure them. In the meantime, Hannah went to get some sustenance while Hayes and Poppy looked for a table.

Waiting in the queue for the refreshments, Hannah inadvertently bumped into a woman wearing a crimson felt hat. While apologising, she realised that it was Martha Potts, who was looking distracted and tense. The queue was long and while they waited, Martha anxiously told Hannah the torrid details of the attack on her son. Hannah was shocked that such an assault could happen at a reputable school. When she enquired about One Ball, Martha pointed to a detached, solitary figure, sitting on a nearby chair.

'He's thrown himself into his work,' said Martha, moving gradually up the queue.

'Well at least that's something I suppose,' replied Hannah, nervously tugging at the waist of her pastel-coloured dress.

'That's his medicine,' rationalised Martha. Beneath the formal politeness, Hannah detected a smouldering anger.

'Have you talked to Mr Aizlewood?' probed Hannah.

'Only on the phone. He told me that my son has been accused of bullying,' confided Martha, while becoming visibly upset.

'Perhaps you should speak to him again now that you're here,' suggested Hannah diplomatically.

'I certainly will,' asserted Martha, pulling herself together.

Hannah and Martha were now at the top of the queue. Françoise smiled warmly at them both and gave them their requested drinks and food. The two mothers then put their refreshments on a tray and affably departed back to their respective progeny.

After giving Hayes and Poppy some time to relish their refreshments, Hannah confronted her son about the assault on One Ball.

'He was a bully, Mum,' urged Hayes. When the young conspirator had finished giving a confident denunciation of One Ball's unacceptable behaviour, he took refuge in his watercress sandwich. For a moment, in spite of his short grey trousers, he appeared as if he was beyond his years.

Hannah, having absorbed her son's condemnation of the monitor, gathered herself and looked him directly in the eye.

'Does that mean that his private parts had to be smeared with black polish?'

Poppy immediately spluttered in her tea and got a fit of the giggles.

'Poppy. Stop it!' implored Hannah.

Poppy's giggling became more obediently muted as she bit her tongue.

'Something had to be done. The school did nothing about his bullying,' justified Hayes, while finishing his sandwich and self-consciously adjusting his blue cravat.

'I see. Were you involved?' demanded an indignant Hannah.

'Yes mum, I was,' confessed Hayes candidly.

'Oh Tommy,' despaired Hannah.

'So were a lot of people,' elaborated Hayes.

'How many?' pursued Poppy excitedly.

'Nine,' answered Hayes.

'You strung him up?' accused an alarmed Hannah.

'Yes, but we didn't hurt him,' explained Hayes.

'What did you do then? persisted Hannah.

'We pretended to be members of the royal family or members of the government. We had masks,' admitted Hayes.

'Who were you?' asked Poppy eagerly.

'Princess Margaret,' revealed Hayes cheekily.

'Poppy, please,' beseeched Hannah, as her daughter giggled expansively.

'We only humiliated him,' maintained Hayes defiantly.

'You assaulted him, Tommy,' countered Hannah rigorously.

While other parents looked curiously in their direction, the Hayes family continued their tea in silence. Gradually, the onlookers turned away as Poppy started plunging into a fruitcake and Hayes relished an almond tart. Hannah rejected the food and became lost in thought. She feared that she had been so seduced by the school's educational standards that she'd glossed over its values. The idea of her son spending more time in an establishment that practised such barbarity, filled her with revulsion. When she'd finished her tea, she decided to search out Mr Aizlewood. She needed to get an explanation from the school. Even if Tommy was right about this One Ball, she was worried that her son had become an institutionalised brute. After telling Tommy and Poppy to stay at the table, she started to leave, only for Hayes to stop her in her tracks.

'Where are you going?'

'To find Mr Aizlewood,' replied Hannah adamantly.

'Don't make things worse mum, please,' entreated Hayes.

'I won't. I just want some answers. Stay here,' commanded Hannah, as she strode towards where the Major was chatting to various parents.

When Hannah reached the Major, she stood on the perimeter of his conversation. He was talking to a bald man, splendidly attired in a cream jacket and a red and white bow tie. As the conversation progressed, Hannah realised that he was Captain Sully, the Biggles of World War Two, and that the woman standing next to him in a pink raffia hat was his wife. The men were discussing discipline while the languorous Mrs Sully, wearing a sleeveless brown summer dress, looked bored. Even though the Major introduced Hannah to the couple, Captain Sully ploughed on about his disciplinary theories. As he finally concluded his exhaustive aria, he stressed that it didn't extend to bullying, which he believed his son had received. Hannah then used the opportunity to describe the action taken by the conspirators. Such revelations severely shocked the Sullys and alerted the Major. The Captain disclosed that their son had just told his parents that there'd been a bit of teasing wearing masks. Although he didn't approve of the Queen and the government being denigrated, initially the Captain found the boys' eccentric strategy rather imaginative. However, on hearing such gruesome details from Mrs Hayes, he was appalled and decided to confront the Major.

'Blackening balls, Aizlewood. That's going too far,' insisted Captain Sully.

'The boys have been punished. Maybe your son didn't tell you that,' suggested the Major.

'Well good. What was the punishment?' pressed Captain Sully.

'Doing public service works,' replied the Major.

'Isn't that a rather liberal response?' added Captain Sully.

'No, darling,' interjected Mrs Sully, 'I think it's a rather constructive one'.

'Maybe,' conceded the Captain sceptically.

'I agree Mrs Sully but I'm concerned about Potts,' admitted Hannah.

'Potts?' queried the Captain.

'The boy called 'One Ball' darling,' Mrs Sully reminded her husband.

'Oh yes. Poor chap. I heard. Dreadful accident. And now having them, I mean one of them, caked with boot polish,' expanded the Captain sympathetically.

'Exactly. My boy took part. He was 'Princess Margaret,' confessed Hannah.

'Really. He must have taken a few drinks and smoked a lot of fags,' remarked the Captain, attempting to lighten the atmosphere.

'Oh darling, please. You know Margaret has been going through a difficult time,' prompted Mrs Sully diplomatically.

'In fact, Potts is concentrating on his exams. He has also seen Dr Meissner,' mentioned the Major, consciously diverting the conversation away from royal scandal.

'Who?' questioned the Captain.

'Doctor Meissner. He's the school's doctor,' explained the Major.

'He sounds German,' commented the Captain suspiciously.

'He's a refugee,' elaborated the Major, trying to disguise his irritation.

'I suppose that's all right,' ceded the Captain.

'He has been carefully monitoring Potts,' verified the Major.

‘How’s his one ball then?’ enquired the Captain sympathetically.

‘Physically he’s all right,’ divulged the Major.

‘Thank God for that. You wouldn’t want to lose both!’ exclaimed the Captain nervously.

‘Darling, please,’ interrupted Mrs Sully, embarrassed by her husband’s barrack room ribaldry.

‘I’m concerned about the psychological effects on the boy,’ expressed Hannah resolutely.

‘Well. Dr Meissner has referred him to a psychiatrist,’ responded the Major.

‘Is he German as well?’ reacted the Captain sceptically.

‘No, he comes from Hungary,’ countered the Major.

‘Not as bad, I suppose,’ mumbled the Captain.

‘And what was the conclusion?’ pursued Hannah.

Just as the Major was about to elucidate on the result of One Ball’s consultation with the psychiatrist, Martha Potts joined the coterie, having left her son listening to Mr Collins’s views on the brutality of ancient Rome. She didn’t waste time telling the Major that Dr Orban, the psychiatrist, had told her that One Ball was suffering from depression as a result of the assault. Her son had become quiet and withdrawn, a hermit compared to his former energetic self. She was concerned that he was now facing a challenging ordeal when he wasn’t well. Although his revising had calmed him down, she was worried that as the exams approached in the next few weeks, he could have a relapse. Therefore, if he didn’t get into Cambridge as expected, she would bring the matter to public attention.

‘That wouldn’t be a good idea,’ intervened the Major hastily, alarmed at the thought of such detrimental publicity.

‘The school should have protected my boy from being assaulted,’ judged Martha.

‘Perhaps he shouldn’t have bullied my son in the first place,’ emphasised Mrs Sully, staring intensely at her.

‘That’s up to the school to oversee,’ retaliated Martha.

‘The masters can’t have eyes everywhere,’ claimed the Captain.

‘That’s right. It’s impossible to be patrolling the house night and day. That’s why we have monitors,’ justified the Major.

‘Then the system needs overhauling. You can’t pretend that young monitors are grownups,’ protested Martha passionately.

Oliver, who had been exhaustively circulating, speaking to each parent in turn, had by now joined the tense group. After listening to Martha’s criticisms, he looked at her with a sense of concern and understanding.

‘I appreciate your comments, Mrs Potts. We should have done more to have prevented such an attack,’ confessed a contrite Oliver.

‘Well, please do so in the future headmaster,’ demanded Martha.

‘We’re going to have an enquiry,’ announced Oliver.

‘I hope that doesn’t mean you’re going to kick everything into the long grass,’ asserted a dubious Martha.

‘Of course not, Mrs Potts. The trustees want a very thorough investigation into what happened and also into the school’s structure. They’re very concerned,’ Oliver assured her.

‘I should think so too,’ replied Martha censoriously.

‘Let’s hope it looks into bullying as well,’ stressed a suspicious Mrs Sully.

‘It will look at everything. Isn’t that so, Mr Aizlewood?’ maintained Oliver, cueing in support for his position.

‘Yes headmaster, it will cover the complete running of the school,’ underlined the Major obsequiously.

‘It damn well needs to,’ insisted the Captain.

‘My boy may be leaving the school, headmaster but I’ll still be watching these developments very closely,’ warned Martha.

‘My son will be continuing here, so we will be certainly looking for change,’ emphasised an imposing Mrs Sully.

‘So will I,’ added Hannah, unequivocally supporting the other women.

‘I’m sure that you’ll see it,’ stated Oliver nervously.

Oliver was beginning to feel like he was in the final scene of a western and that he was being surrounded on all sides by his enemies. Thankfully, the cavalry were on the horizon. And who should come to the rescue but the redoubtable Killer, aided and abetted by Mrs Killer. The junior housemaster had heard the end of the conversation and instantly understood Oliver’s difficulties.

'I think the enquiry will make a fair assessment. I believe that some independent people are going to report to the trustees, isn't that right, headmaster?' said Killer, turning to Oliver for appropriate approval.

'Yes, that's right Mr Roy. We won't be marking our own homework,' confirmed Oliver, laughing nervously.

'I should think not. That would be totally unacceptable,' warned the Captain.

'We need to see not talk about change,' pressed Hannah.

'Yes. After all, the 50s are coming to an end,' said Martha.

'I suppose that's what this rock 'n' roll is all about,' volunteered Deirdre serenely. The red-lipped Deirdre had made herself up to fully play the part of Mrs Killer. She was looking particularly elegant in her light blue dress.

'I don't know much about rock 'n' roll but things can't go on as they are,' thought the formidable Mrs Sully.

'Quite right, darling. I'm a military man and if there's bullying in the RAF, we'd root it out ruthlessly,' chimed in the Captain supportively.

The arrival of the Killers didn't diminish the impact of other parents and their children besieging Oliver. Now, Barrett and his father, a small, tidy man with a thin pencil moustache, approached the gathering. Ryder, the assault's strategist, unaffected by his recently prescribed punishment, followed them with his ample father, who'd previously advised Clement Attlee. Oliver felt imprisoned. He couldn't escape criticism from either more conservative parents like the Sullys or left-wing socialists like the Ryders. He found the latter youth's presence particularly obnoxious, given that the militant insurrectionist had received such minimal chastisement for his latest revolutionary escapade.

Relishing Oliver's unease, the school's Lenin with support from his father, proposed that there should be greater student participation and more staff accountability. He felt pleased with himself. He'd been advocating radical change for some time and now through his actions, it was likely to be on its way. Unfortunately, it'll come too late for him personally. He'll be at Oxford, exams permitting of course. Still, this didn't stop Francis Vladimir Ryder and his father of being so confident of their cause, that they didn't seem to be interested in anybody else's views. Instead, they ploughed on regardless with their ideological vision for the school.

The Ryders' interminable polemic began to bore even Mr Barrett, a committed schoolteacher with more moderate Labour views. Mr Barrett believed in listening and persuasion, so he found the Ryder diatribe rude and disrespectful to the headmaster and his colleagues. He was a schoolmaster, who knew about the difficulties that the school had to face. Nonetheless, he had expressed his displeasure and concern to his son about his role in the assault. He hated bullying but he also had contempt for violence, which he regarded as morally bankrupt. He would talk more fully to his boy about his role in the assault during the holidays. In the meantime, he accepted the conspirators' punishment and that the enquiry would make a fuller judgement. As the Ryders continued to proclaim their revisionist school manifesto, Mr Barrett wondered why people were so attentive to those who just talk and don't listen. Consequently, he welcomed Poppy and Hayes's interruption.

'Mum. We've been waiting for you. It's boring listening to Mr Smallman talk about fishing in Cirencester,' cried Poppy.

'Hello Poppy. How are you? Any marches coming up? mentioned Barrett, delighted to see his fellow protester. He thought she looked rather splendid in her floppy white hat and short skirt.

'There's several happening soon. I'll tell Tommy,' said Poppy coolly.

'Thanks. I'll give him my number,' responded Barrett, disappointed that Poppy wouldn't get in touch with him herself.

'We've been listening to the Ryders' manifesto for revolution,' disclosed Hannah.

'Oh, apologies Mrs Hayes. Have we bored you?' probed an offended Mr Ryder.

'I found it all rather abstract,' declared Hannah.

'I agree. More to do with theory than reality,' perceived Mrs Sully.

'I do think you need to make your interesting ideas more accessible,' advised a more sympathetic Martha.

'We're not Bolsheviks, Ryder,' added the Captain.

‘Who are Bolsheviks, Mum? asked Poppy.

‘The party that created The Russian Revolution,’ replied Hayes, volunteering the answer like a quiz contestant.

‘A section of the Social Democratic Workers Party,’ clarified Ryder, smugly correcting the junior. With his meticulously knotted cravat, carefully combed back hair and assiduously pressed grey trousers, he seemed an unlikely candidate for the barricades.

One Ball, who looked smart but ashen, interrupted this historical conversation. He had been moving glumly from one group to another but decided that his mother was spending too long with the conspirators’ parents.

‘Shall we go mother?’ urged One Ball.

‘Just a minute James,’ said Martha.

‘How are you?’ enquired an inquisitive Mrs Sully.

‘Just working hard,’ revealed a plaintive One Ball.

‘You want to go to Oxford?’ remarked the Captain, eager to know more about the abused boy.

‘I’ve a conditional place at Cambridge actually,’ contributed One Ball quietly.

‘Well good luck with it all,’ wished the Captain.

‘And so say all of us,’ corroborated Killer.

‘Absolutely,’ agreed the Major.

‘Why do you prefer Cambridge?’ queried Deirdre.

‘I think the town’s better,’ answered One Ball faintly.

‘As an Oxford man I’d have to disagree,’ refuted Oliver, while laughing jovially.

‘I prefer Cambridge. My godmother lives there. We punted on the river. Tommy, do you remember when you fell in?’ quizzed Poppy mischievously.

‘Yes, very well. I walked around the town absolutely soaked,’ answered Hayes, recalling that soggy autumnal afternoon with embarrassment.

‘Oh Hayesy, I wish I’d seen that,’ exclaimed an amused Barrett.

As Barrett giggled at the thought of Hayes’s aquatic misadventure, a surly Sully joined the conversation, informing his father that he had been chatting with Sir Malcolm Sargent, who’d now moved to the Dining Hall with his admirers.

‘We wondered where you were Michael,’ claimed Mrs Sully, trying to justify her neglect.

‘It’s difficult getting a word in what with Macready looking to grab all his attention for himself,’ reported a frustrated Sully.

‘Yes, that boy can be a bit vain,’ agreed Oliver euphemistically.

‘So can Sir Malcolm,’ added the hefty Mr Ryder.

‘But Dad, he’s made classical music more accessible,’ contended Ryder.

‘I like Sir Malcolm. He’s got showmanship I love the way he conducts the last night of the proms,’ insisted the Captain.

‘You must meet him, Dad,’ urged Sully.

‘Perhaps I will before we go,’ said the Captain.

‘Well before you do, I’d just like to apologise to you once more for the recent incident,’ announced Oliver, taking the opportunity to make a definitive statement. ‘I’m sure the official enquiry will help us move forward positively. In the meantime, I’d be grateful if you don’t make your views public, otherwise it could prejudice the panel’s deliberations. Of course, in the meantime, we shall do our best to support the boys in their endeavours with their exams, won’t we?’ pronounced Oliver, desperately looking for further support from both the Major and Killer.

‘Of course, we will,’ confirmed the Major hastily.

‘We certainly shall,’ attested Killer, joining the chorus of affirmative action.

‘Well, headmaster, we’ll see what the enquiry says,’ responded the Captain suspiciously. ‘As far as I’m concerned the school’s on trial. I’m not having my son bullied’.

‘And I’m not having my son assaulted,’ stipulated Martha Potts. ‘I shall be the reading the report very carefully.’

Oliver now realised that he couldn’t go any further with the Sully and Potts families. He’d just have to hope the enquiry wasn’t too damning. He departed courteously from the gathering and resumed working the room, mingling with other parents. After introducing himself, he made a general comment about their son’s progress, sprinkled with the odd humorous anecdote, while offering them more food and drink. If they were parents of the boys connected with the assault, he reiterated his faith in the enquiry and his request for privacy. He concentrated on making the parents feel as important a part of the school as the boys. His role was to provide the ambience, the mood music. If the parents wanted to talk further about particular areas of their son's academic performance or behaviour, he referred them to the relevant teacher or housemaster. He made sure that he was above the fray unless something more serious emerged. Unfortunately, bullying and assault qualified easily for that category. Nevertheless, he just hoped that he'd stemmed the flow of complaints and that the enquiry wouldn't make his position untenable.

While Oliver was circulating the room, Sir Malcolm was drinking a cup of tea and intermittently chewing a salad sandwich. Anne was still dutifully sitting by his side, along with Bayliss and Macready. Brown and Bunter, who'd diplomatically extricated themselves from a parental discussion about their career prospects, joined them to hear Anne telling 'Flash Harry' about an exciting classical music talent,

'She's so young but her cello playing is quite extraordinary,' said Anne excitedly, 'her name is Jacqueline Du Pré.'

'Ah yes, the word has got round about her amazing natural ability,' replied Sir Malcolm, who then took a delicate sip of his tea.

'Is she French?' asked Bunter, finding the surname bizarre.

'No, her father is an accountant from Jersey. He's a proud Channel Islander,' mentioned Anne.

'Her name isn't very English,' queried Brown, who remained standing with his fellow rocker.

'I heard her play at the Guildhall School of Music,' enthused Anne.

'She sounds like an exciting discovery,' agreed Sir Malcolm.

'You must hear her, Malcolm, you really must,' proclaimed Anne with the ardent rigour of an agent selling a client.

'Does she rock 'n' roll?' enquired Brown playfully.

'Well, in a way she does Brown,' remarked Anne mysteriously, as if she was haunted by the intensity of Jacqueline's playing.

'Great,' gushed Bunter.

‘So, Sir Malcolm, who’s your favourite rocker? Elvis, Little Richard or Jerry Lee Lewis?’ demanded a provocative Brown.

‘I’m afraid I don’t know that much about them,’ acknowledged Sir Malcolm.

‘Come on Sir Malcolm, which one? insisted Brown.

‘Sir Malcolm doesn’t listen to rock music,’ interrupted Macready diplomatically.

‘Oh, I do. But only a bit,’ admitted the conductor, wanting to keep in touch with the young without seeming an expert.

‘Really? That’s very interesting,’ observed Bayliss thoughtfully.

‘So which one, Sir Malcolm?’ continued Brown, pursuing his prey.

‘None of them. I think that I’d prefer Jacqueline Du Pré. I’ve got a feeling about her,’ said Sir Malcolm, reflecting on the glowing reference.

‘She’ll rock them all right,’ maintained Anne with ferocious certainty.

Suddenly, Root joined Sir Malcolm’s gathering. He was in an ebullient mood and his impeccable beige jacket reflected his buoyant disposition. The tall, blonde Rupert, strikingly attired in a blue seersucker suit, also emerged with an exuberant smile.

‘Sir Malcolm. I’m Reginald Root, the Music Master,’ affirmed Root, moving specifically towards the celebrated conductor. ‘This is my friend Rupert Dixon,’ he added, turning to his companion, ‘he’s an actor’. He then looked directly at the maestro and said earnestly, ‘it’s very good to meet you’.

After the Parents Day social had finished, Martha suggested to her son that they should have a private chat. The public conversations in the Dining Hall meant that it was difficult to have an intimate discussion, so they both agreed to have some further refreshment in a more relaxed environment.

When they arrived at the tuck shop, the formidable Mrs Butcher was arguing with a boy about the price of refreshers. The emaciated junior had the temerity to accuse the tuck shop manager of overpricing her goods. The boy told her that when he bought refreshers at his local shop in the holidays, they were a penny cheaper. Appalled at such insolence, Mrs Butcher tore into the audacious junior with all the rampaging alacrity of a hungry lioness. She told him in no uncertain manner that he didn't know anything about business and that the shop wouldn't exist without her making a profit. She also informed the defenceless boy that she wasn't running a charity and that he could always go and get his refreshers elsewhere. Mrs Butcher was not only forthright but loud. She liked to indulge in full projection and assert her authority around the whole shop. It was her form of a siren, a warning to all her customers not to indulge in unnecessary complaints. She brusquely discarded the junior's protestations as if he was a disrespectful minion disobeying a powerful empress. After such intimidation, the disconcerted junior blushed and left the shop hurriedly with his costly purchase. In fact, Mrs Butcher's involvement in the headstone plot had given her not only considerable amusement but also confidence in dealing with the school. She felt even more strongly that she wasn't going to be undermined by either hypocritical masters or impertinent schoolboys

After witnessing this relentless rant, Martha was cautious about ordering from the enraged tuck shop manager. Martha noted that Mrs Butcher only offered basic refreshments so she politely asked for some tea and biscuits. She then chose to sit near a window where she and her son could observe the serenity of a summer afternoon landscape, as the sun glowed across the nearby playing fields. In contrast to the uplifting weather, One Ball remained darkly subdued and quiet. The ferocity of the attack had surprised him. It took him ages to remove the black polish from his testicle. More profoundly, the psychological scars of his ordeal still haunted him. He often found it difficult to sleep.

'Do you want some tea?' asked Martha, looking to jolt her son out of his reverie.

'Yes. Ok,' said One Ball indifferently.

Martha poured tea from the metal pot and handed him a white porcelain cup. As she started drinking, Martha worried about her son. He was no longer his ebullient self and she was concerned about how the assault had changed him. Nonetheless, she wanted to discover why the other boys felt so much animosity towards him.

‘Were you bullying, James?’ queried Martha after sipping her tea.

‘I don’t think so,’ said One Ball, sullenly holding his cup in both hands

‘But they all began to hate you,’ commented Martha.

‘Yes,’ conceded One Ball passively.

‘Why?’ pressed Martha.

‘They didn’t like my form of discipline,’ acknowledged One Ball.

‘Maybe it was wrong,’ challenged Martha.

‘Then it’s the school’s fault,’ justified One Ball.

‘Why didn’t they attack other monitors then, James?’ demanded Martha.

‘Because I was more efficient,’ stressed a resolute One Ball.

‘Being cruel is a poor form of efficiency,’ retorted Martha.

‘I wasn’t cruel, mother,’ cried out One Ball, dramatically raising his voice.

Immediately, Mrs Butcher’s ears pricked up and she looked severely towards the Potts. At the same time, she wondered what they were discussing. She got a lot of information at the tuck shop. It was the Bletchley Park of the school. Mrs Butcher was good at using such information to advance the position of both herself and her docile husband in the school’s hierarchy. In Mrs Butcher’s case, this meant demanding more money at every available opportunity. She needed it for her pursuit of various consumer goods, not least a transistor radio. Then she could hear Housewives Choice and Music While You Work more easily at the shop. Meanwhile, she wondered why Potts had become so intense. She always knew that he was overzealous and had an unfortunate accident. ‘Mind you,’ she concluded, ‘if you’ve only got one of ’em, you’ve nothing to laugh about!’

Martha responded to her son’s outburst by calmly looking in the teapot. After discovering that there was enough tea left, she replenished both cups. She then offered her son a biscuit. He took a pink wafer while Martha contented herself with a custard cream. When she discussed his revision, he started to become more animated. Studying had obviously become One Ball’s form of redemption Nonetheless, Martha hoped that he wouldn’t permanently bury his feelings in work. Still, this wasn't the time to broach such concerns as she was just relieved that he had some recourse to alleviating his suffering.

'I suppose we can all learn something from this,' reflected Martha, looking for something positive to emerge from the attack,

'Yes. Let's hope the enquiry is fair,' replied One Ball evasively.

'You don't have to wait for the enquiry James,' declared Martha, staring directly at her son.

'What do you mean, mother?' urged a baffled One Ball.

'The world is changing. The days of empire are over, a new era will soon be upon us,' reflected Martha.

'What's that to do with me being assaulted and humiliated, mother?' disputed One Ball.

'I'll tell you. The old truths your father lived by won't hold dear anymore. We can't be as rigid about discipline and power. A new order is emerging and we will need to adapt. We can't go on about the past forever,' expounded Martha.

'Your theories don't mitigate the assault,' rebutted One Ball.

'No. The violence was cruel but I think it comes out of the anger of injustice. I told them I abhorred the attack on you. I think the punishment was too lenient. But why did those intelligent boys decide to risk their futures by planning such an assault? Was it just out of adolescent revenge? Really James?' emphasised Martha, leaning forward earnestly towards her son.

'They wanted to bring down a monitor,' reasoned One Ball.

'But why you, James? Why not the others?' pursued Martha.

'They didn't like me,' admitted One Ball.

'Don't you think it might be more than that?' stressed Martha calmly.

One Ball didn't reply. Mother and son then proceeded to drink their tea in silence, both obsessed with their own thoughts. During this intense conversation, Mrs Butcher was at the counter, pretending to read the Daily Herald. Business was quiet so she had time to relish eavesdropping. She found One Ball's outburst dramatic but not as emotional as the death of Grace in The Archers. Mrs Butcher was sobbing after that broadcast and her husband had to comfort her for several days.

‘You’ve given me something to think about, mother,’ confessed One Ball.

‘That’s good. Mind you, it’s not just about you, James. It’s about everybody. I think we all need to open our eyes more widely.’

The Potts continued quietly drinking their tea and eating their biscuits. Once they’d finished, Martha thought about asking Mrs Butcher to top-up their teapot. Then she quickly dismissed the idea, remembering the tuck shop supremo’s combative attitude towards prices. She feared that she might end up in an argument about paying for hot water. So after dealing with the bill, Martha just gave the assertive vendor a benign smile, while her son conjured up a cautious acknowledgement. As Mrs Butcher counted the money diligently, Martha and One Ball departed from her domain. They then proceeded steadfastly towards the station.

Captain Sully and Mrs Sully accompanied by their son made their way from the Dining Hall to their Hillman Minx, parked outside James B. As the Captain sauntered towards the Avenue, he gathered his thoughts about the bullying of his son. The Captain wasn’t particularly impressed with either Oliver or the Major. There was something equivocating about their attitude to protecting his boy from harm. Still, at least the One Ball boy looked suitably chastened. The Captain had heard that his father died in the war. Maybe that affected him badly and he was trying too hard to prove himself? Perhaps the father put too much pressure on him and was also a bully? The Captain knew examples of this when he was at school. In fact, an oppressive father psychologically damaged one of his best school friends. From that moment, the Captain was liberalised. While he accepted the discipline of the RAF, he also realised the importance of flexibility and consultation.

‘A penny for them,’ enquired Mrs Sully as they reached their car.

‘Just wondering about this One Ball,’ pondered the Captain.

‘He certainly looked depressed,’ observed Mrs Sully.

‘He’s avoided me a lot since the incident,’ revealed Sully.

'That's good. You shouldn't have been treated like that,' affirmed Mrs Sully.

'I was just wondering what made him a bully,' divulged the Captain.

Mr and Mrs Sully got into the front of the Hillman. The Captain then told his son to go to the back seat. Before his father could speak, Sully thanked them both for their support. It meant a lot to him, as his never-ending punishments cast a dark cloud over his disposition. While the Captain was glad that they'd lifted his spirits, he was disappointed that his son hadn't been totally honest about the assault and warned him about getting involved with a mob.

'It could have ended even worse,' contended the Captain.

'What do you mean, Dad?' replied Sully apprehensively.

'He could have been seriously hurt,' indicated the Captain.

'We just blackened his ball,' reasoned Sully.

'That's an assault, Michael,' asserted the Captain forcefully.

'He wasn't beaten up,' insisted Sully.

'But he could have been,' maintained the Captain.

'But he wasn't Dad,' reiterated Sully.

'Michael. You were lucky,' judged the Captain, 'once a group starts an attack like that anything can happen. It can get out of control. I've seen it in the forces.'

'Really?' queried Sully, taken aback by his father's revelation.

'Yes. A sergeant got seriously injured when he was waylaid by some warrant officers,' disclosed the Captain gravely.

Mrs Sully, who had listened intently to the conversation between her husband and son, now decided to intervene.

'Your father has seen enough violence, during the war. He doesn't want you to be a part of anything like that.'

'That's why we voted for Attlee. A new start. A fairer society,' the Captain reminded his son.

'But now we've got Macmillan,' replied Sully dully.

'But he's not radically changing what Attlee started,' argued the Captain.

'We want to make sure that all that fighting was worthwhile,' explained Mrs Sully, earnestly hoping for an optimistic future.

‘I supported you against this One Ball. He was bullying you and the school shouldn’t have allowed it to happen but a mob attacking one person, however repellent, isn’t acceptable,’ articulated the Captain.

‘But father it was a lark. A piece of theatre,’ said Sully exonerating himself.

‘A performance that could have had an even more serious ending,’ accentuated the Captain.

‘But it didn’t,’ Sully reminded his father.

‘Michael, violent criminals have often used dramatic disguises but that doesn’t lessen their vile deeds,’ underlined the Captain.

‘We just blackened his ball as a warning, that’s all,’ clarified Sully.

‘You and your friends assaulted him. That’s a violent act. You got away with a light punishment. You won’t next time,’ cautioned the Captain.

‘You see Michael, One Ball has to learn from this but so do you,’ interjected Mrs Sully quietly

‘Both of you were abused,’ confirmed the Captain.

‘But he started it,’ justified Sully.

‘Yes he did, but ugly revenge isn’t the answer, Michael. It can hurt you as much as him,’ stressed the Captain.

‘What could we do?’ pleaded Sully.

‘Maybe you could have just warned him,’ thought Mrs Sully.

In fact, Sully hadn’t thought of that. He realised that perhaps they had got carried away by an emotional feeling of injustice. The masks and its ensuing ritual made them feel like they were just involved in a ritualistic drama. Maybe, they were so obsessed with humiliating One Ball that the attack did get out of hand. Sully shifted uneasily along the back seat of the car, while his father turned round and looked him in the eye.

‘Of course, the school needs to learn from this, Michael but your mother is right, so do you and this One Ball,’ concluded the Captain.

‘All right, Dad,’ replied Sully, agreeing submissively. He already had plenty to think about so he didn’t want to discuss the matter further.

'I'll always support you son but we need to be honest with each other. So always tell me the whole truth, not just what you want me to hear,' demanded the Captain.

'Ok Dad, sorry. I appreciate that,' responded Sully contritely.

'There'll be no more bullying, so work hard and enjoy yourself,' advised the Captain.

'We love you Michael. You're our only child. We only ask that you do your best. That's all you can do,' urged his mother earnestly.

Just as Sully moved his bulky body towards the door and clasped the handle, his father told him that he'd talked to Root.

'Strange man. Also Rupert, that friend of his. Pleasant but rather effeminate. Apparently, he knows Terence Rattigan-a good RAF man, by the way. Anyway, Root likes your singing. He thinks you can go to a music college. He's got faith in you,' trumpeted the Captain proudly.

'Thanks Dad,' appreciated Sully, with a joyful smile

'And Michael, please tell me the name of this One Ball again,' asked Mrs Sully earnestly. 'I keep forgetting and it could get embarrassing,'

'Potts. James Potts,' reiterated Sully.

'Potts. Yes, we must remember that name before we commit a faux pas,' acknowledged the Captain.

'Absolutely,' agreed Mrs Sully. 'We're not going to Singapore until next month, so we're around if you need us, Michael. Ok, give us both a kiss and away you go,' ordered his mother with an alluring grin.

Sully responded to mother's request, leaning awkwardly towards the front seats. He then said goodbye, adjusted his large body to get himself out of the car, stood on the kerb and waved as his parents started their journey back to the midlands. In the distance, he could see their raised hands responding to his fluttering. When the Hillman Minx receded into the distance, emotion welled up inside him. He hurried through the porch into the house. He then went straight to the toilet, sat down and had a good cry. He just loved his parents so much.

As Hannah left the Dining Hall, she was still worried about her son's role in the assault. She needed to talk to his father about it, that's if he wasn't too busy gallivanting around with his girlfriend. She didn't want to think that such behaviour set a precedent, particularly as she felt Tommy was taking the whole affair too lightly. While the Hayes family made their way down the centre path to the station, Hannah's thoughts were suddenly interrupted by Poppy doing an alarming cartwheel.

'You see, I don't need Eileen Fowler,' cried Poppy, referring to the current TV Fitness Queen.

Hannah and Hayes laughed, as Poppy adjusted her black and white, polka dot skirt and picked up her discarded floppy hat. When her amusement subsided, Hannah elaborated on her son's involvement in the attack.

'I need to talk to Dad about all this,' mentioned Hannah.

'About what?' responded Hayes, feigning disinterest.

'What do you think, Tommy? The assault,' replied Hannah, frustrated by his offhand response.

'We've been punished,' said Hayes dismissively.

'One Ball is a bully, Mum,' interjected Poppy passionately.

'Your father should know about it,' stressed Hannah.

'Do you have to, Mum? Things are difficult enough without you making them worse,' declared Hayes vigorously.

'What do you mean, Tommy?' queried Hannah anxiously.

'Dealing with his floozy and the constant tension between you both,' bawled Hayes, stopping on the path and looking directly into his mother's eyes.

'I don't think she's a floozy, Tommy. She's his girlfriend,' corrected Poppy.

'Well that's the way I see her. She's broken up our family,' continued Tommy, his voice cracking with emotion. He'd always been deeply affected by the hurt the divorce had brought to his mother.

'It's a bit more complicated than that,' revealed Hannah, hugging her son and giving him a kiss on his forehead.

Hannah was worried that the disintegration of her relationship with Phil had affected her son badly. She felt guilty about that. In a society that rigidly upheld marriage and frowned upon divorce, it was difficult being a single mother.

Although Hannah was a committed monarchist, the Queen's rejection of Princess Margaret's request to marry the divorced Peter Townsend, disappointed her. Consequently, she was concerned that family turmoil in such a culture could hinder Tommy's emotional development.

'Why is it more complicated?' railed Hayes.

'Well, Tommy, I think your father's love of his work became more important than his family. Especially after he lost six years during the war,' clarified Hannah.

'His floozy is a jazz singer,' remarked Poppy.

'I thought you said she wasn't a floozy,' Hayes reminded his sister.

'I'm just using your words Tommy,' retorted Poppy.

'Your father wanted to be free,' professed Hannah reticently.

After reaching the end of the centre path, they proceeded across the surrounding road and made the gradual descent down to the station. As they did so, Poppy defiantly disputed her father's notion of freedom.

'He may be free but he's not being very responsible.'

'Maybe but that's the way some artists are,' reflected Hannah.

'But you're an artist, Mum. You play the piano beautifully but you're not leaving us,' stated Poppy.

'It's different for women,' conceded Hannah regretfully, 'we're meant to be the home makers.'

'That's unfair Mum,' insisted Poppy, 'that can't go on forever.'

'I don't know Poppy, I don't know. I'm afraid I'm not a prophet,' admitted Hannah elusively

As they approached the station, Hannah stopped and told her son firmly that she was going to inform his father about the assault.

'Ok,' accepted Hayes reluctantly. 'But what were we to do? Nobody was listening Mum,' he implored.

'Why didn't you tell the parents involved? challenged Hannah.

'They're not at the school,' countered Hayes defensively.

'But they pay the fees or most of them do,' Hannah reminded him. 'And what about those who dish out the bursaries, grants and scholarships?' she asked. 'Why weren't they contacted?'

'Ryder was dealing with the strategy,' justified Hayes evasively.

Hannah then heard more about Ryder and his influence upon the conspirators. While he was evidently articulate and charismatic, with a strong sense of injustice, she wasn't convinced that Francis Vladimir Ryder had thought everything through. It was Hannah's belief that there were other possibilities that hadn't been rigorously pursued. Having witnessed Ryder in the Dining Hall, Hannah got the impression that he was marching to an agenda and lacked flexibility. She had suspicions that he didn't want to pursue other alternatives, because he was obsessed with his ideological message. Hannah concluded that the boys had rushed too easily to judgement, incited by the school's Lenin exploiting their justifiable anger.

'I think more avenues should have been pursued Tommy, before carrying out an assault and threatening a school strike,' pronounced Hannah.

'Maybe,' conceded Hayes reluctantly.

'Next time ask more questions. Don't be led by the herd,' warned Hannah.

'Ok Mum,' agreed Hayes listlessly, wanting to close the conversation.

At the station approach, Poppy wiggling her hips, much to the amusement of some nearby travellers, diverted Hannah's attention.

'Poppy, what are you doing?' demanded Hannah.

'Practising my movements for the hula hoop, you're going to buy me!' exclaimed Poppy.

'What's that, for goodness sake?' enquired her perplexed mother.

'It's a toy hoop. It's becoming all the rage. I saw it on the news,' imparted Poppy excitedly.

'We can talk about that later, darling. But be a little more modest, please,' requested Hannah.

After admonishing her energetic daughter, Hannah turned back to Hayes. He looked vulnerable and confused.

'I'm always here for you, Tommy. Whatever.'

‘I know. Thanks Mum.’

‘So is your Dad. In his own way.’

‘I suppose so.’

‘We may be divorced but we’re still your parents.’

‘I just wish we could be all together.’

‘I’m sorry about that.’

‘It’s not your fault Mum.’

Suddenly, Hannah saw Poppy practising her hopscotch skills in the forecourt.

‘Poppy!’ she shouted. ‘Get ready. We’re going into the station.’

‘Ok but I need to practise,’ yelled her frustrated daughter.

Hannah and Hayes, diverted from their intimate tête a tête, laughed at Poppy’s antics. Hannah then smiled at her son affectionately and probed him about Phil’s recent visit.

‘Anyway Tommy, did Dad’s visit go well?

‘Yes it did’ confirmed Hayes in a non-committal tone.

‘Despite everything, I want you to see him regularly,’ stressed Hannah intimately. ‘How was he?’

‘He was fine. He actually talked to me instead of performing,’ explained Hayes.

‘What do you mean?’ pursued Hannah.

‘He wasn’t just playing Daddy,’ divulged Hayes.

‘I see,’ contemplated Hannah, understanding what her son meant. Her former husband was charming but he could take refuge in making dramatic, sweeping gestures to cover his shortcomings. Like a husband giving his wife flowers after a huge row.

‘You still love him, don’t you?’ asked Hayes quietly.

‘I’m very fond of your father but our marriage is over,’ she uttered deliberately.

As Hannah and Hayes looked blankly at each other, Poppy interrupted them with one of her diversions.

‘Come on, Mum. You said we were going. I’m getting bored.’

Hannah and Hayes took the opportunity to finish their conversation and follow Poppy into the station. Hannah then ordered tickets to Victoria from a thin, genteel man with a long nose. She noticed that amidst his brown suit, a silver chain protruded from his waistcoat, leading no doubt to his pocket watch. A dark peaked hat, with gold insignia in the form of a lion, was lying on a table behind him. Hannah paid for the tickets and they all walked across the bridge to the appropriate platform. Poppy considered sliding down the slim bannisters but then thought better of it. Meanwhile, Hayes took the opportunity to tell his mother that the ticket clerk was none other than Mr Butcher. Apparently, when there were staff shortages, he often took over other people's jobs. Hannah found Mr Butcher, polite and respectful, not qualities that you'd automatically associate with his robust wife and her tyrannical rule of the tuck shop. It was obviously a partnership of different temperaments. She wondered if you needed that contrast to anchor a marriage. In her own case, two struggling, mercurial musicians didn't seem to give her own union a firm foundation.

On arrival at the platform, Hannah discovered that Mr Barrett and his son were also waiting for the London train. The schoolteacher respectfully raised his white straw hat to Hannah and acknowledged Hayes and Poppy.

'It should be here in a few minutes,' claimed Mr Barrett, looking dapper in his cream jacket.

'Good. It's been quite a day,' admitted Hannah, trying to start a conversation.

'Yes. Let's hope everybody learns from this business. My son certainly needs to do so,' replied Mr Barrett, looking towards his boy, who was now chatting earnestly to Poppy and Hayes several yards away.

'What conclusion did you reach about it all?' asked Hannah.

'Bullies can't be tolerated but nor can assault,' emphasised Mr Barrett adamantly.

'I agree. I just hope the school will change,' expressed Hannah.

'Institutions in this country change slowly. It'll happen but not straight away. There'll be some gesture towards change but nothing too extreme,' prophesied Mr Barrett.

'Why do you think that, Mr Barrett? queried Hannah.

'If real change was going to happen, it would have taken place after the war, but the government shied away from abolishing public schools,' argued Mr Barrett.

‘Surely there will be a less brutal environment?’ hoped Hannah.

‘Yes, I think there’ll be a more cautious approach to punishment while these pupils are still here. The school can’t afford bad publicity or persistent rumours. Change that is more meaningful will probably have to wait. I’m a schoolmaster, so I get a sense of the politics of it all,’ concluded Mr Barrett.

‘Still there’s good education here,’ maintained Hannah, looking for some reassurance.

‘Yes that’s true Mrs Hayes. Even so, I was still in a quandary whether to allow my son to come here, rather than go to a state school. The opportunities for boys with parents on a lower income persuaded me,’ admitted an earnest Mr Barrett, uneasy about compromising his principles.

‘Yes, at least they don’t all come from the same background. They’re not all sons of rich people,’ highlighted Hannah, eager to underline the school’s egalitarianism.

‘Exactly,’ agreed Mr Barrett.

Suddenly, the conversation was interrupted by Poppy performing a handstand against a station wall and muddying a picture of Audrey Hepburn on a poster for Funny Face.

‘Poppy!’ shouted Mrs Hayes, much to the hilarity of the boys. ‘Please!’

‘Sorry, Mum,’ apologised a seemingly repentant Poppy.

‘Is your daughter a gymnast, Mrs Hayes?’ mentioned a curious Mr Barrett.

‘Not really. She’s just very active. She’s good at netball though.’

In fact, Poppy was now transferring her energies to talking to Barrett about Operation Grapple, the testing of Britain’s first hydrogen bomb. Both Mr Barrett and Hannah looked on affectionately as the two youngsters tried to solve nuclear proliferation. Undiplomatically, the arrival of a grimy steam locomotive, billowing black smoke out of its chimney, interrupted their negotiations. Mr Barrett courteously opened the carriage door and allowed Hannah and Poppy to enter first. After they were all seated in a carriage, Poppy took the opportunity to roll down the window. Ignoring her mother’s warnings, she continued to engage with Barrett about the imminent dangers of extinction. Their deliberations were so intense that Hannah had to interrupt the summit meeting, in order to say goodbye to her son.

Eventually, the ubiquitous Mr Butcher appeared on the platform in his official regalia, carrying his flag. The guard on the train, a small, stocky gentleman wearing brown-rimmed glasses, started having a chat with the station master about current salaries, which caused a significant delay. Eventually, with everyone safely on board, Mr Butcher lowered his green flag, much to the relief of the despondent driver.

Hayes and Barrett stood on the platform, waving goodbye to Poppy as she leaned out of the window. The train chugged away into the Sussex horizon and Hayes's sister faded into the distance. The two boys followed the civil Mr Butcher out of the station. As they ambled down the centre path, making their way back to their house, they both wondered about their future at the school.

The following Saturday afternoon, Rutter was busy giving Whitgift a cricket thrashing or more accurately witnessing Carson's bowling barrage terrify the opposition. The genial Irishman's sterling performance led to the Croydon boys being all out for a mere 90. The school responded by batting aggressively against modest bowling and polished off the runs by tea time. Only three wickets were lost and Rutter hit a quick 20 not out with some fluent cutting and driving. Fred described the victory as 'a carve up'.

On that Saturday evening, Rutter had more important matters on his mind than his cover drive, like meeting Françoise. His time at the school was drawing to an end and regardless of the urgent demands of revision; he still wanted to see her as often as he possible. That's why he'd arranged to meet her at 6:30 and go for a walk.

It was a humid summer's evening and Rutter waited excitedly at the back of Tickle house. The road to Keats Wood wasn't far away and he hoped for a quiet, intimate assignation. While he strolled around the surrounding asphalt pretending to look occupied, he kicked bits of grit fantasising that he was Johnny Haynes scoring a goal for England. In fact, he'd already spent ages gazing at himself in the mirror, deciding whether to follow Mr Haynes's advice and use Brylcreem or not. In the end, he went for compromising half measures, putting just enough on his fair hair to be in suitably fashionable mode. He also indulged in tying his cravat in various ways, so much so that he ended up literally tying himself in knots. In the end, he settled for something a little fluffy and loose, to create a dilettante look. He thought Françoise would like that, a touch of the left bank and all that. Given that Carson's massacre had given him more time to prepare for his tryst, Rutter had rigorously polished his black shoes. Regrettably, his foolish attempts to emulate football greatness meant that he had seriously undermined his good work. Nervously looking at his watch and realising that Françoise would be arriving shortly, he decided to act. He took out his white handkerchief, spat on the edge of the linen and rigorously looked to restore his shoes to their former glory. After a few minutes of intense rubbing, he saw Françoise in the distance and hastily shoved his sullied hanky back into his pocket.

Françoise in a floral summer dress waved from afar as she moved purposefully towards him. She was carrying a wicker bag and wearing a large sun hat with a red ribbon. They smiled at each other warmly but kept at a distance, so as not to attract any voyeuristic attention from the occupants of nearby Tickle. The two lovers then made their way towards the long school road that led to the wood. On the way, Françoise revealed that she'd bought 'le vin' by pointing humorously to her large bag.

As they rambled along, Rutter wanted to know if One Ball was still abusing her. Françoise divulged that he hadn't written any more offensive letters since the assault but that after emerging from his depression, he was becoming more confrontational. For instance, he'd approached her in the Dining Hall and called her 'a French tart with no morals'. When she'd ladled his bowl with rice pudding, One Ball couldn't resist venomously calling her 'a bitch'. Françoise thought that he found such abuse cathartic as he then proceeded to serve himself, flamboyantly scooping jam out of a metal tin and placing it ceremoniously on top of his dessert, before departing in supposed triumph.

Françoise didn't feel guilty about One Ball. She disliked bullies and found his arrogant exceptionalism repulsive. Yet she didn't think of him as a bad person, just someone full of lost illusions. Although she hoped that he'd change his behaviour, Françoise thought that the conspirators' tactics were wrong. She still found the blackening of One Ball's testicle upsetting and was relieved that Rutter wasn't involved in such a distressing violation.

In fact, Rutter had only heard how the attack had actually transpired, when he bumped into Ryder in the Avenue. The great leader regarded 'physical retribution' as a 'moral imperative' and thought that Rutter's regret at not insisting on greater clarity at the conspirators' meeting was because of 'cowardly vacillation'. Rutter was alarmed when he detected a steely resolution in Ryder's eyes, as he earnestly pronounced that 'the moment had to be seized'. Rutter thought that One Ball should be punished but he didn't think that stringing him up, blackening him and attacking his most tender part was the solution.

When Rutter mentioned his concern to Françoise while walking down the country road, they both started thinking of alternative forms of retribution. Like cutting up One Ball's pyjamas, placing stickers on his clothes, locking him up in his study, refusing to talk to him, instigating mass disobedience in response to his orders, putting ice cubes in his bed, writing derogatory graffiti around his locker and so on. Rutter and Françoise had fun trying to outdo each other with punitive strategies as they jumped around the road at each retaliatory suggestion. After they got exhausted from outbidding each other, they both concluded that even if Ryder saw himself as Lenin, Chairman Mao or God Almighty, they were both much better strategists.

After the euphoria of their antics dissipated, Rutter and Françoise held hands now that they were well away from the school. They sauntered in silence, appreciating the soothing tranquillity of the surrounding Sussex fields. They realised that they might not see each other for some time and that these were precious moments to cherish. They could sense each other's desires, yet they were patient. Their recent necessary restraint only made their rapport more exciting, when they were discreetly alone. As they strolled forward, appreciating the comforting mellow landscape and laughing at the discordant sounds from the nearby cows, they felt totally relaxed in each other's company. Neither of them had ever felt so close to anyone else. Unfortunately, the throaty growl of an approaching motor bike broke their idyllic intimacy. Hastily, the lovers stepped onto a grass verge at the side of the road.

'Hello lovebirds,' cried the familiar midlands cadence of Fred, arrayed in a silver helmet and black motorcycle gear.

'Oh Fred, I thought you'd gone home,' replied a surprised Rutter.

'No Rutter, I had to clean up the pavilion,' moaned Fred.

'Sorry about that,' apologised Rutter.

'Chewing gum all over the place. I think you lot have been watching those Australians too much,' complained Fred.

'I like the motorbike,' complimented Françoise, diverting the conversation away from the 1st X1's refuse.

'Thanks, love. Yes, it's useful for getting around the school. Sometimes I cycle, but recently I've taken to the Ariel. Makes a change from my Raleigh.'

'Looks good. Do you take many passengers?' enquired Françoise.

'I sometimes give the wife a ride into town. She often gets scared and starts screaming for me to slow down,' disclosed Fred, chortling away.

'Carson did the business today Fred,' interjected Rutter.

'He's a bit quick isn't he? I told him to keep pitching it up in the areas,' disclosed Fred.

'In the areas?' questioned a bewildered Françoise.

'It means on a good length,' mentioned Rutter.

'A good length?' queried Françoise.

'So it's difficult for the batsman to hit the ball hard,' elaborated Fred.

'It's very difficult this cricket. Very English,' complained Françoise, frustrated by the game's complexities.

'It's played abroad as well you know,' insisted Fred. 'By the Aussies, the Kiwis, the Indians, the Pakistanis..'

'But not the French,' interrupted Françoise sternly.

‘Well you play..’ said Fred hesitantly.

‘Oh no please, not this French cricket,’ interjected Françoise. ‘It isn’t a major sport in France.’

‘Maybe not,’ conceded Fred.

‘I think it’s a game of the British Empire,’ asserted a buoyant Françoise.

‘The Commonwealth really,’ corrected Rutter.

‘You can call it what you want,’ countered Françoise dismissively.

‘Well it’s better than killing people,’ claimed Fred with a wry smile.

‘Well that’s true,’ agreed Rutter, looking to steer Fred away from further banal generalisations.

‘Well, I’d better get on. The wife will be waiting with the supper. She’ll go bananas if I’m late,’ remembered Fred, starting up the Ariel.

‘Ok Fred. Drive safely,’ advised Rutter.

‘Oh I will, I want to watch Dixon of Dock Green tonight,’ replied Fred cheerily.

‘Nice to see you,’ expressed Françoise warmly.

‘Bye Fred,’ added Rutter, as the cricket coach cranked up his motorbike.

‘Evening all!’ shouted Fred above the rowdy engine, saluting like PC George Dixon. The school’s cricket coach then accelerated down the country road and faded into the distance.

Rutter and Françoise resumed their walk towards the wood. As they passed the green meadows bathed in the shadows of the evening light, they re-established their intimate bond. Rutter liked the way Françoise had defended her country. It made him feel closer to her. She hadn’t done it out of belligerence but an assertion of identity. Yet, Rutter detected a defensiveness in her insistence. The war had brought about considerable humiliation to France. He’d touched on it in previous conversations with Françoise but their chat didn’t evolve very far. It was as if the subject was too painful. Rutter knew that Lyon had been the centre of the French Resistance and that Françoise had family who were members, although he didn’t know the exact details. She was more interested in discussing the new Europe. That’s why she wanted to learn languages and look to the future.

Françoise enjoyed walking in silence with Rutter. As they both absorbed the evening landscape, she appreciated both the space he gave her and the lack of adolescent demands. There was also a sense of adventure and fun in their relationship, as well as a bit of danger. This meant that they both had to be on their toes, which made their romance exciting. To Françoise, Rutter seemed an unusual Englishman as she frequently got the impression that the English were suspicious of foreigners. Some of them seemed detached from the continent and the full impact of the horror that the war had brought there. They gave the impression that they'd won the conflict on their own, as if the Americans and Soviets, let alone Le Maquis and other diverse nationalities, had just minor roles. Of course, she was grateful for their victory at the Battle of Britain and for their part in her country's liberation but not for their presumption. As they approached Keats Wood, she remembered that English romantic poet, who died from tuberculosis at twenty-five in Rome. She wasn't an authority on his work but ever since school she was entranced by his love of beauty. 'Now there was an Englishman with a more universal vision,' she recalled.

As Rutter and Françoise meandered slowly towards the wood, they saw a man in a nearby field sitting on a stool next to an easel, painting a picture. As they moved closer, they discovered that the artist was none other than O'Reilly. Adorned with a Panama straw hat and a green bow tie, he was working furiously on a landscape. When the young couple approached him, he greeted them with an impudent grin.

'Out for a romantic stroll, then?' suggested O'Reilly.

'Just a walk, O' Reilly,' clarified Rutter, not wanting to be embroiled in scandal even in the dying embers of the term.

'Don't worry. I won't tell anyone,' whispered O'Reilly, with a devilish wink.

'I didn't know you could paint,' revealed Françoise, diverting O'Reilly from further lewd insinuations.

'We're not all poets and playwrights, you know,' decreed O'Reilly.

'Sorry. I don't understand,' responded Françoise, bewildered by the Irishman's extravagant generalisation.

'The Irish. Us. We have painters as well. Maybe not as many as the French,' confessed O'Reilly, glancing at Françoise, 'but we do have Jack Butler Yeats,' he announced proudly.

'I've only heard of W. B. Yeats, conceded Rutter bluntly.

'He's the brother of your man,' explained O'Reilly. 'Jack painted beautiful pictures of Sligo. I got inspiration from those.'

'I see,' hesitated a bemused Rutter.

'I've been doing it over the years. It helps me to relax,' claimed O'Reilly, 'I've got a stack of paintings. They're stored at the art school.'

'Are you going to sell them? enquired Françoise.

'I'm more interested in being creative than making money,' declared O'Reilly, offended at the thought of being accused of mere materialistic motives.

'This one looks good,' said Rutter, consciously flattering the Irishman.

'It's not bad but I'm no Jack Yeats,' admitted O' Reilly.

After a discussion about the painting itself, a rather hazy watercolour of Keats Wood, O'Reilly elaborated on recent school developments. He belatedly congratulated Rutter and Françoise on their contribution to Henry V, although he found Bayliss's patriotic production 'a bit over the top', more like that of a colonial Governor. He also couldn't resist mentioning that the Hundred Years' War with the French was an insane amount of time to be fighting. He was aware that the battles over Ireland took place over a longer period but at least there were more breaks between the various encounters or 'time for a jar', as O'Reilly evocatively described it. The caretaker then revelled in school gossip, by informing the two youngsters that Killer had been compelled to pay for the headstone. Apparently, his appeals to both the masonry company and Marian had fallen on deaf ears, he couldn't track down his impersonator and he didn't dare go to court because he feared the consequences of any public revelation of his sexual dalliance. O'Reilly found this so hilarious that when he swayed excessively on his stool, he nearly bumped into the easel. Thankfully, Rutter with the footwork of a natural sportsman, moved nimbly to grab the top of the stand before the Irishman made any contact.

'You've saved my painting!' cried O'Reilly.

'You're welcome,' said Rutter, reassuring the distressed artist, while steadying his easel.

'Good man, Rutter. I really appreciate that,' affirmed O'Reilly, readjusting himself on his stool.

'Well, we'd better be going and continue our walk,' maintained Rutter, looking to extricate himself tactfully from the convivial Irishman.

'Well, listen now. Have a good time. You need to get away from those lunatics running this place as much as I do,' advised O'Reilly, gathering his brush.

'Yes, we all need a break at times,' agreed Rutter diplomatically.

'You know the crazy thing. They don't even know that they're as mad as hatters. They continue running the place as if they're totally sane,' continued O'Reilly, incredulous of the school's establishment.

'Still, it's nearly the end of term. It'll be over soon,' interjected Françoise, hoping to conclude the conversation.

'That's right. I'll be back in Ireland. Mind you, we've got bleeding lunatics over there as well. I mean, this banning of books, what's all that about? The church has the government by the balls back home. It's terrible.'

'Aren't you a good Catholic?' probed Françoise.

'I go to mass. Sometimes,' confessed O'Reilly. 'Are you?' he challenged Françoise, penetrating her brown eyes.

'No,' she replied. 'I'm not.'

'Then we're quits,' asserted O'Reilly triumphantly.

Rutter and Françoise spontaneously joined the Irishman's raucous laughter. They then said their goodbyes and made their way towards the interior of the wood. Just as they were about to pass a nearby copse, the voice of O'Reilly boomed all over the landscape.

'Don't forget Jack Butler Yeats!' he yelled, as he waved his brush chaotically in their direction.

Rutter and Françoise gestured back and ventured into the wood. It was as if they were entering a grotto. The dappled early evening light peered through the tall trees and created an almost mythical ambience. The young couple trod carefully through the narrow paths in search of a place to sit, as the gurgling flow of a small stream accompanied them. They continued gingerly across an old ravaged wooden bridge and ascended a slope, which led to a dry, flat patch of grass, perfect for their purpose. Françoise spread out her African rug while Rutter uncorked the Bordeaux Blanc. She then produced two wine glasses from her wicker bag and proceeded to place several sandwiches on some white plates. Françoise had provided a diverse choice including pâté, mixed salad, brie and tomato, all encased in baguettes, which she'd managed to get from the only delicatessen in the town.

As they ate and drank, Françoise talked more about her family. She had an older cousin, who was in the French Resistance but had been killed, not by the Germans but by Le Maquis, who accused him of being a traitor. Apparently, he was tied to a chair and interrogated for hours before he was shot. Françoise didn't know if he was guilty or not. Le Maquis had discovered that he'd often fraternised with German soldiers and they couldn't risk having informers in their ranks. As they'd lost men through the enemy receiving valuable intelligence, they had a rigorously brutal policy towards suspected traitors. This revelation shocked Rutter as he didn't know much about the French resistance. Hearing about Françoise's cousin, made him realise why France was keen to find new alliances in Europe, to stop such internecine brutality ever happening again. Although Rutter admired his own country's courageous resistance to the Nazis, he thought that the the post-war continental aftermath wasn't discussed sufficiently in Britain. In fact, he discovered that those who'd actually fought in the war were reluctant to talk about it. For instance, his father always changed the subject to topics that were more trivial. Only once, when he'd had a few beers, did he speak movingly of how he saw shot soldiers screaming or in one particular case, pleading for his mother before dying.

As the war children enjoyed their repast, they moved on to discuss the more parochial world of the school. Françoise described how Yvette was continuing to get closer to Barrel. In fact, their increasing addiction to carnal pleasure meant that they were recently discovered clandestinely kissing behind some strategically convenient shrubbery. Rutter thought that such a revelation made his relationship with Françoise seem like the Flying Scotsman when compared to Barrel and Yvette's slow goods train. Françoise refused to be judgemental and had come to realise that everybody needed to find their own speed in life. She also told him that the austere Madame Danvers, was leaving. A college in Brighton had appointed her as Domestic Superintendent, which sounded more like a job with the police than one with an educational establishment. According to Françoise, rumours abounded that Miss Pollard was courting and wanted to be nearer her fiancée, who lived in Hove and ran a dry cleaning business.

Now that she was departing, Miss Pollard had apparently relaxed her frigid veneer and become dangerously frolicsome, cracking inane jokes to her foreign employees, even though they didn't understand a word of her facile utterances. Once, following a liaison with Barrel, Yvette bumped into an inebriated Miss Pollard stumbling down the Avenue after a party, where apparently she'd sung a drunken version of I Do Like to Be Beside the Seaside. Given Miss Pollard's precarious state, Yvette accompanied her back to her flat opposite Tickle. Miss Pollard was so grateful for Yvette's help during the long walk that she gave her a splattering of kisses on the cheek. Yvette became so severely asphyxiated by the smell of beer that the French maid had to diplomatically extricate herself, from the newly designated domestic superintendent's neurotic efforts at affection.

As Rutter laughed at Françoise's description of Mrs Danvers' antics, he gulped le vin with relish. He then looked deeply into her eyes. The fading light danced on her patterned dress as she moved over to him and put her hands around his neck. They kissed for several minutes and then collapsed onto the rug. They didn't mind that they banged into the wicker bag or that they nearly broke a glass. They were alone together celebrating their love. Even though they didn't know what the future held, they were both going to savour their delicate intimacy.

While doing his final exams, thoughts of Françoise haunted Rutter. After their evening in Keats Wood, Rutter couldn't stop thinking about her. When wrestling with a particularly challenging examination paper, images of their most intimate moments interrupted his intellectual ruminations. Although in the mercilessly cold examination environment of Big Hall, such errant meanderings warmed his heart, they weren't conducive to answering a question about the ambitions of Otto Von Bismarck. Later, as Rutter sat on a bench outside Ironside A, enjoying the warm glow of a summer evening, he didn't think that he'd done very well in his A Levels. He just hoped that he'd get sufficient marks to fulfil his aspirations. He also feared that when Françoise returned home, he might not fit into her life across the English Channel. Suddenly, Rutter realised that he hadn't really thought about living without Françoise. Over the last year, they had become inseparable. She'd brought a different perspective to his way of thinking. A way of looking at the world that wasn't limited by the obsessions of suburban Purley.

Rutter loved his parents but he couldn't wait to leave home. Benefitting from an education that they'd never had, Rutter felt alienated from their culture. He didn't want to watch Come Dancing incessantly or listen to the regurgitated editorials of the Daily Mail. Things came to a head when Six-Five-Special started on the BBC and his father switched it off in the middle of Don Lang and his Frantic 5 performing Rock Around the Cookhouse. Mr Rutter found the programme degenerate and Lang a jumped up teddy boy. He also thought that Pete Murray was smarmy and that the demure Josephine Douglas shouldn't be part of such a vulgar programme. Rutter tried to reason with his father, claiming that teenagers needed at least some representation on the BBC but Mr Rutter was implacable. He didn't want such music in his living room.

Eventually, Rutter had to reluctantly accept this censorship and although his mother did her best to alleviate the tension, it didn't remove the cultural scars. The confrontation only gave further credence as to why he didn't invite the family to Parents Day. This estrangement propelled him further towards self-reliance. With Françoise's company, this was manageable but when she departed, he was venturing into the unknown.

A combination of medication and Dr Orban's psychiatric therapy had helped One Ball regain something of his former assurance. As he relaxed in his study, he was confident that he'd done well in his exams and would take up his place at Cambridge. He thought that his self-imposed isolation had produced significant academic benefits. However, such was his total concentration towards exam success that he'd become negligent of other duties. He no longer cared if the lav end stank to hell, that shoes weren't cleaned properly and whether boys were late for parade. He'd had enough. He'd done his best to keep discipline and order but he'd ended up being abused without sufficient support. Boring Beckett and Pound showed concern about his welfare but One Ball found them spineless and servile. What's more, he had no faith in the school's enquiry. It would be a cover-up in the established 50s tradition. Anyway, the result of such official deliberations would be of no benefit to him. Hopefully, by then he would be revelling in higher academia, far away from pious pronouncements that would change very little.

One Ball also realised that his mother seemed to be developing a socialist crusade, if her comments in the tuck shop were anything to go by. Still, he tried to reassure himself that the idea of radicals infiltrating Farnham was as unlikely as a communist revolution in Chelsea. After all, the Surrey town was a bastion of English conservatism and Daily Telegraph readers. Nonetheless, One Ball did know of the occasional renegade, usually imported from the fringes of London, who had parked himself in the middle of the Tory stronghold. One was a middle-aged man with a black beret decorated with hammer and sickle insignia, who went by the name of Marxist Mickey. He regularly gave out leaflets proposing greater common ownership and redistribution of wealth, while yelling through a dilapidated megaphone about the iniquities of the Conservative government and 'our corrupt class ridden society'. The aged Farnham population tended to manoeuvre themselves quickly away from Marxist Mickey's harangues. In contrast, a significant younger crowd, mainly from the local art school, crowded around him with awed reverence. One Ball wondered if Marxist Mickey could have influenced his mother. After all,

One Ball had heard that some other locals, not just anarchic students, believed that he talked some sense.

As One Ball wrestled with such a possibility, he concluded that it was more likely that a deeper thinker than a Farnham street protester would radicalise his mother. Maybe it was somebody on her course. He just hoped that it wasn't the dreadful Peregrine, who only showed interest in himself and his appalling productions. Even though he had encouraged his mother to move out of his father's long shadow, he hadn't expected her to espouse such progressive values. This only made One Ball feel the necessity of being more independent. He became even more cautious about friendship and camaraderie. He was increasingly suspicious and vigilant. People would have to earn his trust. No one was going to bloody well blacken his ball again.

The days edged inexorably towards the end of term. On leaving the Music School after a demanding rehearsal with Root, Ryder bumped into Barrett in the middle of the Quadrangle. Immediately, the school's Lenin couldn't resist sharing his increasing disgust for the rich.

'They live by different rules, those people,' concluded Ryder.

'And the establishment shower honours on them like confetti,' added an aggrieved Barrett.

'Often unjustified honours,' proclaimed Ryder.

'Like the Order of the Bad Egg?' suggested Barrett.

'What's that Barrett?' queried Ryder

'That's what my Dad calls the OBE,' said Barrett with a twinkle in his eye.

'Very good Barrett. I like it,' declared a chuckling Ryder. 'It's a bit stupid to give an award named after an empire which no longer exists.'

'I suppose they had to find something suitably grand,' remarked Barrett.

'Some would say, suitably idiotic. Anyway, Barrett, Let me tell you about the programme for the summer concert,' confided Ryder.

As the two boys sauntered towards the Dining Hall, Ryder went through the various pieces, which included Jerusalem.

'Oh, well done. Brilliant!' exclaimed a delighted Barrett.

'It's replaced Land of Hope and Glory,' revealed Ryder.

'Thank God for that. It's a relic,' claimed Barrett.

'Unfortunately, a very popular relic,' admitted Ryder despondently.

'But one that you've managed to stop,' maintained Barrett.

'Thank you, Barrett. It's good to blow the imperial cobwebs away,' asserted Francis Vladimir Ryder.

The choir's leader then elaborated on the rest of the music, which at least reflected a less relentlessly Teutonic choice by the spiritually rejuvenated Root, who had to reluctantly abort his Missa solemnis ambitions. Ryder finished by informing his young protégé that the main musical event of the school year would end with a speech from Oliver. 'This is where we might become a little active,' divulged Ryder furtively. He then requested the school's baby Lenin to walk towards his house so that he could elaborate on his intentions.

The concert took place during a hot day in late June. As the audience made their way to their seats in Big Hall, the Major entered down the centre aisle with Victoria Wallace. When he'd recently announced their engagement, he mentioned that 'some of you thought that I'd never make it, didn't you?' The boys duly responded to this pronouncement with warm laughter and a rousing round of applause. Now, as the Major ushered Victoria to her seat, the James B fraternity, sitting in the front half of the auditorium, turned round and observed her arrival in an elegant mint green dress with predictable delight. The Major, smartly attired in a biscuit coloured suit, went to sit serenely with his fiancée. The couple were next to Sally, Mrs Hackett's daughter, who was with her redoubtable mother and her permanently disengaged father. Sally's cream lampshade hat, dramatically sailed over the heads of the nearby audience, like the Titanic over a rowing boat. Consequently, it wasn't clear how those behind her were going to see much of the ensuing proceedings.

Marian then made a discreet entrance but couldn't avoid catching the eye of the laconic Boot, the sugar-soiler of her bed. After she blanked him, Boot started laughing and whispered 'witch' under his breath to Binns, who squeezed his hands with glee. Oblivious to such abusive comments, Marian intentionally placed herself directly across the aisle from Killer, in one of the staff areas towards the middle of the hall. The junior housemaster, who was still furious at having to pay for the headstone, refused to acknowledge her. In contrast, Deirdre gave Marian a disdainful stare. The dreaded headstone was still in the garden and the Roys anticipated further removal costs from the intransigent Mr Trueman. Marian revelled in their discomfort. 'Everything comes at a price,' she thought cynically to herself, as she casually leafed through the programme.

Rev Elwyn in familiar clerical collar then entered with his sullen wife, who was attired in a brown lace dress. With Elwyn was Rupert, garbed in an ostentatious, orange and green striped Italian suit. The actor, who couldn't stop smiling as if he was permanently trying to engage an audience, sported an extravagant red handkerchief in the top pocket of his jacket. Rumour abounded that the Reverend Elwyn had been talking to Root and Rupert about their relationship. Rupert was currently 'resting' but still couldn't stop mentioning Terence Rattigan. The fact that the debonair playwright was becoming increasingly unfashionable after Look Back in Anger shook the theatrical establishment didn't seem to bother him. For Rupert, it was enough for 'Terry' to be established and famous. It seemed to boost his self-esteem to be associated with even a fading celebrity. For others, including Root, the Rattigan name-dropping became nauseatingly repetitive, like a record stuck permanently in a groove. Thankfully, the arrival of Pongo Smallman, waddling down the aisle resembling a penguin on patrol, stemmed the 'Terry' flow. The punctilious Pongo joined the audience, accompanied by his devoted friend Collins, who was still periodically rubbing his heart to aid his circulation. Pongo was thrilled that the 1st X1's successful season had elevated his position at the school. In fact, when the formidable Chuck Carson passed him before taking his seat, Pongo greeted him so effusively that the genial Ulsterman blushed profusely.

Meanwhile, more masters piled into the auditorium. Sykes, smartly attired in a blue suit, caught the eye of Sully, who was sitting with James B in front of some of the staff. Sykes reluctantly acknowledged the insolent boy, who when asked by him in his mock French oral as to which French speaking programmes he listened, impudently replied 'Radio Luxembourg!' Le Mesurier and Bayliss then followed. While Le Mesurier was yet again stressing the importance of languages when the country joined the Common Market, Bayliss looked disinterested. After all, the erstwhile theatre director had heard Le Mesurier's views on this subject even more times than the current Kit Kat advert. Eventually, the flamboyant Bayliss excused himself from the European enthusiast and went to sit next to the flaxen-haired, jaunty Rupert, who was with a sombre Rev Elwyn at the back of the hall.

Bayliss felt at ease speaking to performers. He loved their openness, humour, and commitment. There was a creative energy about them, which was seductive. Even their self-obsession was forgivable, when interwoven with gossip and acute perception. He found it a relief after the tedium of the school's bureaucracy and staff infighting. In fact, after what he regarded as his triumph with Henry V, he was seriously thinking of changing his career. However, he'd neither broached this aspiration to Mary nor had he any practical plan as how to achieve his directorial ambitions. Still, at least, he now had Sir Malcolm Sargent's telephone number. Surely, 'Flash Harry' would have some theatrical contacts? And maybe Rupert could get him to meet Terence Rattigan? After all, his beloved 'Terry' would know everybody. In the meantime, Bayliss, blithely ignoring the nearby cleric, became engrossed in Rupert's gossip about the deteriorating relationship between Laurence Olivier and Vivien Leigh, as more staff poured into the auditorium.

Darbishire entered with Bowen and his wife Sarah. The men had dressed for the occasion in light summer suits and Sarah was wearing a red dress, which enlivened her pallid features. Surreptitious schoolboy chuckling and murmurs of 'ok, all right', again confronted Darbishire. In trying to cure his affliction, the English teacher had finally resorted to seeing a psychotherapist, a severe Texan woman, who wore pointed cat-eye glasses and had a humorous bypass. This cerebral practitioner also used abstruse language that seemed to originate from some obscure, theoretical textbook. Nevertheless, for a short time, Darbishire's condition improved and 'ok, all right?' seemed to disappear from his vocabulary. Then, after a few months when he was under pressure, the phrase resurrected itself like an aquatic monster rising from the depths of the ocean. It seemed to be an essential part of his earnestness and desire to please. He knew that many in the school's community regarded him as a rugby playing thicko, who wasn't sufficiently on top of his subject, and in his desperation to prove them wrong, his impediment returned. As a result, Darbishire became more agitated and regretted paying the cat-eyed woman so much money.

In contrast, no one disputed Bowen's teaching ability, particularly with junior pupils, but the small Welshman had become increasingly worried about his future and got depressed. He was approaching retirement and feared that he and his family might not have enough money on which to live comfortably. His initial discussions with the school about his loyalty bonus hadn't gone well and he was drinking heavily. His wife Sarah's nursing experience had helped him to cope with his volatile moods but during the summer, when he wasn't coaching rugby, he became particularly gloomy. Still, he preserved a sociable veneer, genially acknowledging Smallman and Collins, before going to sit next to Sarah and Darbishire.

Suddenly, Basil Ponsonby-Smythe entered Big Hall with a white-suited Perceval, who'd kept a low profile since his controversial refereeing of the house rugby cup final. Basil, sporting a yellow bow tie, inevitably made his way to Bayliss and Rupert. The thespian was now holding forth about Lana Turner's tribulations with her husband, Lex 'Tarzan' Barker'. Basil wasn't so interested in Hollywood, theatre being his first love, so he didn't know much about either Miss Turner or her dramatic love life. He would have much preferred a more serious conversation about the respective merits of Olivier and Gielgud. Still, he had to admit that Lana forcing Tarzan out of the family home at gunpoint was luridly fascinating. While the theatricals gossiped away and Rev Elwyn and his wife listened with bemused fascination, Perceval, whose wife was had generously volunteered to babysit for Deirdre and Killer, appeared bothered and bewildered. He had never seen a Lana Turner film, although he knew that she was abrasively sexy. Consequently, he thought that it was best for him to keep quiet until the conversation diverted to something about which he was more familiar.

As the theatrical gossip went into overdrive and Perceval began to feel ignored and isolated, Oliver appeared with his family. He looked wan and exhausted, his grey suit exemplifying his mood. The blackening of One Ball had obviously taken its toll, especially since the school's Disciplinary Committee had already been critical of the headmaster's management. As the official enquiry hadn't yet started, the effects of the debacle were inevitably going to rumble on for some time. Nonetheless, Oliver's wife and fair-haired daughter maintained a pleasant countenance. They were both wearing white summer dresses. The wife's was plain and the daughter's embroidered with red roses. There was nothing ornate about Oliver and his family. They all politely said 'good evening,' chatted about the hot weather and then went decorously to take up their allotted seats near the front of the stage. On their departure, everybody looked to settle down for the concert.

However, just a few minutes before the start, a harassed Dr Meissner and his stout wife came rushing down the aisle. As they made their way to seats next to Killer and Deirdre, the doctor told them that he'd had to deal with a sudden increase of Asian flu patients. Meissner's news only confirmed Killer's relief that the term was coming to end, while Deirdre impulsively expressed concern about Barney catching the disease. Mrs Meissner, a friendly, talkative woman, wearing elegant horn-rimmed spectacles, reassured Mrs Killer that it was unlikely, given the child's relative isolation. A blushing Long John and an exhausted Endersby, followed the German couple. Fearing that they were late. they parked themselves surreptitiously in the back row, hoping that nobody had noticed their frenetic entrance. Long John, effervescent in a red jacket, abruptly plonked his stick under his seat and the chubby Endersby, sporting a caramel bow tie, leaned back gasping for breath. They both behaved more like guilty pupils than masters.

As they waited for the concert to start, the boys found ways to entertain themselves. Sully decided to extract an elastic band and a ball of paper from his pocket and discreetly catapulted Hayes. The aggrieved junior responded with an impetuous but carefully disguised V sign. Meanwhile, Brown and Bunter discreetly relished their Wrigley's chewing gum as they discussed the merits of the Everly Brothers. Barrett chose a more serious subject, the H Bomb, which the country had recently dropped over Christmas Island. He was against such testing and feared that it could accelerate a nuclear war. Boot disagreed and thought that the UK needed a deterrent, while Binns believed that there should be negotiations with the Soviet Union. As the juniors argued about how to deal with the threat of extinction, One Ball sat silently behind them with monitors Pound, Staines and Boring Beckett. As he ignored his colleagues' chat, his eyes veered across the aisle, only to discover Rutter complacently smiling at him. One Ball blanked his treacherous adversary and took refuge in pretending to read his programme.

The monitors' conversation centred on Beckett winning so many awards. The senior monitor had recently received one prize after another for some form of 'high academic achievement'. Although no one could doubt Beckett's incredible perseverance, one could be equally certain about his lack of imagination. His redoubtable memory was the reason for his success. For instance, he was always the first off the book in plays but he still gave one of the worst performances. Despite his efforts to be more spontaneous, his Duke of Exeter was so rigid that it became a walking monument. 'A performance cast in stone,' said one vituperative local critic. Yet, Beckett didn't seem to mind. He wasn't acting as an entrance to the profession, like the possessed Macready. He took the role to have the experience of speaking in public and being part of a community. When other boys teased him as being a 'three times Oscar winner', he just shrugged it off. He certainly enjoyed being appreciated but he didn't see the awards as being very meaningful, just small stepping stones on a longer journey.

This was the kind of maturity Beckett showed when he discovered the assaulted One Ball. Although he abhorred the violent attack, he thought that Potts had certainly flaunted his authority excessively and that the school had been too indifferent to the boys' concerns. When Beckett tried to talk to the vexed monitor about the origins of the conflict, he was met by a barrier of indifference. It was as if One Ball wanted to erase the assault from his mind and concentrate on the future. Sitting with his fellow monitors, James Potts said very little while remaining quietly aggressive. Beckett didn't believe that approach was going to help him. Beckett just hoped that he'd find the necessary redemption at Cambridge but he feared that similar confrontations would occur, unless he cultivated greater self-awareness.

As the monitors turned their conversation to the Major's forthcoming marriage, Rice, James B's rugby cup hero, was chatting to Barrel in the row behind them. Barrel was frustrated that after finally making emotional progress with Yvette, she was returning to France. He described it like finally getting a pass into the British Library and then discovering that it had closed. The resonance of metaphors wasn't Rice's strong point, he preferred statistics but he did his best to sympathise with Barrel's plight. When Rice told Barrel that France wasn't that far away and that it was possible to visit Yvette in the holidays, the Welsh boy froze as if the English Channel was an impenetrable barrier to l'amour. Just as Barrel was about to elaborate on his romantic difficulties, a round of applause rippled through the auditorium. It was for the arrival of the school orchestra, who like the rest of the boys were in their summer clothes: a dark blue blazer, white shirt, grey trousers and socks. After Jimmy Simmons, an oboist from Wade B with a serious reputation for pyjama parties, gave his colleagues an A, the orchestra replied and got tuned. The house lights then dimmed. The concert was about to start.

More applause engulfed the auditorium when Root, holding his baton, made a dramatic entrance to the conductor's podium. Wearing a white jacket to counter any feeling of formal stuffiness, he looked up at the ornate ceiling and bowed dramatically as if he was in the Royal Albert Hall. After Root raised his baton, the orchestra adjusted themselves to their positions and on his signal, a drumbeat started Johann Strauss Senior's Radetzky March. As the tune became familiar, Root turned round to the audience and encouraged them to clap in time, somewhat to Oliver's disapproval. At the end of the infectious but short piece, there was a swell of applause, mixed with cheers from some parts of the auditorium. It was as if intrusive football supporters rather than concertgoers had appreciated Strauss's attractive tune. Despite his annoyance with the perpetrators, dealing with cultural hoodlums wasn't at the top of Oliver's agenda. The assault on One Ball had seen to that.

After a short pause, Root led out the young soloist for Mozart's Clarinet Concerto. He was the only person of colour at the school. His name was Conrad Worrell, the son of a doctor who had immigrated from Barbados. The ever-smiling Root guided Conrad to the front of the stage, where he bowed in a restrained manner. You could hear a pin drop in the auditorium. There was a feeling that not many people had known that there was such a boy at the school. As far as those in James B were concerned, Wade A, at the end of the opposite side of the Avenue, could have been on the moon. Consequently, to Hayes, Sully, Barrett and co, the appearance of this particular soloist was a revelation.

Conrad shook hands with the leader of the orchestra, a boy called Billy Maxwell, who came from Bradford and was a tiddlywinks champion. Conrad then looked at Root and gave him an apprehensive smile, followed by a nod. Root grinned back, turned to the orchestra and raised his baton. As Conrad listened to the opening introduction, he fidgeted and looked nervous. However, as his entrance approached he seemed to gather focus and concentration. He started with a fluency that gave him confidence and led to a delightful conversation with the orchestra. There was the odd wrong note but his sense of rhythm was impressive. After the orchestra finished the first movement, Root looked at Conrad like a benign father encouraging his son to continue the good work. When Conrad lifted his clarinet, Root cued in the start of the start of the slow second movement. Conrad then played with a touching sensitivity, which complemented Mozart's delicacy. Even though the music dragged at times, Conrad's natural talent won over the audience. There then followed a much shorter pause before the final movement. Root again looked at Conrad supportively and away they went. Conrad seemed to be more at home with the faster, breezy rondo allegro. There was a real swinging, rhythmic pulse to his playing, which inspired both orchestra and soloist to create a compelling dynamic. It was if they were both pushing each other to be more daring. Occasionally the tempo became ragged but no one could doubt their youthful exuberance, as Conrad and the orchestra climaxed with compelling intensity.

On the concerto's completion, the whole audience burst into rhapsodic applause. Macready, who was sitting with Tickle A, histrionically shouted 'Bravo! Bravo!' while Brown and Bunter got to their feet whistling. Others followed, as Root signalled for the whole orchestra to rise and for Conrad to come forward and take a separate bow. As he did so modestly, the audience cheered him ecstatically. Root then let Conrad enjoy the applause on his own before they left the stage together. Conductor and soloist then returned five times to acknowledge the incessant clapping, cheering and whistling. When they finally departed, the ever-vigilant O'Reilly turned on the house lights for the interval.

As the audience lingered in the Quadrangle, the talk was all about Conrad. Oliver in particular felt that it was an historic moment, seeing such an immigrant boy succeed so triumphantly at the school. He was delighted that it had happened on his watch. After all, he deserved some good news, given his current tribulations. He just hoped it would bolster his position with the trustees. He certainly needed some evidence of progress as he was fearful that after the most recent insurrection, they would recommend dismissal for negligence and that the council would just rubber stamp their judgement.

At a short distance from Oliver's fateful ruminations, Rupert was wandering around, enjoying the cool summer evening. However, Bayliss abruptly interrupted his stroll with a request for Terence Rattigan's phone number. After Rupert reluctantly obliged, an observant Macready also charged over to the actor. The nascent thespian wanted advice about agents, regardless of not having gone to drama school. When Rupert made some suggestions, Macready eagerly produced a mangled biro and scrunched paper from the inside pocket of his blazer. He then asked Rupert to repeat the names, which the ambitious artiste frantically scribbled down. After such badgering, Rupert was relieved when O'Reilly entered the Quadrangle, ringing a large bell and shouting like an exultant town crier that the concert would restart in two minutes. Rupert used this interruption to extricate himself from the surrounding theatrical aspirants and walk back to the auditorium with Dr Meissner and his wife. While doing so, he enjoyed sharing his enthusiasm for Conrad's inspiring performance. On retaking his seat, Rupert reflected that it was absurd that he had become a fount of theatrical wisdom. After all, he was finding it hard to get a job himself.

Once the orchestra returned and retuned, the audience settled, the lights came down and Root returned to the stage, bouncing along with amplified energy. It was as if he'd become pharmaceutically enhanced. As he acknowledged the applause, the conductor revelled in the waves of appreciation coming towards him. Such affection inspired him to turn energetically to the orchestra and attack Gustav Holst's The Planets with verve. In fact, Root started conducting with such ferocity that it looked as if he might have a heart attack. His black hair was flouncing so dramatically to every rhythmic beat of Mars, the Bringer of War, that by the time he came to the climax, he appeared completely deranged. Brown loved it and whispered to Bunter that 'this Holst really rocks'. At the end of the first movement, after such manic intensity, Root took out a purple handkerchief from the top pocket of his jacket and dabbed his sweaty forehead. Once he felt that he'd revived, he raised his baton and continued with Venus the Bringer of Peace. This produced a couple of late entries from both the violin and horn sections but Root was now suitably relaxed to let the serenity of the music transcend imperfection. After bringing a playful vitality to Mercury, the Winged Messenger, the orchestra launched vigorously into Jupiter, the Bringer of Jollity.

However, Ryder, watching with the other choristers at the back of the auditorium, felt uncomfortable with the I Vow to Thee My Country section, mumbling intensely 'what type of bloody country are we talking about?' Root then milked Saturn the Bringer of Old Age. Like one of his previous Nazi rallies, he seemed to control the orchestra so rigidly that the music couldn't breathe and the movement took an eternity to end. In contrast, when he came to the Uranus the Magician, it was as if the conductor had taken a stimulant. He loosened his approach and encouraged the young orchestra to play with a powerful, rumbustious invention. The final movement Neptune the Mystic cast a hypnotic spell, while surviving some infectious coughing in the auditorium and various false notes. The finale was particularly moving as Root had strategically placed the choir's trebles far away, in the reception area outside the auditorium, so their song was poignantly transcendental. After the final notes drifted into the ether, the applause rang enthusiastically around the auditorium. Root immediately invited the trebles to come on stage, after which he signalled for the orchestra to rise. He then took four separate bows while the audience cheered the conductor, orchestra and the singers to the rafters. It was a generous appreciation of a significant achievement.

After Root disappeared backstage for the final time, indulging in a triumphant wave to the audience, Ryder led the choir into their position, standing on raised rostra behind the orchestra. He had been waiting for this moment. After all, Jerusalem offered a searing vision of aspiration towards a more just society that the Holst piece lacked. Consequently, Ryder wanted Parry's rousing tune and Blake's prophetic words to be an inspiration to a better socialist future. He was determined to leave his own signature on the school's music.

After a significant pause, Root reappeared. Having meticulously combed his hair, he no longer looked like a crazed Einstein. Sleek and smart, Root bowed obsequiously to the audience, smiled and turned round to face the orchestra and the choir. He then signalled to start the short instrumental introduction. When that finished, Root looked heavenwards and cued in the choir, who responded very robustly. Their singing reached such a fervent intensity that by the time they came to

‘And was Jerusalem builded here among these dark satanic mills’, Oliver feared that some of the boys would break a blood vessel. The headmaster liked the song but was concerned that the content was a portent of some profound change. He would have preferred a rendition of Land of Hope and Glory, especially after the recent traumatic scandal. He suspected Ryder’s influence in the choice, which only accentuated Oliver’s relief that it wouldn’t be long before the school’s Lenin would be propagating his guile and duplicity elsewhere.

As Jerusalem proceeded, Root became increasingly histrionic in his conducting. When the choir reached ‘Bring me my bow of burning gold: Bring me my arrows of desire’, one feared that he might fall off his podium. Blake’s idealistic vision seemed to have driven him into a hypnotic trance that had propelled him into an alternative state. Thankfully, just as he swung his baton with further anarchic abandon, he became aware that his feet had reached the limits of his podium, which was close to the edge of the stage. For a second, he looked at the floor below like a mountaineer staring at a fatal descent. Rapidly, he miraculously propelled himself back from the brink, while still ferociously waving his baton. He precariously managed to regain a stable position and encourage the choir to sing the climactic, ‘Till we have built Jerusalem, In England’s green and pleasant land’ as if their lives depended on it. When the choir and orchestra finished dramatically together, thunderous applause broke out, followed by stamping in the style of the Promenade concerts. Ryder, standing at the end of the choir’s tenor section, looked smug. In fact, Oliver thought that he detected a facetious grin on his face.

In the meantime, Root savoured the riotous applause, bowing incessantly and wiping his face with his drenched monogrammed handkerchief. After taking five bows with the orchestra and choir, Root turned to the audience and asked them if they were ready to sing, to which they yelled back an emphatic ‘yes!’ Under duress from Ryder, Mr Sims had already made sure that Blake’s poem appeared in the programme, so the lyrics were readily available to everybody.

Sims, who was sitting next to his fiancée, the willowy, blonde-haired Beth, became increasingly concerned that Root, intoxicated by the audience's euphoria, would make a fool of himself. He feared that the music master saw himself as Sir Malcolm 'Flash Harry' Sargent conducting the last night of the Proms. As the conductor turned to the orchestra and started the encore, Beth got a fit of the giggles. She whispered to Sims that Root's frenzied physical intensity reminded her of Hitler. Sims then also started to get hysterical, which led to disapproving looks from an intimidating Sykes and a glowering Mrs Hackett, whose disinterested husband was once again falling asleep. As the encore reached its climax, the possessed Root waved his baton towards the audience with heavy dramatic strokes, encouraging them to give everything. They duly responded with such a loud intensity that Oliver feared for the security of the Gothic windows.

Riotous applause greeted the end of Jerusalem. All the boys stood up shouting, whistling and stamping, with the occasional 'bravo' thrown in for good measure. Reluctantly, the masters followed suit like inane sheep, as Root embraced the audience's applause like they were a long lost lover. He then raised his hands upwards, insisting that the orchestra stand up. When they all got to their feet, there was a massive cheer. Root then spread his arms dramatically towards the rostra, acknowledging the choir, who received further acclamation. The appreciation remained in this vein for several more minutes, with Root continually leaving and returning to the stage. He relished every moment, smiling all the time with a childish grin, while wiping sweat away from his fevered brow as if he'd just travelled through a desert. Eventually, after making a dramatic gesture to his heart, which he'd probably copied from one of his favourite Teutonic maestros, he pressed his hands down, requesting everybody to sit. While the audience settled, Root collapsed on a chair, conveniently placed at the back of the first violins. He realised that he'd been too easily transported by the occasion, so he furtively retreated into a meditative cocoon. Meanwhile, as Root searched for spiritual calm, Oliver clambered up the steps at the front of the stage and faced the audience.

The thought of Oliver making a speech after the words of William Blake was an example of how mundanity can sometimes follow genius. He was a poor speaker, who lacked variety in his vocal delivery and droned on monotonously like a British Rail announcement. However, although he had as much charisma as a battered dustbin, a basic decency and sincerity usually emerged from his orations and helped him survive his inept performances.

Oliver started by congratulating Root, the orchestra, the choir and of course Conrad. He then began his formal speech by speaking about Britain and her important role in the war. He proclaimed that as the boys were the beneficiaries of the welfare state, they now they had the opportunity to make society better. He believed that those leaving should particularly focus their minds in terms of what they could contribute. Oliver's egalitarian opening remarks surprised Ryder, who with the rest of the choir were now seated on the rostra. However, it wasn't long before the headmaster progressed to a more nationalistic agenda. He talked about the great contribution the country had made to civilisation through the industrial revolution, its empire, leadership of the Commonwealth, its role in two world wars and how such a background should inspire the boys to great achievements. Ryder's mood abruptly changed to anger as Oliver ignored the more controversial parts of his cleansed narrative.

While the headmaster was making his speech, interspersed with quotes from Shakespeare and Winston Churchill, a strange odour emanated from the stage. Even such a nauseating smell, didn't stop Oliver from developing his committed thesis, which had now moved on to the value of British sport and its importance to the school. As Darbishire and Bowen nodded in approval, Macready looked on with disgust. He hated games and preferred to work for the pacifist Public Services Group. Nonetheless, Oliver ploughed on with his speech, describing how Britain had given cricket, rugby and football to the world. When he tried to make a sporting analogy about how a society should work by stating that 'we all need our goalkeepers and centre halves to keep society stable', Le Mesurier despaired of such naivety. He wanted a more sophisticated analysis of the country's future, not just a regurgitation of the past but something more international and visionary. Although Sykes concurred with Oliver's feelings of national pride, he looked embarrassed by the simplicity of the metaphor. Meanwhile, Darbishire and Bowen, were also disappointed that Oliver referred to football when he was running a rugby school. In fact, Bowen had heard rumours that Oliver was really a closet Arsenal supporter and had been seen hob-knobbing in the directors' box at Highbury. Regrettably, Oliver's facile figures of speech didn't stop him from further tropes as he referred to how he saw the school as 'one family'. He believed that such solid bonds would 'help us overcome any temporary local difficulty'.

As Oliver obliquely mentioned the blackening of One Ball, the fumigation became particularly unbearable. The headmaster started coughing as did several members of the choir, including an aghast Sully, who said 'poo' very loudly. When Oliver tried to continue his speech, others also became rapidly affected by the unpleasant reek. Root suddenly awakened from his pensive reverie and placed his soaked handkerchief over his face. Bayliss also found the smell increasingly irritating and diplomatically asked Rupert if he'd farted. The proud actor took considerable exception to this accusation and the Rev Elwyn had to quieten things down with a holy intervention. Marian perceptively thought that it was a plant and efficiently dispersed any remnant of the unpleasant aroma with a small air freshener, which she'd installed in her bag to combat such an emergency. This freed her to watch indifferently the discomfort of Mr and Mrs Killer, who were periodically coughing and waving their programme around their faces.

While Oliver painted his rosy patriotic picture, it was clear that he was struggling. There were several pauses to accommodate his discomfort as the stink began to overpower him. Still, he was resolutely determined to continue and exemplify the bulldog spirit of the British character, about which he was so earnestly evangelising. In contrast, Boot and Binns started holding their noses and pulling an imaginary chain, as they muttered 'what a stink!' Meanwhile, Rutter mouthed a distracted 'whiffy!' before placing a white handkerchief across his face, pretending that he had a cold.

Dr Meissner took a more scientific approach and tried to analyse the smell but had found it hard to come to any conclusion, especially as his thinking process was impaired by the power of the stench. Mrs Meissner had a habit of continually eating fruit and occasionally she put peel away in unexpected places. Consequently, she started rummaging urgently through her handbag, but much to her relief she found nothing suspiciously odorous. As she extracted a yellow handkerchief to cover her mouth and nose, she pronounced herself not guilty. Elsewhere, the Major was sure that he hadn't farted and he certainly wasn't going to ask his fiancée if she'd experienced any flatulence. He suspected some form of sabotage and hoped that Oliver would stop his increasingly rambling speech.

Meanwhile, Smallman and Collins were bewildered by the malodour and becoming very uncomfortable. In fact, Collins was feeling ill and Smallman became concerned about his friend's welfare, given his poor health. During Oliver's address, Mrs Hackett had forcibly alerted her dozing husband to a 'ghastly pong', while Sally implored her parents to leave the stinking hall instantly. Eventually, Oliver decided to curtail his speech, abruptly concluding by wishing leavers the best of luck and everybody an enjoyable summer holiday. As a postscript, Oliver commented on the suffocating smell and reluctantly instigated an immediate exit. Consequently, his lengthy speech only received a splattering of lukewarm applause.

Oliver and his family left in haste with the rest of the asphyxiated audience. The beleaguered headmaster now foresaw his doom when the trustees learned of another uprising On exiting Big Hall with his family, Oliver bumped into the mischievous O'Reilly guarding the main entrance. Between coughs, he told him to look into the cause of the awful smell.

'I will do sir. Nice speech if I may say so,' said O'Reilly ingratiatingly, while using his linen handkerchief to combat the dreadful tang.

'Oh, thank you, O'Reilly,' acknowledged Oliver, grateful for at least one positive response.

The headmaster then ushered his family out of Big Hall and into the Quadrangle. As the boys followed him, Barrett, who'd been observing events with a strategic eye, came over to O'Reilly. He had a protective scarf wrapped over his face, which made him look like a formidable terrorist. When O' Reilly saw this alarming vision he moved discreetly away from the entrance, to avoid the departing audience hearing any scandalous revelations.

'Thanks O'Reilly,' Barrett whispered, 'it worked a treat.'

'Didn't it? The timing was great. I got under the stage before Jerusalem to open all those stink bottles,' revealed O'Reilly in a conspiratorial tone.

'Will you get rid of them soon?' asked Barrett anxiously.

'That'll be part of my usual clearing up operation,' muttered O'Reilly furtively.

'Oh, I see,' replied an impressed Barrett.

'Before I leave,' disclosed O'Reilly, 'I'll take them away and get rid of everything with my own rubbish. Just in case there's an official investigation and they look through the school bins.'

At the end of the caretaker's ingenious explanation, Barrett was about to leave when Ryder appeared with his scarf protectively entwined around his face. The school's Lenin looked less a man of the people and more of a smooth, manipulative Mr Big, revelling in the success of his plan while others did the work.

'Thanks O'Reilly,' Ryder murmured softly,' I loved the way the stink started to rise just as Oliver was rambling on about the British Empire.'

'I found that bit particularly bloody offensive. There was no mention of Ireland's colonisation,' protested O'Reilly vehemently.

'Nor the Amritsar or Malayan massacres,' added an outraged Ryder.

'Nor recent atrocities in Kenya or the Suez debacle,' stressed Barrett, not wanting to be outdone.

'History as written by the powerful. But then we Irish are used to being an afterthought in the British narrative. But our time will come,' prophesied O'Reilly slyly. 'Anyway, boys, I can't keep doing such stuff. You played mercilessly upon my republican instincts.'

'We really appreciate it O'Reilly,' said Barrett.

'So you bloody should,' exclaimed the caretaker adamantly.

‘All changed, changed utterly, a terrible school is destroyed,’ recited Ryder in a poetic tenor voice.

‘That’s enough of that. Away with you,’ retorted O’Reilly dismissively.

‘Irish poetry, O’Reilly,’ insisted Ryder.

‘Bugger off!’ exclaimed the indignant Irishman.

The two boys left Big Hall laughing and waving at O’Reilly, before disappearing into the darkening summer night. As they were the last to leave, O’ Reilly locked the door and went back into the auditorium. After putting away his hanky, the caretaker put on a black mask that he used for refuse collection. He then gathered the dishevelled programmes, chewing gum, sweet wrappings and elastic bands from around the seats. Having deposited the rubbish into a bag, he descended under the stage. On his arrival, he proceeded to meticulously restore the surrounding plastic tops onto a plethora of ammonia bottles, which lay amidst that dark, subterranean, theatrical underworld. When he’d finally transferred them all into several large bags, he covered them with the general refuse. After closing the gaps under the stage that he’d created for the fumigation to transport itself easily to the audience, he emerged defiantly into the deserted auditorium. Next, O’Reilly carried the bags to the entrance, whistling cheerfully with a look of nonchalant innocence. At the threshold, he put the mask in his pocket, turned off the lights, opened and locked the large door, before looking carefully left and right like a master criminal anticipating possible confrontation. Once O’Reilly had established that the coast was clear, he walked at an even pace towards his pickup truck, which he’d parked at the back of Big Hall. He then hauled the bags onto the back of the vehicle, which was conveniently provided by the school, got into the cab and started to depart. ‘Not 1916 exactly but at least a prick on the British establishment’s posterior,’ reflected O’Reilly, while driving down Open Way. ‘The family would be proud,’ he persuaded himself as he started singing a song of Irish rebellion.

One Ball reclined in his bath as superciliously as ever. He believed that he’d fully recovered from the unjust assault. He no longer needed to listen to either Killer’s paternal advice or Dr

Orban's views about irrational thoughts. Now, he was off his medication and ready to make sure that his detractors wouldn't humiliate him again. The final days of the term gave him complete freedom to flex his muscles. He'd become newly invigorated and was going to fully relish his authority before the boys broke up and he left the school forever.

'Squit!' he yelled as he lathered his arms self-consciously with Palmolive soap. 'Squit!' he shouted again, so he could penetrate the lav end doors.

Eventually, Hayes answered the monitor's screeching.

'Yes Potts? enquired Hayes with feigned naivety.

'Have you packed everything?' asked One Ball forcefully.

'I think so, Potts,' said Hayes vaguely.

'What about stuff here in the settle?' challenged a relentless One Ball.

'Oh right. I'll do that,' agreed Hayes reluctantly.

'Come on Hayes. No slacking,' yelled the demanding One Ball, who was now washing his chest with a blue flannel.

Hayes quickly gathered all the items in the settle and placed them in a trunk, next to One Ball's bed in the senior dormitory. He then returned to the lav end to confirm that everything was packed.

'All right, squit, take the trunk downstairs. Leave it in the corridor, ready for collection.' As Hayes was about to depart, One Ball suddenly called him back. 'Just one thing, Hayes,' shouted One Ball.

'Yes, Potts?' responded Hayes warily.

'Who put those stink bombs under the stage?' demanded One Ball.

'O'Reilly says it was the smell of a dead animal,' reported Hayes.

'Rubbish. That certainly was not the smell of an animal,' refuted an outraged One Ball

'Well, apparently a lot of rats got under the stage,' mentioned Hayes, casually putting his hands in the pockets of his short grey trousers.

'Who said that?' countered One Ball, angered by Hayes's disrespectful posture.

'O'Reilly,' revealed Hayes nonchalantly.

'For God's sake Hayes, that bloody Irishman has a complete disconnection with the truth,' proclaimed One Ball.

'Perhaps he should become a politician,' joked Hayes, attempting to bring levity into the conversation.

'Hayes, O'Reilly is a professional rebel. He couldn't organise a..' One Ball stuttered, lost for words.

'A piss up in a brewery?' suggested Hayes.

'No, unfortunately he'd be rather good at that, given his extracurricular habits,' declared a frustrated One Ball, consciously displaying his muscular chest to the younger boy. 'No, Hayes, O' Reilly has a pathological dislike of the British establishment,' maintained One Ball.

'He's good at his job,' claimed Hayes, who had affection for the Irishman's pranks.

'He needs to be; otherwise he would have been sacked ages ago. He's like a bloody rash on the body of the school,' claimed One Ball, swishing his towel either side of his remaining ball.

'Well at least he's a rather good painter,' divulged Hayes, publicising the Irishman's recently discovered talent.

'Who told you that?' replied One Ball dismissively.

'Rutter,' disclosed Hayes.

'Rutter! What does that bloody dwarf know about painting, apart from the decoration of school toilets?' yelled One Ball maliciously.

'I don't think he's a dwarf, Potts,' said Hayes, challenging One Ball's derogatory description.

'Well he is to me,' emphasised One Ball with a withering stare.

'Anyway, Rutter saw O'Reilly when he was on a walk, painting a picture in a field,' remarked Hayes, diverting One Ball from his innate prejudice.

'He's not paid to be Picasso,' stated One Ball.

'I think O'Reilly is more interested in landscape painting,' specified Hayes.

'Whatever. He's my main suspect for the stink bomb affair. As soon as Oliver mentioned the British Empire, the place began to poo to high heaven. That's the work of a skilful, rebellious plotter,' reiterated One Ball, dramatically discarding his towel and momentarily appearing stark naked, before putting on his white underpants and shirt. 'Oliver might not be the greatest speaker,' continued One Ball, having initially clothed himself to his satisfaction, 'but we're currently in a cold war and to ridicule our history in such a manner was contemptible.'

'It probably was the rats,' presumed Hayes.

'Nonsense, Hayes. That odour didn't smell like dead rats,' affirmed One Ball vigorously.

'Are you familiar with a rats' smell, Potts?' asked Hayes impertinently.

'No, but I know the smell of a stink bomb,' asserted an obstinate One Ball, pulling up his long grey trousers.

'Did you plant one yourself, Potts? enquired Hayes cynically.

'No I didn't Hayes but somebody let one off during assembly at my primary school. Miss Russell, the headmistress, went berserk,' clarified One Ball.

'You make O'Reilly sound like Guy Fawkes, Potts,' commented Hayes.

'He could be more efficient than Guy Fawkes,' contended One Ball, dramatically fastening the final buttons of his trousers. 'Look at those bombs going off around the border in Ireland.'

'O'Reilly isn't a member of the IRA. That's too far-fetched,' reacted Hayes incredulously.

'How do you know?' questioned One Ball, sitting on his settle, momentarily staring at Hayes before putting on his ashen socks.

'So are you going to tell the Major of your suspicions?' enquired Hayes.

'No, I'm not. I'm leaving in twenty-four hours. They can sort it out themselves,' pronounced One Ball bitterly. 'I've given up on the Major. Anyway, it's only a hunch but instincts can be right.'

One Ball got his wooden shoehorn out of his settle. He then started to put on his shiny black shoes while Hayes remained in the lav end, indifferently observing the ritual, looking for an opportune moment to leave.

‘You did a good job with the shoes, Hayes,’ admitted One Ball, supposedly looking at his own reflection in the toecaps.

‘Thank you, Potts,’ responded Hayes, disinterestedly accepting the compliment.

‘Better than Sully but then that wouldn’t be hard,’ judged One Ball.

Hayes refused to be drawn into criticism of his reinvigorated friend, so a tense silence ensued as One Ball finished putting on his shoes. When Hayes tried to depart, One Ball immediately stopped him.

‘Wait, Hayes. Tell me one thing. Who were you?’ pressed One Ball, as he got up from his settle.

‘What do you mean, Potts?’ queried Hayes, turning his head away from the monitor.

James Potts checked that he was comfortable in his shoes and then vainly stared at himself in the mirror, before turning to Hayes.

‘Which mask were you wearing, I wasn’t sure?’ resumed One Ball, while extracting a black comb from his blazer, which was hanging on one of the clothes pegs next to the settle.

Hayes was reluctant to reply but decided that if he didn’t, One Ball might resort to more primitive methods to get an answer.

‘I was ‘Princess Margaret’ Potts,’ confessed Hayes.

‘I thought so, Hayes. You not only denigrated royalty but abused me, you cruel bastard,’ accused One Ball, while rigorously combing his crinkly locks.

‘You were cruel to Sully, Potts. Everybody agreed about that,’ highlighted Hayes, resolutely confronting One Ball’s vitriol.

‘People were bloody cruel to me,’ snapped One Ball, as he continued his robust combing. ‘Rough kids at my primary school turned on me. They thought I was too posh and that I’d stolen some cigarette cards. They threatened me. I was terrified and ran out of the playground. When I reached an alleyway, they cornered me. I panicked. I tried to climb over a wall but lost my balance and fell across barbed wire. I cried in agony. Blood was everywhere. That cowardly bunch fled, while I was trapped bleeding on the wire for what seemed like an eternity.

Eventually, an ambulance arrived. Now I only have one bloody ball and you and your mob covered it with black polish to humiliate me again. You hung me up like a pig in a slaughterhouse, you bloody bastards,' screamed One Ball, completing his combing and turning round from the mirror to vent his spleen directly at his traitorous squit.

Hayes was becoming increasingly fearful of One Ball. He'd emerged from his treatment more angry, bitter and defiant. Despite Potts's childhood trauma, Hayes was determined to stand up to his vengeful barrage. He resorted to trusting his instinct for justice.

'You still didn't have to punish Sully for nothing,' said Hayes resolutely. 'You used fancy phrases to mask your cruelty. You relentlessly bullied him until he was a gibbering wreck. You offered him hope of a reprieve if he spied on Rutter and Françoise. When he failed, you punished him further because of your jealous anger. You wanted to condemn Sully forever. When he looked for help, he was refused. He had nowhere to turn. Nobody would listen, so he appealed to us. We had to defend him from your cruelty. We had no choice. We gave him the courage to resist.'

'Shut up Hayes!' yelled One Ball, glaring menacingly at the insubordinate junior. 'I did my duty.'

'You go on about duty. What does it mean Potts?' demanded Hayes, who refused to buckle and defiantly eyeballed the irate monitor.

'I'll tell you what it means. It means being efficient not careless,' declaimed a fiery One Ball. 'It means being on time and not late. It means being disciplined and not negligent. It means achieving standards and not being lazy. It means being honest not deceitful. It means being independent and not just reliant on others. Above all, it means order not anarchy. All I did was what the school wanted. That's all.'

'Sully was vulnerable,' retorted Hayes. 'You abused him until he was totally demoralised.'

'We're all vulnerable, Hayes,' claimed One Ball angrily. 'I'm bloody vulnerable. My father, whom I adored but hardly knew, had a brainstorm and got killed. My family collapsed. My mother struggled to start a new life. I've lost a bloody ball. But this place is meant to teach you how to deal with all that. Self-reliance can't be conjured out of thin air, Hayes. You need to learn it and be prepared for living in that bloody jungle out there.'

One Ball finished his angry invective with a departure to the urinals. While he waited for him to return, Hayes remembered the rumours that in order to sustain his recovery, Dr Orban had encouraged his patient not to withhold his anger rather than remain an introverted recluse. Obviously, One Ball had been unleashed. Hayes just hoped that he wouldn't expand his vitriol and outdo the operatic climaxes manifested in the music of his beloved Wagner. He was alarmed that somebody as disturbed as One Ball was likely to rise to the highest echelons of the establishment. Thankfully, the sight of the disgruntled monitor returning from the lavatory, self-consciously zipping up his flies, interrupted such alarming thoughts.

'Did you brush my blazer, Hayes?' queried a seething One Ball, still angered by Hayes's criticism.

'Yes Potts, I did,' confirmed Hayes wearily, eager to extricate himself from the belligerent monitor.

'Good,' acknowledged One Ball, who then moved towards the dark blue blazer, with its silver crest adorning its top pocket. He removed the hanger from the peg and inspected Hayes's work with meticulous rigour. Although he looked at the blazer with relentless intensity, he was unable to find any blemish. This frustrated One Ball as he desperately wanted to pour further vitriol on the cruel conspirator. Unfortunately, he reluctantly had to concede defeat and return the blazer to the peg.

'I must admit Hayes, that overall you're not a bad squit.'

'Thank you, Potts,' stated Hayes blankly.

'I'll miss your work, Hayes,' admitted One Ball.

'Maybe you'll have to be more self-reliant,' challenged Hayes facetiously.

'Yes, I will,' accepted One Ball obstinately 'and I'll manage Hayes, you'll see, I'll bloody manage,' he reiterated emphatically.

One Ball was now looking intensely at his squit, while struggling to resist the temptation to instigate another aria about individual survival. Eventually, he managed to change the subject.

'How's your mother?' he asked casually.

'She's well,' responded Hayes automatically.

'Nice woman. How's the music teaching? mentioned One Ball.

'She's got a lot of private pupils now,' Hayes asserted proudly.

'Good. And your sister?' pursued One Ball.

'She has a very active social life'. I can't keep pace with it,' remarked Hayes with a slight giggle.

'I see,' pondered One Ball, with the vaguest hint of a smile. 'Is she against nuclear armament?' he enquired more gravely.

'Maybe, I'm not sure,' replied Hayes vaguely.

'Well, remind her that we still need a deterrent to stop those Soviets,' insisted One Ball.

'All right,' agreed Hayes, while not intending to inform Poppy of any such conservative views. 'Anyway, how's your mother?' he reciprocated, consciously avoiding further discussion about his sister's political beliefs.

'She's got a new beau, thank God. A divorcee, on her course. She's not on my back so much,' disclosed a relieved One Ball

'Good. She must be happy,' suggested Hayes sympathetically.

'I suppose so,' thought One Ball.

The monitor then proceeded to take his cravat from one of the pegs and fastidiously tie it around his neck. He always liked to look his best for meals.

'Squit. Do a check to make sure I haven't forgotten anything,' ordered One Ball peremptorily as he completed his necktie ritual.

Hayes looked cursorily on the pegs, the floor, the top of the elongated basin, in the urinals and lavatory. There was no evidence of any of One Ball's belongings. Finally, he opened the settle and discovered a packet of durex lying unopened.

'The Johnnies must have fallen out of the Bible, Potts,' concluded Hayes.

'Not so loud, squit!' whispered One Ball, turning round from the mirror where he'd been admiring the deterioration of his acne.'

'You didn't use them?' suggested Hayes slyly.

'No, I didn't,' countered One Ball defensively.

'Can I ask why not, Potts?' probed Hayes mischievously.

'No, you bloody can't,' proclaimed One Ball indignantly.

'It wasn't because of Françoise, was it?' mentioned a roguish Hayes.

'No, of course not,' denied One Ball.

'You played tennis with her,' cited Hayes.

'How do you know that?' exclaimed a shocked One Ball, suddenly turning round, after popping an aggravating pimple.

'Everybody does,' divulged Hayes casually.

'This place is more scandalous than Tit-Bits!' exclaimed an affronted One Ball.

'So you had no luck?' indicated Hayes impertinently.

'I was betrayed by not only that French woman but bloody Rutter,' maintained a vengeful One Ball.

'So you didn't use the Johnnies?' asked Hayes, cheekily looking for corroboration,

'No, Hayes, I did not use the Johnnies,' confirmed an increasingly incensed One Ball.

'What shall I do with them then?' enquired Hayes insolently. 'I mean it says here that they're guaranteed until 1961. So you've still got quite a few years to use them.'

'Pack them, squit. As you should have done already,' decreed One Ball impatiently.

Just as Hayes was about to open the lav end door to start entering the dormitory, One Ball called him back.

'You can't take them like that!' yelled a distressed One Ball.

'What do you mean?' questioned a bewildered Hayes.

'Wrap them up, now the Bible's packed,' instructed One Ball. 'I don't want them exposed to all and sundry.'

'But no one is here,' reasoned Hayes.

'Someone might come in, like Killer for instance,' feared an apprehensive One Ball.

‘Maybe you could give them to him. He might need them when he’s visiting the Witch of Wigan!’ exclaimed Hayes, laughing hysterically.

‘Stop it, Hayes. I know the end of term is often a time for levity but just wrap up the bloody Johnnies,’ dictated One Ball urgently.

Hayes paused to control his mirth. He then went into the lavatory and wrapped up the Johnnies in the finest of bog paper. When he came out, he proudly presented his artistic handiwork.

‘I think this will do, Potts,’ said Hayes, thrusting the wrapped Johnnies towards One Ball.

‘I suppose so,’ conceded One Ball grimly.

‘Well, Potts. Good luck,’ uttered Hayes perfunctorily.

‘Not so fast. Remember the trunk, squit,’ declared One Ball, reminding him of his duty to the last.

‘I will. I’ll collect it after tea and put out it for collection,’ Hayes reassured him.

‘Maybe, you can get one of your conspirators to help you,’ suggested One Ball bitterly.

‘I will,’ verified Hayes cheerily.

‘Who will it be ‘The Queen’ or perhaps ‘The Duke of Edinburgh’?’ queried a cynical One Ball.

‘Probably ‘Lord Home,’ proposed Hayes jocularly, thinking that the lanky Boot would be a suitable removal man.

‘Not the brightest in the cabinet,’ commented One Ball.

‘But a good lifter,’ enthused Hayes.

‘Let’s hope so,’ responded a sceptical One Ball.

‘Ok Potts. I might not see you tomorrow, as I’m off early to catch the train. So I’ll say goodbye now. Who knows when we’ll meet again?’ posed Hayes, echoing the celebrated song.

‘Yes. Who knows? reiterated One Ball evasively.

‘Good luck, Potts,’ said Hayes in a dull tone.

‘Good luck Hayes,’ repeated One Ball blandly.

Hayes then opened the door but just as he was to leave, One Ball stopped him again, whispering urgently.

‘Don’t forget to pack the Johnnies.’

‘I haven’t forgotten. Potts. I’m going to pack them now,’ answered Hayes tersely.

'Just checking. I don't want to leave amidst any further controversy,' emphasised One Ball, still wanting to keep his status despite his disillusionment with the school.

'Don't worry One Ball, I mean Potts, I'll pack the Johnnies,' assured Hayes, looking to alleviate his semantic deviation.

'You'd bloody better, squit,' insisted One Ball, relishing Hayes's position of servitude with venom.

After his linguistic aberration, Hayes left swiftly, and deposited the Johnnies in One Ball's brown trunk, next to his treasured LP of Tristan and Isolde. He locked the trunk with JP embossed on its front and as arranged put the key in the settle next to One Ball's bed. He then exited the dormitory and quickly went downstairs. He couldn't wait to finish being a squit and carrying out submissive duties. He just wanted to see his mother and Poppy and go on holiday to West Runton.

Relieved of his squit, One Ball renewed his acquaintance with the lav end mirror, readjusting his cravat and checking his youthful face for any more defiling spots. He knew his nickname so the revelation wasn't a surprise. Normally, he would have punished such an abusive junior for 'sheer impudence'. After all, he was good at finding phrases for infantile, ill-disciplined behaviour but now it was too late for such retribution. As he was confident of getting into Cambridge, he reassured himself that he would soon be among mature students, away from the facile, juvenile mayhem of the school. He put on his blazer and took one last look in the mirror to confirm that his appearance was sufficiently spruce. He then left the lav end, walked confidently through the dormitory, descended the stairs, entered the dayroom and vigorously rang the bell. It was time for tea and taking his last parade.

On the day of his departure, Rutter moved purposefully down the centre path towards the station. He wasn't surprised by the 'the great stink attack' and its ensuing chaos but now he was only interested in saying goodbye to Françoise. As he proceeded, carrying a canvas holdall containing the essential items he needed before his trunk arrived at Purley, he just hoped that Françoise would be at the station as arranged. It was going to be difficult to talk to her intimately on the train but he would certainly do so before she finally departed. The hurly-burly of the final weeks of term had meant that their recent meetings had been intense but fleeting. This made him desperate to be close to her again

Rutter increased his speed, excited by the thought of seeing Françoise. Nonetheless, when he reached the top of the centre path, he couldn't resist turning round and taking one last look at the school: the extensive playing fields, Mrs Butcher's tuck shop, the cinder athletics track, the baronial Dining Hall and the back of all the red-bricked houses, with the chapel's spire overseeing the whole landscape like a beacon of calm. 'I've been here eight years,' Rutter reflected. 'Eight bloody years,' he repeated, 'that's a long time, longer than some people have been married.'

Before he started to get sentimental, he crossed the road and gathered pace as he passed the gym on the way to the station. Unfortunately, romantic anticipation made him lose concentration and he dropped his holdall in a puddle. Immediately, he took out some paper hankies from his pocket and cleaned up the mess. After depositing the accumulated rubbish in a nearby bin, he proceeded down the familiar sloping path. In the distance, he could see a huddle of people outside the station, distant figures gathered together like a small, remote community.

As they gradually came into focus, Françoise emerged distinctly among the assembled throng, holding a green travel case. Her casual khaki trench coat and tightly belted waist, made her look as distinctive as ever. Instinctively, Rutter hurried down the stony path. He didn't care anymore if he dropped his holdall or fell down. He was propelled by a greater force. Now that Françoise was leaving, he was increasingly aware of how important she was to him. He wanted as much time as he could with her. While he rapidly descended, he also saw not only Françoise but Yvette with Barrel as well as Hayes, Sully and Barrett, among those congregating outside the station.

On Rutter's arrival, Françoise greeted him with a beaming smile. Although he refrained from embracing her amidst the school coterie, he could still feel their shared emotions. After, acknowledging the others, Rutter realised that there were only ten minutes before the London train arrived. Once again, Mr Butcher was in the ticket office, complaining that a certain Mr Bartleby hadn't come to work because he was indisposed. Mr Butcher implied that this was a euphemism for being hung-over, as apparently his wife had witnessed the aforementioned worker drinking excessively the previous evening. Rutter found this remark somewhat ironic, given Mrs Butcher's inveterate history.

Walking over the bridge, carrying both his and Françoise's luggage, Rutter concluded that the industrious Frederick Butcher seemed to enjoy being a victim. It gave him something about which to converse. When they all arrived at the platform, a large crowd of noisy boys greeted them. This welcoming committee included Binns, Boot, Brown, Bunter and Rice. Rutter now feared that there would be even less chance of a meaningful conversation with Françoise, while all the boys were in such an effervescent holiday mood.

The train to Victoria duly arrived and everybody clambered into a carriage. Thankfully it was open, unlike the older closed compartments, in which smokers often suffocated passengers by puffing away indiscriminately in a constricted space. Rutter put the luggage and the women's coats neatly on a rack, while Françoise and Yvette sat down opposite Barrel and a place reserved for himself. Meanwhile, Hayes, Sully and Barrett, found seats across the aisle, where a chubby, grey-haired woman with brown glasses attached to a chain, had already ensconced herself with a book. The inconvenienced woman gave the boys disapproving glances, as if intruding barbarians had invaded her private space.

Boot, who was sitting in a seat in the next section of the carriage, whispered to Binns that he could espy Margaret Rutherford next door, trying to read an Agatha Christie thriller. Binns, who was going to stay with an eccentric aunt, squeezed his hands and laughed so loudly, that the ample woman gave a withering glance in his direction. Brown and Bunter, who were sitting opposite those two boys, were more interested in their summer music schedule. They were arranging to meet at the 2i's and go to the Flamingo, where some black American blues musicians were going to perform. They wanted to get to the heart of the London music scene as they'd read in the Melody Maker that exciting developments were taking place.

On the opposite side of the aisle to the music fans, Rice was reading the New Statesman, which he'd discovered on his seat. He was absorbed in an article that implored people to take notice of the connection between cancer and smoking. Despite being in one of the few non-smoking carriages, it certainly did nothing to alleviate his apprehension about such a fatal link. Eventually, Rice discarded the periodical and started thinking about how he could get hold of that live recording of Frank Sinatra at the Grand Blackpool. That was just the project he needed to get away from school, the bomb, the cold war, the class divide and gloomy articles about cancer.

Meanwhile, the obsessed thriller reader was totally absorbed in the twists and turns of Dead Man's Folly, avidly turning pages in imaginative expectation. However, when Hayes mentioned the words One Ball, the large, haughty woman's concentration was broken and she reacted like an outraged duchess, aghast at hearing such abusive language. Hayes formally apologised to her ladyship, which she reluctantly accepted and returned to Hercule Poirot's investigation of a macabre murder at the home of Sir George and Lady Stubbs. Hayes then continued to talk about One Ball but only by referring self-consciously to his surname.

'Potts seems to have reverted to his old ways.'

'His period of detachment was short lived,' concluded Rutter.

'He's still very angry with me,' admitted Françoise.

'About the tennis match? suggested Barrett.

'About everything,' confirmed Françoise.

'He feels abused and everyone must feel his wrath,' added Rutter, taking out some wine gums from a trouser pocket.

'He wouldn't speak to me in the Dining Hall,' said Yvette disdainfully, leaning back in her elegant plaid dress.

'He also ignored me as if I didn't exist,' claimed Sully.

'I'll always be just a squit to him,' maintained Hayes.

Rutter then unwrapped the wine gums, leaned forward in his seat and offered them around.

'Don't take the green ones as I love 'em!' he pleaded.

Only the boys accepted Rutter's invitation, diplomatically opting for those of a different colour.

'Maybe you've made him worse,' reflected Françoise thoughtfully.

'Do you really think so?' queried a concerned Barrett while sucking a black wine gum.

'I wonder if he'll ever really change,' contemplated Françoise.

'Who knows?' pondered Barrel as he chewed on his yellow pastille.

'France needed a violent revolution to change,' Françoise reminded everybody.

'And that led to a reign of ghastly terror and the tyranny of Napoleon,' proclaimed the duchess, who couldn't resist pricking up her ears at the talk of such a bloodthirsty event.

'You're right Madame, although eventually it did lead to progress,' insisted Françoise politely.

'But at too high a price. I hate extremity. I believe in moderation at all costs,' pronounced the imperious duchess, before she returned to her book to discover who killed Marlene Tucker.

'Do you think we shouldn't have attacked him, Françoise?' asked Barrett.

Suddenly the Agatha Christie devotee peered over her book at the mention of real violent action.

'Maybe not,' replied Françoise thoughtfully. 'Still, he was a bully and should have been punished. But if he's unrepentant, he could go on to bully others,' elaborated Françoise.

Rutter had been listening intently to Françoise while admiring her swing red dress, with its black bow neatly tied at its top, and her smooth brown hair hanging attractively on both sides of her face. She not only talked sense but looked stunning. She'd certainly made everybody reflect upon their actions, including himself. He was just relieved that he hadn't been part of the assault. Although Brown wanted to commemorate the attack by forming a band called The Jacobins, Rutter wondered if the insurrection would alter anything. No doubt, the experience will inform Ryder's future political career but whether the school's ethos will radically change remained to be seen. Whatever the future brings, Rutter just hoped that Barrett would learn to relax more with Lonnie Donegan and not become the next resident Lenin. Otherwise, he thought that the school could experience more confrontation rather than progressive dialogue. He also feared that Françoise might be right in thinking that the likes of One Ball could descend even more brutally upon the wider world. Rutter certainly didn't look forward to being employed by a person with those rigid values.

As the train puffed through the sunny, desolate Sussex countryside, the boys chatted about their families, holiday plans and aspirations. Everybody was glad to be on vacation but anxious about the future. They were all venturing into the unknown. In Rutter's case, there was a strong emotional resonance. When the train left East Croydon, his heart started pounding. He looked at Françoise and the reality of not seeing her again intensified. In half an hour, the course of their lives would never be the same. As they reached the perennially busy Clapham Junction station, with its hustle and bustle of passengers changing trains, Rutter started to get emotional. He took out a white handkerchief from his blazer pocket to pretend that he was blowing his nose, while furtively wiping his eyes. He wasn't listening to the other boys as they continued talking about their hopes and dreams. The only important person to him was Françoise. Not only was he losing a lover but also his best friend. Despite the many obstacles put in their way, their love had survived and Rutter couldn't bear to think of losing her. He'd never before felt such grief. Sensing Rutter's feelings, Françoise broke away from conversing in French with Yvette and gave him a radiant smile. In that moment, he decided to become fluent in her language and travel to Lyon. He couldn't let Françoise go. She'd brought something different and challenging to his life that he wanted to keep forever.

When the train reached Victoria and finally screeched to a sudden halt, the duchess's book spilt onto the floor, just as she was coming to the final revelatory pages. Rutter helpfully picked up the Christie tome and handed it to the distressed reader. After the crime-fixated duchess thanked Rutter profusely, everybody gathered their belongings, said their goodbyes and scrambled out of the carriage as soon as they could. Rutter helped Françoise into her coat and they both departed, followed by Barrel and Yvette. The two boys were going to accompany the women to the Dover train.

Rutter and Françoise held each other's hand tightly as they moved silently down the platform. A youthful rail official checked Françoise's ticket and took Rutter's. They then continued to the indicator. The train to Dover would leave in five minutes. As they went towards the appropriate platform, they saw Barrett and Hayes being embraced by their families and Boot, Binns, Sully, Brown, Bunter and Rice meandering to the tube or a train connection. Rutter wondered how they'd progress at the school. While waving them all goodbye with Françoise, Barrel and Yvette, he hoped that their intelligence and good humour would ultimately supersede both their own transgressions and institutional shortcomings.

Nearby, a newspaper seller was shouting in broad cockney 'Star, News and Standard!' 'Asian Flu Spreading!'. As the two couples approached the Dover platform, a young girl wearing a red headscarf was talking animatedly to a teenage boy with a big wavy quiff. She was very excited by a group she'd seen in Liverpool called The Quarrymen. Rutter had never heard of them and wondered if any of those musicians would ever make it.

After Rutter got a platform ticket, he and Françoise, still firmly holding hands, made their way to the train. The official at the barrier, with his black peaked hat and British Railways badge on his lapel, was speaking about cricket to a colleague. He was extolling the virtues of someone called Collie Smith, an exciting, young West Indies cricketer playing in the current test series. The animated official punched Rutter and Françoise's tickets and waved them through, all the while maintaining his sporting outpouring. Yvette and Barrel followed behind them but neither could they stem the man's loquacious enthusiasm.

Rutter and Françoise made their way to the middle of the platform. They stared at each other momentarily, put down their luggage and kissed passionately for some time. When they paused, they hugged each other closely so that their bodies intertwined. Over Françoise's shoulder, Rutter could see Barrel kissing Yvette. As Rutter kissed Françoise again, some nearby workers on another track started wolf whistling. They both laughed dismissively and ignored the ensuing bawdy comments.

'I'll miss you,' said Rutter quietly.

'I'll miss you too,' replied Françoise, giving him a light peck on the cheek.

'We must meet soon,' declared Rutter, looking deeply into her dark brown eyes.

'Yes, we must,' acknowledged Françoise.

Suddenly, the brutally sharp sound of a guard's whistle awoke them from their intimate reverie. Françoise looked towards Yvette, who'd disentangled herself from Barrel's smothering kisses. The two women then made their way with their cases to the train. There followed a pause while they disappeared from view. The boys looked on anxiously as if Françoise and Yvette had vanished miraculously in a puff of smoke. Eventually, after finding some seats, Françoise pushed down the carriage window and they both reappeared. Various late passengers were now scurrying down the platform. Several squeezed past the two women as the boys watched helplessly. After the final packages went into the goods van, a uniformed guard blew a whistle to signal imminent departure and then raised a green flag. After a lull, he lowered the flag, and the train started to depart.

Rutter immediately ran down the platform, his holdall swinging in his hand. Françoise was now on her own at the window, her hair flowing in the wind. As the train increased speed, Rutter ran faster. Stopping breathlessly at the end of the platform, he shouted with all his might:

'I love you! I bloody love you!'

He looked out into space for some time as the train receded into the distance, steam billowing into the air. When he eventually turned round, he saw Barrel sitting on his duffle bag, looking bewildered and forlorn. Rutter walked slowly but deliberately towards him. After he arrived, they both ambled back down the platform. As the two boys passed the urbane ticket collector, he was still talking about Collie Smith.

www.ingramcontent.com/pod-product-compliance
Ingram Content Group UK Ltd.
Pitfield, Milton Keynes, MK11 3LW, UK
UKHW021931080925
7790UKWH00031B/767

9 781917 293068